The

THE DEITY
DOZEN

Andrew Harman

LEGEND

Published by Legend Books in 1996

1 3 5 7 9 10 8 6 4 2

First published in the United Kingdom in 1996 by Legend Books

20 Vauxhall Bridge Road, London, SW1V 2SA

Random House Australia (Pty) Limited
20 Alfred Street, Milsons Point, Sydney,
New South Wales 2061, Australia

Random House New Zealand Limited
18 Poland Road, Glenfield
Auckland 10, New Zealand

Random House South Africa (Pty) Limited
PO Box 337, Bergvlei, South Africa

Random House UK Limited Reg. No. 954009

A CIP catalogue record for this book is available from the British Library

Papers used by Random House UK Limited are natural, recyclable products
made from wood grown in sustainable forests. The manufacturing processes
conform to the environmental regulations of the country of origin

ISBN 0 09 968101 3

Typeset by Keyboard Services, Luton
Printed and bound in the Great Britain by

Contents

Dedication

A bit of an International Feel this time!

A huge 'vielen dank!' to all the folks at Heyne Verlag, especially to Friedel Wahren, Wolfgang and Rosemarie Jeschke and certainly not least, Jakob Leutner. The headaches are over ... until the next translation! Ha ha!

A bit nearer to home, a massive thumbs up to Jonathan Sissons for sorting out the deal. Cheers! Now, about Russia ... and Japan and America and the Bahamas and Thailand and Mars and...

And so the finger of thanks wriggles its way Midlands-ward. Step into the spotlight Claire and Annie in Dillons UK. Quite simply, thank you for all your support. Without you, I think I would've had to hang on a bit longer before being 'Number 1'. Now, about this next promotion, I've got a great idea...

Even closer to home, thanks are definitely in order for the two Johns. Messrs Jarrold and Parker, take a well-earned bow for continuing excellence in the pock-marked fields of editing and agenting. Hoorah! Now then, about this comedy thriller thingy...

And, at home. Love and hugs to the one with the thumb! Er, was it a double brandy you wanted, Jenny, dear? Or simply a foot massage? Both? And a candlelit dinner for two? Hmmmmm, we'll have to see about that ... ahhh, no, not the half nelson, please!!!!

The Death of a Soulsman

An early morning gecko squinted at the shadow creeping across the sundial, shrugged its scaly shoulders and scuttled out of earshot. Years of first-claw experience of life in the Mountain City of Axolotl had taught it that things wouldn't remain tranquil much longer. They never did, first thing in the morning in Hyh'd Park.

Today was no exception.

There was a crunch of eager feet on the sun-bleached stones of the Xhen rock-lawn and a figure in a long black cassock and matching skull cap scuttled across the swirling grooves of the fifty-foot square, his hand clutching a large case. Eyes scanned left and right, checking for any other movement, any other competition. He hadn't come this far to lose his place at the last minute, oh no. Not after lugging that damned case across those endless mountains for the last three days. No way. It was worth *far* too much.

Suddenly, he caught a movement out of the corner of his eye – the flicking of a branch and the flash of a toga. His heart skipped a beat as he gritted his teeth and lurched forward. The toga'd one erupted from a hedge of cactus, spotted him and immediately doubled his pace, shouting. Flints of whitened stone scattered from his heels as he accelerated on an intercept course towards a gleaming pillar of marble.

Desperately, the man in the cassock swung his case in a scything arc and released it, thrilling as it frisbeed towards its prey. The holdall landed with a spray of rubble, bounced and impacted a pair of sprinting ankles with irresistible momentum, sending the man in the toga arcing into a distant fence of cactus on a vapour trail of obscenities.

The Mostly Reverend Vex Screed punched the air victoriously, snatched up his case and leapt onto the bottom step of the pillar in Preacher's Corner. He had done it, staked his claim for the day, secured as much preaching time as he wanted until nine the next morning when it would all start again.

He panted a heavy sigh of relief and began to unpack his case feverishly, prepared to take full advantage of the finest spot in the whole Mountain City of Axolotl.

The gecko tutted to itself, wondering idly why they went to so much effort at this time of day. Why didn't they just find a suitable rock and get down to some serious basking like any decent being should? Shaking its head and muttering reptilian things about the stupidity of mammals in general, the gecko slithered away as a man in a dark grey tunic puffed his balding way across the Xhen rock-lawn.

'What d'you mean by running off like that?' he gasped at the Mostly Reverend Vex Screed of the Haranguist Mission. 'What if I'd got lost, or...'

'Competition, Pedlah,' answered Screed and pointed to the toga'd man scowling as he tugged cactus spines from tender anatomy.

'What competition?' the balding man squawked, and then added, 'And that's *Mister* Pedlah to you!'

Vex Screed ignored the last few words and unfolded a large jointed board covered with glossy coloured illustrations. 'It's like I told you on the way up here,' he mumbled. 'Ancient Axolotian tradition. "First up, most saved."'

Pedlah wiped his brow and stared about him. 'You're saying *this* is Preacher's Corner?'

'What did you expect? Flashing candles? Amphitheatre perhaps?'

'But it's so *small*.'

2

Screed tutted. 'As I keep trying to tell some of my dwarvish friends, that doesn't matter. It's what you do with it that counts. Believe me, in a few short minutes this place will be heaving.'

'Not if I can help it,' challenged the toga'd one, glaring at Screed. 'You're here every week, trotting out the same old...'

'Ah, shut up. You're just naffed off that I beat you to it, again! I was here first. It's mine for as long as I like, as decreed by the Holy Ruler.' Screed tossed his head dismissively and glanced at the sundial. Less than a minute left.

Pedlah looked baffled. 'Beat him to it?' he asked in confusion. 'Do I take it that there is a double booking here?' He wiped his brow again, his knees weakening. Had he spent three days struggling all the way up here just to be stopped by some clerical error?

The Mostly Reverend Screed threw back his head and laughed. 'Booking? Oh no. Like I said first come...'

Pedlah's glistening brow wrinkled into furrows of suspicion. 'Then what, pray tell, was the hundred groats "booking fee" for? Hmm?'

'That's really none of your concern, is it? The Harang-uist Mission's Policy, as you well know, is to preach "Any Time, Any Place, Any Word!" So here I am, on your behalf, ready, willing and completely able to preach *your* word here. Unfortunately, as yet, that word hasn't got very far. I know it and you know it but we have to make sure that the audience knows it and they won't know it if they ain't here. See?'

Pedlah's palms twitched skywards in a state of baffle-ment.

'Have to make sure they turn up, haven't I?' Screed rubbed his thumb against his first two fingers as if there was a coin there. Then he turned and unfolded another illustration board, lining it up for maximal visibility, grinning at the displays of indecently erotic underwear being modelled by equally indecent figures of both sexes.

'You ... you *bought* an audience?' accused Pedlah as he worked through the speech.

'Oh no, no, no. Nothing so crass. Please do give me some credit.'

'Then where is the hundred groats?'

'Spent,' tutted Screed, pulling display samples out of the case.

'Where? On what? Did you get a receipt?' flustered Pedlah, thinking of his business account.

Screed glanced at the sundial and decided he really had to make this explanation quick. 'Tuatara Street. Column and a half in "Omen Corner". And, yes.' He turned away and continued fiddling with his growing display.

'Look, I don't understand any of this,' spluttered the balding man.

The Haranguist Missionary raised his eyes heavenwards and gnashed his teeth. Then trembling with the thrill of an impending preaching, he fixed Pedlah with a wild stare and a wagging fingertip, leaning forward imperiously over the four-foot marble pillar. '*If* you'd been paying *any* attention to what I have been saying these last three days then the truth would be revealed to you in a blaze of grail-shaped glory and you would let me get on with last-minute preparations. Instead, it appears I'll have to reiterate for the terminally hard of thinking...'

'There's no need for sarcasm...'

Screed made an angry noise in the back of his throat and began to wonder if this contract was really going to be worth the hassle. 'What is the first thing any Axolotian does in the morning?' he enquired, folding his arms and adopting the tone of voice more normally associated with pedantic teachers addressing stupid six-year-olds.

Pedlah stuck his finger in his mouth and looked vacant. 'Go to the toilet?'

'No, no, no! Think!' He mimed opening a newsparchment and reading.

'Do the crossword?' spluttered Pedlah.

'Gah! Does the name *Scryin' Out* mean nothing to you?'

'Oh, yeah. You told me about that.'

'May Ahnikdote, the Memory Deity, bless your shiny little neurones. You remembered! And what section do they turn to first?' Screed glanced at the sundial and realised that perhaps he didn't really have enough time for this approach. '"Omen Corner"' he answered himself.

'Yeah, yeah, I was gonna say that,' protested Pedlah, suddenly remembering it all. Two nights ago Screed had explained. Whether it was too much inbreeding, or the sun, or something in the water, no one knew, but for some reason ninety-nine percent of the Axolotian population had 'the Gift'. Be it by using a handful of ancient shrew bones, or staring at the pattern in the froth of a pint of ale, or squinting myopically into a glowing crystal, whatever method used the result was the same. Axolotians could see the future.

There were those with a penchant for seeing flames, like 'Snuff' Douser and his trusty donkey Dennis, who worked for the Fire Prevention Service. They'd saunter up minutes before *that* spark flinted off *that* llama's shoe and engulfed *that* dry haystack in a swirling inferno of combustion, preventing disaster with a deftly hurled bucket of water. Others, with a more culinary foresight, found employ in the myriad fast food emporia dotted around Axolotl, turning their minds to ensuring the correct meals were delivered to the door moments after a spark of hunger appeared. Then there were the Litter Predictors, getting a strange tingling in their noses and dashing out into the streets to place receptacles anywhere stray garbage was about to fall.

And some worked for the weekly parchmag *Scryin' Out*, poring over signs and portents and piecing together

'Omen Corner'. It went way beyond the vague fuzziness of the classic horoscope, taking the risk out of the day to come. 'Omen Corner' was specific. Over-Seers whose concern was the foresightings of Portentous Creatures issued warnings of Dreaded Black Mantric Geckos, giving place and time of their appearance, ensuring that nobody had to have their paths crossed by one. Chromotherapists declared what colours would show off your personal aura to its best advantage. For the hyperstitious Axolotians, *Scryin' Out* was essential reading.

'But what's that got to do with my hundred-groat booking fee?' asked Pedlah, still in a state of confusion.

Screed snarled, tugged this week's edition from his pocket and hurled it at him. 'Page twelve. Now move unless you *want* to get trampled.'

'What?'

'They're always punctual, too frightened to be late.'

In the background he could hear the sound of a crowd gathering from all corners of the city.

The Mostly Reverend Vex Screed of the Haranguist Mission, (Contract Conversions Division) raised his eyes to the shimmering golden roof tiles of the Grand Municipal Temple, donned his mitre and cleared his throat.

When he looked down again a minute later the entire expanse of Hyh'd Park was a sea of expectant faces, some of them familiar from many previous weeks.

'People of Axolotl,' declared Reverend Screed, his hands raised with evangelical fervour. 'So glad you could come.' He grinned inside, bathing in the ruddy warm glow of the approaching mass conversion.

Pedlah spluttered as he began reading the specially placed 'prediction' on page twelve. Now he realised the source of Screed's confidence in the crowd's appearance. How could they not turn up when faced with such a deliberately ambiguous and hyperstitionally terrifying prediction?

You've never been happier.
You've never thrilled this much before.
And you'll never be this free again.
Unless...
Unless you're at Preacher's Corner 9 am tomorrow.
Be there ... or weep for eternity!

Pedlah looked up at the sea of eager bodies, each of them desperate to know what was the cause of their pinnacle of happiness, each terrified of the future. The air was thick with ferments of trepidation. He had to admit it was a good turnout. He'd had his doubts for a few moments there, but he was satisfied. It had been a hundred groats well spent.

'My dear people, I hope you understand just how privileged you all are,' oozed Screed, palms upright, his arms sweeping the crowd in welcome. 'You stand here now, poised on the brink of a new and terrifying revelation.'

There was a gasp.

'Terrifying, that is, for those not present here. It will be they who will tremble when the realisation hits of wasted security, the peace of mind they have lost by *not* attending here this morning.'

Pedlah grinned and felt a wriggle of anticipation and relief squirm through his intestines. Screed *was* good. He'd heard that he was the best of the Haranguist Missionaries, but until that moment he hadn't been entirely convinced. The vast amounts of money he'd parted with to get Screed spreading the good news about Pedlah's latest product looked like it was going to be worth it. He knew experience cost, and Screed had plenty of that: twenty years spent converting nomads and heathens to the true ways of faith, only to return three years later and convert them to something shiny, new and even more soul-saving. But now things were different. Gone was the noble reward of simply igniting the pilot light of faith into the full conflagration of devotion, standing well back and getting a couple of groats of thankful donation. Now devotion was leaner, meaner and commercial.

Two years ago the Haranguist Mission had ceremonially binned the financial suicide of dealing in deities and leapt onto the bandwagon of bankable baptisms and economic communion. Overnight they became contract missionaries, or 'mercionaries' as they liked to be known. There was nowhere they wouldn't storm in spreading mercy to all and making a killing.

And now the Mostly Reverend Vex Screed was in full swing. He whirled and spun as he spat forth strings of words, like a dervish with acute verbal bowel problems.

'Just *look* at those pictures!' he declared, pointing to the glossy images of buxom babes and tanned hunks of masculinity, each clad in items of erotic lingerie. 'I know what you're thinking now. Do the words "carnal", "lust" and "sex" spring to mind? Do they?' With a twinge of satisfaction he saw a plethora of guilty expressions. 'Carnal thoughts of sweat-glistening bodies rolling together on beds of feather and lust! Well, it's disgusting, I tell you! You are all victims of your deepest darkest desires! All being manipulated by that distracting devil of sex!' Faces dropped in shock.

Screed relaxed his lightning-striking pose for a moment and lowered his voice to a more conciliatory tone. Folding his arms he leant over the top of the pillar of Preacher's Corner. 'Have you ever stopped to consider how dangerous this is? Yes, *dangerous*! One moment of distraction considering a curvaceously proportioned body clad in satin and straps, one slip, and who knows where it will end. An absent-minded turn down a badly augured street bringing you face to face with untold danger ... Who's to say there isn't any one of a dozen different portentous creatures lurking in the shadows, ready to bring doom and dread into your life? Yes, it is true. There is no greater hazard of the devil than ... Underwear!'

8

His index finger waved frantically skywards as he ranted to the sea of awestricken Axolotians. 'Yes! And the risks are worse if that underwear is incorrectly secured. Think of the disasters waiting to happen when distraction strikes as an incorrectly secured strap rides inopportunely up towards a sensitive region.'

Several of the more youthful men in the audience winced. Ha! thought Screed with a breath of relief. His information was correct. The fashion for fetishistic undies was still going strong. By their reaction he knew he had them.

'But fear not, people of Axolotl. I can save you from the evils of underwear. No more will that stray lustful thought turn your head, no longer will you risk wandering straps. Take full control of your future and wrap yourself in the comforting cosy embrace of fleecy-lined warmth. Yes! For a donation of only five and a half groats a pair I can introduce you to the snugly satisfying support of *these*!'

With a practised flick of his wrist he unclipped two catches on a pair of display boards, one on each side of the pillar. They unfurled dramatically, covering the initial lingerie images, and revealed an extensive range of full-length ready-to-wear undergarments for both sexes, blue and pink.

Screed wound himself for one last evangelical push, stabbing the crowd with hard stares and the seasoned end of his fingertip. 'Yes! Dispense with the dangers of silken lingerie, rid yourselves of the creeping evil of straps and buckles, and embrace the one true way. Enter an eternity free of rude urges.' His voice soared and shifted into a sing-song pattern as he delivered his final message. 'Yes! You'll feel so happy, never need to be bare. The future's a joy dressed in Wonderwear!'

Pedlah was ready to applaud, the crowd eager to shell out their donations when ...

'Why should we?' screamed a toga'd man on the edge

9

of the crowd, stray strands of cactus protruding from his collar.

'What?' spluttered Screed.

'Why should we believe what you say?' the man shouted back, with more confidence.

Screed's fingers gripped the rim of the pillar. 'Because ... because it is the one true way...' He was flustered. Nobody had ever answered back before.

'Give it a rest, Screed. You know that's not true. Over the last two years you've harangued us with well over a hundred different "true ways". If we were mugs enough to listen to your every word, and believe that guff you spout every week, then we'd be using Hale Mayorie's Extra Virgin Olive Oil in our cooking, Dom Esto's Pure Angelic soap flakes in our washing, we'd drink endless gallons of Dr Kharie's Spiritual Envoy Ale and we'd...'

'Okay, okay. Just what is it you're trying to say?' snarled Screed from behind the marble pillar.

'Every bleedin' week you come here, stand on that step and rant on about the only true way to salvation. One week it's through McVicar's Holy digestive biscuits, the next it's "Stay out of hell, drink Crucifix Coffee as well". Why can't you be consistent?'

A crescendo of murmured assent came from the crowd.

'There *is* a point to this, I take it?' Screed attempted to assume an air of superiority and looked down his nose.

'Oh yes,' grinned the man in a manner which made Screed very uncomfortable around the collar. 'The point is ... you're a fraud!'

The crowd booed and readied themselves for a bout of hissing.

'I ... I ... the gods work in mysterious ways, and there are many, many paths you can go by,' blurted Screed, glancing down and shrugging apology at Pedlah. The wild gaze of fury which was returned looked less than friendly.

The hissing started.

'Er ... now look, I'm only doing my jobs showing paths so that you are free to choose. Now, I *can* offer a small donational discount on bulk conversions to Wonderwear...'

There was a scream of anger from the crowd and a Crucifix of Coffee whistled towards Screed's high fore-head. At the last second he ducked and stood upright, the seeds of panic decorated his face.

'Now, just wait a minute here, let's not be too hasty...'

The cruciform jar vanished into a distant row of cactus hedging, caught on a large succulent leaf and was catapulted back with frightening force. The crowd seethed, acutely irritated that their hyperstitional beliefs had been used to manipulate them so callously.

'Look, this stuff is good, alright. I'd be quite happy to drink it and...' The jar of Crucifix Coffee hit Screed on the back of the head, sending his mitre flying into the mob. His erstwhile audience cheered noisily and, as if the jar was a trigger, began to press forward.

It was at that moment that the Mostly Reverend Vex Screed suddenly wished he had gone on that Imminent Riot Avoidance Course he'd been offered by the Mission.

A chant of 'Fraud! Fraud!' germinated from the back of the mob, roots and tendrils of contagion spreading rapidly across the entirety of Hyh'd Park.

Screed, palms sweating, edged nervously backwards.

'Okay, okay. I can see you need to think about Wonder-wear. Tell you what, for the first ten of you who want it I can offer a free trial period. No, no, please don't *all* rush at once. I ... I...'

Pedlah winced. And then he realised that perhaps there was more at stake than his profit margins.

With a squeak of alarm, Screed whirled on his heel and sprinted towards the cactus hedging. Distracted by

11

the roar of the mob, he barely noticed the spikes as he plunged through to other side.

Pedlah stood stock-still for only a moment as he watched the riotous assembly surge unstoppably towards him like some wild tidal wave of anger. In a flash he was hard on Screed's heels, springing through the gap in the hedge, sprinting for his life and the chance to beat seven shades of retribution out of Screed. He was supposed to be the best!

Explosions of dust erupted from Screed and Pedlah's heels as they clattered down Tuatara Street and skittered around the far corner on one leg each. The crowd surged through the gap in the cactus fence and swarmed after them, driving them forward like panicking surfers on a screaming wavefront.

Street after blurring street flashed by beneath their feet, twisting and turning as they dashed towards the edge of the city. They rounded a final corner, and there ahead of them stood the sandstone gatetower, its massive reinforced palm-wood doors standing open. Vision blurring beneath torrents of sweat, Screed and Pedlah ran on. They had little choice – the mad mob behind saw to that.

In a flurry of cassock and a flash of tunic they sped through the squat gatetower, one question firmly in the upper reaches of both their minds. Just how much further would the Axolotians pursue them?

Still screaming, the mob powered on towards the gatetower, blazing a trail of dust. All eyes clamped on the fleeing pair.

Suddenly two men galloped a cart out of a side alley and screeched to a halt in front of the gate, blocking it securely. The driver fastened the reins and leapt down, waving his hands and ringing a bell. In an instant the mob had recognised the distinctive peaked cap and matching white uniform. They were men from the Accident and Emergency Foreseervice.

The mob backpedalled frantically, shedding momentum and desperately ground to a halt.

12

'Sorry to spoil your, er ... fun,' said the man in the uniform, 'but you'd have all had a very nasty accident if you'd carried on like that.'

Everybody knew of the Accident and Emergency Foreseervice and their uncanny knack of appearing just in the nick of time, placing mattresses under falling window cleaners, or fixing the handbrakes on imminently runaway carts poised at the top of steep inclines. But few had ever seen them at first hand. Almost all anyone really knew of them was their motto, 'Prediction is Better than Cure!'

The crowd shuffled restlessly as the mercionary escaped across a narrow wooden bridge.

'I'm sorry,' apologised the Foreseer. 'If I'd let you all go pounding across that bridge you would've all ended up in a nasty heap at the bottom of the ravine. Wood rot, see? Support strut would never've held you all.'

The man in the toga stamped angrily forward, still bristling with cactus spikes. 'Me,' he growled, 'let me go. I'll give that fraud a good...'

'Sorry, mate, can't do that. Too risky.'

'What?'

'Knuckles. Right mess they'd be in by the time you'd finished. Not to mention the twist you'd get in your ankle when he pushed you. Oh no, can't let you go. More than my job's worth. Now clear off. We've got to keep a little princess from pricking her finger on her spinning wheel.'

The crowd gasped.

'And if you don't get there in time?' growled the toga'd one, cactus spines vibrating in sympathy with his mounting frustration. 'Does she fall asleep for a hundred years awaiting a kiss from a handsome...'

'Grow up' grunted the Foreseer dismissively. 'It's tetanus she gets. Rusty needle, see? Now come on, you lot. Shift. I don't want to run over anyone's toes.' And with that he sprang onto the cart, his colleague snapped the reins and they galloped away.

13

The mob tutted and dispersed, irritably vowing that next time they'd wear boxing gloves and reinforced kneepads.

Part way down the mountain, it was Screed who first noticed the lack of pursuit as he glanced in terror over his shoulder. Within seconds he had collapsed in a panting heap, trembling pathetically with relief.

Pedlah stood, hands on knees, gasping as sweat drooled off his brow. 'Brilliant' he choked. 'Just brilliant! Entire stock lost. No money!'

'Wasn't my fault,' spluttered Screed.

'Why didn't you tell me you go there every week?'

'Didn't ask,' muttered Screed between vast gulps of air.

'Well, that's it. End of contract. You'll get no more work from me and as soon as I get back to the office, I'll sue!'

'No, you can't...'

'Just try to stop me. I want full reimbursement for the lost goods. Now, gimme your purse!' snarled Pedlah. His crimson face added a certain forcefulness to his words. 'Think of it as a down payment.'

Screed lay on the ground, immobile.

'Give!' Pedlah lurched forward and snatched Screed by the cassock, his knuckles whitening as he tugged the collar tight.

'Stop! You're choking...'

'Gimme your purse!'

Gasping for breath, Screed emptied his pockets. Pedlah snatched the tiny bag of cash and weighed it in his hands. 'It'll do,' he grunted. He stepped back and picked up a large stick, hefting it angrily in his hands. 'I'm setting off down the mountain and you're staying here in case that mob decide to follow. If I catch any glimpse of you on my way down I will use this, clear?' The tip of the stick waggled inches from Screed's nose.

'Perfectly.'

The sales manager of Wonderwear growled once more

14

and set off miserably down the mountain, cursing as he thought of three days of hiking and nothing to show for it.

Screed collapsed on the ground again and whimpered pathetically.

As usual, Manna Ambrosia's was packed to the gunnels. Every table was full, and the glasses were rapidly emptying. Waitresses hovered attentively in the noisy atmosphere of the celestial pizzeria.

'Here, love, bring me another flagon of my favourite, there's an angel,' slurred Sot, leaning over the back of his chair and holding out his vast leather mug. The waitress tutted and fluttered across the bare boards clutching a huge jug.

'Why do you insist on drinking that filth?' jibed Lush from the next trestle table. Behind him a fresco of two cherubs leered from the bare plaster walls. 'This wine is far superior. And better for your waistline.'

'You would say that, you're biased,' grumbled Sot as the angelic waitress slopped a gallon or so into his flagon. 'Anyway. I *like* my waistline. Been cultivating it for years. Shows real devotion that does.' He tapped his vast corporation and grinned. The waitress smoothed her apron and fluttered away to another beckoning diner.

'Shame you don't pay as much attention to cultivating faithful droves of devotees,' grinned Lush, his interesting nose curling into his goblet of wine.

Sot, the Deity-in-Command of Ales, took a long draught and grinned. 'Never takes you long to get back to that, does it?'

'It should be a thought at the forefront of your mind, dear Sot. How else can one hope to advance up the ladder of promotion if not by increased devotion quotients? Wouldst thou not desire a seat on the Top Table, eh? Best garlic manna and pizzas anywhere, cut crystal flagons *and* the tablecloth changed once a month. Not to

15

mention the tastiest-looking waitresses in the whole of Heobhan.' Lush, the Arch-Idol of Wines and Spirits, cast a scathing glance of envy at the seven deities on the Top Table and knew that some of them were on the slide this month. But his mind fizzed with one single question. Had he secured enough converts to his alcoholic cause to get him up there, eating and drinking on the Top Table before the day was out?

Lush crossed his legs as a shapely brunette fluttered back towards the Top Table and filled Letch's flagon with finest wine. Silently Lush cursed the Deity-in-Chief of Adultery's way with angels. 'Look at them all,' he growled in the privacy of his mind, 'five of the tastiest ones flitting around him like flies. Well they'd forget him quickly on his way down.'

They always did.

'I shouldn't be choosing your seat so quickly,' grinned Sot. 'You can never tell what this month's souls figures will be until they're announced. Might be a few surprises in the Believer Beacons.'

He scrubbed a fistful of stubby fingernails on his suede tunic as Lush sneered and thought about his own particular Believer Beacon. Sot wondered what colour it was currently glowing. He'd only seen the room they were stored in once, but the memory lingered in perfect, intact detail. How could he forget the shelves and shelves of individual flasks glowing in a myriad of colours, each with a name tag underneath, each reflecting the intensity of belief held by a deity's following? The brighter it glowed the better.

Only the top seven were allowed onto the Top Table, there to sit and 'rule' until the next souls figures were announced. It was a system which seemed to work. They'd tried having one single Top God, but, after a few hundred centuries of listening to the same old ideas being trotted out in the same old tone of voice, some of the more militant deities had staged a coup, ousted him unceremoniously and imposed the current system of seven constantly rotating deities. So far, the last few hundred millennia had chugged along fairly well under a deimocracy.

Lush hurled back his head and laughed again. 'Surprises? You? Ha! The day you get on Heobhan's Top Table is the day Letch keeps his hands to himself.'

'I wouldn't be so hasty if I were you. I've had a few conversions to the glories of the amber nectar. Just you wait till the figures are announced.'

'Ha! You reckon you can finally overtake me?'

'Oh yes.'

'Dream on,' chuckled Lush, thinking of his own recruitment drive, which had recently been highly successful. Carousle, Goddess of Parties and Binges, had thrown a stack of raging near-riots at the beginning of the month and by the end of each one Lush had hooked vast swathes of alcoholic novices into the delights of vinic and spiritual inebriation.

Lush narrowed his eyes and squinted at d'Luge sipping nervously at his wine on the Top Table. The word was out that he'd lost a stack of devotees due to dumping a series of badly timed torrential downpours on his normally faithful followers. He claimed it was a clerical error, but that was no way for the Chief Deity over Rain and General Precipitation to treat his flock. Twenty-three days' solid sprinkling was severely taxing the faithful. Even the most hydrophilic of folk could have too much of a good thing – and recently they had stayed in drinking.

Suddenly there was a pounding of a large pizza dish on the dented surface of the raised Top Table, and a vast figure hauled himself upright and cleared his throat. 'Gods, idols, deities,' declared Scran, the hundred-and-three-stone Supreme Being-in-Charge of Savoury Supplies. 'Welcome once again to Manna Ambrosia's for the announcement of This Month's Souls Figures.'

There was a ripple of applause. This introduction was far from necessary. Not only had all those present heard

Scran mumble it on countless occasions, but it seemed faintly ridiculous nowadays to welcome folk back to a place they hadn't actually left for more than eight hours or so. A quick kip or the odd blessing was all that normally kept them away.

Several centuries ago it had been different, of course. Then there'd been a choice. The Kingdom of Heobhan had been dotted with tiny eateries serving all kinds of supernatural snacks and finger-licking nirvanic takeaways. Gods and goddesses flitted about, sampling this new recipe, meeting at that hostelry and generally having a pretty heavenly time. All was fine and dandy, century after century. Every decade or so the manna would be served up in a slightly different way, or the nectar was dished up with ice-cream, or the ambrosia was meringued. Everybody was perfectly happy, until...

One fateful day the Supreme Being-in-Charge of Savoury Supplies, Scran, had received an innocent enough request to zip down into the mountain city of Axolotl and give a brand-new restaurant the quick once-over before its grand opening the next day. It was the usual thing – the whole Eternal Blessing lark for trouble-free prosperity and a bunch of luck in return for a large portion of the Dish of the Day in his own tiny temple out the back. Dutifully he'd nipped off into the brand-new, old-fashioned eatery, its insides decorated with olde-worlde cobwebs, cracked plaster, bare boards and cherubic frescos, and his deitic nostrils had quivered with intense excitement. Never had he smelled anything quite like it. A musty, sweet aroma at once subtly distasteful and yet captivatingly delicious. And it was there, in the restaurant. A complete disc of golden bread gently steaming beneath a sheen of garlic and herb butter. Before he realised it he had shovelled a wagonload of grated dragonzola cheese on top and wolfed the lot.

The manna in Heobhan that night was the worst he had ever eaten. Every mouthful elicited wails of mourning

18

from his tongue, knowing that eternity wouldn't be worth living without Tohnee Fabrizzi's Infamous Dragonzola Garlic Bread.

The Supreme Being-in-Charge of Savoury Supplies knew that something had to be done.

In the final few hours before the grand restaurant opening, Fabrizzi was working alone on the finishing touches of a secret pizza recipe involving careful use of the rare and highly volatile Murrhovian dragonzola cheese.

Precisely where the tiny spark appeared from nobody mortal ever knew, but appear it did, scant inches from a large pot of dragonzola cheese. In seconds the entire place was ablaze, beams tumbling from the roof and adding to the fire, engulfing everything in a few infernal minutes.

That night there had appeared in the Kingdom of Heobhan a strangely round angel complete with chef's cap, odd accent and the uncanny ability to do the most amazing things with a bit of bread and a few cloves of garlic. Taste buds throughout Heobhan tingled with joy as they were treated to curling triangles of garlic manna. In less than a month a replica of the restaurant was made and every other takeaway had given up and folded. Nowadays no one left Manna Ambrosia's. Well, there was nowhere else to go.

Scran chewed absently on a breadstick and unfastened a large envelope he held in his hand. 'Gods, idols, deities, for the last month you have all been watching this Top Table with a potent mixture of good healthy envy and the overwhelming urge to steal our places. Each of you has been working your hardest to secure a fresh influx of devoted followers, each of you hoping that you can come and join me here on the Top Table.'*

* Although Scran hadn't actually spelt it out in so many words, every one of them knew horribly well that he had a place on the Top Table for as long as he wanted. Heobhan would be a miserable place indeed if he were to leave with Fabrizzi the amazing garlic-bread cherub.

There was a flurry of interest as Scran slid the souls figures out of the envelope.

'Oh!' he declared, as if he hadn't actually spent most of the previous day sorting out the numbers. 'There have been some moves this month. Two vacancies up here.' He glared around the table with a little too much relish for one so ostensibly theological. 'Sorry, d'Luge. It's been just a little too wet for even the hardiest of believers to think you hadn't got it in for them. Out. And...'

The remaining five swallowed nervously and debated snaffling another special recipe bread breadstick before it was too late.

'What has been top of the mortal mind again this last month, eh? Well ... I'll tell you what hasn't. D'Mure? Stand up please.'

At the furthest corner of the restaurant a small and particularly frail-looking deity shuffled to his feet and looked around in terror.

'My dear d'Mure,' Scran intoned, 'you should be ashamed of yourself. Not one new follower of your particular way. I know Chastity is pretty unpopular these days, but ... What d'you have to say for yourself?'

D'Mure looked at his feet and made an odd mewling sound before looking up. 'It wasn't my fault,' he blurted. 'I nearly got one.'

Chuckles rippled around Manna Ambrosia's.

'And I would've done too, only ... only...' Suddenly, d'Mure's head came up fully, and he pointed an accusing finger at Letch, the Deity-in-Chief of Adultery, who sat grinning beneath a cloud of flittering waitresses. 'He stole my follower!' challenged d'Mure.

Letch threw back his head and laughed. 'What? I didn't steal him, he came willingly.'

'That's not true. After the way his girlfriend had treated him he was ready to renounce women for the rest of his life.'

20

'Oh, come on,' yawned Letch. He devoured a coyly offered grape from a hovering waitress. 'Haven't you heard of "playing hard to get"?'

'Is that what you call it? Flirting at him from her balcony in enemy territory, driving him to fake his suicide and then killing herself with feigned grief. Oh, sure, six foot under *is* pretty hard to get, isn't it? I'm telling you, he'd never have trusted another woman, rich family or otherwise, if you hadn't had him seduced by all those flower sellers. Poor Romeo...'

Manna Ambrosia's erupted in a flurry of laughter, sending d'Mure mewling back into his seat. He knew he was pretty well on a hiding to nothing with his cause. Now if only he could turn the Chastity Belt into a fashion item, then maybe...

'So who else, I hear you asking,' demanded Scran from the Top Table, 'is going down?' His eyes seemed to focus on one very hirsuit being who took a last swig of wine from a crystal flagon. He had known it wouldn't last. One freak period of wildly misbehaved and untrainable llamas just at the opening of Kruff's Obedience Show and his droves of believers had swollen considerably. And then, inevitably, when these new recruits to his way of Enlightenment through Llama Training hadn't won any rosettes they'd gone in search of salvation elsewhere. Generally down the pub, much to Sot's delight.

'Yup, you guessed it!' declared Scran, hands on his belly, staring at Paca the Deity-in-Charge of Ungulate Control. 'Out!'

As expectancy rose, the noise levels grew and the two usurped Deities stood and trudged miserably to the back of the restaurant, waiting for the places which would become available.

'So, three of our number have done remarkably well this month, each almost equally worthy of a place up here...'

Lush flashed Sot a smirk of overconfidence. Sot sneered back.

21

'And who are those three? I can hear you begging to know,' continued Scran in his now traditional attempt at injecting the proceedings with some sort of tension. 'Well, the candidates for promotion are, in no particular order, on table number three, Spirin...' A thin and surprisingly ill-looking goddess sprang unsteadily to her feet, clutching her head.

'On table five we have a newcomer to the possibility of a month's Top Tabledom, over there, Lush...' With a sickening sneer Lush grinned at Sot and leapt to his feet punching the air joyously.

'...and on table seven, another newcomer who has made amazing improvements this month. Stand up, Sot!'

Lush's self-satisfied sneer tumbled from his face as the Deity-in-Command of Ales hauled himself to his feet and thumbed a vast nose at him. It seemed that three weeks of almost continual rain and the disappointment of losing at Kruff's had kept folk in the pubs a lot recently, introducing them to the delights of ale. A surge of adrenal excitement coursed through Sot's body as he realised that this was his big chance. He knew he'd had a big conversion rate this month but secretly he hadn't expected to do so well. But now, here he was almost head to head with Lush.

He racked his brain and tried to remember exactly what it was that Spirin did. What danger was this unknown outsider?

'So,' continued Scran, chewing on another tranche of garlic manna, 'out of these three worthy candidates, who is about to step forward and take up their place, to be wined, dined and spoilt something rotten for the next month?' He pointed to the empty placements, aching for a dramatic roll of drums.

Manna Ambrosia's was hushed.

'The first successful candidate, with a conversion of fifteen thousand six hundred and eight souls to the ways of enlightenment through wine and spirits this month, yes, Lush, come on up!'

22

Applause erupted begrudgingly from the rest of the restaurant as they watched the Arch-Idol of Wines and Spirits stride arrogantly towards the Top Table, already peering imperiously over his interesting nose. He took a napkin and settled himself at the table, beaming.

'A bit too zealous on occasions, Lush,' chastised Scran. 'I was forced to remove several hundred claims due to them being under age. Still, a valiant result. And so...' He paused for effect '...We have two candidates left for one place. Who will it be?

Sot found his mouth feeling unpleasantly dry.

'Who will join us here?'

'Get on with it,' muttered a voice from the back of the restaurant. 'I want some pudding!'

Scran tutted, ruffled the envelope in his hand and tugged a fresh sheet out. 'Before I announce the other successful candidate, the loser, with fifteen thousand six hundred and five souls converted this month, Sot the Deity-in-Command of Ales, leaving...'

Sot didn't hear the end of the speech. His head pounded in torrents of frustration. Three souls, he'd lost to Lush by three! It was so unfair. For the whole of the next month he would have to put up with his sneering smugness as he revelled in his reaching the Top Table. He would never hear the last of it. Suddenly eternity looked like being a very long time.

He sank miserably into his seat and stared at the dark pool of his ale.

And then it hit him. In a flash of realisation he knew why the name of Spirin was so familiar. It was obvious now why she had reached the hallowed stool. With him and Lush converting so many new recruits to the delights of inebriation it was more or less inevitable there'd be an upturn in Spirin's particular Deitical responsibility.

Spirin, the Idoless-in-Chief of Hangover Cures, hobbled forward clutching her head and took her place at

23

the Top Table amid a tumult of apathetic applause.

And in that instant Sot vowed to succeed next month. Somehow he would find a way to usurp Lush. All he needed was a whole wave of thirsty souls desperate for the quenching delight of heady ale.

Miserably he stared into his flagon and began to plot.

The Mostly Reverend Vex Screed sat forlornly on the side of the mountain out of sight of Axolotl and filled a large tankard out of his flask. A humourless smile slithered across his face. He was glad that Pedlah, the damned sales manager of Wonderwear, hadn't found his stash of ale. He recorked the flask and took a large consolatory swig, his tongue cheering as the bitter-sweet liquid wrapped it in an alcoholic security blanket. Why, with only a dozen more pints of the same stuff he could even start to feel happy again.

Miserably he looked around him and sighed. Mountainous tundra spread away in all directions, littered with directionlessly flittering grouse and aimlessly grazing ibex. His inside security pocket felt worryingly conspicuous by its lack of reassuringly heavy cash. The shadows were getting longer, and the prospects of gainful and profitable employment were far from healthy and far away. In short, he had been hit in the back and trampled on by the hardest of times.

He swigged hard on his ale, stared into its fathomless peaty depths and thought of a time when his word could fire entire nomadic tribes into wild flurries of excitement. His mind drifted back to before the contract commercial preaching, before the creation of the mercionaries, returning to the halcyon days of the Haranguist Mission. The pure harsh beauty of one man and his book, striding out in search of nomads and wanderers ripe for conversion.

Oh, he had been good. Once. A wistful tear sparkled at the corner of his eye as he swigged his ale again and recalled his one-man bid to bring the word of St

Lucre the Unwashed to the D'vanouin Tribesmen of the Ghuppy Desert. And as his eyes stared into the dimensionless eternity of the bottom of his flagon, images swam upwards towards him.

A flock of goats had stared boredly at him back then as he had crossed the final few yards of the Ghuppy Desert towards the brightly coloured tents of the nomads. In his pack he had dozens of the new D'vanouin translation of the Red Proselytic Manuscript of St Lucre the Unwashed. Their pristine spines rubbed affectionately against his ancient battered tambourine. Oh, he mused, if he had a groat for every 'Kumbayah' that instrument had started he'd be a rich man.

He moved on through the ale-tinted memory replaying in the bottom of his tankard.

Unknown to him, he wasn't alone in there.

At that very instant another being was staring forlornly into his ale as a deity with an interesting nose wittered unstoppably in a speech of acceptance. Sot, the Deity-in-Command of Ales, blinked in surprise as something moved in the depths of his flagon. He rubbed his eye, glanced furtively around the interior of Manna Ambrosia's, shook his head and stared harder as a herd of goats shimmered into full ale-tinted view. Ignored, Lush's acceptance speech continued like so much hot air in the background.

The Mostly Reverend Vex Screed watched his ale as his past self snatched at a tent flap, whisked it aside and ducked quickly within. 'Have you heard the Word?' he declared and began handing out the newly printed books. 'Take one, pass them along. If there aren't enough you'll have to share them, one between two.'

Ah, that was the way to do it, complete confidence. In, grab their attention and convert them before they knew what had hit them. A tray of sheep's eyes hovered unpassed between two enblanketed tribesmen.

'But first, a short lesson from the Book of Apophthegms,' declared the peat-dark image of Screed, before starting to read heartily from the tome in his hands. Sot, an unfathomable distance above, watched in awe as the events unfolded. In a matter of minutes this black cassocked man had battered down any resistance the D'vanouins had and was turning them, moment by inexorable moment, towards a state of firm belief in his words.

He had been extremely lucky that the D'vanouins hadn't lynched him as soon as they'd recognised him as a man of the cloth. The wanderers of the Ghuppy Desert were always being bombarded by new religions – stay in the wilderness for anything over forty days and missionaries were flocking in from everywhere to save them. The D'vanouins were heartily sick of flocking missionaries. Now it wasn't that they were incapable of embracing faith at all, far from it. All they needed was some sort of system that allowed them to carry on with a bit of debauchery now and then, as well as running up any debts necessary for a damned good time. Once they found that their piety would know no bounds.

The ale-tinted image of Screed took a breath and read in pidgin D'vanouin. It had to be said, it was close. In fact it was a perfect representation of what was on the page. But if Screed had been fluent in D'vanouin he would have noticed that the words which had just left his tongue weren't *quite* what had been initially written. The words floated through the tent and wriggled their way into a host of D'vanouin ears.

Yea though I walk in the Alley of Debt, I don't give a damn.

The ears pricked up.

Blessed is the pure grain spirit for it is the water of life.

The shrieks of reformation rang loud as he solemnly stated the last offer the D'vanouins couldn't refuse. An

26

offer of the security of religion and the promise of a chaotic havoc-wreaking session to put the word 'mayhem' to shame, the infamous call to arms...

Let ye lambs of devotion burn bright.

Sot watched in awe as the D'vanouins snatched at this new religion, clutching it firmly to their faithful chests. It had to be good: to their ears it offered parties, it demanded sacrificial lambs and a bonus of kebabs afterwards. In seconds the tribesmen were hooked.

And so was Sot.

He knew how hard it was to convince the D'vanouin to do anything. He'd given up trying to turn the bedsheeted nomads on to the delights of an overwhelming belief in the teachings of the Deity-in-Command of Ales, 'Drink, drink, drink and be merry.'

But with this black cassocked missionary on his side ... Sot grinned. He knew for certain he would be on the Top Table next month.

He stood, swayed out towards the 'Little Gods' Room' and shut himself in a cubicle. There was no one there to see the blinding flash of light and the plume of smoke as he disappeared.

The Reverend Screed stared at his ale once more, bathing in the warm glow of his finest moment of one hundred percent conversion, and then shrugged. With a flick of a long hand he drained the tankard's contents and whispered a quick psalm of passing.

What he would do with himself now he hadn't a clue. Well, not beyond hiking back down the mountains and drumming up some more business, anyway. The chances of that would be greatly reduced when Pedlah's claim to sue became widely known. Screed stood, stuffed his flask back in his pocket and screamed as the air suddenly exploded before him and a single vast wall of chapped skin appeared. Huge ridges arced across its surface, mounted above a six-foot high foundation of leather-coloured material.

The air erupted in a crack of thunder which, if Screed really had to be honest, he would have admitted did sound disturbingly like the noise a three-hundred-foot tall giant would make if he'd just appeared suddenly.

Screed yelped and peered accusingly into the bottom of his tankard as the sky exploded again and an eight-foot tall figure appeared before him wearing leather sandals and the type of loose-fitting togas beloved by deities everywhere. 'Sorry about that,' said the intruder, rubbing the edge of his bulbous nose and trying to look nonchalant as he shrank another two feet. 'Always have trouble with scale. Didn't mean to scare you. Er, have a drink.'

'C ... can't. I've just finished ... oh. Cheers,' answered Screed as his tankard glowed and filled suddenly with frothing ale. 'H ... how did you do that?'

'Oh, just a little something I, er, picked up,' hedged Sot warily. 'It's an interest of mine.'

'What is?' asked Screed around a mouthful of celestial ale.

'You're drinking it,' grinned Sot.

'You made this? You some kind of brewer, or something?'

'More or less,' the deity answered and a tankard of his own coalesced out of the thin mountain air.

'A wizard?' whispered Screed.

'Cheers,' responded Sot enigmatically and raised his now-frothing tankard. They both drank.

Screed looked at the stranger's normal-sized chapped big toe and felt his head spin. Unreal images of walls of skin flitted around his mind. He took a steadying swallow of ale. It was followed by half a dozen more. In quick succession. Over the space of a few significant gulps he began to start doubting if he had in fact witnessed this stranger's arrival in as spectacular a manner as he had initially thought. It had been a hard

28

day, his mind could be playing tricks. And he didn't look exactly dangerous. With a tattoo of gulps he drained his tankard.

As if by magic, it flashed again, and was full.

Screed blinked and concluded that this stranger couldn't possibly pose any danger. Throughout the vast expanses of history no dangerous persons had ever been famed for dishing out free ale.

'Where *did* you learn that?' he begged. 'I've seen a few magicians in my time and they never did anything that useful. Rabbits out of hats or cutting folk in half, but never ale on tap. Can you do anything else, you know, nice drop of red wine or cask of whisky?'

Sot's jaw clenched tighter as he imagined Lush's expression of smugness at Screed's question. 'What's the matter? Don't you like the taste of my ale, eh?'

'Hey, I only asked. No, it's really good. And very kind of you. How d'you do it?'

'Ooooh, it's all in the wrist action,' answered Sot vaguely, and settled down to a figure that looked about five eight and weighed far too much to be hiking up and down mountains without oxygen. 'Takes ages to perfect.'

'I've got plenty of time,' said Screed and waggled his tankard. 'I can learn.' It probably wouldn't be as morally rewarding as introducing souls to new and improved ways of life, but if he learned to conjure ale out of thin air he'd be set up for life. More party invites than he could shake a stick at.

'Sure you wouldn't rather find yourself a new contract, Rev?' asked Sot with that grin again.

Screed took a sudden step backwards, his mind flitting to the all-too-recent events which he had already christened The Wonderwear Debacle. 'Hey, now look. Back there in Hyh'd Park, that wasn't my fault I'm only trying to make a living, you know. I mean, come on, everyone has their bad days!'

'Yes, I'm sure you were...'

'Wasn't my fault. I said it was going to be hard to make the Axolotians believe in that stuff, but he wouldn't listen. The guy you really want is down that way. If you run you'll still catch him. Beat him up. And while you're at it could you get my purse back and persuade him not to sue?'

'I'm not interested in that sort of thing, Reverend Screed, I'm here to offer you a commission that you can't refuse.'

Screed scowled suspiciously at the stranger. 'How d'you know my name?'

'I know a great deal about you.' Sot, knew that eavesdropping on an ale-soaked reverie didn't really count as a 'great deal', but it *was* more than nothing. Besides, it did sound somewhat more impressive. 'And I can offer you a great deal.'

'Oh yeah?' asked Screed somewhat sceptically and shook his empty tankard again.

'Yes,' grinned Sot as Screed's tankard flashed and filled. 'Something you've been dreaming of, I'll warrant. Something you'll never get up the road there.' He pointed a thumb in the general direction of where he hoped Axolotl was.

Screed raised a curious eyebrow. 'And that is?'

Sot leaned forwards and whispered, 'Virgin territory. Somewhere your face isn't known. Somewhere filled with folk just aching for what I want you to, er, promote for me.'

Screed's mind spun, intoxicated by the ale and the stranger's promise. His heart skipped as he thought of it. Virgin territory, pastures new. 'How filled?' he asked.

'Packed. Er, captive audience, you might say. And their numbers are growing all the time.'

Screed's eyes flashed with excitement.

Sot leaned closer, snaking a companionable arm around the Reverend's cassocked shoulder. 'In fact you could spend an eternity converting them all.'

Screed whistled and his eyes lit up. 'An *eternity*? There's *that* many of them? Where is this place, how come I don't know about it?'

'Oh, but you do,' grinned Sot. 'You just might not have thought of it in these terms before. You know, er, out of bounds.'

'Ha! Now you've done it. Said too much. I know exactly where you mean,' gloated Screed. 'Huge place, hard to get to, massive population, three-headed dogs on the gates.'

Sot nodded, impressed that a man of the cloth had harboured similar thoughts to himself.

'You want me to go and preach to the Murrhovian Empire!' declared Screed with an anticipatory smile. He'd heard all the legends about that place...

Sot burst out laughing. 'Ooooh no, no. I've somewhere better than that in mind. Bigger and just a little hotter.' He pointed a finger at the ground.

Screed scratched his head as he tried to remember his geography. 'Bigger and hotter ... south?'

'No!' Sot pointed at the ground again, forcefully.

Screed's jaw dropped as realisation hit. 'You *can't* be serious...'

'No? And why not? Like I said, it's a captive audience, just ripe for conversion. More ale, Reverend?'

Screed gulped another mouthful and shook his head. 'Are you really standing there and suggesting I preach the good word to the wailing souls in the ... the Underworld Kingdom of Helian?'

'Yup. Good, eh?'

'Good?' he squeaked and gulped at his ale. 'In case it had slipped your mind, there is one very major snag about preaching down there.'

Sot sipped nonchalantly at his tankard. 'And that is?'

'Nobody ever gets out alive, that's all!' growled Screed. 'It's hell down there!'

'Hmmm, wondered how long it would be before you started with the trivial objections,' mused Sot.

31

'Trivial? *Trivial!*' flapped Screed. 'It's my life you're talking about here. I don't particularly fancy popping my clogs just yet, thank you very much.' He threw a mouthful of ale down his throat, attempting to shore up what he felt was his rapidly diminishing sanity.

Sot shook his head, arms crossed. 'That's a very short-sighted outlook, you know. Very blinkered.'

'What?'

'Have you ever stopped to think about the Big Picture – your place in the grand scheme of things, eh?'

'Of course I have. I've devoted my life to mission-ary...'

Sot tutted. 'There you go again, wittering on about life as if it's the *most* important thing...'

'Well, I wouldn't be much fun at parties without it, would I?'

'Don't be too sure about that. I had a great time at a couple of barn dances the other week.'

'What?'

'Yeah. The real soul of the party ... Hey, what's up? Why you backing away?'

'I know what you're doing. Keep away from me.' Vex Screed squirmed up the hill, suddenly recalling the stranger's entrance. Okay, so he didn't have black scaly skin, curly horns and a pointy tail to mark him out, but he could be in disguise. 'It's sick and disgusting, that is. Trying to seduce a man of the cloth into Helian. You'll never get me to enter a pact with you...'

'Me? Pact? Oh no, you think I'm ... Ha ha! Relax, pal, I'm not from down there.'

'Don't believe you.'

'Oh, come on. How many devils d'you know that go around handing out free beer, hmmm?'

Screed's tankard flashed full again.

'Besides,' continued Sot, 'where's my black scaly skin, curly horns and pointy tail, eh?'

'Disguise,' muttered Screed.

'Stop being so paranoid. Trust me. I'm one of the good guys.'

'Make your mind up!' snapped Screed, his head whirling. 'You said you were a mage before.' Angry now, he slammed his hands on his hips and spilled ale down his cassock. It did little to improve his mood. 'I don't know what your game is, but I'm telling you, if you think you can just breeze in here and buy me with free beer then you've got another...'

'My dear Reverend Screed, it was you who said I was a mage. Would you like a refill?'

'You didn't deny it!' Screed shouted, his mind fixed on the mage question.

'I'm sorry if I misled you by my enigmatic failure to answer, but folks don't normally cope well with being greeted out of the blue by a god unless they've had a few beers beforehand. Don't know why that should be, really. We're not such a bad bunch...'

'Wh ... what did you just say?' asked Screed, having slapped the side of his head forcefully a few times with the heel of his hand.

'Which bit did you miss?'

'Folks being greeted by g ... g...' Screed whimpered.

'Gods. No, the public don't cope at all well sometimes. Some of the faces I've seen would make your skin crawl. I ask you, it doesn't make sense. I'm not *that* bad-looking, am I?'

'You? You're trying to say *you're* a g ... You're from H ... H...' Pathetically Screed pointed a trembling finger skywards.

Sot looked up. 'Well, I think it's up there somewhere. I really should find out.'

'You saying you're a god?'

Sot smiled deitically.

'No, no, no. That can't be right,' Screed floundered. 'Not right at all. What was all that about life being trivial? I can't imagine gods normally wander about with such views.'

'I'm only trying to be helpful. No, don't look at me like that. Trust me. I'm only trying to make sure you achieve your full potential. Look, have another ale, dry yourself off and I'll explain.'

A curiously warm glow stroked Screed's thigh as steam rose from his ale-soaked cassock. Shrugging, he held out his tankard again as he realised that in fact he didn't have anywhere to run and that he was, despite a large hoard of reservations, very, very intrigued. If this guy really was a god and he walked away ... he'd never forgive himself. It wouldn't do him much harm to listen for a few minutes.

Keeping images of what happens to the proverbial curious kitten firmly in the forefront of his mind for reference, he said, in as healthily sceptical a voice as he could manage, 'Alright, fire away. I'm listening.'

'Goody, goody. Well, it's all a case of mathematics really,' said Sot enthusiastically. 'See, you know that right now, you're far from immortal, alright?'

Screed nodded doubtfully.

'And once you've shuffled off this mortail coil, then it's afterlife time, agreed? The rest of eternity twiddling your thumbs and getting bored, right?'

Screed nodded again.

'Wrong!' insisted Sot. 'Common misbelief, that one. The afterlife's busy, busy, busy. No chance to rest. Well, it wouldn't be right, would it? I mean, just 'cause you're immortal doesn't mean you don't still have needs. You know, going down the pub, or a night's theatre. Somebody's got to supply it. But the good bit about Heobhan is that you get to choose what you want. You for instance, I reckon the perfect afterlife for you would be to spend eternity preaching to your heart's content.'

Screed's eyes misted over. 'Yes...' he whispered dreamily and a kitten of wary curiosity was toasted.

'And that's where the mathematics come in, see?'

'No.'

Sot took a breath and hoped he could pull this off. 'It's

34

all to do with efficiency. How many souls have you converted in your lifetime?'

'Hundreds,' answered Screed happily, thinking proudly of droves of D'vanouin Tribesmen.

'Hmmm, not bad,' mused Sot, rubbing his bulbous nose. 'But just think of how many you can convert between now and the end of eternity, when you don't have to muck about with wasting time sleeping and stuff. Hundreds of thousands of millions, that's how many.'

Screed's jaw dropped.

Sot readied himself for the awkward bit, the bridge of belief he had to build to make his cunning scheme a gleaming reality. 'Just to put that into context we need to do a bit of maths. You any good at maths?' Screed shook his head. Inside Sot grinned. That would make things easier.

'Well, a couple of hundred divided by hundreds of thousands of millions is near as dammit nothing, so, in short, your life is a waste of time. You're better off dead, see?' Sot grinned. 'Far more effective.'

Screed looked crestfallen and mouthed the word 'dead'. Three more kittens expired.

'Look, it's nothing personal, just good management, see? Have some more ale.'

Screed sipped and looked as if he was struggling with a series of complex calculations in his head, his fingers twitching.

'I wouldn't have mentioned it if I didn't know it was true,' offered Sot, hopefully. 'The sooner you start working at full efficiency the more souls you personally will have saved. Do you realise that every day you cling to your grossly inefficient way of life then three dozen more souls are left unconverted?'

'I ... I never thought about it like that before.'

'Oh yes. Thirty-six, every day, for eternity. Lost. Shocking really, but there you go. Still, if you want to carry on the way you are then...'

'No, no. You're right!' declared Screed, the light of

35

understanding flashing on behind his eyes. Millions of souls cheered in his imagination. 'Absolutely spot on. Oh, why didn't I see it before? Such selfish inefficiency. I can't let them go unsaved. *Can't* let that happen to them. It's my duty!' he extolled evangelically, tugging a dagger out of his cassock and holding it quivering before his belly.

'Wait! Wait!' shouted Sot, flapping his hands in alarm. 'No, not that way! Helian for sure that way!' He knew the rules on suicide. Straight to the torment of Helian, no appeal.

'But I must. Think of the souls I should be saving. I cannot deny them...'

'No, you can't do it yourself!'

Screed tutted, shrugged his shoulders and held out the dagger to Sot. 'Fair enough. You'd better do it then.'

'No, no...' The colour drained from Sot's cheeks.

'I won't struggle, it'll be fine. Just jam it there in between my ribs. C'mon, don't be squeamish.'

'No, I...'

'I'll look the other way if you want.'

'I can't,' panicked Sot, thinking about the stink there'd be if the truth ever got out that he'd murdered a missionary. It was bad enough embroidering the truth with such dodgy twists of fact to coerce him this far, but...

'Well thank you very much!' snarled Screed, angrily stamping his foot. 'That's really kind, that is. You pop out of nowhere, tell me my life's a waste of time and then you won't help me do anything about it. You sure know how to make a Reverend's day!'

'I didn't say I wouldn't help.'

'Take the dagger then, come on.' Screed was tugging his cassock open feverishly and pointing to his chest. 'There, quick stab and I'll be on my way...'

'I'm not going to do it, either. Look. I've got a plan. Now, if you promise not to do anything stupid with that dagger, I'll make sure that you snuff it tomorrow, alright?'

Sot sipped at his ale and looked at the Mostly Reverend.

'Morning or afternoon?' growled Screed begrudgingly.

'First thing in the morning. How's decapitation suit?'

'Marvellous.' Screed decided to make full use of his throat's last few hours. With a grin he downed the ale, wiped his mouth with the back of his cassock sleeve and waggled his tankard for a refill. 'Now then, just what is it you want these tormented souls converted to, eh?' he asked.

'You've been drinking it,' smirked Sot. He knew that Lush's days on the Top Table of Manna Ambrosia's were definitely numbered. 'Now, I've just got a few things to do before tomorrow. Just a couple of little details to make sure of. Don't go away!' And with a flash of light Sot, the Deity-in-Command of Ales, vanished.

One of the huge advantages which Axolotl offered those of a more spiritual origin was that having to sneak about inconspicuously wasn't necessary. Since the entire population of the Mountain City of Axolotl were utterly hyperstitious and held an unshakable belief in everything omenical and significant, none of them was ever surprised when odd beings popped up unexpectedly.

And Xxoe was no exception. She sat up in her hammock and stared at the spot where a second ago a captive lightning bolt had writhed explosively and coalesced into a large and extremely solid-looking form.

'Hello,' she said to the beer-bellied deity standing in her hammock-room. She flicked a strand of black hair over her shoulder and swung in her hammock.

'Hello, little girl,' answered Sot with what he hoped was a reassuring smile. 'All ready for the morning?'

'I will be when I've had good night's sleep,' replied Xxoe. 'What d'you want?'

'I'm here to make sure you have a nice sleep.' He grinned in the darkened room. It wasn't really a lie. When he'd finished with her she would be, quite literally, dead to the world.

'That's nice. Are you going to tuck me in? Or read me stories?'

'Ooooh no, dear, I've got something *far* better than that.' There was a tiny flash of light and a large flagon of ale appeared in her hands. 'Drink it up,' urged Sot. 'It'll help you sleep.'

'Like chocolate?'

'More or less.'

'But I've already had my chocolate,' answered Xxoe, puzzled.

'Well, that's not chocolate, that's ale ... er, a little something extra for a special little girl,' he insisted. 'And you *do* deserve something special. It's not every morning that you get yourself sacrificed, is it?'

'No, just once a year.' Xxoe grinned proudly. It was an honour to be selected for the Annual Undertakers' Festival parade. Not only for her, but also her parents. Even though they were fast asleep in the next room, rocking gently in their hammocks, they grinned proudly. Tomorrow they'd get the head of the table at the Feast *and* what's more Xxoe's mother could hold her head high and look down her nose at all the brazen rejects of teenagerdom who could never, ever take Xxoe's place. Sacrifices were only for good girls, chaste girls, not wanton promiscuous harlots.

Quickly, Xxoe jumped out of her hammock and pattered across to the curtain. Tugging it back, she pointed across the square to a darkly silhouetted temple, its serrated sides rising like a stepped pyramid.

Sot could make out the equally dark silhouettes of two vast guards as they patrolled the flat roof with a pair of flaming torches. It was tradition that no one be allowed near the sacrificial device until dawn had risen and Xxoe was led up there to be sacrificed. Again.

38

Six times she'd faced the gleaming blade on the top of
that temple and six times she had gone to the party
afterwards. It had started centuries ago when the Grand
Union of Undertakers had decided it was grossly unfair
they were missing out on all the parties in Axolotl.
Farmers had their harvest festivals where they'd all cook
up bits of their crops as an offering for next year. At least
that was the excuse. Once the service was over it was
bibs on and tuck in. And similarly there was the
Brewers' Annual Bash, the Confectioners' Pick'n'Mix
Party ... the list was endless. Everybody went to
everyone else's do's (except the Undertakers, who were
snubbed). And so they started their own Annual Undertakers' Festival Parade. Everyone received invites to
the Ritual Sacrifice and Dance on the Temple. Nobody
knew what was going to happen.

The crowds gathered in the square looking up at the
odd bamboo device with the suspended blade, curious as
to its function. The drums rolled and the Undertakers
dragged the young girl out screaming, slapping her down
onto the stone slab, drums beating wildly, and then with
a cry of delight from the Head Undertaker – and a squeal
of anguish from the girl – he had released the scream-
ingly sharp blade. Slack-jawed, the whole of Axolotl
watched as it plunged down the vertical rails, accelerating unstoppably toward the maiden's silk-smooth neck,
eager to snatch her life...

It took three whole minutes after the blade thudded to
a stop for the crowd to realise the girl was still breathing.
The Undertakers hauled the blade back to the top of the
rails and tugged out the chock, holding it up for all to
see. Well, they couldn't actually sacrifice her, could
they? It would have ruined the Party. Especially for her
parents.

Following the vastly debauched party which ensued,
the Annual Undertakers' Festival Parade and Dance had
rapidly become a regular fixture on the Axolotian party
calendar.

'Can't wait for it all to be over,' said Xxoe with a glint in her eye as she looked across at the temple. 'The party afterwards is always good fun. I want two pieces of chocolate pudding this year. I deserve it.'

'And you deserve that too,' urged Sot pointing to the flagon. 'Drink.'

Xxoe took a large gulp, crossed her eyes and spat it out, ale aerosoling across the curtains in a fine spray. 'Yeuch. That's horrid!' she complained. 'You trying to poison me?'

'No, no,' panicked Sot. 'Er, it's an acquired taste.' He flicked his wrist, the flagon flashed and he said, 'Try that. It might be more to your taste.'

Xxoe sniffed uncertainly at the frothy liquid.

'It's good for you,' urged Sot, smiling in a very untrustworthy manner. 'Go on.'

She sipped cautiously, rolled the liquid around her mouth and looked thoughtful. Then she swallowed. Sot exhaled, relieved.

'Not too bad,' said Xxoe begrudgingly. 'Any chance of a bit more ginger?'

Sot's wrist flicked once more and he upped the flavouring by a few points. He also took the liberty of adding an extra five percent alcohol. Xxoe sipped and swallowed, coughing as the ginger ale burnt the back of her throat. 'Phew!' she choked. 'That's *good*!'

The Deity-in-Command of Ales inclined his head graciously and beamed as the heart-warming sound of a guzzling girl reached his ears.

'Another?' he asked a few moments later as Xxoe wiped her hand across her mouth. She grinned a mite lopsidedly and nodded.

Dispensing another flagon of eighteen-percent proof ginger ale with a nonchalant wrist flick, Sot relaxed. A couple more of those inside her and nobody would be able to wake her before mid-afternoon.

Would the Undertakers ever find a willing sacrificial

replacement? Sot grinned to himself. He knew the answer to that one.

The figure in the black long-tailed toga and matching cylindrical cap raised his staff, twirled it between his fingers and shattered the early morning stillness of Axolotl.

'Alright, alright,' came a cry from within the hovel as the staff's ferule took gouges out of the door. 'I'm coming.'

The door was snatched open and a worried-looking man cannoned out and pulled it shut behind him.

'I have come,' declared The Undertaker, twirling his staff.

'Yeah, well, go round the block again will you, we're not ready.' babbled the worried-looking one, still unshaven and in an obvious state of distress.

'This is the appointed time,' intoned The Undertaker, looking imperiously down his nose at Xxoe's father.

'I know that! Appointed time, appointed place. No appointed daughter.'

The black-clad one took a step backwards. 'What? But that can't be ... she ... We need her! The Party! She must come.'

'How good are you at raising the dead, eh?'

'This is no time for jokes.' The Undertaker scowled and tugged at the collar of his toga, which suddenly felt worryingly tight. 'Out of my way,' he barked and swept into the hovel, his sandals pounding on the stairs as he sprang towards Xxoe's hammock-room.

Kicking open the door, he gasped as the scene hit him full in the face: the curtains tightly closed, wreathing the room in catacomb gloom, the mother rocking back and forth muttering forlornly, close to tears. And the body motionless in the hammock, bereft of life. Dead to the world.

No! wailed the Undertaker's mind. Not today. It's my day off!

41

Xxoe's mother looked around, eyes rimmed with tears, knowing instinctively that their invite to the party was cancelled. 'I'm sorry...' she sniffed.

The Undertaker strode across the room, head whirling with unanswered questions, boiling with annoyance. He snatched the covers back and stared at the pale figure.

'G'roff,' mumbled Xxoe into her pillow as she tugged back her blankets. 'Leevmeeyalone. I'm dying...' She clutched her head and groaned horribly.

The Undertaker's knees collapsed with shock and he crumpled to the floor, his head reeling with the irony of it all. It wasn't fair. What was his announcement going to be? 'Sorry, there'll be no sacrifice today. The victim isn't feeling very well!'

Why hadn't anyone foreseen this happening? The Editor of *Scryin' Out* would have some severe questions to answer.

But right now that wasn't important. Right now he had an entire city of party-goers to entertain. Where was he going to find a stand-in at such short notice?

Snarling, he stood and whirled out of the room.

'Well?' asked Xxoe's father as the Undertaker whisked by, toga-tails flapping.

'No it's not. Far, far from it,' he growled, then vanished into the street, angry sandals stirring clouds of sand.

At that very instant a certain black-cassocked Reverend was entering Axolotl across the rickety bridge and trudging up the main street, stifling a worried yawn. It was, to his way of thinking, far too early to be up and about.

The large beer-bellied man at his side denied this heartily.

And amazingly, the residents of Axolotl agreed with him. Baffled, Screed watched as flocks of people swarmed out of side alleys and sped off enthusiastically, all in the same direction, buzzing with excitement.

'Well, go on then,' urged Sot, pointing after the dashing crowds.

'You think this is really a good idea, me showing my face back here so soon after the Wonderwear Debacle?' asked Screed nervously.

'Trust me,' oozed Sot. 'Everything is sorted. Just relax and do as I say.' He gave Screed a secretive wink.

'Sure,' muttered the Reverend, feeling unconvinced. 'I just hope nobody recognises me from yesterday. They'll kill m...' A flash of realisation flared behind his eyes. 'Ahh, right. Good one. I understand.'

'Good. Now hurry up. You don't want to miss it. Timing is absolutely critical.'

Vex Screed followed the rapidly gathering crowd and squeezed into the packed square just as a wave of excitement flooded the area with adrenaline.

Sot grinned and pointed towards the vast temple which dominated the square. A single black-toga'd figure climbed slowly up the stepped side wringing his hands desperately. A stone slab lay at the summit between two vast torch-bearing guards, its head crowned by an odd-looking device lashed together from bits of bamboo.

The crowd murmured restlessly, and occasional bursts of cheering and whistling exploded spontaneously from all directions.

For such an early hour, mused Screed, they were very lively. Must do good breakfasts round here.

At last the black-toga'd man reached the top of the temple. He fixed the angle of his tall cylindrical cap, then approached the crowd. All eyes were swept up towards him, focus forced by the perspective of the steps, ears ready for his announcement.

The Undertaker swallowed nervously and wrung his hands. He still hadn't a clue what he was going to say. A hundred different options had been thought of and rejected outright. He had considered just not turning up, pretending he'd forgotten about it, or spouting some guff about it not being an auspicious day for a party and trying again tomorrow. He'd even thought about volunteering himself but, well, the sacrifice was supposed to be a virgin and there had been that grief-stricken nymphomaniac widow a couple of years back who had just begged for a good comforting and ... well, he didn't really count any more.

Taking a gulp of air, the Undertaker raised his hands and addressed the crowd, a passenger to his mouth's whims.

'Ladies and Gentlemen, er...' he began impressively. Thick silence fell over Axolotl, broken only by the deadly crackling of the guards' torches.

'Er ... unaccustomed as I am...' he hedged. One or two of the crowd shuffled restlessly. Something was amiss, they could tell.

'Er ... in a change of plan I'd, er, like to try something new, alright?' The Undertaker tried to inject a feeling of vitality into the proceedings. He failed. 'For the past six years we've sacrificed the same little girl. Now Xxoe's been a good sport,' he crossed his fingers, 'but, well, we've heard her scream a bit too often, don't you think?'

The only answer was the restless shuffling of feet.

'What is this?' muttered Screed in confusion.

'Shut up and pay attention,' growled Sot.

'Well, I think it's about time we had a brand-new sacrifice,' continued the Undertaker. 'So, have I got any volunteers?'

Silence swept the temple square as sceptical thoughts raised ugly heads. What had happened to Xxoe? A mistake at rehearsals? Could that happen to them if they volunteered?

'Now come on,' begged the Undertaker. 'Just think of the prestige. The honour of giving your life here, now...'

Screed's ears pricked up. 'Did he say what I think he said?' he asked Sot.

The Deity-in-Command of Ales nodded casually in the knowing way of one whose plans had just taken a massive step forward along the road to glorious completion.

'Come on,' pleaded the Undertaker. 'Just one volunteer in the audience? Won't somebody just...'

'Me, me, me, me, me...' yammered Screed as he shoved his way through the crowd and raced towards the temple. He couldn't believe his luck. This was his chance to achieve his full salvational potential. *And* help a chap out of a jam. Oh, joy!

Sot grinned to himself. In a few minutes it would all begin. A bit of careful timing would be needed up at the Gates of Heobhan for him to intercept Screed, then he could whisk him out the back steps straight to work. It was perfect. And when the increased souls figure started coming in, why, there'd be no stopping him.

'Me ... me ...' panted Screed as he staggered onto the top of the temple. 'I volunteer!'

The Undertaker scowled. 'You? But you're not Axolotian.'

'So what? Nobody else's come forward. C'mon, off with my head.'

'But, I ... I can't. You won't be allowed.'

'Why not? I'm as good as anyone.' He turned to face the crowd. 'My head. My head!' he cried, punching the air. A ripple of a chant took hold.

'You don't count,' flapped the Undertaker. 'You ... you're not a virgin!'

'Excuse me, my man. Are you suggesting that I don't take my vows seriously? I'm a man of the cloth! Off with my head!'

'But ... oh, alright then. Since you insist.'

Almost before the words were out of his mouth, four vast bearers snatched Screed and slammed him onto the slab, knocking his breath away.

And then a terminal feeling of worry flooded his body as he looked up the parallel rails to the gleaming hatchet blade suspended above him. Behind his head lay a basket, splattered with dark fruit juices for that touch of realism. The guards held his limbs firmly to the slab of stone, immobilising him. The crowd were cheering now.

Alarm swelled in Screed's heart as his gaze fell on the wooden chock jammed in the rail to his left. What was that doing there? If it remained in position then the blade would stop an inch above his neck. Panic seized him. He struggled, trying to snatch the chock away, trying to make sure that here, now, would be the first day of the rest of his afterlife.

The guards pressed him onto the slab, their feathered headdresses flapping colourfully. And then the vast beer-bellied bully clinging to his left hand winked, reached into the rail and grabbed the chock. In a second Sot had it in his pocket.

Nearby, behind a large statue of a mountain coypu, the real fourth guard chuckled as the flagon of ale in his hand flashed and refilled itself miraculously. It had been very nice of that large chap to swop his uniform for this magic flagon.

The crowd in the temple square below seethed and cheered wildly as the Undertaker strutted towards the bamboo blade-wielder and grasped the release rope. He unravelled it from the cleat and immediately felt the deadly weight of the blade. The rope arced up to a primitive wheel, down through a hole and there was tied to the blade. All he had to do was let go and gravity would do the rest.

'In celebration of the party to come,' shouted the Undertaker in the traditional words, 'release the rope!'

Reverend Screed braced himself as he watched the rope slacken momentarily above the blade. A glint of sunlight reflected off the razor edge and it rumbled towards him, accelerating, screaming sparks out of the rails, hungry to taste his neck, to sink its dread fangs in his throat. Unstoppably it whistled towards him. His heart pounded with the excitement of it all, thrilling as his toes dangled over the edge of eternity.

The crowd squealed as the blade jarred and shuddered to an abrupt halt.

'Bugger!' screamed Screed, staring at the blade shuddering half an inch above his throat. 'What happened? What went wrong? Why aren't I ... Oh.' Disgustedly he stared at the vast knot jammed in the hole at the top of the framework.

The Undertaker was rubbing his hands in alarm. 'I'm so dreadfully sorry. That should never have happened. Never. There should be a chock in the rail. I ... I don't know where it could possibly have disappeared to. I'm so glad the safety knot was there. I ... Ooooh!' And then he heard the crowd's cheers. Grinning skeletally he strode to the front of the temple and bowed low.

Screed snarled in angry frustration as the guards released him and tugged the blade back to the top of the frame, tying it up safely. 'How dare you let that happen,' he growled, prodding Sot in the chest and walking him towards the back of the temple roof. 'You promised me I'd...'

'Yeah, yeah. Look...' Sot winced as he backed up towards several hundred feet of sheer drop. 'Don't let a little hitch like that get you down. I said I'd do it and I will, alright?'

'This morning,' snapped Screed, striding forcefully across the temple top. 'Just think of all those souls I should be saving!'

'Yeah, yeah. I'll deal with it, okay, just give me a...'

Suddenly Sot's foot stepped into mid-air. Reflexively his hand flashed out and grabbed Screed's prodding arm. In an instant both Screed and Sot realised that the temple was not constructed with the classical symmetry one normally associated with this ilk of building. It had steep steps on three sides of its near pyramidal form, but none on the back. It was a cost-cutting exercise. Since nobody would ever view the temple from anywhere but the front, the Axolotians simply hadn't put any steps on the side facing away from the square.

It was one hundred and fifty feet straight down.

Screed screamed as he fell and Sot realised he should really have had more control over his reflexes. If he'd stopped for a millisecond and actually thought about it he would have just fallen for a few feet and then swooped upright to land deitically on the temple again. But now...

Screed tumbled on, his beard streaming back from his face, his cassock flapping like a loose sail in a hurricane. And as he fell he grinned, spreading his arms like a love-lorn sweetheart sprinting towards her long-lost fiancée. Eternity here I come!

Briefly, as the ground whistled towards him, he wondered in a detached sort of way just how much it would smart when he hit the dirt at terminal velocity.

And he was only seconds from finding out when a cart came screaming around the corner of the temple on two wheels and skittered, surrounded by a dust-cloud, to a halt.

The Mostly Reverend Vex Screed hit the crash-mat-cart of the Accident and Emergency Foreseervice in a flurry of abuse. His fists pounded the spongy mattresses with acute indignation. Saved! *Saved!* How dare they!

'Alright up there?' asked the man in the white uniform, looking up as he set his ladder against the cart.

'No!' snapped Screed with frustration.

The Foreseer looked shocked. 'What's up, then? Twisted your ankle? Sprained your wrist?' It was a matter of extreme pride amongst the Emergency Fore-seers that a rescue wasn't a real rescue unless it was completely scratch-free.

'No! That's the problem. I'm fine, thanks to you!' Screed swung onto the ladder and began scrambling irritably down. 'Bloody selfish, that is, assuming that just 'cause someone's in imminent mortal danger they want rescuing!'

'Nobody's ever complained before,' the Foreseer protested.

'Pah!' snapped Screed. 'Did I *ask* you to save me? Was I screaming for help as I plummeted down, eh? Was I?'

'Well, I didn't hear ...'

'Exactly! Bloody do-gooders,' grumbled Screed as he stormed off.

'Bloody tourists,' said the man in the uniform, tugging his ladder down. 'Ungrateful git!' he shouted. 'Don't you go thinking I *wanted* to save you. It's not my fault it's policy, you know. Just something we Axolotians do, 'cause we can! Just think on, the next time you find yourself plummetin' groundwards you'll be on your own. Then who'll be sorry, eh? It won't be me!'

He got no answer from the grumbling missionary as he swept around the corner, avoided the party as if it was plagued and stomped out of the city, his blood boiling.

It was a full ten minutes before Sot deemed it safe-ish to approach. He swooped out of the clouds as Screed stomped onto the rickety bridge to the south of Axolotl.

'Look,' began the god, 'I'll fix it. I'll sort it out, okay?'

'Go away,' snarled Screed, stopping in his tracks, hands defiantly on his hips. His face was purple with blood.

'It'll be alright.'

'You said that last time!' fumed Screed, tapping his foot. 'I thought gods were supposed to be able to control mortal happenings – part crimson seas and drop supplies to starving tribes lost in the wilderness, that sort of thing.'

'Wouldn't believe everything you hear,' Sot grumbled. 'But look, I *nearly* got you snuffed, didn't I? If it hadn't been for those Emergency Foreseers, then ...'

'I know!' Screed stamped his foot. A rotten beam directly below his feet creaked and sent a dozen wood-lice tumbling into the black ravine below. 'You don't have to rub it in! I could have started my mission by now.

49

I could have rolled up my sleeves and been up to my elbows in my afterlife's work! But no. That's too much to ask, isn't it?' He stamped his foot again. 'I've failed.' he stamped.

'Fancy a beer?' offered Sot.

'No, I don't want a beer!' Screed yelled and stamped again, for all the world looking like a small boy on the verge of a tantrum. Unheard, the rotting beam creaked again.

'You sure? It'll calm your nerves, help you think straight.'

'I don't want a beer now!' Stamp. 'I don't want a beer in ten minutes!' Stamp. 'In fact I don't want to see your face ever again in this lifetime!' Stamp.

The bridge trembled sickeningly and seemed to slip sideways.

'Uh-oh,' muttered Screed, looking at the gaps beneath his toes.

'One last beer?'

Nervously Screed shook his head as the final fibres of wood unravelled beneath him. The planks split and with a shriek of 'Yipppeeeeeeee!' the Mostly Reverend Vex Screed vanished into the ravine.

A figure in a white uniform and matching cap tutted from the Axolotian gatetower. 'Told him,' he muttered to himself. 'I did warn him.'

He turned and wandered off, heading back to the party where he knew he'd be needed to tug a cocktail stick out of a woman's throat in ten minutes.

HEL and Efficiency

The unmistakable sound of hooves clicking on obsidian tiles echoed down the corridors of the Sinful Service. Outside, the Underworld Kingdom of Helian continued oblivious to the events about to unfold. Never had anything like this been done before on such a scale. Things would never be quite the same again.

With a squeal of hinges the door to Immigrations was kicked open and a nine-foot demon lurched in beneath a stack of Nognite parchment. It was followed by a smaller demon with a large scaly brow, wearing a long black cloak.

'Alright, you lot, sit up and listen!' bellowed Seirizzim, the Undertaker-in-Chief of Mortropolis, dropping the wad of perforated parchment onto the nearest desk with a dramatic crash. The office of demons peered nervously around their stacks of parchmentwork and shuddered. Seirizzim was at it again. Another change in works practices, it had to be. Almost at once all minds focused on two questions: 'Now what?' and, 'Who's the dweeb in the cloak?'

'I've got a question,' declared Seirizzim joyously, his curly horns barely missing the low, roughly carved ceiling. 'And the question is, what's the difference between this parchment and the stuff you're used to?'

A thick silence filled the office, broken only by the crash of a sheet of crimson lightning outside. They all recognised the tone of the question. Ever since he had been elected Undertaker-in-Chief of Mortropolis, Seirizzim had burst in here, and many other departments of the Sinful Service, with the same eager quiver in his voice. The entire office drooped. It always meant two things. The introduction of a brand-new hyper-efficient system. And a shedload of extra work because of it.

'C'mon,' bellowed Seirizzim angrily. 'What's the difference?'

'That stuff isn't covered in writing,' grumbled the demon sitting at the back of the office, who went under the name of Nabob. He stared out through crimson eyes, scowling over the interminable mound of Immigration forms stacked on his desk and demanding attention.

'Wrong!' declared Seirizzim and turned the pile of parchments end on. Helpfully he snatched the top sheet with a careful claw and tugged it into the air. Another three sheets followed in a string. 'Try again!' he sneered sarcastically.

'Er, they're all stuck together,' grunted a clerk from the front row.

'What's this, a cost-cutting exercise at the parchment works?' grunted Nabob.

'No!' shouted Seirizzim. '*This* is efficiency!'

'Still looks like a pile of parchment to me.' Nabob shook his horned head miserably.

'*This* is the future!' bellowed Seirizzim wildly, his nostrils flaring like a stallion in a stud farm.

'Why? Does it fill itself in?' mumbled Nabob.

'Can it file itself?' enthused the clerk at the front. 'That would be marvellous.'

'Creep,' muttered Nabob, exploring his nostril with a practised nine-inch talon.

'Neither of those,' shouted Seirizzim. 'This is much more ground-breaking. Moloch, explain.' With a flourish of claws, Seirizzim grabbed the cloaked demon and thrust him forward.

'Th ... this is b ... brand-new,' he stuttered nervously. A lifetime spent fiddling with interesting crystals in dark rooms at all hours of the day and night had never prepared him for public speaking. He folded his scaly arms and tapped at his ribs.

'Just show them. They wouldn't understand the explanation anyway.' Seirizzim landed a deft hoof in the small of Moloch's back. 'I didn't carry that parchment all the way down the corridor for this. C'mon!'

Moloch trembled nervously as a bruise welled up around his kidneys. 'Ahhhh ... well ... simply b ... by utilising one's index digit in a piercing manner one c ... can...'

'Show them, I said!' snarled Seirizzim. 'You, Nabob,' he growled, pointing imperiously at the back of the office. 'What's the name of your latest immigrant?'

'Stobart Dentressangle,' grunted Nabob, reading the latest soul tag. Moloch, on hearing this, made a frantic series of tiny holes in the top sheet of parchment with his index talon.

'Cause of death?' rapped Seirizzim, trying to mask his excitement.

'Rhino,' answered Nabob.

'What?' spluttered Seirizzim.

'Sorry, that should be rhinos, I suppose. It takes six to pull a forty-ton wagon train, doesn't it.'

Moloch shrugged and put a single extra punch hole next to the second line he had just pricked out. Seirizzim barked a whole series of questions regarding Dentressangle's previous life, recent death and future of eternal torment here in Mortropolis. It was all pretty routine stuff. A lifetime spent overcharging the customers of his haulage company for excess baggage met with twenty hours a day shoving rocks up an endless incline for eternity, with four hours a day suspended sentence. Suspended, that is, head first in the excrement pools for the lies. At every answer Moloch skewered a series of carefully chosen holes in the parchment.

The office of demons watched in bafflement.

'O ... of course, once you get the h ... hang of it it'll be m ... much faster.' Moloch grinned as he held up the perforated sheet.

'So what's the point of that?' Nabob scratched his pointed ear. 'I can't read it.'

'Aha!' declared Seirizzim. 'Maybe *you* can't. Follow me!'

The fifteen demons stood, shook their heads and followed. 'Nabob, bring the parchments,' shouted Seirizzim through the door as he left.

'Bring the parchments,' grumbled Nabob. 'Pah!' It was always the same. "Clean my hooves" or "fetch me a drink" or worse. He got all the dirty jobs. Gah! What had he done to deserve it all? Well, apart from lose the Undertaker-in-Chief elections to Seirizzim, that was.

Accepting the inevitable command with a tick on the blackboard of mounting revenge, Nabob struggled through the door, after the retreating crowd of demons. His heels clicking on the marble surface of the stairs, he followed in bafflement as they turned down a series of unfamiliar corridors and eventually stopped outside a particularly insignificant-looking door. By this time his arms were aching from the weight of the stack of Nognite parchments.

Seirizzim kicked open the door with a joyous flourish of shining hoof and beckoned everyone into the dark.

The air, like everywhere in Helian, reeked as badly as a three-month-old egg mayonnaise and hovered in the high six hundred and sixty degrees fahrenheit.

'Moloch, the lights!' Seirizzim ordered and, with only the briefest of fumbling, a dozen lava lamps melted into life. 'There...' whispered the Undertaker-in-Chief with exaggerated awe. 'Behold, the future!'

'Where?' asked Nabob.

'There!' Seirizzim pointed to what looked like a large and regularly shaped lump of rock.

'But it's just a large and regularly shaped lump of rock,' grunted Nabob, staring at a vast slab of obsidian. For his troubles he received a swift hoof in the stomach.

'Ignorance. That is why you are where you are. Show them, Moloch!'

The cloaked demon pushed his way through the clump of office workers and perched himself on a suitable lump of rock. Flexing his talons with a sickening click, Moloch turned a small circular valve and smiled as a familiar whoosh of hyperheated steam surged into the slab. Inside, a whole series of complex valves and steam switches slid and clicked smoothly. Moloch opened another valve and a current of magma slithered invisibly upwards in pulses. In a matter of seconds a crimson glow shone through a window of obsidian, pulsing regularly at the bottom of a large stretch of crystal. If any of the demons had looked really closely they would have been able to see a forest of capillaries etched behind the translucent black glass. The cloaked demon tugged a lever, there was a clicking of valves deep inside the crystal and a flow of magma was directed to the back of the screen.

The office demons gasped as a wave of crimson letters swam into view on the seamless black screen.

READY ... it said.

Moloch turned and grinned. 'The Parchment, please.'

'Nabob!' bellowed Seirizzim over the constant whoosh-ing of the obsidian crystal. 'Move.'

With a shake of his head Nabob lurched forward under the weight of the perforated parchment. Moloch pointed to a thin slit around the side of the black device. 'Feed it in there,' he added by way of ex-planation.

Confused, Nabob obeyed, threading the sheet into the narrow opening. With a shriek he leapt backwards, spread-ing himself inelegantly across the floor as the parchment was slurped inside. Jets of steam erupted from within, valves and switches clattered noisily and suddenly the screen filled with a host of angular letters.

Nabob's jaw dropped as he looked up and saw the words.

And there was more. Everything in fact that he had read out to Moloch a few minutes earlier.

'But h ... how...?' gasped a demon, awestruck.

'The placement of the holes is highly specific and is used to direct tiny jets of steam to a bank of highly sensitive...' began Moloch.

'It reads it! That's all you lot need to know,' interrupted Seirizzim. 'That's the future.' His curling talon shook as it pointed towards the vast black slab.

'What? Intelligent rocks?' sneered Nabob as he picked himself off the floor.

'Ahhh, strictly it's not intelligent as such, but...' began Moloch.

'Shut up,' snarled Seirizzim then rounded on Nabob. 'The future is automation. That thing can process thousands of new arrivals in a fraction of the time you lot take. It won't make mistakes and it doesn't take lava breaks. In short ... efficiency!'

Nabob swallowed nervously, suddenly feeling that he could be replaced by a shiny black lump of rock.

'You lot, back to the office,' ordered Seirizzim. 'Moloch'll show you how to input everything into that ... that...'

'Er, Moloch's Analytical Crystal,' offered Moloch with a flush of modesty not normally associated with those of a demonic nature. 'Or...or you could just use MAC for short.' He grinned pathetically.

Nabob tutted and headed towards the door.

'Not so fast,' snapped Seirizzim, snatching him firmly by the throat. 'I'm not having my new technology, my lovely new chunks of Moloch's Analytical Crystal soiled by your filthy talons, not in the week before Foul Lord d'Abaloh's Annual Assessment anyway.'

'Surprise, surprise,' the demon muttered under his sulphurous breath.

'I've got something *much* more suitable for your, ahem, elevated level.' Seirizzim's black scaly lips curled into a sneer of satisfied evil.

Nabob shrugged and chalked up another couple of revenge points on his blackboard of hatred. Whenever Seirizzim introduced any of his new 'efficient' systems they inevitably meant a shedload more work for someone. And that someone was invariably him.

'There are fifty-three filing cabinets in the cellar that need clearing out. I need room for more of Moloch's Analytical Crystals. Get on with it!'

Nabob was handed a set of directions and propelled from the room with a swift kick from the Undertaker-in-Chief.

Snarling imprecations, Nabob shoved his shoulder against the cellar door and pushed. And once again the damned thing refused to budge. Surely this was the right place? Seirizzim wouldn't send him off on a wild stalag-mite chase, would he? Nabob began to wonder.

There was only one way to find out.

Gnashing his fangs, he strode away from the expanse of slate, clenched his fists and charged. Sparks struck off the ancient marbled floor as he accelerated, turned sideways and hit the portal square in the middle. With a seismic squeal of stone it shot open and Nabob was catapulted bodily into a pitch-black net of silicon webs, landing unceremoniously against a far cabinet, his legs halfway up the wall. Dust tumbled from what passed as the ceiling in a choking storm of grey flakes, clogging his nostrils.

For a moment he lay there storing up the feelings of detestation for Seirizzim deep inside his mind, saving them for the day of revenge, the time when he, Nabob, would take his rightful place as the Undertaker-in-Chief of Mortropolis.

He whimpered as he sucked cautiously on a throbbing talon. If only things hadn't gone so wrong before.

He still couldn't really believe he'd failed. It had all

seemed completely foolproof. Everyone knew of Foul-Lord d'Abaloh's 'loathing of crowds' and the fact that Helian was almost completely overcrowded after accepting centuries of souls for torturing. Everyone also knew of the dubious ways of the Helian Electoral System – absolute bribery, complete corruption. D'Abaloh's vote, the only vote, was readily available to the highest bidder. Centuries ago this nod of approval could simply have been secured by waggling the biggest sack of obuls in front of his snout, but these days it required a touch more finesse. And even that had gone way beyond giving d'Abaloh the pick of recently deceased female companions.

Now only the best would do, something like the offer of an entire world, heated to a cosy six hundred and sixty-six degrees fahrenheit for d'Abaloh's own private use.

And Nabob could have given it to him. If only he'd had a teensy weensy bit more time. And a stack of proof.

Nabob swore profusely and hurled a filing cabinet across the room in angry frustration as he recalled the sneer of mocking disbelief spreading across Foul Lord d'Abaloh's vast face. Without proof he could never make d'Abaloh believe that he, Nabob, had been directly responsible for starting a raging Holy War. And now that his scheme to raise the ambient temperature in the Talpa Mountains, a thousand feet above, by hundreds of degrees had also been utterly destroyed, well ... it was completely hopeless. He had no choice but to spend eternity as the pathetic butt of Seirizzim's humiliating schemes, detesting every moment, hating himself almost as much as he despised Seirizzim.

But somehow, deep inside his swirling pools of despair a small glow of hope glimmered. There had to be a way out of this, a way to turn the tables. All he had to do was find it and then Seirizzim would...

'Done yet?' bellowed Seirizzim, sneering as he kicked

the door aside and stood silhouetted in the doorframe, his arrow-headed tail flicking like an angry tabby's. 'Not slacking, are we? Not deliberately slowing my efficiency drive?'

Nabob looked up from the floor and gnashed his fangs. For a moment his internal rage cast a glorious hallucination on his retinas. He leapt to his feet, spun around and lashed a striking hoof across Seirizzim's grinning face. Black blood trickled from the broken nose as Nabob clenched his fists and launched a volley of blows at his enemy's overfed belly. Seirizzim collapsed, groaning, whimpering beneath the victorious Nabob.

Then the doors burst open and a swarm of guard demons sprinted forward, fists circling, ready to leap to the lucrative protection of their beloved Seirizzim...

'Bugger!' grumbled Nabob, defeated even in his dreams. There had to be a better way.

'Work, damn you!' screamed Seirizzim, his curling horns quivering malevolently. 'Clear this room, now!' Nabob stared at the fifty-three filing cabinets and cursed. There was a shuffling of hooves outside the door and a massive thug of demonkind blocked out what little light seeped in. 'Or do you need a little persuasion?' sneered Seirizzim.

At that moment Nabob knew he had only two choices. Do the job. Or do the job in extreme agony.

With a shrug he stood, trudged to the first drawer and tugged it open. Behind him a gurgling snarl of hunger echoed from the corridor outside. Nabob spun on his heel as a five-foot high, bloated creature scuttled sickeningly through the doorway.

'Wait. I *said* I'd do it!' protested Nabob. 'I don't need persuasion ... yeurch!'

With the gut-wrenching sound of claws on blackboards, the bloated creature flexed its complex mouthparts and sighed like a chainsaw. Nabob caught a worrying glimpse of what appeared to be saliva soaked blades deep inside the cavern of its throat.

'I'm telling you, I *don't* need that much encouragement,' squeaked Nabob, backing away.

Seirizzim burst out laughing, his head arcing backwards evilly. 'That's not for you, although it is a tempting idea. That's for the contents of the drawers.'

'Eh?' spluttered Nabob.

'Well, you can try burning Nognite parchment if you really desire it. Just not on my time, hear? Feed it everything, I want this room cleared by tomorrow!'

'But what ... what is it?'

'Latest development in the Office Ecology Department. Started as a cross between a stalag-mite and a parchment beetle, but they've fiddled about with it since then. I've called it a parchmite. Like it?'

'Cute name,' grunted Nabob warily. 'Catchy.'

'It hasn't been fed for a week, so I'd start work if I were you! I'm not sure how good it is at telling the difference between parchment and certain portions of your anatomy!' Cackling evilly, Seirizzim turned on his hoof and headed away to introduce a no-smouldering policy into the flame pits of suffering.

The parchmite gurgled hungrily and scuttled a few paces forward, its antennae twitching as it sensed edible somethings in the vicinity.

Nabob squeaked in alarm and backed into a cabinet. Grunting with the effort, he snatched a drawer out and hurled it towards the salivating parchmite. Eagerly it smacked its mandibles and looked up expectantly, locking onto the airborne treat with deadly accuracy. A grin flashed across it's mouth-filled excuse for a face. Hundred-century-old parchment matured in slate casks, coming its way ... what a treat!

In seconds Nabob had emptied another drawer into the gaping maw, cringing as razor mandibles slashed and whirled in a frenzy of devouring. Its throat bulged, eyes screwed shut and the entire drawerful was swallowed in a single nauseating gulp. The parchmite grinned, opened its massive mouth and belched eagerly. There was no mistaking the message. It wanted more. More. More! *Now*.

A low gurgling echoed through the cellar as the parchmite licked its mandibles and plucked a piece of spine binding from between its teeth with a grotesque claw. Nabob stared for a moment and was suddenly worryingly aware of the expression on its face. Somehow he had the distinctly unnerving feeling that if he didn't shove another mass of parchment down that throat it would have his leg off in a matter of seconds.

Swallowing desperately, he spun on his hoof and sprinted towards the next drawer, tugging it free from the runners and flinging it towards the parchmite. Unknown to Nabob a single envelope of parchment documents slipped out from behind the drawer and tumbled to the cobwebby floor. If it had been in possession of eyes it would have lain there, blinking, trying to adjust to its first sight of lava-light in centuries.

The parchmite, in its frenzy for more of the ancient documents, snatched the drawer from Nabob's claws and gnashed the lot in double time, ending with an awful smacking of razor-sharp implements. Nabob wheeled around, shocked at the rate of mastication, and headed for another load.

Spying the thin envelope on the floor, he grabbed it, aimed at the parchmite and would have hurled it into those jaws had his slitted crimson eyes not focused on the large red letters grinning across the front.

Utterly, utterly secret! Don't even think about
  reading this!
Yes. This means you!

Nabob froze, looked nervously around him and grinned as he made to open the cover.

Suddenly he squealed in alarm and stared at his talons. Bright sparks of icy fluorescence zapped between his clawtips in a haze of burning cold. Reflexively he hurled

61

the envelope away, shoving his claw into his mouth with an explosion of hailstones.

The parchmite's compound eyes locked onto the tumbling document, judging trajectory and velocity with greedy precision, and, in a flash of black, a tongue lashed out, plucked it from the air and whiplashed it into the capacious belly of the creature. Nabob stared from his talon-tips to the creature in a state of baffled shock. His claws throbbed with icy cold, his mind whirred with annoyance. What had that been? Could it have been useful to him? Now he'd never know.

The parchmite's complex jaw still gaped eagerly, chewing at the air like some starving hake with a cleft palate, desperate to fill its belly.

Nabob snarled, tugged another drawer out of a cabinet and made to hurl it at the parchmite. He never quite got that far.

It was only as the parchmite's antennae shot erect, it slammed its mouth shut and its compound eyes started to quiver that Nabob realised something was wrong. Slack-jawed, he watched as the parchmite's claws clutched worriedly at a bulge in its abdomen, the exact spot where he would have guessed its stomach would be. Its compound eyes crossed embarrassedly as there was a muted belch, its cheeks puffed out and a small wisp of frost curled around the edge of what passed as lips. A claw slammed across its mouth and Nabob's reflexes decided it was time to take cover.

And not a moment too soon.

With a final hiccup, which sounded disturbingly like 'Uh-oh', the cellar filled with a deeply intestinal rumble and, preceded by a wet eruption, the air became a mass of all-too-recently chewed parchment. Fragments of soggy documents splattered against walls and filing cabinets; strips of saliva-soaked inventories parchment-mached themselves throughout the entire room.

For minutes, Nabob lay trembling behind a cabinet, his talons a-throbbing with burning cold, the only sound the regular pattering of gobs of wet parchment slipping to the floor. Nervously he peered out into the chaos and caught his breath. Across the room the parchmite sat forlornly in a carnage of documentation, its antennae flattened against its head, moaning like a puppy that had eaten something which didn't agree with it.

But for Nabob, more surprising and interesting than the acutely woeful parchmite with acute indigestion was the strange object glowing gently before it. There, apparently unharmed by its recent ingestion, sat the thin and secretive envelope. His talons throbbed in sudden recognition and his spleen quivered excitedly.

Somehow, he felt certain that nobody else knew of this ... this ... what?

He sprang over the cabinet and stalked towards the document, pointedly ignoring the pathetically admonishing eyes of the parchmite who blamed him in no uncertain terms for its accident. Picking up a fragment of drawer from the wreckage the demon reached out with it and gingerly touched the cover. Steam erupted wildly from its surface as he pushed it open and peered curiously at the mysterious contents.

His slitted pupils clicked wide in alarm as he stared at the strangely angular old-fashioned writing and distorted pictures, entirely unaware of the significance of the message held therein.

Figures with long flowing beards hid behind large clumps of strange shaped rocks and peered furtively around. Over the page a group of them crawled towards a vast hole in the ground. And still further on they peered from behind other rocks at stick figures with tails, horns and large tridents held in their talons.

That there was something odd about Nabob's find was blindingly obvious, and whilst he couldn't put his talon on it (he winced at the thought) he knew he had to find out more.

Wrapping the envelope and its contents carefully in a bundle of parchment sheets, he hid it deep inside his tunic pocket and set to tidying the room, eradicating any

63

evidence that anything even remotely unusual had transpired. Absolutely under no circumstances was he prepared to let Seirizzim start asking awkward questions about his find. Well, not until he knew what it was he had got his talons on anyhow.

Volubly cursing the vomiting parchmite, Nabob cringed as he began to peel sodden strips off the ceiling.

A crimson flash of lightning erupted in the murky atmosphere and rumbled noisily away across the Underworld Kingdom of Helian. A plethora of inchoate ferries ploughed sticky furrows through the ooze of the River Phlegethon, belching clouds of chthonic fumocarbons high. The cries of tormented souls writhed ignored through the boiling heat.

In short, it was a typical chewsday afternoon.

Well, it would have been a typical chewsday afternoon had it not been for the crowd of nine-foot black scaly demons that were milling about furtively on the river bank. Normally they'd have been down 'The Gamorrah' necking lava martinis like there was no tomorrow. But today was different. Something odd was going on.

Their numbers had been swelling gradually as they had watched the activities of another small group labouring busily away on a desolate patch of river bank. Fascinated, and not a little suspicious, their slitted eyes had snatched every detail of activity and tried to figure just what it was that was ahoof.

'So, figured out what it is yet?' grunted one of the observers from Immigration.

'Nope,' grunted Captain Naglfar, taking a huge drag on his belching pipe. 'But I don't like it, don't like it one bit. Should've been informed of any building work. Especially so close to the jetty.' Nervously he rubbed the badge that marked him out as the representative for the Underworld Ferrymen's Coalition of Arguing, Shouting and Generally Being Narked. He should have had his due opportunity to reject any development proposal outright from the start. He should have been consulted. Should have been given time to call a meeting to decide on a date to have a meeting to discuss this proposal, cancelled the meeting on a technicality and reconvened it in a few decades' time when all the fuss had died down. This just wasn't right. It smacked of efficiency, and under edict ninety-three of the Coalition Rules: 'efficiency, as a theoretical model of work practice, is recognised providing that it does not interfere with current systems operations'. Everybody knew that. At least Naglfar thought everybody knew that. But ever since the new Undertaker-in-Chief had been elected, things just hadn't been handled in the proper bureaucratic manner.

A ripple of interested gasps bounced around the group as one of the labourers dragged a large cage towards the site. In a flash, the demon had laid a small trail of rocks away towards a marked area, leapt behind the cage and opened the door with a scrabbling of nervous talons. The black carapace of the multi-legged creature inside flashed into view as it pounced on the rocks and shredded them into oblivion, scuttling forward eagerly to begin gnawing at the marked areas. In moments the stalag-mite was cheerfully excavating the foundations of a small kiosk.

It was suddenly too much for Captain Naglfar. Cursing profusely under his breath and exhaling vast plumes of rancid pipe smoke, he clattered across the rocks, his hooves striking-sparks off the surface and his tail twitching.

'Who's in charge here?' he demanded moments later as he spun one of the labourers round and sneered halitotically into his face. The demon pointed to a minor devil who, at that moment, tugged something vermilion and shiny out of his pocket and began talking frantically into it. Behind Naglfar a pair of labourers demon-handled something long and heavy off a flat truck.

'Do you mind telling me precisely what is going on

here?' snarled Naglfar above the noise of the gnawing stalag-mite. The devil wagged a talon dismissively and continued talking. Naglfar's spine spikes rose in extreme irritation.

'Do you know who I am?' he bridled.

The devil turned, put a claw to his black lips and continued talking.

Naglfar, as was his wont, ignored the request for silence. 'For the last twelve centuries I have been the duly elected representative of the Underworld Ferrymen's Coalition...' he ranted imperiously.

'Look. Can't you see I'm busy?' grunted the devil. He quickly whispered a few last words and added, 'Now go. Top priority!' Then with a single underarm lob he launched the vermilion mhodemm into the air. Naglfar's jaw swung limply open for a moment as he watched the insect-like creature take to a quartet of tiny silicon wings and power away towards the centre of Mortropolis. He'd never seen anything like that before.

'The name's Maentwrog, site manager,' said the devil matter-of-factly. 'What can I do, eh?'

Twelve centuries of experience snapped into play within Naglfar as he pointed a curling talon at the foundations chewed out of the rock. 'What's that?' he snarled.

'Don't tell me you ain't seen foundations before,' began Maentwrog. 'Strewth. Thought everyone knew 'bout that sort o' thing...'

'What are you going to put there,' sneered Naglfar, rapidly losing what passed for his patience. A curl of smoke drifted out of his nostrils as he drew himself up to his full nine feet. 'What's it going to be, eh?'

'You mean you don't know?'

'I wouldn't be asking if I did.'

'Nah, s'pose not,' mused Maentwrog and fell silent. High above, the vermilion mhodemm flittered rapidly towards the stratascrapers of Mortropolis.

'So what is it?' growled Naglfar.

'Can't tell you,' grinned Maentwrog. 'Rules.'

Naglfar's spine spikes flexed angrily. 'Rules?' he bellowed. 'As duly elected representative of the Underworld Ferrymen's Coalition of Arguing, Shouting and Generally Being Narked, the rules say that I am informed of every development which has any bearing on our working practices.'

'Sorry, mate. All interested parties have been inform ... uurgh!' Maentwrog dangled by the throat at the end of Naglfar's claw.

'Except me! Show me the plans!' Naglfar screamed.

And as Maentwrog began to turn gradually purple and wonder just how much longer he could keep quiet, away across Mortropolis, high up in the offices of the Sinful Service a set of curling crimson claws tapped irritably on a parchment-strewn obsidian desk.

'Damn him!' snarled Seirizzim as he stared once again at the recently delivered note. 'That's not an offer, it's an insult! How much does he think tortures cost these days? Look at it!'

He thrust the note across the desk at his Chief of Finance, Asmodeus.

'Hmmmm,' grunted the demon over his half-moon crystalline pince-nez. 'It seems our friend does not yet understand the concept of the free torture market.'

'Friend? Sheytahn's no friend of mine.' Seirizzim snatched another sheet of Nognite parchment from a heap and stared angrily at it. The strings of figures swam before his slitted pupils.

'Perhaps if he was informed of the consequences of not paying you for use of our unrivalled torture services he might come around to a more amenable viewpoint,' oozed Asmodeus.

'Such as,' snarled Seirizzim.

'Well, if, for example, a little anonymous mhodemm was to whisper in the shell-like ear of our dear Foul Lord d'Abaloh during his forthcoming inspection that perhaps the damned souls of the Arrhenius Basin weren't being

67

tormented quite so, er, harshly as they should be, maybe steps would be taken. How many torture establishments does Sheytahn currently operate?'

'Well, I . . .'

'Are they capable of delivering a constant barrage of pain, anguish and suffering as befits the name of Helian? Does not everyone know that for that all-round professional eternity of damnation, Mortropolis cannot be surpassed? Why, we can provide extensive excrement pools offering upright or inverted accommodation, a whole range of boulder-rolling hills fitted with the latest No-rest Moving Perspective Summit, en-suite bogs of boiling pitch, pits of flames . . . the list grows almost daily.'

'Perhaps with a little more marketing . . .' Seirizzim said thoughtfully.

'Has it not been proven that insufficient levels of said pain, anguish and suffering is a direct causal link in the fostering of . . .' Asmodeus leant across the desk and whispered into Seirizzim's pointed ear. '. . . frivolity?'

'Sssssh! Don't *say* that. Don't even think it! It's disgusting!'

'And I'm certain that His Vulgarity, Foul Lord d'Abaloh, feels even more strongly about it.'

Seirizzim trembled and stole a quick glance over his shoulder. The 'F' word, he thought in panic, he mentioned the 'F' word in my office.

Asmodeus leant back in his swivel throne and grinned slyly to himself, sensing victory once again. 'So, once it is revealed to Sheytahn that his kingdom is grossly underequipped in the eternal torment department, following several centuries of concentrating on the expanding extraction of a surfeit of natural resources, I am certain he will see the continued sense in paying a small fee for his tortures to be carried out here.'

'And that's exactly what this is all about,' snarled Seirizzim, hurling another sheet of recently received parchment at the Chief of Finance. 'Those natural resources you were referring to ... Sheytahn, the bastard, wants *me* to pay for them!'

'But they are only lava and brimstone. One can surely do without...'

'Oh yeah? And how often have you tried scorching tormented souls' tender particles into vast suppurating sores of agony with a cold poker, eh? Do you really expect vats of boiling pitch to be truly effective at a gentle simmer? I'm sure d'Abaloh would be wonderfully impressed if he found out that Mortropolis was offering health-giving saunas!'

Asmodeus tapped a nervous talon to his pince-nez. 'I see the dilemma,' he muttered cautiously.

'Oh, you do, do you? Well, let me tell you another thing...'

Fortunately for Asmodeus, he never did find out what that other thing was. There was a sudden rattling in a small tube through the plate quartz window and a tiny vermilion insect-like creature buzzed in through the mhodemm portal.

'Parchment. Parchment, quick!' shrieked Seirizzim as he spotted the agitated action of the silicon winged creature.

Asmodeus dropped a wad of parchment on the obsidian desk and watched in amazement as the mhodemm swooped down and settled in the top left-hand corner. In a flurry of victorious research and development from the newly formed Mortropolis Office Ecology Department a needle-sharp tail swung out from beneath its abdomen and began stabbing a series of tiny pin-holes in the parchment. As each character formed the mhodemm leapt sideways and began again, pounding its tail pneumatically through the parchment with devastating efficiency. Seirizzim's face grinned wide as he watched the creature's performance, revelling in the stunning advance this represented in communications.

It was only as he actually read the message that his face soured.

'Damn those bloody ferrymen!' he screamed and tore out of the office in a flurry of scathing curses.

Asmodeus gulped and squinted across at the message, screwing his eyes tight to read it upside-down.

His eyebrows raised a few inches as he looked.

To: Seirizzim, Undertaker-in-blah-blah-blah. Oh, he knows who he is. I haven't got time to faff about remembering all that guff about addressing him properly. Not when that lot up there are looking so suspicious ... uh-oh. Here they come.

Ahem. Calm, keep calm. Dear Seirizzim, Er, we got trouble. Naglfar's on his way. I'll try to hold them off as long as ... Look, can't you see I'm busy? ... Get here, quick. Out.

Now go. Top priority.

In the bowels of the Sinful Service Stratascraper Nabob wiped the back of a scaly claw across his equally enscaled forehead and watched the parchmite gnash its sickening way through the final fragments of the last filing cabinet.

One thing he had swiftly discovered was that the parchmite had the memory capacity of the average goldfish. Six seconds after suffering the most explosive vomiting session of its life the parchmite blinked, looked around and wondered where all the mess had come from. It had also clearly forgotten several other pertinent facts. Little things like it shouldn't have a raging bellyache, it really detested the taste of mouldering flame-proofed parchment and it wasn't supposed to be able to chew through slate filing cabinets. As a result it hadn't taken much coaxing to persuade the pathetic creature that it really did want to eat everything in the room, except Nabob.

This lack of anything even remotely approaching total recall was completely unsurprising. The damn thing was simply made that way. Since the Mortropolis Office Ecology Department had mercilessly honed its massive hunger reflexes and relentlessly tweaked what passed for its brain, it was now constantly ravenous and recalled almost nothing.* The latter was a security measure insisted upon by Seirizzim who had reasoned that "it probably wouldn't be completely helpful to have parchmites wandering freely about the place spouting entire passages from acutely sensitive documents like senile thespians recalling ancient monologues." In short, it was way too risky.

Nabob scoured the cellar for any evidence of his recent mysterious discovery, grinned at the bare walls, spun on his heels and vanished through the door. The parchmite watched him go, rocking gently on its now vastly distended belly. For a few seconds it clawed desperately at the stone floor, eager to follow and get fed something else tasty, but suddenly it stopped, blinked and wondered what it was trying to chase. Idly it looked around the room and seeing nothing edible for the first time in its life, forgot that it was supposed to be hungry.

Nabob, clutching his parcel close to his chest, sprinted along the corridor, dashed up a dozen flights of steps and erupted through the rotating doors of the Sinful Service

---

* Early on, the attempts at breeding the perfect parchmite hadn't been without their share of mishaps. One entire litter had been hatched which were completely incapable of recalling what it meant to be cavern trained. Fortunately, it was discovered that sheets of Nognite, having passed through the bowels of a parchmite, formed quite the most remarkably potent fertiliser for Dethfodils, Red Hot Pokers and other plants resident in Helian.

The entire litter was herded out to Foul Lord d'Abaloh's palace by the Styx. Right now his ornamental borders were the envy of the whole of Helian and the floors of the Mortropolis Office Ecology Department were a lot safer underhoof.

Later generations of parchmite were all equipped with the instinct to visit the Excrement Pools of Stench and Depravity when the need arose, thus ensuring that everyone, except the unfortunate souls sentenced to a spell within said pools, spent an eternity free from unpleasant gooey patches on the pavement.

stratascraper at full tilt. His rapid progress didn't last very long though. In seconds he was up to his armpits in moaning souls shuffling forlornly towards their next torture session. Snarling about the state of the over-crowded streets, he clawed his way through the mass of bodies and forged on towards a certain insanitary outflow just round the back of 'The Gamorrah' in downtown Tumor. It wasn't normally a place he'd choose to frequent after work, but tonight was an exception.

Up to his waist in it, Flagit the demon tried his best not to think about what all this stuff had been before it had passed through he intestines of the patrons of 'The Gamorrah'. It seemed that a heavy session of lava martinis loosened more than just demon's tongues. He readjusted his noseclip, picked up his shovel once more and attacked the distant bank with resigned conviction.

'Community service,' he snarled under his seething breath. 'Damn Seirizzim!' His shovel grated against the rocky bank and chipped off another tiny fragment. At this rate it would probably take him a good decade to redirect this outflow into the reservoir tank which supplied the Excrement Pools of Stench and Depravity. It had been three months since his sentence had started and he'd so far managed to get three inches.

He gritted his demonic fangs and cursed again. Things would have been so different if everything hadn't gone so horribly wrong and he hadn't been caught red-clawed. If d'Abaloh had turned up on time for the damned election instead of three days early then they could have offered him the finest bribe he could ever have received. For his vote, he would have got the Upperworld. All of it. The direct link was already in place and working: a thousand-foot fissure, belching massive volumes of Helian's atmosphere into the pristine Talpa Mountain skies. The temperature was rising rapidly; things were flaking out all over the place. It was going to be so perfectly inhospitable.

If only d'Abaloh's stupid dactyl hadn't caught its wings in the escaping vortex of gas and crashed into the penthouse offices of the Transcendental Travel Company Ltd. And ruined it all! Now his and Nabob's chances of Undertaker-in-Chiefship were less than those of the average parchmite winning a memory master's quiz.

There had only been one thing that had gone right. The Transcendental Travel Company Offices were such a mess after it all that no one had been able to piece together the truth of what he and Nabob had been up to. Amazingly, Seirizzim had believed his tale about using dodgy illegal immigrants to extend the offices. Flagit had expected to be banged up for a couple of hundred years on various counts of extending property without planning permission, utilising non-standardised labour for said purpose and causing excessive trauma to d'Abaloh's personal transport. Instead he had been sentenced to community service. He looked at the work ahead of him and winced. Three centuries of solitary looked almost appealing in comparison.

He snarled once more as he looked around him. Seirizzim had gone too far this time. Community service? Damn him! And damn Nabob! Keeping his mouth shut about their partnership just 'cause he'd lost. Damn the weedling sneaky son of a slime-ridden...

'Hello, Flagit,' called Nabob with forced cheeriness. 'Nice day, isn't it?' His talon brushed the package of parchment deep in his pocket.

'Oh sure,' snapped Flagit, slopping his shovel down and folding his arms across the handle. A serpent of writhing anger squirmed in his lower intestines. Play it cool, he told himself. No sense rushing into a frenzy of revenge. If, as they say, it was a dish best served cold then Flagit knew that he who dined last savoured it longest. Or something. 'A perfect day! Just the best for standing waist-deep in *this*!' he sneered with a shovelful of what he hoped was withering sarcasm.

'Er, I didn't mean it quite that way but...'

'What d'you want, eh? Come to gloat, have we? Come to feel superior and smug about not being sentenced to bloody community service, hmmm?' A curl of angry smoke licked around his nostrils, escaping despite the noseclip. Flagit was, it had to be said, miffed.

'No, I...'

'Three months I've been here and not once have you come to visit! Well, thank you very much.'

'I would have come but...'

'You should be in this with me!' growled Flagit.

'Ah, now let's not be too hasty, shall we? I've got a favour to ask.'

'A favour? Oh, that's nice,' snarled Flagit, dripping with sarcasm and sewage. 'You leave me well alone to paddle about in here but as soon as you need a favour, it's "Hello, Flagit. Nice day!"' Despite his seething exterior there was a small fragment within which was bursting with acute curiosity. A favour, eh? That was Nabob's way of saying he had a problem he couldn't figure out. If he was asking Flagit, risking being seen with him, then it must be something pretty serious. And weird. Flagit specialised in the weird. And for the paddleless demon in the creek, Nabob's 'favour' was intensely interesting.

But right now there were more immediate, if childish, things to get off his chest first. It was time to take Nabob on a guilt trip he would, hopefully, never forget.

'I hope you're happy with the way it all turned out,' he began, slopping pathetically. 'Or are you ashamed, eh? I mean, you never even tried to get in touch. Not even a note of condolence or sympathy...'

'What for?'

'You heartless ... for Flinty. She's gone!' moaned Flagit. 'I've lost my pet stalag-mite!'

'Well, they don't normally last very long...'

'I had her years...'

'But there's plenty more in the scree,' insisted Nabob.

'Not like Flinty. That little diamond of pure white on

74

her foreclaw, the way she'd grind her mandibles with delight when I'd sand her belly...' Flagit sniffed. There were times when he wasn't sure which of his current situations was worse. This community service, or the fact that they'd dragged Flinty away kicking and squealing.

'Tell you what,' grinned Nabob, Flagit's pathetic attempts at tugging his heart strings having totally failed. (This was almost certainly due to the fact that he'd had them surgically removed at the age of three thousand. Heart strings were as much use to the average demon as a constantly complaining appendix in an anatomy class.) 'If you do me this favour, I'll get you another.'

'I don't want another! I want Flinty back!'

'Look, it's tough being immortal. Face it. Pets snuff it...'

'What?' shrieked Flagit, shocked. Had Flagit some news of his dear pet? Suddenly the last three months without Flinty weighed heavy on the demon. Could Nabob be right? Had she curled up her claws for one last time? 'You saying she's d ... d...?' and then came a surge of cold anger. 'Why didn't you tell me? You heartless...'

Nabob looked momentarily confused. 'Tell you?' he asked, warily wondering if community service had more long-lasting psychological effects than he had at first imagined. This was worse than he had thought. Flagit was in denial. And all over a stupid stalag-mite. If the demon was in this state would he be able to solve the mystery in Nabob's pocket? Had coming here been a bad mistake? If there were any prying eyes that linked them together ... uuurgh, he shuddered to think of what joyous community task Seirizzim could dream up for him.

'I knew those pet pounds were unhealthy,' sobbed Flagit angrily. 'They said she'd be alright...'

'Wait a minute.' Nabob shook his head as he tuned back into Flagit's rantings. 'Pet pounds? What are you on about?'

'Flinty. They took her away. Said I didn't deserve privileges.'

'Oh, that's alright then,' answered Nabob with a sigh of relief. Flagit still retained at least a good half dozen of his cognitive marbles. He would be useful after all.

'Alright? How can you say that when you tell me they've k ... k ... hurt her, irreparably. Argggh, just wait till I get my claws on those murdering ... !' Flagit waded through the outflow, his talons wrapped tightly around the handle of his shovel, black scaly knuckles turning grey.

And Nabob's confidence in Flagit's sanity flipped once again. Which half dozen cognitive marbles did he still have? 'You told *me*, didn't you?' he began feebly, as he attempted to retrace the conversation in his head, now utterly confused as to the demise of said stalag-mite. Flagit swarmed angrily up the bank, dripping, just as Nabob figured it out. 'No, wait!' he cried, grabbing Flagit's arm. 'It *was* you who told me she'd gone. I was trying to comfort ...'

Flagit wheeled around, anger reaching boiling point. 'Comfort? Is *that* what you call it? Well, you just try this for comfort.' The sodden shovel arced through the seething air and caught Nabob across the side of the head, sending him spinning. The parcel of parchment flew out of his pocket, hit a sharp rock and split, hurling the envelope away along the bank, where it came to rest against a tiny knoll.

And there it lay, glowing eerily, fixing Flagit's attention completely and firing his curiosity setting to inferno. 'What the ...?' he grunted, shovel high over his head in preparation for another volley at Nabob's person. For a few moments he trembled, dithering between taking out three months worth of fury on Nabob's anatomy in a frenzy of wild shovelling, or simply forgetting it and finding out more about that curious, oddly steaming document.

Nabob's ear was eternally relieved he chose the latter.

With a clatter the shovel fell to the ground and Flagit, entranced, drifted towards the eerie envelope. His claws reached out...

'Wait.' grunted Nabob around a nastily swelling lip. 'Don't pick it up without...!'

The scream of demonic anguish indicated that Nabob's warning had probably come a little too late.

'...gloves,' finished Nabob, as Flagit discovered this for himself. As he shook his talons with almost as much shock as agony the envelope arced into the air, spun for a moment, and plunged steaming into the outflow.

Nabob's jaw dropped in alarm. Then, without thinking, he snatched the shovel and sprinted towards the bubbling plume of vapour. With a fortunate thrust and twist of demonic wrists he hefted the file, and a large shovelful of yesterday's chilli, onto the bank.

And there they both stood for a moment, staring at the steaming pile. The mysterious envelope was lying in solitary splendour, a few inches to the right, and it was gleaming in the pristine manner of a polished first edition in shrinkwrap.

'Now, how d'you suppose it did that?' spluttered Flagit, enthralled.

'Dunno,' confessed Nabob. 'Even a parchmite didn't muck up the dustcover.'

'What? That's been inside a parchmite?'

'Yup. Didn't stay there long, though.'

'Wow!' grunted Flagit, consumed by wonder.

Nabob grabbed the remains of his parchment bundle and cautiously wrapped the envelope up again.

'I think you've got some explaining to do,' muttered Flagit in hushed tones. 'And I think you'd better start at the beginning. What's a parchmite?'

Having studiously ignored the suffering of Maentwrog, their site manager, as he dangled from the claws of Captain Naglfar, the labourers had continued with their

77

project. They were all too horribly aware that the chances of getting a fraction of an obul out of Seirizzim's tight fist if they didn't finish on time were about as high as being hit by a low-flying snowball. So, keeping their heads down and thinking of the emptiness of their collective pockets, they had beavered away behind the seething mob of irate demons and hastily assembled a pair of large kiosks, each featuring a slot in one side and a horizontal arm still swathed in thin bubbly material. Already a length of parallel fencing was being assembled in a straight line towards the end of the ferry jetty. A huge demon was perched on top of the two kiosks, attaching what appeared to be a large board. It too was covered in the peculiar bubbly sheet.

'Show me the plans!' insisted Captain Naglfar, his back to the continuing toil as he waggled Maentwrog meaningfully by the throat.

'Can't,' groaned the now purple-faced devil barely audibly. 'Rules!'

'Tell me what it is,' snarled the fuming Captain around a cloud of acrid pipe smoke. 'Tell me now, or I'll personally...'

'Look for yourself,' exhaled Maentwrog in a gesture of defiance. 'You're too late anyhow. It's almost finished.'

'What?' Naglfar wheeled around and stared, dropping Maentwrog without a further thought. At that very instant the wrappings were tugged off the barriers.

The entire crowd of angry demons took a step backwards and gasped. The black and yellow chevrons emblazoned along the barrier could mean only one thing. Efficiency had arrived on the banks of the Phlegethon.

'So the rumours are true!' croaked Naglfar. 'Soul Booths!' He'd heard hushed whispers about these infernal things over in 'The Gamorrah'. Tongues loosened by one lava too many had let slip the awful truth – once issued their passmorts, damned souls need never look a demon in the eye until they were whisked through that

78

barrier. Immigration was no longer necessary. Replaced by automation.

At that instant the bubble wrap was hauled off the sign above the booths. The demons stared at the gaudy letters.

Helian Enterprises Limited (that's HEL to you) welcomes you to Mortropolis.
Despair, despond, distress. We've got the very best!

Naglfar's screams of anger were drowned by the rest of the mob. 'You can't do this!' he squealed, snatching Maentwrog by the ankle as he scuttled away.

'Not my fault,' pleaded the site manager, squirming wildly, his talons raking furrows in the rocky bank as Naglfar tugged him backwards. 'Orders. Seirizzim told me...'

'Seirizzim! Damn him!' snarled Naglfar. 'How dare he...'

The rest of his words were drowned in a roar of fury as the rest of the mob heard the name of their detested Undertaker-in-Chief. Without a word of command being uttered they suddenly knew what had to be done. Almost as one the demons surged past Naglfar, snatched tools from the ground and began attacking the brand-new structures. Talons wrenched the barriers from their hinges, hooves battered against walls, striking thousands of blue sparks, and in a fraction of the time it had taken the building team to erect them the Soul Booths were torn to the ground, the fencing shredded. The mob whirlwinded towards a flat truck, overturning it in a frenzy of riotousness. A large cage flipped off, tumbled to the rocky floor and cracked open. Unseen, the multi-legged stalag-mite within blinked, saw its chance and scuttled to freedom for the first time in three months.

'Feel better for that, do you?' yelled a monster arrogantly from in front of a newly arrived and panting force of helmeted demons. The chain of Undertakership glinted officiously around his scaly neck. The crowd froze.

Naglfar dropped Maentwrog in a heap and grinned wryly as the devil scuttled frantically away towards Seirizzim and his team of specially bribed Malebranche. It was common knowledge that Seirizzim felt far more efficiently protected with this loyally bribed force, rather than relying on the standard Mortropolitan response. Okay, so it was a little on the expensive side, but so what? Asmodeus had taken the necessary obuls out of half a dozen public accounts.

Seirizzim folded his arms, cocked his head five degrees to the left and peered down at the now stationary mob trying to pretend that the rubble beneath their hooves didn't really exist.

'I said, do you feel better for that?' he snarled.

'No,' began Naglfar. 'And neither should you. The standard of building was very, very shoddy. Tsk, tsk. Had to be pulled down. Dangerous. Could've caused a very nasty accident if we hadn't been here to, er, stress test it.'

For a second Seirizzim looked confused. Naglfar caught the look and pressed on. 'Should never have been put up on such dubious foundations. Somebody didn't check on planning permission very efficiently.'

Behind Naglfar a few demons stifled giggles as Seirizzim rounded on the crawling Maentwrog. 'Is this true?' he snarled, stamping his hoof on the site manager's claw.

'Ahhh. Th ... that hurts ...'

'Pardon?' Seirizzim leaned forward and added more pressure to Maentwrog's scaly digits.

'Arrrgghh. No, no, stop!'

'Is what he says right?' roared Seirizzim.

'No, no! They just went mad and attacked it!' screamed Maentwrog.

'Thought so,' growled Seirizzim under his breath and turned back to face Naglfar. 'So. Damage Mortropolitan property, would you?' he bellowed.

'My claw,' whimpered Maentwrog, tapping gently at Seirizzim's heel. 'Could you move your hoof ... please?'

Naglfar drew himself up to his full height and yelled, 'Since I, as duly elected representative of the Underworld Ferrymen's Coalition...'

'My claw...' whined Maentwrog unheard.

'...was not informed of any planned buildings,' continued Naglfar, 'it seemed entirely within my rights to assume that it was an unauthorised structure and therefore...'

'You took it upon yourself to tear it down?' completed Seirizzim.

'Something like that,' replied Naglfar around a haze of rancid pipe smoke.

'It had absolutely nothing to do with the fact that it will put you out of a job?'

'Me? Hah, no,' answered Naglfar with a grin. He was fine, at the moment. As captain of a trans-Phlegethon ferry he would always be needed to ship new arrivals across the river. Unless of course the rumours about the proposed sub-Phlegethon tunnel with moving walkways were, in fact, true. He swallowed.

'So,' mused Seirizzim over-theatrically, 'if I was to inform you that a structure *will* be built there you will allow it?'

'Well...'

Seirizzim's pupil-slits narrowed with barely hidden anger. 'No, listen carefully. If I was to inform you that a structure will be built over there, you *will* allow it!' he bellowed.

'Hey, I thought this was a demonicracy, you know, one demon, one vote,' protested Naglfar.

'It is,' declared Seirizzim with a grin of supreme triumph. 'And I'm the demon with that one vote!'

With a final grinding of Maentwrog's knuckles Seirizzim spun on his heel and stomped away from the seething mob of demons, his head thrown back with a peal of victorious braying laughter. There were times when it

81

was *so* good to be Undertaker-in-Chief. And that had been one of them.

Maentwrog writhed around on the ground clutching his mangled claw and burning one of a huge number of killing looks into the back of Seirizzim's oblivious skull.

'So that's it. Weird, huh?' whispered Nabob eagerly as he concluded his explanation to Flagit.

'And nobody else knows about it?' gasped Flagit with a tremble in his voice. His eyes had never left the steaming document in the last half hour.

'That cellar's been locked up for centuries. It's our secret.' Nabob patted the parchment parcel almost affectionately. 'So, c'mon, what's it mean?' he pressed eagerly.

'What's it worth?'

'Eh?' blinked Nabob.

'"Do me a favour" I think you said,' growled Flagit, amazed that he was not actually leaping in with both hooves and agreeing to tell Nabob all about the mysterious file. Could he be learning? 'Favours cost,' he reiterated. 'What's it worth?'

'Well, just take a look at the first few pages and, er, I'll think about it.'

'No way,' grunted Flagit despite the fact that the tips of his curly horns were itching with intense curiosity. He knew damn well that he'd be lost if he even peeked inside. There was something compelling about that sheaf of parchment. Not least the fact that it was Utterly Secret.

'What d'you want?' asked Nabob nervously.

Flagit looked up for the first time, fixed Nabob's gaze and directed it deliberately to the far side of the bank.

'Oh no. No way. I can't do that!' whined Nabob as he realised what Flagit meant.

'I can't leave here until it's done. Seirizzim's pretty tough on community service jumpers. Or so I hear.'

82

'Yeah, but there's favours and there's favours,' whimpered Nabob pathetically, 'And that's ... uurgh, well, it's just not hygienic.'

'You don't have to tell me,' grinned Flagit as he watched Nabob writhe in acute distaste.

'No, no, I couldn't possibly...'

'I don't want *you* to do it. That would take even longer than if I did it myself,' said Flagit.

'Eh? Then what *do* you want?'

'Seirizzim never said how I should dig through the far bank,' offered Flagit with a glint in his eye. 'Now if I could just think of something that would hurry the job up...'

'Aha! I understand?' declared Nabob, brightening visibly. 'You'll tell me about this file if I get you a pickaxe.'

Flagit slapped his palm against his scaly forehead and groaned. 'No, think. What'll go through that rock in a few seconds?'

'Well, apart from a stalag-mite I can't think...'

'Bingo!' sighed Flagit.

'What? Hey, good idea.'

'Get me Flinty back.'

'But you said she was...'

'Don't start that again,' growled Flagit. 'She was taken away to the pet pounds. And if Seirizzim's efficiency mania is as bad as I hear then she's probably having to earn her keep, digging foundations or the like.'

'It might take a while to find her,' offered Nabob with a wheedling edge in his voice. 'Er, in the meantime, how about just having a little look...'

'You'll get her back,' insisted Flagit.

'Yeah. Now, page one...'

'You sure?'

'Cross my heart and hope for reincarnation. Flinty'll be back in no time, you'll see. C'mon, open the cover and tell me what it all means...'

'Ssssh,' hissed Flagit, suddenly aware of something approaching rapidly.

83

Nabob's ears pricked up in alarm. Was this the Malebranche coming after him? Had they discovered the fact that a secret document was missing? Were they coming to retrieve it with maximum unnecessary force? Had Seirizzim set him up, knowing that he'd take it? The clattering of running increased in volume.

The reds of Flagit's eyes showed at the edges in fear. 'If they catch me here ... I should be over there ... this is all your fault.' In a second he was on his hooves.

At the same instant the sprinting reached a climax. Nabob turned in alarm, expecting a dozen Malebranche to come whistling around the corner, tridents and batons raised. He almost screamed. Flagit beat him to it.

'Flinty!' he cried as the stalag-mite scuttled into view, gathered its momentum and sprang joyously into his arms. Twelve legs hit his scaly chest and knocked him flying, claws waving in frantic greeting. With a muscular flip Flagit righted himself, snatching a rock and scraping it affectionately across the underbelly of the grotesque creature. Seconds later Flinty was grinding her mandibles in delight.

'You swine,' grinned Flagit at the shaking Nabob. 'You really had me going there. Had her all the time.'

'I ... I did?' he whimpered, then added with a little more confidence, 'Of course I did. Er, had to see if I could still trust you. Now, er, what about your side of the deal, eh?' He pointed at the parcel.

'Yeah, sure,' grunted Flagit and started whispering a stack of guttural croakings at Flinty. There was a gurgle of confirmation and she was off, heading for the far bank with overwhelming enthusiasm.

And as fountains of shrapnel erupted into the murky Helian air, Flagit began unwrapping the mysterious file.

A misty haze tumbled down from its surface as he gingerly opened the cover with a chunk of stone. Even from that range the cold touched his talons and in turn his memory. That cold was unnervingly familiar. Flagit had only once felt such a magnitude of chill before. On a

84

highly illegal visit to the Talpa Mountains one thousand feet above their heads, through solid rock.

'Well? Can you do it?' pressed Nabob. 'D'you know what it means?'

Flagit rubbed his chin and growled thoughtfully. 'This may take a while,' he grunted, his slitted pupils not moving from the angular text, the illuminated borders and the sketchy drawings of strangely haloed figures present on every single page.

The Wrong Talons

The Mostly Reverend Vex Screed lay in a crumpled heap
at the bottom of the ravine and shook his head. To his
intense irritation he had regained consciousness a few
minutes ago. Cursing his current predicament he looked
up a couple of hundred feet to the thin crack of daylight
and the remains of the rotten bridge he had recently
fallen through.

It really wasn't fair. How could he have survived that?
And so painlessly? He shook his head again and sat up,
tutting as his gaze ferreted amongst the knobs and
crannies of the ravine walls, searching for handholds and
a possible means of escape. He couldn't stay down here.
He'd starve. If he didn't expire through severe frustration first. All those souls he could be saving! He
whimpered pathetically.

For a brief few seconds he wondered if sitting here,
doing nothing and wasting away from lack of food was
tantamount to suicide. He concluded that he wasn't
willing to risk an eternity's suffering finding out.

Nope, he decided. Up, up and away. No choice. Too
many souls needed to hear the Good News for him just
to stay down here bathing in the endless lakes of self-
pity. He had to get up, get out and then find another,
successful way to gain the essential terminal entry
qualification.

He stood shakily, placed one foot against one side of
the ravine, one against the other and readied himself to
push, chimney-style, all the way up two hundred feet.
He took a breath, braced himself and screamed as both
feet vanished up to his ankles in the rock. Claustrophobic
terror seized him, grabbing at his windpipe and making

him choke. He felt as if the rock walls were pressing in all around him, constricting, clutching.

Of all the places he'd spread his many lucrative variations of the Good Word, he'd never done it in such a narrow hole. No wonder his mind was playing tricks.

It wasn't a pleasant thing for one to discover suddenly that one had a screaming hysterical phobia of being two hundred feet down an extremely narrow ravine with no way out. Especially when one was in fact two hundred feet down an extremely narrow ravine with no way out.

Just as he was about to relax his grip on his mental faculties and slip unstoppably into the manic relief of total panic, a flash of blinding light opened above him. It surrounded two pairs of beating wings, expanding rapidly, sweeping the ravine as if searching.

Screed's jaw fell open as the million-lumen spotlight intensified and was joined by a thin, swirling chord of angelic voices counterpointed by the frantic strumming of a harp.

With a suitably ethereal whooshing sound two members of the Parangelic Service swept out of the light, snatched Screed under the armpits and hooked him skywards, a dozen sirens in tow.

'Naughty, naughty,' admonished Agnus, the angelic interceptor, from his left arm, her wings powering them upwards. 'Trying to save yourself, were you? Well, you shouldn't! Good job you didn't get far or we might not have found you, might we, Florrie?'

'Oooh, no,' answered the other angel, struggling to be heard above the wailing of the sirens behind.

'It's so easy to get confused and go wandering off in any direction. D'you know, over ninety percent of all souls get lost in the first ten minutes,' chattered Agnus, her white apron flapping in the breeze.

'Ninety-five,' added Florrie, then turned and bellowed at the sirens. They subsided and flew off to chase another emergency.

Screed was having real trouble with all this. 'What d'you mean, lost souls,' he spluttered.

'You,' answered Agnus. 'Few more minutes and you'd have wandered off. Lost soul, see?'

'But how? I'm still alive...'

'Oh, dearie me,' smiled Agnus angelically. 'Would we be here if you were? Would we? You wouldn't need us, dear.'

'But...' It was as far as he managed to get for a few moments as he tried to figure out this new strand of information. Despite all the teachings and preachings that had dribbled unstoppably from his mouth, one thing he had never actually done was sit down and work out quite what stepping into the afterlife would really be like. He hadn't expected to be claustrophobic, for one thing.

'But ... I can move and ... What about my body? I want to see my body!' he squealed, looking down between his toes. By now the ravine was almost out of sight. His stomach churned. Oh gods, vertigo, too! 'Where's my...'

'Now, don't you go worrying yourself about your body. It's fine. Fully biodegradable,' reassured Agnus. 'Few years and you wouldn't even know it was there.'

'What?' Realisation didn't so much dawn in Screed's mind as come screaming over the horizon, lights blazing, horns sounding, banners waving madly. 'So you're telling me I'm actually dea...?' he asked, a quiver of excitement in his voice.

'We prefer the term "animationally challenged",' advised Agnus. 'It's less worrying for some folk.'

'Say the word "corpse" to some old dears and they go all weepy,' added Florrie with a tutting noise. 'It is sad. Should see the state of some souls if you let slip the word "cadaver" by accident. Oh, dearie me, floods of tears, wailing and gnashing of teeth. It's shocking behaviour. Shocking. Oh, I see that you don't seem too perturbed by such vulgar epithets?'

Florrie looked at Screed's grin and a whole host of questions sprang to mind. Only a few times before had she met anyone who looked so cheerful about being here.

'Hard life?' she asked, then added quickly, 'No, no, don't tell me, dear. Let me guess. Er, you're so happy 'cause that good-for-nothing wastrel son of yours didn't get a chance to alter your will and so inherit the company now that ... oh, no. Wrong clothes for that one, er ...'

'Ahh, here we are,' interrupted Agnus, relieved that she could stem Florrie's wittering flow of wild speculation. She pointed ahead as they swooped out of a large bank of cloud.

'What?' spluttered Screed. 'Here already?' In all his years of missionary work he had never realised that Heobhan was actually so close. 'But I'm not ready yet!'

'Hey, we don't hang about, you know,' answered Agnus.

'Can't now they've introduced that Impatience Charter,' grumbled Florrie. 'Nuisance, it is. According to Head Office we've got to get to all the recently deceased in under three minutes, otherwise, they reckon, they start to get all fidgety and ratty. And things like that just aren't allowed in Heobhan. Still, me and Agnus, great team!'

With a flurry of wings, they slowed down and swooped through a vast gateway which seemed to be floating in its own bank of cloud.

'Pretty, that, isn't it?' suggested Agnus, pointing to the gold filigree of the decorative inlay panels.

'Always makes Agnus' day, that,' said Florrie. 'But then, she's a real softy for a bit of twenty-four carat and a few barnfuls of dry ice. I think they should've kept the old portcullis – it had a certain rustic charm – but no. Blinkin' Impatience Charter again.'

'The powers that be reckon it's more reassuring to have this nice familiar entrance. Less traumatic,' interjected Agnus.

'Give the public what they know. Keep 'em happy,' grumbled Florrie. 'What I want to know is, who thought this whole gold and pearly gates thing up in the first place?'

'It was the prophets, wasn't it? And good on them. I think it's pretty,' enthused Agnus, as she adjusted trim and settled in on a perfect approach. It was obvious to Screed that she'd done that before.

'Whoever thought it up had no idea of budgeting, I can tell you. Do they think we're made of money up here?' complained Florrie. She turned to Screed, adding, 'Nearly had to lay off a few hundred cherubs 'cause of that thing. It cost a fortune!' It wasn't hard for him to imagine her trotting out the same complaints over some chest-high fence between neighbouring banks of cloud.

With the gentlest of touchdowns the two gossiping angels dropped Screed off and marched him towards the back of a long queue stretching away across the large landing pad.

Florrie's complaining erupted again. 'That's typical, that is!' she groaned as she stared at the string of latest admissions. 'We do our bit to get you folks here as quick as we can and what happens? We've got to wait around while they check you in! Pah! D'you know, according to the Impatience Charter this should take less than two minutes and what with...'

'Afternoon, ladies,' came a richly intoned voice from close behind.

'Now you've done it,' whispered Agnus harshly out of the corner of her mouth. 'You and your mouth. I've told you about criticising. They don't like it, you know...'

'Busy today, isn't it?' interrupted the large bearded figure, thumbing the side of his nose.

'I was just saying that to my colleague here...' began Florrie before her angelic shin received a swift kicking from an innocently grinning Agnus.

The bearded one stepped between the two angels, placed an overly affectionate arm around each of their very muscled shoulders and smiled. 'Would you care for a little refreshment?' he asked, pushing Screed behind him with a well-placed sandal.

Before the angels could answer, a fizzing flagon of nectared mead appeared in their hands, pleading to be drunk.

Sot grinned as they curtsied demurely and, in a second, swigged the lot. It was thirsty work being a member of the Parangelic Service. In a flash, another flagon for each appeared and again mewled for immediate glugging.

This time, as Agnus and Florrie's attention was firmly focused on the content of their mugs, Sot turned to Screed and pointed to a distant rock in a dark corner. 'Hide,' he whispered.

'Well, this *is* kind, I must say,' smiled Florrie in a way that can only be described as angelic. 'One does get rather thirsty bringing the likes of this chap up ... Hang on. Where's he gone?' She spun around desperately as she looked for Screed. 'He's vanished! I knew he was going to be trouble as soon as I laid eyes on him.'

'He's wandered off!' echoed Agnus. 'Typical!'

'Brilliant! That's just great, that is. That'll really muck our average time up now if we've got to go and look for the ungrateful little...'

'Ladies, please,' soothed Sot, assuming an abashed expression of guilt. 'I'm so sorry. This is all my fault. How can I make amends?'

'You can go and find the little...' began Florrie.

'No,' snapped Agnus. 'That's our job.'

Florrie grabbed Agnus by the shoulder and yammered a hoarse whisper in her ear. 'Look, if he hadn't come here and distracted us then...'

'She is right,' sighed Sot, eavesdropping for all he was worth. 'It is all my fault. Please, leave it to me. I shall find him.'

91

'I don't really think we should leave you to...' began Agnus.

'And I don't see why my interruption should cause you to lose your highly-struggled-for collection average...' offered Sot.

'He's right you know,' insisted Florrie. 'Spot on. Just like I said. C'mon. We've got souls to save!'

'Yes, but he's...' began Agnus.

'He's okay,' blustered Florrie. 'Just think of the panic that our next customers will be feeling when they wake up dead with no one to explain what's up. You want to leave them in confusion and panic?'

It was too much for Agnus. 'Find him,' she pleaded to Sot and handed back his flagon.

'See you later for a refill, big boy?' asked Florrie, handing her mug back.

'Perhaps,' grinned Sot and watched the angels of the Parangelic Service take to the wing and swoop through the Gates of Heobhan.

Rubbing his hands eagerly as the flagons tinkled into nothingness, he whirled on his feet and dashed across to the boulder in the corner. 'This way,' he grunted, tugging Screed through a small door.

'Is it far? I'm really rather keen to get on and save a few...' Screed spluttered, preferring the treatment meted out by the angels.

'Yes, yes. And so you should be. You are off on your greatest mission after all,' grinned Sot. 'Going down,' he added, clapping his hands, and with an odd fizzing sound the Mostly Reverend Vex Screed of the Haranguist Mission vanished.

It was the shortest visit ever made to Heobhan.

In the vast pyramidal cavern of the Axolotian Grand Municipal Temple the air was tingling with electric excitement. Every seat of the steep-sided amphitheatre was groaning under the load of a fidgeting Axolotian citizen, ready and fizzing with pent nerves as the curtain-up on this afternoon's show rumbled ever nearer.

Buried deep in the buzzing noise, the three taps of a tiny bamboo cane on wood were missed by almost everyone. The sudden eruption of the band wasn't. A cacophany of kazoos and ocarinas blasted into the instantly recognisable jaunty theme tune and the crowd was on their feet, screaming and cheering, hurling skullcaps into the rafters.

Behind the heavy curtain, the stage manager signalled to two figures in the wings. Each leapt up their respective ropes and tugged. Simultaneously the crimson curtain began to rise and a vast mirror slewed sideways high in the roof. It snatched the afternoon sunlight, bounced it off its glinting surface and sent it cascading across a carefully aligned series of other mirrors and lenses. And at the exact moment that the curtain revealed the stage, a spot of light flashed into being.

The cheering rattled the roof tiles as the grinning figure of their host Tehzho Khonna stepped into the pool of light, raised his hands and declared, 'The future's here now...'

And the crowd yelled back, 'The future's nice!'

After he had somehow patted the audience into semi-calm, Tehzho Khonna raised his hands joyously and shouted, 'Ladies and Gentlemen, Welcome to today's session of "Play Your Stars Right!", the Astrological Game Show that puts *Your* Future in *Your* Hands!' Needless to say the crowd erupted in a cacophony of clapping.

The consummate professional compere that he was, Tehzho strolled around the gaudy set for a few minutes while the audience worked their excitement out like a colony of seals. He knew he could work them up into fervent, frenzied fanaticism at the flick of a deft catchphrase. Especially today: The 'Play Your Stars Right!' Grand Final.

Nonchalantly he rummaged in his pocket as a table

was pushed on by a shimmering assistant in an equally shimmering toga. With a wry grin and a cheeky wink he produced a handful of ornately decorated bone cubes. 'It's time to "Take Advice from the Dice!"' he declared, shook his hands and scattered them across the table. The crowd looked on with a modicum of confusion. What was he doing? He shouldn't be 'Consulting The Cubes' to find who was to be today's contestants – he already knew the answer. This was the final. The contestants were...

'And the contestants are...' he announced, peering mystically over the scattered bones. Then he stood, shrugged and grinned yet again. 'But we already know, don't we, Ladies and Gentlemen? Say "Yes, Tehz!"'

And dutifully the audience yelled back, 'Yes, Tehz!'

'Yes, indeedy-doo. We've seen them before, we've cheered them on, we've begged the fates to be kind ... Here they are, back again in the Head to Head, the lovely Cheiryn Roon and the beautiful Khrystal Gehyz. Give them a big hand!'

The shimmering assistant led the two girls on and placed them centre stage, one each side of Tehzho Khonna. His eyes bulged as the voluptuous Khrystal strode past in front of him. His palms began to sweat.

'Now, turning to you, Cheiryn. You won through against tough competition three months ago after "Aligning Your Signs" *most* fortuitously to correctly predict a place in the final and a month's free groceries courtesy of the Fruit Preservation Company Ltd. Say "Yes, Tehz!"'

'Yes, Tehz,' nodded Cheiryn plainly.

His eyes steered his body around to linger longingly upon Khrystal Gehyz. 'And ... and the stunningly beautiful Khrystal,' he announced. She fluttered her darkly curling eyelashes with deft precision. 'You ... er, you are 38–24–32, single, devastatingly blonde, all natural it says here,' he waggled a small sheet of sun-dried bamboo leaf and leered at the crowd. Dutifully, they laughed. 'And you won through to the final easily. Say "Yes, Tehz!"'

94

'Oooooh yes, Tehz. I am delighted to be here,' she cooed in her sultriest voice and gave a demure wave to the audience.

Cheiryn Roon sneered angrily. Tehzho's knees went weak. The orchestra of kazoos and ocarinas erupted suddenly into a four-bar variation of the theme tune, snapping Tehzho out of his mental undressing of the lusciously leggy Khrystal.

'And that tune means that it's time for "The Divination Game"!' He turned, put his arm around Khrystal and led her to the waist-high wooden temples emblazoned with their names. Frowning, Cheiryn trotted behind.

Without delay Tehzho Khonna launched into the now familiar introduction. 'We asked one hundred different prophets a string of questions and asked them to choose one correct answer. I'm going to ask you two lovely contestants ... sorry, finalists the same questions and I want you to choose the one which you truly believe to be correct. Okay here we go, question one...' He picked up the pack of parchment cards on his temple top, flexed them and cleared his throat. Khrystal fluttered her eyelashes.

'Ahem, question one. We asked one hundred prophets whether they have ever used their divinatory powers to pull a bird. Their answers were, A) Of course not, that would demean the entire standing of prophetic visons within our society, how dare you ask such a rude question!, or B) Yes, but only if my aftershave and offers of recently deceased floral tributes had failed to melt her frozen heart. Just don't tell my wife!, or C) Sure, every time. If you've got it flaunt it! You now have thirty seconds to decide which answer *you* think was the most popular. Starting now.'

The band blew up another raspberry-based tune as the two contestants pondered carefully beneath the fascinated gaze of the packed audience.

All too soon the music stopped and a taut silence gripped the temple.

'Ladies, "Reveal your leaves,"' urged Tehzho with a grin. Khrystal thrust a bamboo leaf bearing a proud 'C' high above her head as Cheiryn clutched an 'A' to her chest. The crowd gasped.

'Well, a touch of disagreement there, ladies. Will one of you be right and gain a valuable advantage, taking you one step closer to the ultimate prize on "Play Your Stars Right!", or will both of you be wrong? Who knows? Only the Cards will tell!'

The shimmering assistant scuttled across the stage proudly bearing a single gold envelope on a velvet cushion. She halted downstage of Tehzho, curtsied and fluttered her eyelids at him. Ignoring her, his attention fixed on Khrystal's cleavage, he snatched the envelope open and caught his grin just moments before it fell. An unblinking 'A' stared back at him.

'Oh ladies, one of you is wrong. And I'm dreadfully afraid to say that, much as it pains me, it's you, my dear Khrystal.' He was holding her hand and staring into her eyes like a devoted suitor comforting his lover. 'Are you alright? Say "Yes Tehz."'

'Yes, Tehz. It's only the first round,' she observed. 'Plenty of time to catch up.'

Tehzho beamed as he patted her hand and spun around. "So brave, so brave!' he thought devotedly and sprang back centre stage.

Cheiryn scowled.

'Well, Ladies and Gentlemen, let's see Khrystal catch up, shall we? Question two. We asked one hundred and fifty seers what they used to keep their crystals gleaming. A) Spit and polish, B) Divine-Light No-Scratch Scrying Crystal Cleanser and Hand Conditioner or C) A quick scrub with a handy chamois. Ladies, there are your choices, start thinking. Now!'

The band dutifully chimed up again and Tehzho turned to the audience. 'Our guest Khrystal doesn't seem to need any advice about keeping herself clean. Just look at her, beautifully groomed, beautifully...'

Suddenly the music stopped and the shimmering assistant scuttled on with the answer on the cushion. The contestants held up their answers for all to see, Cheiryn brandishing a definite 'B' and Khrystal waving an eager 'A'.

'Oooh, another difference of views,' observed Tehzho, his gut w'rithing in excitement. 'Now then, this *is* interesting. Will Khrystal pull back neck and neck?'

"And *what* a neck!" his mind leered as he fumbled with the envelope and tugged out the answer. With acute relief he held the 'A' aloft for all to see, waggling it under Cheiryn's nose. 'Wrong. Ha!' he scoffed.

'Question three to decide who goes through to play "Align Your Signs" for tonight's star prize! We asked five dozen aromafuturists to name the essential oil most likely to bring success in tonight's show. Did they say A) Patchouli, B) Gopher, or C) Ylang Ylang? Ladies, choose your smell!'

The band dropped their instruments, clenched their fists and pounded frantically on the edge of the stage in a makeshift drum roll. Unfortunately the percussionist had been so excited by the Final that he had clean forgotten to pack his tympani.

Thirty seconds of pounding later Tehzho Khonna flashed his palms high in the electrified air, waving them for the contestants to stop thinking and raise a letter. The girls dutifully obeyed, Cheiryn thrusting an angry 'A' skyward, Khrystal simpering beneath a 'C'.

Over a low drumming from the band and a hushed expectancy from the fizzing audience Tehzho declared, 'Ladies and Gentlemen. Only one of our finalists will go through to challenge the stars in the Grand Climax "Align Your Signs". Will it be the vivaciously beautiful Khrystal Gehyz? Or Cheiryn? Two different answers, only one is correct. Which is it?' He held out his hand and the shimmering assistant trotted dutifully on with the envelope.

Snatching the envelope dramatically and striding to the front of the stage with it clutched tightly to his chest he asked in hushed tones of melodrama, 'Which will it be?'

The audience held their breath.

Of course, the actual answer didn't matter a damn. Tehzho knew the outcome. He'd been planning it for weeks. Ever since he'd laid his lecherous eyes on the cleavage of a certain Miss Gehyz.

With some of the audience turning blue, he eased open the envelope, slid out the answer and held it against his pounding chest. Quickly he glanced over his shoulders to remind himself of the girls' answers. It wouldn't do to get it wrong now. Not after all the effort he'd gone to.

'If this card says "C" then I will be joined in the Grand Climax by the delicious Khrystal who'll be playing "Align Your Signs". "A" and it's Cheiryn' he added dismissively. 'And the answer is . . .' He tugged the card away from his chest and was hit in the face by an accusing 'A'.

The . . . the answer is "C"!' he declared, screwed the card up, stuffed it deep into a secret pocket in his toga and skipped joyously across the stage to snatch Khrystal Gehyz around her waist and waltz to the strains of the theme tune.

'Congratulations, Khrystal Gehyz!' he declared a few minutes later as he found his spot centre stage and patted the audience to mere fever pitch. 'Congratulations, you're through to the finale of "Play Your Stars Right!"' Reluctantly he turned away and addressed the loser. 'But Cheiryn Roon, you don't go away empty-handed. Oh no. Today's show was brought to you by those lovely people at Divine-Light. Yes, you will go away with one year's worth of Divine-Light No-Scratch Scrying Crystal Cleanser and Hand Conditioner. Please, give her a big hand, she's been a . . . a contestant!'

And in an instant Cheiryn Roon had been hauled off

the stage by the sequinned shimmering assistant to spend several weeks attempting to figure out precisely what she could do with a year's worth of Divine-Light No-Scratch Scrying Crystal Cleanser and Hand Conditioner.

The stage turned around, the mirrors and lenses re-angled and Tehzho Khonna and the voluptous Khrystal Gehyz re-entered on a vast wave of tumultuous applause. Khrystal pouted and preened in audience-loving fervour. It had to be said that describing her as a shyly wilting wallflower was as accurate as describing the average terrapin as a perfect aeronaut.

'So, Ladies and Gentlemen of Axolotl, here she is, this year's finalist and winner of "Play your Stars Right!", Miss Voluptuousnessly Curvaceous Herself, Khrystal Gehyz. Big hand, big hand.'

Only one pair of hands didn't join in the devoted slapping of palms and they were Cheiryn Roon's. She stood in the wings, snarling.

It was almost more than Tehzho could cope with. The crowd were utterly wild. But somehow, over the next few minutes, with yells of 'Please, please. Don't get carried away now,' he gradually coaxed them into a mere boiling frenzy of voyeuristic pleasure.

Eventually, when he knew that everyone would be able to hear him again, he turned to Khrystal, his tongue salivating lustily, and declared, 'So, congratulations! You've won. How does it feel?'

'Ooooooh, I'm thrilled!'

'So, shall we find out what golden prize awaits you?'

Khrystal nodded her tresses of blonde hair enthusiastically and Tehzho felt stirrings in potentially embarrassing regions.

'Well . . . well, let's play "Align Your Signs". Come this way, please!' And with a trembling hand tightly wrapped around her two-foot waist he fairly skipped across the stage to face the vast array of cards held face down against a multi-coloured wall.

'Well, Khrystal, I'm sure you know how to play "Align

Your Signs" by now, but for those who have let it slip their minds...'

He turned to the audience, beckoned and they yelled back, 'Shame on them!' as they did every day.

'...I shall remind them. Khrystal, my darling, you are allowed four cards, chosen from any of the card holders, and, using these you must arrange to bring about the finest and happiest of futures, be that financial, touristical or even matrimonial! Do you understand? Say "Yes Tehz!"'

Again Khrystal nodded. 'Yes, Tehz. I do.'

'Course she does!' hollered back the audience in well-drilled response.

'Very well, make your choice, my love. Here's your chance to snuggle up in the lap of luxury. Good luck!'

'I ... I'll have the third one off the top row, the second in off the third and the rest from the fourth,' pouted Khrystal sultrily. In a corona of flashing sequins the shimmering assistant snatched the indicated cards, whirled on her sandals and placed them face down on the table centre stage.

And then, for the first time in the entire day, the amphitheatre was silent with apprehension. They had all watched Khrystal Gehyz work her way up through the ranks of hopeful contestants on "Play Your Stars Right!", gradually gaining in confidence and wearing more flamboyant, and shorter, togas at every appearance. Now it was doubtful if the toga she was currently sporting held enough material to stop a nosebleed. The men loved her for her ever more apparent attributes and the women loved her for having the guts to flaunt them. Everyone wanted the absolute best for her. And that included Tehzho Khonna.

Clattering crazily on her heels, Khrystal rattled towards the four cards to see what she had chosen.

'Let's see what's on "Tehzho's Table", shall we?' the compere declared and turned over the first four-foot

100

high card. It showed a single enormous bunch of flowers. The crowd shuffled closer on their stools. The second card was an open-topped cart drawn by three majestic pairs of ibex. The crowed 'oohed' appreciatively.

'And the third?' Tehzho flicked it over expertly to show a single blue garter. The men in the audience made suitably lecherous noises. 'And lastly...' Two letters sprang into view: 'T' and 'K'. Rumoured rumblings rattled around the temple.

'Now, Miss Khrystal Gehyz, Winner of "Play Your Stars Right!" it is time for you to choose...' The band pounded their fists on the stage again and the lights lowered to a single concentrated spot focused on her and Tehzho. 'You know now that you have ten seconds to reject one of these predictions and arrange the others in the order in which you feel the fates will prefer. Do you understand?'

'I ... I do,' she whispered, the tension at last getting to her.

'Course she does!' shouted a few die-hard participators who hadn't been gripped by the poignancy of the moment. In ten seconds Khrystal Gehyz would have to choose her future. The last year of countless appearances had all been leading to these last few moments.

'Are you ready? Say "Yes, Tehz!"'

'Yes, Tehz,' she nodded nervously.

'Very well, your time starts as soon as the crowd begin to count. Good Luck. Ten! ... Nine...'

She leapt at the table and stood dithering, clueless as to the symbols' meaning.

'...Eight ... Seven...'

She picked up two cards at once, flapped and dropped them again.

'...Six ... Five...'

She snatched the bunch of flowers and frowned.

'...Four ... Three...' The countdown was deafening.

She dropped the flowers, snatched the cart...

'...Two...'

101

She flung the cart away and shifted the other three around randomly.

'...One ... Stop!' Tehzho snatched at Khrystal's slim wrists and quivered. Quickly he released them before his palms started sweating.

'Well, you've rejected the open-topped cart with ibex entourage. Now is this touristic or ... matrimonial? Have you just rejected the finest of romantic Axolotian transports, ready to whisk you off towards the wedding of the year with you as the star? No! You have thrown away an all-expenses paid three-day trip around the known world!' The crowd moaned in commiseration. She had lost the chance to see the mountain next door and visit the dark side of the one beyond that. Oh, shame!

'But what have you chosen and in what order? How have you "Aligned Your Signs"? Well, here we have a huge bunch of flowers, held together in such a way that they can be carried easily and ... thrown perhaps?' Some of the older and more romantically inclined women gasped. 'The garter, here in blue, one of a trio of signs, the others being old and borrowed, perhaps?'

Khrystal slapped her hands across her mouth and squeaked.

'Yes.' declared Tehzho expansively. 'Some of you have already guessed. This is it. Miss Khrystal Gehyz you are going to announce the name of the man you are going to marry. And we at "Play Your Stars Right!" will pay for the whole thing. Oh this is *so* unexpected. What a fairytale ending!'

Tehzho was trembling with terror and lust. It had all worked so perfectly, so far. Now the final push.

'But who is the lucky man? These two letters hold the answer. Who could it be? Who could possibly have the initials "TK"?' Tehzho mused theatrically. He stared longingly at Khrystal and winked.

She stared into space, thinking. '"TK"? Sure it's not "KT"?'

102

'NO!' squealed Tehzho. 'Er ... ahem, no. It's quite clearly someone with a first name beginning with "T".' He flashed her a grin and winked.

And then her eyes widened, her gaze focused and she made a strange choking noise in the back of her throat. 'I know what it means,' she whispered, staring at him in a new light, overwhelmed by the pressure of the occasion. The cards had spoken, and here before everyone it had been revealed.

Silently her index finger uncurled and pointed at him. 'Tehzho Khonna!'

They were the two words he was desperate to hear. 'Me?' Ever the consummate milker of audiences, he stepped back, turned to the crowd and mugged it up for all he was worth. '*Me*?' He clutched at his chest as if in complete shock.

'This is a complete shock!' he yelped dramatically. 'But the cards *have* spoken,' he added before anyone, least of all the stage-shocked Khrystal, could disagree. 'It is my duty to obey. Miss Khrystal Gehyz, darling,' he fell to his knees, 'Will you marry me? Say "Yes, Tehz!"'

'Yes, Tehz,' she whispered and the amphitheatre erupted in tears and applause.

With a lecherous grin Tehzho leapt to his feet and grabbed Khrystal around the wrist, whisking her off stage left and heading for his dressing room.

The stage manager would get his backhander later.

A crimson flash of lightning flared across the expanse of Mortropolis at the end of a flamestorm, lighting the plumes of chthonic fumocarbons rising from the infernal combustion engines of the ferries. Somewhere a valve was changed, hyperheated steam surged down miles of piping and the shift-change Klaxon drowned out all sound.

In moments, the push hour would begin. The streets of Mortropolis would be heaving with dispossessed souls hurled out of one torture, heading off for another eight hours of screaming agony elsewhere.

It was just a normal day for the residents of the Underworld Kingdom of Helian.

And this included the street-wise Pact-men.

'Okay, we all know what we're meant to be doing?' asked a tall, thin man with a goatee beard. A violin was tucked nonchalantly under his arm.

'Course we do, Fithel. You've told us enough times,' grumbled an extremely wasted-looking figure wearing a rictus grin.

'Listen, Phaust, I just want to make sure it all goes nice and smoothly, alright?' snapped Fithel. 'I'm the one causing the distraction. I'm the one on the line. All eyes will be on me. If anything goes wrong...'

'Yes dahling, but you like that sort of thing. The peril, the chase, the worshipping audience,' snapped Bahbz, fluttering her eyelashes harshly. 'I could take the pressure off with a little vocal accompaniment.'

Fithel's eyes widened with alarm. Vocal accompaniment. No! Just as well she hadn't tried to call it singing. Her throat's ventures into music made fingernails on blackboards sound positively operatic.

'No singing,' he spluttered.

'You've only yourself to blame if you won't let me share a bit of the limelight, luvvie,' she continued. 'I can take their minds off you, you know? If you don't let me sing I could...' She shimmied her far from unattractive figure and pouted. 'Ahhh, they could never keep their eyes off me...'

In the shadows a miserable figure in the habit of an Abbey Synnian monk rolled his eyes and tutted grumpily.

'And they still can't,' growled Fithel. 'Look at them!' The entire cluster of Pact-men stood with their tongues drooling pathetically.

Much to his disgust the Abbey Synnian monk flushed and had to think of cold showers and dead dogs.

'Ooooh, ain't they sweet,' cooed Bahbz.

'Pathetic,' tutted Fithel. 'Snap out of it, you guys. C'mon!' Irritably, he swung his violin up under his chin and assaulted their ears with a swift flurry of the glissandic crescendo from Queazx's Erotic Symphony in B Minor.

'Owww. Give it a break!' barked Phaust, wincing. 'Bloody racket! I've heard more melody from a boiling kitten!'

'Musical poetry!' declared an enraptured ex-composer standing with his hands clutched to his chest. 'Play some more, dear Fithel!'

Phaust shook his head, 'Damn, I forgot you wrote that din. What were you thinking of to sell your soul for that?'

'Achh, heathen. Those four bars of nine-eight are *the* most technically demanding fingering in the entire history of the fiddle! If you knew *anything* about post-modernist neo-classic symphonic works, you would appreciate its full value,' nagged Queazx in a well-rehearsed manner.

'Oh, I do,' grunted Phaust. 'Four bars a day can really clear out earwax, I'll tell you. How come you didn't sell your soul for something more worthwhile.'

'The way you did, you mean?' snapped Queazx.

'Got a better deal than you did, matey. Given the choice between writing a screechy racket or spending twenty-four years indulging in the *very* finest pleasures a body can stand, I know which I'd go for.' Phaust grinned in an exceedingly lecherous way.

'My name is famed throughout the whole of the Talpa Mountains. Famed as an interkingdomnally recognised genius. Are you as widely known?'

'Oh yes,' grinned Phaust. 'My name appears in more regularly read books than yours ever will.'

'What, what?'

'I was on the first page of every interesting woman's little black book. They'd always call on me first if they wanted a good time!'

Bahbz's eyes lit up.

'I sold my soul for art,' said Queazx.

'And I had much more fun,' grinned Phaust.

Every one of the so-called Pact-men was there for fundamentally the same reason. They had all missed something so desperately, or needed some skill, some talent so urgently, that they had succumbed to the ultimate temptation. They'd whispered their greatest desires three times in the shell-like of their local devil and there they were. Sold out, homeless, tortureless. They were Helian's Illegal Immigrants. Hoisted on the petard of their own desires.

All except the miserable monk in the shadows, that is. He had been conned one fateful night in the silent chapel of St Absent the Regularly Forgotten and now he was stuck there, treated with the same tarred brush as the others – constantly harassed for vagrancy and unwarranted busking by the nine-foot coppers in the Malebranche. And worse, in every waking moment – which meant in fact every moment – their pacts were at the forefront of their minds. Fithel, the finest violinist ever to have lived, owing to a slight helping claw from his local demon, was now constantly gripped in a state of desperation to leap up and perform his finest works and simultaneously struck almost incapable of doing so by an incessant, stomach wrenching attack of stage fright.

'Look, if you two will stop arguing we can get on with the job, alright?' barked Fithel. 'It's Cassoh's turn for the raid today.'

The now colour-blind artist nodded enthusiastically. 'I promised Bahbz a portrait,' he grinned, hiding a large canvas behind his back. 'A full frontal portrait.'

'Hey, we'll get you everything you need, matey,' leered Phaust. 'Just so long as we can watch.'

Cassoh was trembling at the thought of his first nude model in centuries. He had found it abominably difficult as a pre-pact artist. Since he was covered in dreadful acne, no model would come near him for fear of contagion on. But three little pleas demonwards and it had all been solved. Well, sort of. His acne had cleared up nicely but there weren't exactly very many models down here. The painting he was forced to carry with him everywhere was a barely recognisable self-portrait buried beneath a festering heap of oil-painted pustules and sores. 'Spectators' he muttered nervously. 'I think that's up to Bahbz.'

'Oh, what a gentleman.' She grinned and fluttered her eyelids. 'That's so nice it really makes me want to sing...'

'No, no. It's time to go. C'mon!' interjected Fithel desperately before Bahbz could get started. Having been incredibly popular in the regular daily theatrical matinées of the ongoing show 'Crossbows' she had decided to break into serious culture and become a folk star. Her only mistake was in her choice of devil. Although she had asked him three times to make her singing voice into the most beautiful sound he could imagine, the problem was she didn't have any idea precisely what that was. Now she sang like an entire amateur operatic chorus of lovesick wolverines.

Clutching his violin tightly under his arm, Fithel led the band of Pact-men out of the tiny alley opposite the entrance to the Pit of Burning Coals. Any second now the vast door would be flung open and waves of tormented souls would come streaming out, heading off to their next torture. Already the flow of souls shuffling along the street was increasing as push hour began.

With a signal from Fithel, leader for this raid, Queazx and Phaust squirmed into the crush of bodies and wriggled across to position themselves on each side of the entrance. Spruce, the ex-holder of the only million-groat note ever printed who had died penniless and starving because nobody had any small change, Bahbz and the miserably habited ex-Reverend Unctuous III

107

positioned themselves carefully as lookouts for any approaching Malebranche.

They were bound to come. The only variable was how long it took them and from which direction they appeared.

Suddenly, with a roar of devils and the cracking of whips, the vast security door of the Pit of Burning Coals screamed open and gasping souls in torment spilled out. The heat singed Phaust's eyebrows. Incredibly, it was even hotter in there than the average inferno of six hundred and sixty-six degrees fahrenheit they had become used to.

Right on cue, and trembling with terror on top of a small hut, Fithel scraped his bow across the strings. It was unmistakably the opening discord of Queazx's Erotic. In seconds he was sawing furiously at the instrument, hurling licks of alarming atonality at the surging mob of tormented souls pouring along the street below. Cracked fifths and flattened ninths bombarded their ears and, as with every other public performance of the work there had ever been, they were halted in their tracks. They stood there rooted to the spot, stunned, trying to believe it was music that they were hearing. In moments the entire street was a solid mass of miserable souls.

Wasting no time, Phaust and Queazx squeezed themselves in through the door of the Pit of Burning Coals, heads down, hunting. Charred coals littered the floor, its uneven surface showing where bodies had been buried in eight-hour stretches. The two raiders tugged sacks off their shoulders, grabbed at coals and hurled them rapidly into the gaping draw-string mouths. Ten, fifteen pieces, then out, squirming back through the crowd.

Fithel was enraptured, his body snaking wildly as the music took control. Phaust and Queazx dashed down the alley through which they had entered the street, whistling cheerily in signal to the lookouts. They dropped thirty pieces of charred coal into Cassoh's lap.

108

'There you go, enough art supplies for another month,' grinned Phaust. 'Now, about Bahbz posing for you...'

He never received an answer. At that very instant there was a sudden and unexpected flash of screaming white light and a tall black-cassocked figure appeared on the roof next to Fithel. By his side a large box appeared, stuffed with Nognite parchment cups. The violinist squealed and stopped in mid-glissando, his bow quivering with shock. 'Who the hell are you...?' he began.

'Er, ah, hello everybody,' declared the interruption, trembling with excitement. All those eager faces to save. There were probably more desperate folk jammed into that single square than he had seen in his entire life. A lesser missionary would have gaped in spiritual stage fright, but not him. This was it. Time for action. 'I'm the Mostly Reverend Vex Screed of the Haranguist Mission and I'd very much like to have a chat to you about a little something that will really make life, ahem, or death, er, a lot more pleasant for you all down here.'

The ears of the ex-Reverend Unctuous III leapt into quivering excitement and almost instantly began to doubt what they had heard. Surely, there couldn't *possibly* be another man of the cloth down here? He wheeled around on his sandals, heart pounding, desperate for some less theologically-challenged company, steeling himself for the disappointment he was sure would soon be revealed.

The demons on the gate of the Pit of Burning Coals snarled and surged forward. Screed twitched nervously on the hut roof. Demons! This really was in at the deep end. 'Er, even you could benefit,' he added and shrugged. 'I ... I suppose.'

Unctuous's jaw dropped onto his chest as he stared at the cassocked figure. He looked the part, he sounded right ... but dare the ex-Reverend believe it was true?

Screed waved a hand in front of his face in the age old,

and ineffectual, gesture of someone who was far warmer than they really want to be. 'Bit stuffy down here, don't you think? Well, I've got really Good News for all of you. I stand before you with the answer to your dreams.' He tugged a large frothing flagon of ale out of his pocket and took a long draught.

'Yes, it is your lucky day, for I am the envoy of Sot the Deity-in-Command of All Ales.' This announcement got a very mixed reaction. The demons, on hearing the word "Deity", screamed and began clawing their way towards Screed. The crowd, on hearing the word "Ales", screamed and, interestingly, also began clawing their way towards him. And the ex-Reverend Unctuous III, on hearing the word "Envoy", became transfixed with shock. It *was* true!

'Please, please,' declared Screed happily, holding up his hands with evangelic piety. 'There's no need to push. There is plenty of Good News to go around. Simply be patient and listen as I explain...'

And with that he launched into a Speech extolling the virtues of a true belief in Sot. He held the crowd totally enraptured by the flagon in his right hand, mesmerising them completely.

'So what d'you reckon it means then?' snapped Nabob once more as he and Flagit pushed their way through the crush of bodies on the streets.

'Gimme a chance,' barked Flagit, clutching the package secretively inside his tunic, changing talons regularly as the cold seeped through the parchment. Flinty the stalag-mite clattered along eagerly behind him, seemingly not noticing the swathe of souls she was trampling under her fast-moving legs.

'You must have some sort of a clue,' pressed Nabob, elbowing his way through the armpit-deep mob.

'Nothing definite,' muttered Flagit noncommitally.

In actual fact this wasn't true. Flagit did have something very definite. Confusion. Complete and total.

110

Whoever had written whatever it was they had written in the secret file obviously hadn't wanted just anyone to read it. If it hadn't been for the generously included sheafs of diagrams and illustrations then Flagit would have been utterly clueless. Right now things just didn't make sense. Mind you, even if they had he wouldn't have admitted it to Nabob. Didn't want to make it look like it was *too* easy to translate ancient mysterious secrets.

Being able to translate a *little* more easily would help though, he mused, as he mulled over a strange series of six pictures he had recently stared at confusedly. The first had shown a stick figure with a beard and cassock digging a small hole in the ground. The second showed him placing a small cross-shaped device in the hole and covering it over. The third frame showed a curiously familiar demonic figure sprinting wildly over the ground yelling obscenities and brandishing a trident violently. The fourth illustration was a close-up of a hoof striking freshly dug ground. The fifth, an explosion of clouds and light and possibly an angel or two. And the sixth, and most baffling, image was of the demon on his knees, talons clasped joyously together, face a hideous picture of ecstatic evangelism and apparent sudden conversion.

To Flagit it was almost meaningless. He could see that something had happened to the demon, but what?

Nabob's grumbling snatched him back to the present with a jolt. 'Damn push hour. I hate it! Did you have to spend so long in "The Gammorah"?'

'Yes. Course I did. I deserved it!' Flagit snarled righteously.

'Deserved it?' spat Nabob. 'You?'

'Having spent so long seeing what comes out of the place I thought I'd explore the inside properly.'

'But you had five lava martinis!'

'Who's counting?'

'Me!' protested Nabob. 'I had to pay for them all.'

111

'Good job I didn't fancy a snack then, isn't it?'

Nabob made a guttural growling noise, turned to face forwards and realised that they hadn't moved in the last few minutes. Snarling, desperate to get out of the crowd and back to his cavern so that Flagit could have a proper look at the secret file, he dug angrily through the mob and ploughed his way around the corner.

There he saw the reason for the tormentous jam.

Screed, atop the small hut just across from the Pit of Burning Coals, was in full evangelistic flow. He knew he had already converted the vast majority of the mob to the joys of Ale Worship. Mind you, it hadn't been that hard, since most of them knew of those pleasures from a life long gone. Wildly, they were distributing frothing Nognite parchment party cups to all who said they'd believed in Sot. And at the back of the crowd Unctuous struggled on the horns of a critical dilemma. Exactly half of his body desperately wanted to hurl himself at the crowd and muscle his way to the front, leap up onto the roof and embrace every word of the new Rev-on-the-Block; and exactly half of him was utterly convinced that it was a trap. He dithered in the shadows, one step forward, one back like some desperate six-year-old with a full bladder who is embarrassed by the word 'toilet'.

Gasping, and looking warily around them for any members of the Malebranche, the demons from the Pit of Burning Coals sipped cheerfully at the crimson cups with balloons on the side. The conversation that had passed between them moments before accepting their first drink had gone something like...

'What d'he jus' say? Believe in Sot and the drinks are free?' asked demon one.

'Yeah, reckon so,' grunted demon two.

'But that's blasphemy, isn't it? You know, talkin' about gods and deities an' stuff down here.'

'Yeah, reckon so,' mused demon two.

'But didn't he say summat about seein' is believin' jus' before?' said demon one.

'Yeah, reckon so,' grunted demon two.

'Well, I can see there's loadsa beer over there. Now, I didn't see anyone bring it in and, unless things have really changed around here, I can't imagine old Seirizzim givin' away booze to the tormented. So, to recap: I can see it. And as seeing is believing, er, I ... I ... over here, mate, pass us a big one, will you?' he called. 'You 'avin' one, mate?'

'Yeah, reckon so,' grinned demon two.

That had been three cups ago. Now they were true believers.

A few yards away the pair of demons which went under the names of Flagit and Nabob stared open-mawed at the scene. It was unbelievable.

'This is unbelievable!' declared Flagit with an uneasy sense of excitement. There was an indefinable 'something' in the air.

'Is he doing what I think he's doing?' spluttered Nabob, scratching a wickedly-curving talon across the top of his scaly head.

Flagit nodded. Years ago he'd heard of this sort of thing going on in Upperworld*. But down here? It was horrifying.

But somehow he just couldn't ignore it.

Somehow the very voyeuristic thrill of it made the scene all the more compelling. Flagit knew that he absolutely should not be listening, knew also that his

---

* When Flagit had worked in the Transcendental Travel Company Ltd, one of the most popular vacations amongst the more perverted demons had been two-week Possession Tour breaks to attend various religious happenings. At the drop of a hat, it seemed, normal straight-laced devils would shell out hundreds of obuls, jump into the body of an innocent attendee and see how the other half lived.

There were still some deeply affected demons loose in Mortropolis, the seeds of conversion planted deep in their psyche, ready for the trigger. Nobody knew how many.

demonic duty was to rush away screaming and report this to any local Malebranche on the beat, but . . .

His pointed ears tingled as he listened, and his slitted eyes seemed unable to pull away from the black-cassocked figure gyrating enthusiastically above the heads of the motionless audience.

'People of Helian,' declared the Reverend Screed, his hands flailing with further doses of evangelical fervour. 'It fills my heart with corruscations of wriggly delight to see how you have adopted the Words of Sot with such open throats. Drink, drink and be ever merry, my little sheep!'

It had to be said that Screed had become a little carried away. Everything that Sot had promised him was in fact coming true. Countless conversions in a matter of minutes, a captive sea of believers. It was Heobhan in Helian.

But there was one tiny little cloud of unrest flittering across his clear blue sky of eternal bliss. Now that he had in fact achieved one hundred percent conversion of the mob at his feet . . . what was there left to do with them? He couldn't just fold his arms and cry 'Bring on the next mob!' Couldn't just throw an eager audience away. But what more could he tell them about Ale Worship?

And then it hit him. Why limit it to Sot? He had a willing audience – if you've got them, milk them!

'People of Helian,' he continued, and clutched his hands to his chest in ecstatic delight, staring at the dreadfully shabby appearance of the garments worn by the souls before him. 'You are indeed privileged today! Yes, you stand here now, poised on the brink of a new and terrifying realisation.' There was a gasp. 'Terrifying, that is, for those not present here. You will be amazed at their reactions when they next see you, transformed in all your glory!' Screed strode to the edge of the hut roof and pointed to a near-naked man of incredible scrawni-ness, his beard singed, his skin covered in burns and

114

streaks of blackened soot after a shift in the Pit of Burning Coals.

'You, sir,' he declared. 'Yes, you! Step forward, come up here. Join me!' He held out a hand and tugged the man up onto the roof before he had a chance to refuse. Oh, the joys of captive audiences!

Hardly realising they were so doing, Flagit and Nabob leaned forward, their interest snared.

'Sir,' continued Screed. 'I trust you will not take it as impertinent of me to ask if you are overjoyed with your incredibly shabby appearance?'

'What?' croaked the tormented soul.

'Dost thou wear this abhorrent demeanour through choice?'

'Eh?'

'Want some clothes, mate?'

'Well, er, if you're offering I wouldn't say no. I mean, it's not as if it's that cold down here, but...'

'...A man has his pride!' interrupted Screed, steering.

'Yeah, I suppose that's...'

'The absolute truth! A man's body should be his secret. Not a piece of public property to be stared at, poked and ridiculed. People of Helian! If one's ribs stick out, like this chap's do in such a dreadfully repellent fashion – er, no offence, mate – then that is his business. If one's legs are scorched and wasted by excessive deprivations, and here by my side is a perfect example of such neglect...'

''Ere, d'you mind?' objected the man. 'I think they've got the message. I know I'm not what you'd call sexy or anything but...'

'At least if you were covered up there would remain a tangible sense of mystery to your bodyshape. A sense of mystery which one could utilise to a sexually attractive advantage if the situation so arose.'

Nabob felt a cheer of agreement form in his throat.

'Really? Attractive? Me?' spluttered the shabby soul on the roof.

There was a gasp from the crowd as they looked to their own state of appearance. Even Flagit caught himself smoothing his forehead scales self-consciously.

'With the correct covering, you could take your pick!' announced Screed and with a flourish he tugged a piece of coloured parchment out of his cassock, unfurling it with a flick of a wrist and not pausing to thank Sot for ensuring that somehow this had been prepared, as he had himself, for survival in an ambient temperature around the high six-sixties.

The crowd gasped as they feasted their eyes on the full range of ready-to-wear undergarments for both sexes, blue and pink.

'Yes! You'll feel so happy, never need to be bare. Helian's a joy dressed in Wonderwear!'

Flagit was stunned. He pushed forward into the crowd for a few moments, desperate for more information on Wonderwear, clamouring to feel its fleecy texture against his shiny black scales.

And then he caught sight of Nabob's expression. Instantly, like a bolt of lightning between fingertips, he recognised it. True, it was only a pale imitation of the sixth frame of the illustration he had recently contemplated, but it was all there: the talons clasped together, the face a partial picture of joyous evangelism and almost conversion.

There and then Flagit knew for certain that this ranting encassocked creature on the hut roof was somehow linked with the secret. Could he translate it? Was *he* it? A secret weapon of ultimate disruption?

Flagit stared at the scene from a suddenly altered viewpoint. It was true. Something powerful was happening here. All normal systems had broken down in this square. Demons were drinking ale with the tormented souls!

He simply had to have that man. He surged forward into the melee.

Nabob, now yards ahead of him, was only saved from

116

imminent conversion by the scream of whistles, the galloping of Malebranche hooves and the sudden scattering of everyone in the area.

Both he and Nabob watched in awe as eight truly massive monsters waded into the fleeing mob of once-transfixed souls, unfurling lengths of rope. In moments, and despite the screamed protests of the watching Pactmen, the Malebranche had lassoed the three vandals on the roof of the small hut with practised ease.

In seconds Reverend Vex Screed, the innocent model from the crowd and the violin-touting Fithel were snatched to the ground, bound and dragged away.

'No, you can't take him yet!' screeched Unctuous, surging forward against the tide of scattering souls, his mind made up, fists whirling, ready to take on all of the Malebranche. At once if necessary.

If Phaust hadn't leapt on him from behind and pinned him to the scorching ground he would have been in the thick of a one-man melee. 'Not yet,' snapped Phaust in Unctuous's ear. 'We'll get him back, don't worry. We won't be without Fithel for long.'

And in that instant, a germ of a mission hatching in his fervid mind, Unctuous went limp and allowed himself to be led away as Screed vanished around a distant corner between two vast demons.

'Naughty, naughty,' admonished Mabin the devil, clutching Screed's left shoulder. 'Tryin' to save some folk, were you? Well, you shouldn't! Good job you didn't get far or we might not've been able to stop ourselves from mashin' your 'ead in. In't that right, Ogion?'

Screed struggled pathetically. 'No, you don't understand. I'm on a mission from a god . . .'

'Oh, now that is a good one, in't it, Ogion? I ain't ever 'eard that one before.' He turned and bellowed over his shoulder to the pair clutching Fithel; ''Ere, this one says 'e's on a mission from a god! Ever 'eard anythin' so ridiculous? I ain't.' The Malebranche behind burst out laughing savagely.

'I'd keep quiet if I was you,' growled Mabin seismically. 'You's already in enough trouble for starting a riot without rantin' on about gods and stuff.'

'It wasn't a riot,' protested Screed, his legs thrashing ineffectually between the two giants. Somehow this situation felt worryingly familiar. 'It was a quiet meeting of...'

'Shut up,' snarled Mabin, and dragged him away. 'It *was* a riot, see? An' I'll tell you why. We's Riot Squad, yeah? We was called 'ere to deal with a disturbance, yeah? They wouldn't call Riot Squad unless it's a riot. Stands to reason, dunnit?'

Around a far corner, Flagit and Nabob were fleeing rapidly in extreme embarrassment. They had no intention of waiting around to be asked any searching questions.

And as Flagit sprinted, his heels clattering demonically down the backstreets of Mortropolis, his head whirled in panic.

Something very odd had just happened there. For a few moments he lost control of his willpower. And that wasn't all. For a few moments all the naturally dictatorial nature of Helian had ground to a clawing halt. Just for a few moments Seirizzim had lost control of a small section of Mortropolis.

Though Flagit hadn't a clue what it meant he knew it was a chink. A tiny dent in Seirizzim's armour.

A seedling of revenge planted itself in this thought, settled itself down and began to grow roots.

As the door to his workshop was kicked open by a volley of hooves, Moloch flicked his head up reflexively and smashed the back of it into a pattern recognition filter.

'Well, c'mon. Where are you?' shouted a worryingly familiar voice. 'It's that time of day again!'

Moloch groaned quietly to himself and wriggled out of the inside of the latest mostly completed Analytical Crystal.

118

'I'm waiting!' snarled the voice.

Brushing his talons down the front of his cloak, Moloch stood and scuttled around the front of the vast obsidian block.

'Hiding from me?' Seirizzim glared as the short demon appeared, rubbing the back of his head. 'Progress report not ready yet?'

Asmodeus, standing at Seirizzim's side, grinned as he clutched a vast abacus. It was always nice to see someone getting torn off a strip. Oooooh, just being in Seirizzim's vicinity when that happened was so exciting. And it didn't do his standing any harm either. It gave a banker a bit of power simply to hover in the aura of the Undertaker-in-Chief of Mortropolis. Soon, when all of those below him had been on the receiving end of one of Seirizzim's beatings, they would no longer cause him problems.

'Ahh ... well, I was still adjusting the...' began Moloch.

'Woops,' tutted Seirizzim, intensifying his glare. 'Wrong answer!' The Undertaker-in-Chief's fist whirled out of nowhere and cracked across Moloch's snout. It seemed that a recent meeting with a vandalistic bunch of ferrymen on the banks of the Phlegethon had done little to foster Seirizzim's feelings of calm and well-being. "Miffed" didn't even get anywhere close to his current mood.

Asmodeus rubbed his talons together cheerily. That was another handy deposit in his evil futures market. A few more assaults like that and Moloch would be trembling every time Asmodeus strolled past the door to his workshop.

'There is only one answer right now,' growled Seirizzim to Moloch. 'And that is "The MAC is ready to run." Alright?'

Moloch's lip quivered as he nodded.

'Good. So let's try again, shall we?' Seirizzim grinned with an ostentatious display of fangs. 'Progress report.'

Moloch took a nervous step backwards and glanced quickly at the latest of his eponymous Analytical Crystals behind him. Not a fragment of light glinted on its monolithic surface. Just around the corner, out of sight, oddly coloured guts spilled everywhere.

Seirizzim tapped an irritable hoof. 'Well?'

Asmodeus grinned sharkishly.

A bead of apprehensive sweat struggled for release at Moloch's temple.

The gentlest of coldly imperious sighs slipped out of Seirizzim's mouth as his eyes flashed upwards for a split second. 'Progress report!' he bellowed, covering the twenty feet between them in one raptorial bound and snatching the trembling scientist by the throat.

'Ahhhh ... well ...'

'Wrong!' screamed Seirizzim, his nose a scant inch from Moloch's. 'You know the answer I want!'

Moloch struggled and answered. 'The ... the MAC is ready to run.'

'Good! Well done ...'

'O ... only I've still got to adjust the ...'

It was a tiny miracle that Moloch's eardrums didn't explode under the decibel pressure of Seirizzim's scream.

'In your humble opinion, Mr Moloch,' whispered Seirizzim coldly after a few frantic minutes spent pounding the scientist against his latest piece of work, 'when will it be ready for use on the Phlegethon Admission Site? There is absolutely no point in rebuilding the Soul Booths until the Torment Allocation System is completely ready, I want this up and running for d'Abaloh's visit. Understand?'

Moloch's eyes rolled into the top of his head and, with a sad gurgling, he collapsed.

'Damn him! You just can't get the staff these days. I only tapped him a few times. Alright, you,' he dropped Moloch and whirled on Asmodeus, 'what'll this delay cost?'

'Assuming that his memory is not affected by that unfortunate ...'

'Don't get funny!' threatened Seirizzim, looming.

'I ... I don't know how to be funny, sir,' whimpered Asmodeus, looking at the floor. 'Accountancy does not teach such skills.'

'What'll it cost?'

'For every day's extra cost for the full construction team it'll be ...' Asmodeus's talons clattered over the obsidian spheres on the abacus, moving with lightning blurs of fiscal dexterity. 'Should I include the wages paid to the soon-to-be-redundant admissions clerks on a daily or hourly basis?'

'Daily, idiot! It's a bigger number!'

'Very well, then.' There was another flurrying of talons and after a few moments Asmodeus cleared his throat. 'For every day that the latest of Moloch's Analytical Crystals is not installed and working in the Phlegethon Admissions Site, thus preventing full automation in the acceptance of new arrivals and, consequently, not freeing up labour for utilisation in the acquisition of readily available alternative fuel supplies, it will cost twenty-two thousand three hundred and five obuls.'

It was a figure that surprised even Seirizzim. 'Are you saying that every day we keep demons in Immigrations and out of my proposed lava and brimstone mines it'll cost us twenty-odd grand?'

'Spot on, sir,' grinned Asmodeus.

Seirizzim snorted angrily and kicked the groaning form of Moloch. 'Take it out of his wages!' he commanded. 'Then close Immigrations down now and get those boilpoint pen-pushing wimps over to Rubor and down the mines!'

'But, sir? The delays at the far side of the Phlegethon will be enormous ...'

'So what? The recently snuffed have got eternity to look forward to down here. A few weeks in the waiting room won't exactly do them any harm.'

'Ah, that is correct, sir ... but won't the Ferrymen

121

get a little uppity when there aren't any souls coming through?'

'Are you questioning me?' snapped Seirizzim, rounding on the banker.

'Oh, n … no, sir. Er, accountancy does not teach such things.' Under pressure, Asmodeus' needle was getting stuck.

Seirizzim's upper lip curled, trembled and then broke into a fiendish grin. 'But you're right about the Ferrymen. Oh, it will be so sad. They're still paid by the number of souls shipped, aren't they?'

Asmodeus nodded, sensing Seirizzim was onto a revelation.

'Looks like they're about to enter a particularly lean period, then.'

The sound of babbling voices rattled around the inside of the ancient abandoned ferry's disused hull as the group of Pact-men huddled in their hideout and panicked.

'What are we going to do?' barked Phaust, for what seemed like the twenty-fifth time.

'Where have they taken him?' wailed Queazx. 'They'd better not harm his fingers. Oh, if I never hear my finale again…'

'It'll be too bloody soon,' groaned Phaust.

'Don't say that! We've got to rescue him. I can't possibly endure the rest of eternity without Fithel's playing to comfort me,' spluttered Queazx desperately.

'We've been over this a hundred times. Has anybody got anything useful to suggest?' asked Bahbz.

'Er, I could draw the plans,' offered Cassoh the artist. He was ignored.

'You, Unctuous. You've been very quiet,' barked Phaust.

The Really Reverend Unctuous III shook his head and looked up through shocked eyes. 'I don't believe it,' he croaked. '"Envoy", he said. "Envoy"! Never thought I'd see another man of the cloth down here! We've got to help him. He'll be way out of his depth, horrified, lost, feeling betrayed...'

'He seemed to be managing alright to me,' muttered Phaust. 'It's Fithel I'm worried about. That other guy had them eating out of his hand with his preaching.'

'It'll be different when he realises where he is,' said Unctuous meaningfully. And he should know. He'd been through it all himself. It had only taken one unguarded moment of desperation in the Chapel of St Absent the Regularly Forgotten. That fateful day it had simply been too much for him. For the fiftieth year running, the entire congregation battering down the door in eager readiness for prayer had numbered exactly zero. And then he'd said it. He hadn't realised he'd been talking to himself, it just sort of came out. Which, after fifty years of his own company, wasn't that surprising, really.

'Oh, what I wouldn't give to do that to real people!' he had declared after several rats had turned up looking for cheese, summoned, he believed, by the power of his thoughts alone.

'What, precisely, *would* you give?' the voice had buzzed in his head.

'Oooh. Anything!' he had said without thinking.

'Anything?'

'Absolutely anything!'

'Absolutely anything at all?' parroted the buzzing voice in his mind.

'Yup! Absol...' The floor of the chapel had exploded, plumes of superheated steam had billowed out, dozens of scaly black claws had snatched at him...

Phaust's voice snapped through his reverie, tugging him back to the time at hand. 'I think he probably already knows where he is. Being dragged off kicking and screaming between two monsters like that might be a bit of a hint. Man of the cloth like that'll spot it a mile off. Just you see.'

Unctuous shuddered. 'It must be such a shock to him. He must be terrified.'

'But what about Fithel?' reminded Queazx. 'Let's not forget him.'

'I told him he should've let me help,' grumbled Bahbz irritably.

'Oh yeah, then I'd be without a model,' protested Cassoh admiring Bahbz through a rectangle of his fingers. 'You'd have been dragged off with him.'

'Dragged off where?' asked Queazx.

'Malebranche Headquarters,' groaned Unctuous. 'Probably manacled to the walls even as we speak.'

'Ooooh, I'm *so* jealous,' scowled Phaust. 'If he's been whipped I'll detest him forever! And thumbscrews ... ohh, bliss!'

Queazx's hands were in his mouth, fretting as he thought of Fithel's fingering hand ruined for eternity. 'Oh, his pitching! Nightmare! We've simply got to save him.'

Suddenly, deep inside Unctuous's brain the small section that dealt with conniving subtlety leapt into action and began flinging orders at his speech centres with wild abandon. 'Queazx is right. We cannot leave captives at the mercy of the Malebranche,' he declared, his mind firmly on Screed. 'I, for one, would never be able to live with myself!'

'D'you say "live"?' asked Bahbz pedantically.

'Oh, you know what I mean,' countered the Reverend. '"I couldn't be dead with myself" just doesn't sound the same, does it?'

'Stop arguing. We need a plan!' shouted Queazx.

'Agreed,' confirmed Unctuous with a secret smirk. It would be terribly unfortunate if that plan just happened to accidentally save a certain cassocked captive at the same time.

Cassoh grinned, smoothed out a sheet of Nognite parchment, rolled up his sleeves and licked a lump of freshly stolen charred-coal.

The underfloor heating whooshed and gurgled through the foundations of Nabob's cavern as Flagit angled a lava-lamp onto the sheaf of mysterious documents. Cold fingers of vapour licked off their surfaces and trickled down the legs of the obsidian desk.

In the far corner Flinty was gnawing contentedly at a large boulder, licking out the amethyst crystals from the middle with noisy slurps.

Flagit grunted thoughtfully and, using a pair of tongs, turned a sheet over.

'Well?' asked Nabob impatiently over his shoulder.

Flagit waggled his talon dismissively and stared harder at the complex text shimmering under cloud. Flinty crunched another chunk off the boulder, sending shivers of revulsion up Nabob's spine.

'Have you found anything useful?' he pestered.

Flagit turned and opened his mouth as if to dispense some soothing unguent of wisdom. He yawned, rubbed his chin and waggled his wide-brimmed crystal cup. Nabob snarled, took the hint and trudged over to the drinks cabinet.

'You've been poring over that for hours,' he complained as he mixed another lava martini irritably. 'Haven't you come up with anything?'

'Well,' grunted Flagit, sitting up and rubbing his eyes. 'I have got something.'

'Yes, yes, yes?' begged Nabob.

'Neckache.' He rubbed his aching cervical vertebrae.

'I knew I should have left you to suffer the full term of your community service, you ungrateful . . .'

'Hurry up with that drink. And then I'll tell you what I know,' dictated Flagit, spinning around on his swivel stool.

'So, you've been lying all the time. You do know what it is.'

Flagit snatched the boiling lava martini and tipped half of it down his throat. He rubbed his neck again, stood and walked across to the far wall in the manner beloved by Belgian detectives just about to make a dramatic revelation: chin out, hand in the small of the back, that sort of thing.

'Well, what is it?' groaned Nabob after two minutes of Flagit pacing up and down.

'Weird.'

It was all Flagit said.

Nabob slapped the crown of his forehead and sobbed. '*I* could have told *you* that!' he snapped. 'Gimme something definite. Why's it steaming like that, for instance?'

'Ah, well that's something I do know. What you've found there, regardless of the information it holds, is probably worth a fortune to the right collector.'

'What?'

'It's ancient. Way back before the invention of Nognite Parchment (scorch-free at ambient temperatures; will not wrinkle, char or calcine – honest) and boilpoint pens to write on it, they had to use that stuff.' He pointed to the documents. 'Normal flammable parchment wrapped in a dedicated refrigeration field. It's a couple of centuries old, at least.'

For the first time in a very long while Nabob was lost for words.

It didn't last.

'Marvellous,' he declared, clapping his talons after a swig of lava martini. 'Well, I'll just pop off to the right dealer and earn myself a few bob. I fancy a good haggle right now...'

Flagit's eyes widened. 'If you want to fritter that document away on the price of a few bottles then go ahead. I'll give you fifty obuls for it.'

'Fifty?' grinned Nabob, rubbing his claws. 'Well, alright then, that seems like a decent enough... Hold on. You? Give *me* money for it? What's the catch?'

Flagit swept across the room and stood disturbingly close to Nabob, his slitted pupils darting sideways in search of listening ears. 'The catch? It's probably worth *far* more than you can even guess at, in the right claws, that is.'

'Whose claws? When can we sell it to them? Show me the way and...'

Flagit wiggled his claws. 'Don't you see? This is *our* chance! We don't sell it on any account!'

'You've had too many of those,' grunted Nabob, pointing a curling talon at Flagit's empty cup. 'You're hallucinating.'

'I'm telling you, this is our chance!'

'Okay. Chance for what?'

'That's just it, don't you see? I ... I ... I haven't a clue.'

'Marvellous.'

Flagit suddenly began to get desperate. The last few hours had taken their toll. In the back of his mind Patience lay bleeding and bruised under Frustration's angry fists, the victim of seemingly wasted hours. Flagit had lost count of the number of times a million random and disconnected thoughts had whirled around inside his mind. Fragments of hints of something useful shone, then vanished. Tiny particles of clues to something bigger had welled up through the murk of misunderstanding, glinted once and sunk without trace. Helplessly his claws of comprehension had plunged into the silt of ignorance and come up filthily empty, dripping with the dredgings of despair. In short, he was scuppered.

'I've got some of it figured, but they're such fiddling little...'

'Tell me!' snarled Nabob.

Flagit glanced around furtively again. 'Nobody shoves the words, 'Utterly, Utterly Secret! Don't even think about reading this! Yes. This means you!' on something unless ... well, unless it's something secret, right?' His voice fluttered nervously.

'Give him a pat on the head,' groaned Nabob sarcastically.

127

Flagit glared. 'If you're going to be flippant...'

'Alright, alright! Do go on.'

'And nobody leaves secrets hanging about for just anyone to read, do they? They normally try to do something to stop them falling into the wrong talons and stuff, 'cause there'd be trouble if they did.'

'The point?' groaned Nabob wearily, beginning to wish he hadn't bothered getting Flagit involved. He could have been doing something really exciting now, like watching lava set.

'The point is that, according to whoever wants this kept secret, *we're* the wrong talons!'

Suddenly Nabob had a twinge of understanding.

'We've got to be,' continued Flagit, his voice slightly too high in pitch, flung there by the constriction of his excited larynx. 'I mean, it stands to reason. If we're not the right ones, which by definition we can't be since we'd understand in a jiffy exactly what that stuff's all about... then we *must* be the wrong ones!'

Nabob nodded eagerly, still clueless where all this was supposedly leading.

'And there's two things we can do with this stuff which makes it really valuable.'

'Yeah, yeah?'

'Blackmail...'

'Oooooh yes!' cried Nabob, punching the air enthusiastically. 'Of course, we just extort stacks of obuls out of the folks that don't want this secret public. And the other...?'

'Buggered if I know.'

'Oh, c'mon, don't give me that. You've been squinting at those pictures for hours. You must know something!'

'Alright, alright, but they're only guesses!' Flagit waved his claws dismissively and grabbed at the tongs. 'Look, here, er ... where is it, here. Look at that.' He pointed to a series of odd stick figures, some tall with pointy tails, hooves and horns, some smaller with beards and long cloaks and odd flat rings around their heads.

'These ones,' mused Flagit, pointing to the taller figures, 'are devils.'

'What makes you think that?' asked Nabob.

Flagit harrumphed and glared at his pointy tail, hooves and horns. 'Like I said, it's just guesswork.' He aimed his gaze towards the withering end of the spectrum.

Nabob's body did have the decency to apologise for his mouth and blush momentarily.

'These,' continued Flagit, pointing at the smaller figures with cloaks and head-rings, 'I think that they're some sort of enemy. See, here they're facing up to each other.' He pointed the tongs at the top of one sheet of parchment, then skipped over a wedge of indecipherable text and waggled the tongs above another. 'Here they're fighting...'

'Could be dancing,' offered Nabob. 'I've seen that grip used in a fair few cavern dances...'

'Shut up.' Flagit flicked over a few pages to another illustration. Here there were fewer standing figures, and the ground was littered with prone beings of both types. 'The battle continues?' he suggested.

'Or they danced till dawn and...'

'I shall ignore that with the arrogant flippancy it deserves,' grumbled Flagit, turning over a few more sheets. 'Now this is where I get a headache. So far it's all sort of made sense. It's a battle. But this is ... what d'you make of it?'

The scene showed the strange stick figures sitting cross-legged around what looked like a large campfire. They held almost headsized rings in each hand, decorated with smaller rings around the circumference. They appeared to be waving these strange rings. Alarmingly, some of the mouths had been drawn in an open position. Above them, in the sky, was written one single word.

'Any idea what that means?' asked Nabob, pointing at the word 'Kumbayah!' in the picture's sky.

'Like I said before,' grunted Flagit, rubbing his chin noisily, 'buggered if I know!'

It was a typical afternoon in the Grand Municipal Prediction Hall. The group of five ageing prophets sat around a curiously shaped marble table asking important questions in the echoing room and then hurling omenical bones to divine the answers. Things like the burning issue of when to hold the Axolotian Primary Prophets Sports Day, or whether it was more fortuitous for the forthcoming re-run of 'The Thing and I' to last two weeks or three weeks and one day. And so it would have remained, had not a pair of feet clattered frantically down the corridor, propelling a desperate man at an extremely high rate of knots. He hit the solid bamboo doors, swung around them and slid to an undignified halt against the far wall, cursing the highly polished nature of the floor.

The leader of the Grand Municipal Prophets, Captain Maehap, peered over the edge of the table and grunted, 'Do come in.'

The man scrambled to his feet, rubbing a pair of rapidly blue-ing buttocks, and looked pleadingly into Maehap's eyes. 'I need a date. A date of absolutely maximum auspiciousness. And I need it now; things to plan, you know?'

'And you are?' grumbled Maehap, not entirely certain he was overly chuffed at being disturbed by such a hasty being. Propheteering was a relaxing, stately profession. One didn't normally have to fling one's self around with such wildness. Especially if your arthritis was as bad as his was.

'Khamran M'kyntosh, producer of "Play Your Stars Right!"' announced the intruder cheerily.

'Play your what? What's that?' grumbled Maehap.

'The Astrological Games Show Where Your Future is in Your Hands, starring Tehzho Khonna. It's very popular. Oh, never mind. I expect you're busy when it's on.'

'Not one of those daytime theatre things, is it?'

'Yes ... I...'

'Gah, never watch it. I remember a time when nobody would dare to put on a theatre show until the sun was way over the back of the Temple. People have *far* too much spare time these days, don't you know?'

'Yes, I'm sure they do. But I'd really like that date now, please.'

'Ahhh yes, I remember. Now give me the details.'

'Well, I don't really know quite how he pulled it off, but Tehzho Khonna somehow managed to get the winner of "Play Your Stars Right!" to "Align Her Signs" in such a way that she asked him to marry her. No, actually he asked her because he had to ... er ...'

'So you want an early wedding for three?'

'Eh?'

'Had to marry her, you said. Get 'em hitched quick before it starts to show, is it? Gah, the morals of the young!'

'No ... well, I don't think so.' Khamran rubbed his chin thoughtfully. 'The old devil,' he mused under his breath.

'Let's see what we can do, eh?' Maehap struggled to his feet, rattled his suitably warmed omenical bones in his wrinkled fist and shuffled to the top of the table. It was about twenty feet long and, oddly, had an eighteen-inch wall at the far end. He blew on the bones in his wrinkling hands as he leant his hip against the table and, with almost none of the ceremony Khamran expected, he hurled the trio of runic cubes backhand down the length of the table. They bounced once, hit the back wall and came to rest amid an expectant silence, broken only by the incessant tooth-sucking of Captain Maehap.

He shuffled down the far end of the table and peered at the runes, sucking his teeth as he considered their significance. 'Most auspicious, you say?'

Khamran nodded.

'Hmmm ... soon as possible?'

131

'Yeah, we need to keep this an event very much in the public mind and start to sell tickets as soon as...'

'Happy outcome for the happy couple?'

'Yes, er ... I suppose so.'

Maehap sniffed, grabbed the runic cubes and shoved them in his pocket. 'Week next Tuesday,' he sniffed, and shuffled back to his chair.

'What?' squeaked Khamran. 'So soon?'

'You wanted soon. Said so yourself. Running in like that all unannounced. I remember when folks used to knock. Week next Tuesday or nothing!'

And inside Khamran's mind a whole host of problems appeared. Clothes ... presents ... guest lists ... costumes, er, clothing...

The list grew. Panic hovering imminently over his shoulder, he spun on his heels and sprinted out of the Grand Municipal Prediction Hall, skidding a full five paces before he gained traction fully.

'That's the trouble with the youth of today,' grumbled Captain Maehap, dripping melancholy. 'Hasty. Can't wait to get everything done. I remember in my day we'd take a girl out at least once or twice before all that marriage lark reared its ugly head.'

'It shouldn't be like this. He promised me a captive audience, not that I should be the captive,' complained the Reverend Vex Screed miserably to himself as he dangled from the manacles on the wall of the Malebranche Prison.

'You should've run away when you had the chance,' grunted Fithel dangling next to him. His words were half addressed to Screed and half to himself.

'Never,' declared Screed. 'I will never leave. This is my mission, my...'

'You still complainin'?' grunted Mabin, the nine-foot-six devil boredly filling in the requisite parchmentwork behind a stack of large reference manuals.

'I'm not supposed to be in here!' shouted Screed. His voice echoed coldly on the bare walls.

'Don't worry, soon as I've found the right torment, you're out.' Mabin turned his gaze back to the Torture Tables, his talon scraping down the left-hand edge of the tome while his mouth worked. 'Perversion. Prostitution. Perjury. Gah! No Preachin'. How come preachin's not in 'ere? Fat lot o' use this is. How'm I s'pposed t'work out what torture t'stick you in if preachin's not in?'

'Guess?' suggested Screed.

Fithel dangled admiringly. It was good that Screed was being awkward. It would take all the longer to sentence him and dangling on the end of a pair of manacles was probably a real holiday compared to where they'd end up.

'Oooh, no. Can't guess. More than my job's worth. No. It's got t'be a proper torture to fit the crime, see? Gah. I really hate sentencin' you bloody Pact-men, damned Illegal Immigrants!'

'What did you just call me?' squeaked Screed.

'Illegal Immigrant! Well, it's what you are, isn't it? Didn't come in the proper way, you know, feet first!'

Any queries the intellectual side of him had about the 'Pact-men' was squashed beneath the thundering roar of hope. Amazing himself, he heard his voice say, 'Well, since I'm an Illegal Immigrant why don't you just deport me?'

Fithel grinned, despite his throbbing shoulders and smarting wrists. The logic was faultless. Now if the devil was in a reasonable mood...

The roar of derisive laughter told them both instantly he wasn't.

'Nice one,' grinned Mabin horribly. 'But it doesn't help. You're here for eternity. Now then, about this sentence. Let's see, preachin'. What's like preachin'?'

'Try looking under "evangelism",' growled Screed. 'Just hurry up and get me out of here. I've got work to do!'

133

'You'll have more than enough once I've found the right torture,' chuckled Mabin, his talons scraping backwards through the Torture Tables. 'Evangelism, why didn't I think of that? G. F. E. 'Ere we are. Now then. Euthanasia. Extortion ... oooh, that's a good one. Er ... Nope, not there either.'

'Look, just let me out! I shouldn't be here!'

'Can't you think of anythin' more original? I've 'eard that one before.'

'But it's true, I tell you,' protested Screed. 'Let me out, I've got a contract.' For a sneaking moment he wished that he had thought of putting a reincarnation clause in his agreement with Sot. Right now even being reborn as a mollusc seemed far preferable to this. At least molluscs were free of manacles.

'Funny, I didn't find nothin' like a contract in my search o' your pockets.'

Fithel was baffled. He'd never been offered a contract when he'd entered his pact. Were they getting more organised these days?

'But I was promised!' pleaded Screed.

''Ow many times?' grinned Mabin. 'Three?'

'Well, as a matter of fact...'

The scaly Malebranche Officer hurled back his head and laughed raucously. 'You been 'ad, matey. Ha! Welcome to the real Underworld.'

'I tell you, I shouldn't be in here.'

'Oh, no? Jus' s'ppose you tell me where y'should be then. I could do with another laugh,' growled Mabin, twirling his boilpoint pen casually. 'It'll make this parchmentwork a bit easier.' He thumped the Torture Tables irritably.

'Well, well, I should be free to go anywhere I like. Seeking out crowds of lost souls, big crowds. It's always better when there's a decent lot of willing ears to listen to my message.' Screed's thoughts somehow drifted back to his mission. 'That's always the hard bit, I find. Making sure there's enough people ready to listen to the Good

News, finding people who need it most. That's why I'm here, see? Amazing potential down here. Everywhere I look.'

'Pull the other one,' mocked Mabin.

'No, really.' The fire of evangelism flared in Screed's mind 'Just look at you, for example, strong and yet gentle – my shoulders are healing up nicely – handsome profile.' Screed winced as he looked at the mawful of teeth. It was stretching the truth, but it was all in a good cause. 'Responsible ... but, with all that on your side, can you honestly say you are happy?'

Fithel was amazed. Did this guy never give up?

'Happiness?' mused Mabin. 'Well, I'll tell you, that's something I never really think about for long. I'm a bit busy, you know?'

'Not many really professional folks, such as yourself, do have the time. Now if you could just spare a few minutes, right now, I'd like to read you a few passages which may help you. Would you be an ange ... er, devil, and pass me that little red book from that bag over there.'

Mabin was on his hooves and half way across the cell when he realised what was going on. 'Hey, what you doin'? Stop that!'

Snarling, he snatched the sheaf of parchments and the Torture Tables off the obsidian desk and, slamming the cell door behind him, found peace and quiet outside.

'How did you do that?' asked Fithel.

'Not very well, it would seem,' tutted Screed. 'I've got to get out of here. I promised Sot I'd convert...'

'Oh, come on, you can drop that now. He's gone.'

'Drop what?'

'This Mission-from-the-gods nonsense. Who really is this Sot guy? Where's he come from?'

Screed pointed a finger towards the ceiling.

'You don't have to keep this up, you know. Just admit it, it's easier in the long run.'

'What are you talking about...'

135

'Look, we all feel guilty as hell when we first realise we've been had. Embarrassed, too, I'll bet, but at least it's better than being the likes of him. We don't get tortured so much.' Fithel pointed to the third dangling body on the wall, the unconscious one covered in scorch marks and burns. 'Okay, so we've got to carry the guilt for eternity but, hey, the sooner you admit to being a Pact-man the bett...'

'A what?'

Fithel tried to swing closer, curiosity burning. 'What you in for, eh? What's your pact? Go on, you can tell me. I certainly couldn't work it out with all that ranting about beer and knickers earlier. You were probably confused, disorientated, hell-shocked, you might say. What was it, eh? Wanted to live forever? Or be the best lover? Or...'

'No! Certainly not! And I wasn't confused. I am the Mostly Reverend Vex Screed. I'm a missionary! I'm here to spread the Good News!' There was a shrill edge of hysteria to his voice. None of this seemed to make sense to him.

'Yeah, pal, whatever you say,' said Fithel condescendingly. 'Er, just one more thing though. Got any more of that beer?'

Flagit wasn't sleeping very well.

Having spent the last few months kipping next to a certain insanitary outflow under the unblinking canopy of rock that covered the entirety of Helian*, the unaccustomed racket of Nabob's underfloor heating was keeping him in a state of thrashing restlessness.

He had hovered for hours like this, falling gradually into a shallow doze, unleashing his dreams and then being snatched back to wakefulness as a particularly noisy belch of gaseous lava spumed by underneath his ear. It was like being the REM equivalent of a flying

---

* Known affectionately, if geographically inaccurately, as the Stratasphere.

fish: one minute zipping effortlessly through the clear calm of the ocean of dreams, the next, flapping and gasping wildly in the spray-ridden surf of semi-alertness. And Flinty wasn't helping much as she snuggled affectionately next to him. Her breath stunk of pyrites and brimstone.

But as much as the physical disturbances bothered him, the mental ones were worse. Flagit could probably have been tucked up, alone, in complete silence, in the comfiest cranny in Helian, and he still would have been tossing and turning fitfully. Having wound the cognitive cogs of his mind up to full screaming activity and fuelled them with so much mental energy, trying to figure out precisely what that secret file of Nabob's hinted at, he simply couldn't get them to slow down.

Tall, horned, stick figures danced with lashing tails and wrestled with the short, bearded ones, alternately tangoing then throttling each other in lethal-looking martial arts grips. Knots of ethereal suppositions writhed and squirmed in murky pools of unfathomable obscurity. Packs of wild assumptions brayed and galloped across prairies of incomprehension, herding bare facts into rocky corners and diving in for the kill.

And across all of this mayhem strode a single figure, black cassock swirling, oblivious to the surroundings, sandals crushing the squealing bodies of writhing assumptions, red book clutched firmly in his right hand and decapitating wild suppositions in scything evangelical sweeps, advancing unstoppably, inexorably, relentlessly . . .

Flagit squealed, and his eyes flicked open, unseeing. Sweat erupted coldly across his forehead as he scuttled backwards across the floor. His horns hit the far wall before he realised it was all in his head.

He leapt to his hooves and sprang raptorially across the room, snatching Nabob awake and shaking him desperately.

'I've got it!' he shrieked. 'I've got it.'

'Don't give it to me,' gasped Nabob, jolting alert and

137

staring at Flagit's fevered brow. 'Don't breathe on me! What is it? Luciferosis? Stalagmonella? I knew "The Gamorrah's" food was dodgy!'

'Secrets!'

'No, you've got to tell me. I've got some tablets in the cabinet. Catch it quick enough and it'll be easy to cure. Whatever it is.' His hooves struggled for traction on the stone floor as he tried to back away and keep out of infection range.

'No! *Those* secrets.' Flagit swept a curling talon towards the steaming sheets of ancient parchment. 'I know what they mean now. It's obvious! Come and look.'

He dragged Nabob across the floor, flung him onto the swivel stool and pointed.

'It's just like I was saying,' Flagit brandished the tongs above the stick pictures, his eyes bulging with fizzing gallons of hyperactive adrenaline. 'This is our ticket to what we've been waiting for. This ... this holds the key! I know what these small bearded ones are. Oh, when Seirizzim finds out about this! Ha, ha!'

'What? Tell me.'

'No time. Must act now before it's too late! Flinty!' Flagit whistled around a mouthful of claws and the stalag-mite leapt awake. Eagerly she clattered to heel.

Nabob had taken enough. With one leap he bounded across the room and stood across the door, blocking Flagit's hasty exit. Above him a coloured plaque read 'Hole Sweet Hole.'

'Out of the way,' begged Flagit. 'It could already be too late.'

'For what? I'm not letting you out of here before you tell me the answer to that secret.'

'You're wasting time!'

'Tell!'

'Ahhhh,' gnashed Flagit impatiently. 'Okay, look, its complicated but...' He gathered his whirling thoughts, struggling to hold them like some amateur camper

138

wrestling with a flapping tent on a stormswept clifftop. 'Remember that feeling you had earlier when that guy in the cassock almost persuaded you to have a pair of Wonderwear...'

Nabob flushed. 'How did you know...?'

'Never mind that. Did you see the guards over the far side? They were completely gone. There was something odd in the air. Something secret!'

'You can't be serious?'

Flagit's eyes flashed with the strength of his seriousness. 'Imagine that secret something, only infinitely more powerful. And under *our* control!'

Nabob scratched his head, his slit-pupils fizzing with shock like tadpoles on a barbecue.

'Going to open the door?' asked Flagit.

A split second later he and Nabob were clattering down the street, their hooves striking sparks off the stone surface. Flinty was hot on their trail.

A small clump of six Pact-men huddled in the shadows of a tiny alley and stared worriedly at the imposing exterior of the Mortropolitan Malebranche Headquarters. Somehow the fact that few lava-lamps glowed in the arching windows made it far less inviting, despite the fact that it meant most of the Malebranche were out on duty.

'You sure this is going to work,' muttered Spruce, the starved owner of the only million-groat note in existence.

'Course it will,' chorused Unctuous and Queazx.

'What's up, babe, don't you trust me?' oozed Bahbz, adjusting her cleavage for ultimate drop-dead appeal.

Phaust clapped Spruce on the shoulder and leered unhelpfully. 'Look at it this way. If we get caught, it's eternity in irons and shackles and centuries of discipline. How delightful!'

'Pervert,' grumbled Spruce.

'Oooh, never knew you cared.'

'Shut up, you two,' snapped Queazx. 'Now you *can* keep a lookout, can't you?'

Phaust tutted and Spruce snarled.

'I'll take that as a "yes",' grunted the composer eager to get his violinist back from prison. 'Right, everybody ready? Let's go.'

The four dashed out of the alley, sprinted across the street towards the threatening mouth of the Headquarters and, at the last minute, ducked sideways and sprinted around the back, bent double to keep out of the windows' line of sight.

Four heads appeared at the corner of the stratascraper, took in the scene and ducked back out of view. They glanced at Cassoh's charred-coal sketch and mumbled approval. It was perfect in every detail, showing a guard slouching outside a small round stone structure. In front of the guard was a heap of large tomes. In fact if one was to look closely at Cassoh's illustration one would have quite clearly been able to see the words 'Torture Tables' on the spines.

There was only one aspect of Cassoh's scenario which differed from reality — a sweeping arrow arcing out of the stratasphere and ending an inch or so above the tiny stone structure. It trailed the word 'Prison'*. He had thought it might be helpful just to clarify matters.

Unctuous peered around the corner once more as a

---

* Since by the very nature of Helian's extensive torment system most of the population is either suffering eternal torture, or ensuring that those who are *meant* to be suffering eternal torture are so doing, there is very little time or inclination for what is loosely termed crime. Robbery is right out. There's nothing to nick.

Murder? Well, it's a bit too late really.

Crimes of passion are unheard of since potential perpetrators are either too knackered to do anything about it, or can't find any subjects worth getting worked up about. This is probably due to the ravaging effects which an eternity of flames and suffering can wring on sensually arousing curves.

In fact, there was really only one class of Helian's denizens who ever wound up in there.

The Pact-men.

And they only, literally, hung around until a more permanent eternity of torment could be procured.

final check, then flicked his hand impatiently. The coast was clear. Time to go, go, go.

Bahbz swallowed nervously, adjusted her cleavage once more and strolled, with forced casualness, around the corner of the Malebranche Headquarters, swinging a small handbag.

The other three reluctantly tore their eyes off her gyrating buttocks, swivelled on their heels and dashed back around the stratascraper, pausing only momentarily to pick up a vast club they had brought with them.

Mabin gasped and looked up from his parchmentwork as Bahbz giggled seductively and whispered sultrily, 'Well, hello, big boy.' She pouted the very pout that had made her the starlet she had once been.

Mabin's talons flashed to his throat and fiddled about there for a moment in the way all males do when confronted with an eyelash-fluttering blonde wearing far less than is practical and only slightly more than is rude.

'Well, 'ello.' He grinned in what he hoped was a suitably becoming manner. Simultaneously the logic centres of his brain were shouted down and gagged by the wolf-whistling lusty bits for having the audacity to ask, "Hang on. What's *she* doing there? Shouldn't she be engaged in an eternity of tortu ... urggggh?"

Bahbz fluttered her eyelashes once more for effect.

It was the last thing Mabin saw for a while. A vast club wielded by three of Bahbz's colleagues arced out of the sky and ricocheted concussively off the back of his skull.

The cluster of tiny pink dragons whirled and tweeted around his head for several hours.

Scant seconds after Mabin had tumbled heavily off his stool, scattering parchments and Torture Tables hither and yon and raising a single enormous cloud of dust as he hit the deck, Queazx, in a rare moment of practicality for one so artistic, snatched the vast bunch of keys from Mabin's belt, leapt onto Unctuous's shoulders and burst in through the prison door.

The sound of razor-jaws on manacles, and the squeals

of terror as Screed vanished kicking through a hole in the far wall, hit them first.

This was followed swiftly by a barrage of yelling from Fithel as he dangled in helpless horror, screaming, 'Don't let it get me! The claws! The teeth! Just exploded through the wall and grabbed him! Get me down!'

The Really Reverend Unctuous III stared at the rapidly vanishing backs of two gigging devils through a hole framed by stalag-mite teeth marks, his lower lip quivering.

Behind them scuttled a black-carapaced monster.

Between them dangled a black-cassocked missionary.

The Deity Vanishes

Precisely how many ells of Nayburn High Tensile Hemp were would around the Mostly Reverend Vex Screed's body, anchoring it firmly to Nabob's swivel stool, it was hard to tell. But it had taken a wildly shrieking Flagit a good ten minutes to bind him securely enough for his satisfaction. Right now, Screed looked like the sick result of a madman's idea of genetic recombination; a Reverend's head grafted to a squirming, giant rope-coloured maggot.

'I want some answers and I want them now!' snarled Flagit, slitted pupils staring into Screed's terrified eyes. 'Who sent you?'

There was no reply.

'Why are you here?'

Silence.

'We *can* make this difficult, you know?'

Still the steely silence of Screed's non-reply.

'Right! Now you've done it!' Flagit whirled on his heels, sprang across Nabob's cavern and snatched a lava-lamp off the wall. With a terrifying crash he slammed it onto the obsidian desk and angled its orange beam at Screed's eyes. Now he would start to get answers. It was common knowledge that any decent interrogation only really got going when the lamp was angled into the victim's eyes. Flagit hadn't a clue how this chunk of inquisitorial alchemy actually was supposed to work, but ... well, he'd done it now. Time for results!

'Who sent you?' he barked, his face inches from Screed's, a black silhouette crowned by a lava-lamp corona.

There was no reply.

'Why are you here?' The heat of the lamp burnt into the scales on the nape of Flagit's neck.

And from Screed? Silence.

Flagit snarled and edged closer. 'What do you want...?'

'Ahem. If I could make a suggestion,' interrupted Nabob, who was slouching on a pebble bag at the far end of his cavern.

'No!' yelled Flagit, his slitted pupils not moving from Screed's optical pools of terror.

'I think it would be helpful,' Nabob said wearily. This interrogation had been going on for hours and there had been no reply from Screed during that time. Not a peep.

'What is it, then?'

'Now, I'm really not trying to be picky, but ... well, it's the lamp.'

'What about it? It works every time. The perfect tool for every inquisition. Common knowledge!' protested Flagit, somewhat too much.

'Yes, but isn't it supposed to be shining straight into his eyes? Don't you think that perhaps your head might be getting in the way just a bit? I mean, if you really do want to interrogate the back of your skull then feel free, but...'

Flagit snarled and rubbed the hot patch on the back of his head. Angrily he wheeled on his heels, jammed his fists into the small of his back and strutted around the cavern. Nabob had the distinct impression that he could hear the enamel grinding off Flagit's molars as he stalked past him.

'Now then,' Flagit declared after a few moments' gnashing. He hurled the words across the cavern at Screed. 'We start again from the beginning. You! Who sent you?'

The beams of lumens from the lava-lamp struck Screed's terrified face, seemingly drilling their way into his skin, boiling his eyeballs, toasting his nasal hairs. Screed swallowed and...

Silence.

A tiny glint of light reflected off the scales at Flagit's temple, flashing in time with the angry pounding of an artery. A morse code pulse of severe fulmination.

'Why are you here?' he bellowed.

The sweat on Screed's forehead evaporated in sizzling wisps.

'Ahem,' interrupted Nabob.

'What is it now? Can't you see I'm busy?'

'Far be it from me to criticise,' said Nabob. 'But don't you think it's about time you removed his gag now?'

Sparks erupted from Flagit's back molars as he attempted to control his spitting fury. In one spring he was over the table and ripping the makeshift gag out of Screed's mouth, hurling the now damp pair of Nabob's underclothes across the cavern with disgust.

For Screed it was as if three weeks' worth of verbal laxative had suddenly taken devastating effect. Torrents of words flooded past his lips, garbled evangelisms spuming unchecked, consonants and vowels pounding in a white water flood of vocabulary. After three minutes without a breath he was quite exhausted.

'I'm sorry,' said Nabob. 'Didn't quite catch that. Could you run it by me again?'

Screed gurgled pathetically.

'Why are you here?' snarled Flagit once more.

'Oh, give it a break,' snapped Nabob. 'It doesn't matter why he's here or who sent him. All I want to know is what I can get from those sheets on the table there.' He stood with a rustle of pebbles and pointed a curly talon at the condensation-coated sheaf of Secret Documents.

'I was *coming* to that,' snarled Flagit, stamping a hoof pettishly. 'These things must be done in the right order. You don't just start an interrogation with the first thing

145

you want to know. You've got to work up to that over a few hours, get them into the swing of answering, confuse them with conflicting questions...'

'And take out the gag.'

'And take out the ga...' Flagit scowled and attempted to pretend he hadn't just said that. Irritably he smoothed down the scales on the front of his stomach, picked up a pair of tongs and snatched one of the sheets of ancient parchment. With a flourish he flashed it before Screed's eyes and barked, 'This. Tell me what it means!'

His talon hovered beneath the oddly lettered title.

Screed stared at the ornately calligraphed words and shook his head. This was definitely not what he was down here for. This was not spreading the Good News.

'What does it mean?' snarled Flagit intensely, waggling the parchment. The illuminated initial letters of the four words writhed before Screed's eyes, chrominent lizards and glittering serpents wrapping around each obscured and distended character.

'What's it worth?' asked Screed almost casually.

It wasn't the reply Flagit had been expecting. Pleas of desperation urging mercy, maybe, heart-rending grovelling, almost certainly ... but this? Never.

'Worth?' spluttered Flagit. 'Well, I ... what d'you *think* it's worth?'

'Freedom,' smiled Screed and wriggled in his bonds for effect. 'I tell you everything you want to know about that lot and you let me get on with my mission.'

At the back of the cavern, perched on his pebble bag, Nabob was hooting with derisive laughter. 'You serious? You want to strike a bargain with us?' he crowed. 'You do realise that we are in fact devils and that you are the one currently in *our* grip. You're in no position to bargain!'

'Oh, but I am,' grinned Screed with practised calm. Inside, his stomach was seething with sheer fifteen-denier terror. It was only years of experience in similar situations which enabled him to appear calm. It was a constant source of amazement to Screed how the reaction of primitive tribes to missionaries always seemed to revolve around placing them in large pots of vegetables over a roaring fire. The number of times he had talked his way out of said pots was almost into three figures. Right now he was trying desperately to convince himself that these ropes were just a subtle variation on the cooking pot theme. 'If you don't want to bargain then I might not tell you what that collection of Secret Documents actually says.'

'How d'you know it's secret?' snarled Nabob, suddenly scared.

'It says so, clear as anything,' smiled the Reverend. 'Of course my understanding of Ancient Tallian is a little rusty, but...'

'You can read it?'

'Of course. Language training is rather important if you're going to try spreading Good News to as many diverse tribes as possible. Now, about that bargain?'

Nabob's face creased grotesquely into a sneer of scorn. 'You must be joking...'

'...if you think we won't agree,' interjected Flagit abruptly.

Nabob stared at him with unblinking alarm. Flagit winked knowingly back as if to say 'Sit back and watch an expert in action!' He strolled across to Screed. 'As bargains go that is most reasonable,' he lied. 'We both stand to gain exactly what we desire. Perfect.'

Flagit smiled. Inside he beamed with the intensity of a million lava-lamps. Why not tell him he could go free at the end of it all? Keep the sucker sweet until the documents were translated. After that it wouldn't matter to anyone if the dear Reverend wound up smouldering for eternity in a handy brimstone pit.

'So come on, what's it mean?' growled Flagit, waggling a sheet of parchment emblazoned with the words:

Ye Feleftele Ouyrrlode Finnaryo

147

And again it was total nonsense to Screed.

'It's total nonsense to me,' he said. Okay, so he hadn't exactly lied about being able to translate Ancient Tallian, but he hadn't exactly told the truth either. Word for word his translation was perfect but his interpretation left a lot to be desired. From what he'd seen of the document up until now it was way beyond his comprehension, littered with oddly technical references to objects and stratagems he had never heard of.

'Nonsense?' shrieked Flagit. 'Don't toy with me!' He screamed as he swung an arcing slap at Screed's face. The Reverend screwed up his cheeks, pushing his eyes shut, and braced for the collision. Flagit's claws whistled through the air, plunging down, down ... and stopped. A slim inch from his cheek Flagit's claw trembled and withdrew.

A flash of confusion crossed the devil's face as he trembled with indecision. 'Now ... er, that was a warning, see? N ... next time you'll really get it and then you'll be sorry.' He waggled an unconvincing talon as if trying to re-establish his authority.

He felt as if something in the back of his mind had reached out and stopped him delivering the blow. Something unnervingly familiar.

Nabob raised a questioning eyebrow, harrumphed and began to wonder once again about Flagit's mental marbles.

Growling, Flagit waggled one of the stick pictures in front of the Reverend's face. 'This! Explain this!' he barked. Nabob stalked around behind the Reverend and stared at the illustration.

Screed writhed uncomfortably, blinked and stared, his hands turning red with the tension of the burning ropes. He shifted nervously. Explanation! He gritted his teeth and started to bluff. 'Er, well it looks to me like a bunch of devils, er ... dancing with...'

'They're not dancing!' snapped Flagit. 'They're fighting. Look closely. They're holding tridents. See, they're tridents.'

148

Nabob leant closer to Screed's shoulder and squinted at the picture.

'Sure they're not pitchforks?' asked Screed. 'It could be a barn dance, you know. I've seen that hold used a few times. Strip-the-Willow, I think it is. Could be wrong though...'

'See?' grumbled Nabob over Screed's shoulder. 'Told you, didn't I? Cavern dance.'

Suddenly the pain of the ropes clawing at Screed's wrists was too much. Agony swept the recollection of a double Ancient Tallian class aside, hurling it into obscurity. He grunted and shuffled uncomfortably in his cocoon of constricting hemp.

'Those ropes hurting?' asked Nabob and Flagit simultaneously with a shocking degree of genuine concern.

The next second they were at the opposite end of the cavern trembling with fear. The sheet of parchment floated in see-saws to the floor. Nabob was biting his tongue trying to stifle the urge to offer some words of comfort to Screed. He wrestled with himself, fighting back the almost overwhelming desire to spring across the cavern, cut Screed free and offer him a double vintage brimstone liqueur.

'W ... what's happening?' he spluttered as he clawed at his pebble bag.

Seeing the terror and alarm that inhabited Nabob's features, Flagit's face became a study of hysterical relief. 'There. You felt it, didn't you?' he whispered intensely, clutching at Nabob's shoulders. 'Don't deny it. You can't deny it. You wanted to help him, didn't you? Wanted to pull the ropes off, shower him with as many creature comforts as you could lay your talons on, marinade him in complete snugness...'

'It was disgusting,' confessed Nabob, shaking his head in shame.

'Face it. You wanted to be good!' accused Flagit. 'And you felt happy because of it. You could have skipped across the room singing. You wanted to be frivolous!'

'Ssssh. Quiet. My reputation! I ... I don't know what came over me!'

'You lost control again. Just like in the street when he was preaching, remember?' jabbered Flagit with an odd note of victorious terror in his voice. It was the type of quivering note with which a six year-old-boy would yell, 'Got it, Daddy! See?' as he flashed past their picnic clutching a roaring tiger by the tail.

'How could I forget?' Nabob turned pale grey with the memory of the urge to convert to using Wonderwear. 'But what does it mean?'

'Haven't you figured it out yet?' spluttered Flagit trembling like someone ready to explode with excitement.

Nabob, reluctantly, shook his head. He really was beginning to hate it when Flagit knew things he didn't. It was so degrading.

'It's ... it's a secret weapon!'

Nabob erupted with relieved laughter. Flagit had done it now, he'd flipped this time. No doubt.

'What are you laughing at? Stop it!' snarled Flagit petulantly.

'Oh, that's funny. Oooh, my ribs. A secret weapon?' shrieked Nabob in a state of hysterical derision. 'What? Like, "Stand and Deliver. Hand over your money or I make you want to offer me tea and biscuits"? or ... no, I know. Yeah, you could grab Seirizzim round the neck, hold the Reverend to his head threateningly and yell, "Make me Undertaker-in-Chief or I make you want to devote the rest of eternity to helping the homeless in Downtown Tumor"? You tellin' me it's that sort of secret weapon?'

'Yes,' said Flagit flatly, 'I would have thought *that* much would have been obvious, even to you!' And with that he scurried across to the table again, keeping as much distance as possible between him and the Reverend, and began riffling through the stack of parchments. With cold satisfaction he snatched a single sheet firmly with the tongs.

150

'Look at the picture!' he declared, waggling it furiously at Nabob. The devil peered at a series of oddly instructional scenes.

'Feel familiar?' crowed Flagit.

'Wha ... what d'you mean?' hedged Nabob, fishing warily.

'The expression on that demon looks not too dissimilar to the one you were wearing a few minutes ago. *Don't* deny it! And see anything else? Any similarities between him and that?' He pointed to Screed and then one of the stick figures in the first two frames. 'He could've been the model!'

'There is a passing resemblance...'

Screed's ears were burning with a heady, toxic cocktail of curiosity and alarm. What were they shouting about?

'It's a perfect match!' shrieked Flagit. 'Bald head, beard, cassock!'

'But what about that funny thing in the picture above his head?'

'Screw your eyes up and tell me it isn't there,' snarled Flagit, trembling on the brink of discovery.

Nabob screwed his eyes up and suddenly it appeared. It was very faint but undeniably there. A pale translucent ring of purple light. Just like in the parchment.

'Alright, alright. So what are you trying to say? What's the point?'

Flagit vibrated with tense excitement. He waggled the sheet of parchment triumphantly under Screed's nose at a careful arm's length. 'What's this word?' he snapped and pointed a quivering talon.

'Er ... against,' muttered Screed, then. 'No, it's "Anti".'

A flash of over-excited triumph raced across Flagit's face. 'And this?' Another word.

'Personnel,' answered Screed uncomprehendingly.

'This?'

'Er ... oh, that's easy, "Shrine".'

Flagit almost cartwheeled across the cavern with

shrieking excitement. 'I knew it! I know what this means,' he whispered intensely. 'I suspected it before from what little Tallian I've figured out, but dismissed it. I was wrong. Now I understand. Now I *know*! Now I see it for what it is!'

'Well, are you going to let me in on it? Or do I have to guess?'

'You've got no sense of occasion, have you?' grumbled Flagit, shaking his head. Here I am about to tell you *the* single most useful bit of info...'

'Get on with it!'

Flagit shrugged. 'Alright, alright, have it your way. Now listen carefully. These six pictures show the correct deployment techniques and field strategy for the use of an Anti-Personnel Shrine.'

Nabob, despite himself, made a strange, shocked, gurgling sound.

'One false hoof-fall,' ranted Flagit unstoppably, 'the device is triggered and "Wha-Booooom!" – any unbeliever in the blast area gets *the* biggest dose of shrine waves ever, falls to his knees, starts yodelling in plainchant and gets urges to run around in cloisters and cassocks.'

Nabob stared at the translucent sheet of parchment through new eyes. Could this be as valuable as Flagit said? Was he right? 'B ... but this doesn't make sense,' he whimpered. 'What's this doing down here?'

'I don't know. Filing error? That's not importan...'

'What is it?' Nabob's slitted pupils were wide with nervous alarm.

'Secret,' insisted Flagit cursing the thickness of Nabob's skull. 'Look, I don't know what it is, exactly. Could be a kind of scenario, you know, Just to make sure folks are ready for an invasion. Or something.'

'What! From...?' Nabob pointed an index finger vertically upwards.

'We don't exactly see eye to eye, us and Heobhan, now do we?'

Nabob's face flashed complete alarm. 'You mean they're coming to get us? Invading?'

'Relax,' dismissed Flagit with a wave of a talon. 'This parchment's centuries old. We're not in any danger. I think this is only hypothetical. War-games. The devils who wrote this have probably forgotten all about it. And *that* is our advantage!' His face writhed into a scheming sneer.

'Advantage? What are you on about?'

'Just look at what one of those Anti-Personnel Shrines can do! Other sheets show there's lots of them. Enough to take out a whole army!'

'So,' asked Nabob after a few moments under the intense stare of Flagit.

'Aaagh!' he squealed in frustration. 'So, *we* find them and we start to get our just desserts! We call the shots!' Flagit's dictatorial grin flashed back onto his face again.

'Now,' he continued in a strangely macho tone of voice, 'Need more info. Going in again. Need you to keep watch. Any signs I'm startin' to get too nice, you get the hell in there and pull me out. Okay?'

Nabob nodded his head, still full of confusion.

Flagit punched a clenched claw into his open palm, shrugged his shoulders and stomped off across the cavern. 'Alright, Screed. What's the word "Kumbayah" mean to you? He a spy, huh? That where the Anti-Personnel Shrines are stored?'

The journey across the Phlegethon in a belching ferry had done little to raise the cheers of Seirizzim. Especially since the captain had been one Naglfar, the foul pipe-smoking representative of the Underworld Ferrymen's Coalition of Arguing, Shouting and Generally Being Narked. Of course, he had smelt scandal a mile off and wouldn't desist hectoring Seirizzim with a barrage of questions.

153

'So, nice day for a trip 'cross the river. Goin' anywhere nice?'

'Gahenna wharf.'

'I see. That's not *too* far from the Admissions shed, is it?'

'How d'you know?'

'I *should* know. I ply this route every day. What you goin' to the Admissions shed for anyhow? Business or pleasure?'

'I didn't say I was going to the Admissions shed, did I? Stop blowing smoke in my face.'

'All them Malebranche goin' too, are they? All twelve o' them?'

'They are accompanying me.'

'Must be important. I mean, you don't normally just pop across the Phlegethon wi' twelve strappin' Malebranche in tow for a laugh now, do you?'

'How I amuse myself is my concern.'

'What's it to be then, fishin' for pookas off Gahenna wharf or somethin' a little more sensitive?'

'Won't this crate go any faster?'

'It might if I knew what the rush was. Want to borrow some fishin' tackle?'

Captain Naglfar had spent the rest of the journey under the watchful gaze and heavy breath of three of the larger Malebranche. His collar and the back of his neck were soaked with condensation by the time they docked at Gahenna wharf. And just as he had suspected, they had left his entire stock of fishing rods untouched on deck.

The first that any of the demons in Admissions knew about their imminent change of career was when a size thirteen hoof burst through the door and carried a vast Malebranche officer in with it.

'Shut up. Don't move!' he bellowed, as the rest of his highly paid team escorted Seirizzim into the shed.

Some of the demons weren't sure if they should bow,

154

or something. A surprise visit from the Undertaker-in-Chief should surely be marked by some gesture. In a few moments that gesture would almost certainly be two talons.

'Does the phrase "corporate downsizing" mean anything to you pathetic creatures?' asked Seirizzim imperiously. There was silence in the shed. Outside, of course, there was the usual sobbing and wailing of confusion as the soon-to-be eternally tormented souls realised precisely where they were and noticed the distinct scarcity of exit signs.

'How about the words "efficiency"? "Automation"?' The silence continued. Seirizzim tutted noisily. ' "Sack"?'

A hand shot up. Seirizzim sniggered. He had intended this to be entirely rhetorical. Hence the Malebranche.

The demon with the erect hand looked too pleased with himself for Seirizzim to ignore. After all, he was about to have a very bad day.

'Yes?'

'Sack, sir. I know what that is, sir.'

'Well, aren't you the bright one?' smarmed Seirizzim, dripping derision. It went right over the demon's eager head.

'Sir, it's what you let cats out of,' blurted the demon.

'Wrong,' sang Seirizzim with a dismissive gesture. 'The sack is what *you* are about to get...'

'Presents!' squeaked the demon, missing the point completely.

'...or more precisely, since I am who I am, you're all totally redundant as from this moment on. You are not needed here any longer. I have machines! Get out!'

'Thank you,' shouted the demon clapping his hands. 'I really needed a holiday! Oooh, presents and a holiday!' He looked around, baffled at everyone else's odd lack of enthusiasm and realised that maybe it wasn't such good news.

'Well, go on then, get out! Go and do something else!'

shouted Seirizzim with a cackle of delight. The Male-branche took a menacing hoofstep forward.

'Oh! I forgot,' grinned Seirizzim, devilishly. 'You haven't got anything else to do, silly me! Tell you what, I know of a perfect place where all your idle talons can be put to perfect use. Follow me. It doesn't pay half as much, of course, but, well, you have very little choice.'

His voice hardened into the dread tones of command as he led the way towards the long abandoned Lava and Brimstone Mines of Rubor, his ears deliberately deaf to the grumblings of dissent.

Nabob was shaken rudely awake by a cascade of banging and crashing and slipped off his pebble bag.

Backlit in a corona of orange lava-lamplight, Flagit's scaly fist pounded a large hammer against a sheet of thin metal, shaping it, warping it into profound useability. All around him odd structures were scattered, some assembled, some the twisted, mangled wreck of rejects.

Nabob watched in raised-eyebrow bafflement as Flagit pounded feverishly at the metal fragment, turning it carefully on the makeshift anvil of the arm of Nabob's favourite armchair. Then Flagit stood, angled the item carefully over a sheet of parchment and grunted approval as he compared it with the ancient blueprint.

'What in Helian are you up to now?' asked Nabob, staring at the wreckage of metal.

'Ahh, so you've finally come to help?' snapped Flagit barely glancing up from the steaming parchment.

'Help? Do what?'

'This! The key to our successful future!' Flagit waved an enthusiastic talon across the wasteland of what looked like badly misshapen shoe-horns.

'Not another one,' grumbled Nabob under his breath. 'Dare I ask. What is it?'

'Isn't it obvious?' snarled Flagit. 'We want Anti-Personnel Shrines, yeah?'

Nabob nodded in as noncommittal manner as possible. He knew Flagit when he was in this pioneering sort of mood – one false nod and he'd find himself roped into yet another wildly incomprehensible scheme.

'So, how d'you find a secret stash of Anti-Personnel Shrines, hmmm?' asked Flagit gleefully. 'Simple! A shrine detector!'

Nabob had to admit that the argument did have a certain logic to it. It was completely unbelievable, though. He made a mental note to make sure that Flagit went to see someone who knew about things beginning with 'psycho-'.

'There's only one problem,' piped up the Reverend Screed from the far end of the table.

'Shut up,' snarled Flagit. 'I've told you!'

'There's no such thing as Anti-Personnel Shrines...'

'Shut up.'

'...so there's no point making a shrine detector, is there?' finished Screed.

'You would say that! You're just trying to keep them secret. That just proves how useful they are. A vital weapon!' ranted Flagit with a wild glint in his eye.

'Hold on, hold on,' begged Nabob. 'You're serious? Shrine detectors? Where d'you get such a ridiculous idea...?'

The sheet of freezing parchment was thrust in front of his nose. It was covered in complex diagrams illustrating precise dimensions, principles of operation, user instructions.

'It's all there,' announced Flagit. 'Detailed manufacturing instructions to build your own detector as translated by our very own captive Reverend ... What's this say?'

Screed shrugged resignedly. The sooner he finished this translation the sooner he could get back to his mission. It wouldn't be his fault if they were on a wild chase for fictitious Anti-Personnel Shrines.

'"Mount the gimballed shrine wave indicators (g)

on the pivots (h), add the theophobic agent (j), – not supplied – and with only the minimum of fuss your shrine detector will be ready for field trial." But I really wouldn't bother, it'll be a complete waste of...'

Flagit towered above Screed and growled. 'What's "theophobic"?' he demanded.

'Just like you!' snapped Screed defiantly. 'Totally scared of religion.'

'Thought so,' grunted Flagit and whirled around the cavern, snatching various bits of crudely shaped metal. In seconds he was holding up the remains of what had once been Nabob's lava-lamp holder. He had jammed two nine-inch nails vertically up through the base. Carefully he placed a pair of what had until recently been dessert spoons on the two almost friction-less points of the nails. The spoons spun freely, shimmering as they wobbled like compass points in a magnetic storm.

'And now for the finishing touch,' grinned Flagit under the withering gaze of both Screed and Nabob. 'The theophobic agent.'

'It'll never work,' insisted Screed. 'There's nothing to detect.'

Flagit rolled his tongue around the inside of his toothy mouth, sniffed noisily and grinned with ominous confidence. With a sickening choking sound he ejected two globs of spit into the spoons and stood well back.

'Was that really absolutely necessary?' asked Nabob, his mouth wrinkling in disgust.

'Oh yes,' answered Flagit cheerily as the spoons quivered, and eventually settled down to point in a steady direction. 'Ha! It works! I knew it! Such detailed instructions had to be right. Here it is, a shrine detector! My darling theophobic spit is trying to stay as far away as possible from anything inherently holy, like Anti-Personnel Shrines! Couldn't be simpler!'

Screed stared in stunned surprise as the handles of the spoons pointed directly at him, the quivering globs of Flagit's spit straining to get as far away from him as possible. The two metallic indicators held their accusatory position. And slowly the significance of it dawned on Screed.

'Now wait, hold on a minute. If you think that shows I've got an Anti-Personnel Shrine in my pocket you are totally wrong. I tell you, they don't exist. There's no such thing. Never has been!'

Nabob stared helplessly from the bound Reverend to the devil with the wild grin and his brain failed to understand any of it. Then his eyes drifted back to the cobbled-together shrine detector. He was staring at a device that was clearly detecting, here in his cavern, the presence of an item, or items, which, according to all logic and common sense didn't exist. The need for a stiff lava martini loomed large.

'I knew it!' shrieked Flagit, his brain galloping freely off on the back of a dozen wild conspiracy theories. 'I've done it! This is showing traces of contamination on him. He's been handling Anti-Personnel Shrines, I tell you! C'mon, it's time for action.'

'Wait a minute...' pleaded Nabob.

'No time to lose. If he's been handling them that means they could be moving them. If we don't act now we could lose them. Forever.'

Flagit raced towards a distant cupboard and started hurling its contents across the cavern. 'Where are they? Where are they?' He slammed the door and whirlwinded towards another.

'What do you want? Stop!'

More of Nabob's belongings arced off stone shelves and crashed to the floor, victims of Flagit's mad search.

'Hey, that's my favourite toaster!'

'You can have a new one! Have three! Twelve! You can have all the toasters you'll ever need. Just tell me where they are!'

159

Nabob grabbed Flagit by the shoulders and pulled him away from the cupboard. 'What are you looking for now? Haven't you destroyed enough of my stuff?'

'I need blankets,' cried Flagit wildly, ignoring Nabob's accusation. 'Where are your blankets?'

'Third shelf down on the lef...'

'Got them! Oh yes! C'mon, c'mon!' Flagit snatched his detector, flew out of the door and clattered off along the street, whistling Flinty to heel.

Nabob stopped for a moment, stared at the still thoroughly bound Reverend, shrugged in sheer twenty-denier confusion and sprinted off after Flagit.

Somehow Flagit seemed to know what he was on about and there was, after all, only one way to find out what was on his mind.

'Oi! Come back. Wait for me!'

High in the Mountain City of Axolotl, the single black finger of the Hyh'd Park sundial swept to ten arc-degrees past dawn and carried on beyond, silently. To the north, pale reflections of silver wriggled on the slowly oscillating surface of the nearby Lake Averjinn. The miserable cry of a bucket crane resonated off the distant scree slopes as it arced in on lazy wings and settled on one leg in the shallows. It deliberately ignored the gathered crowd of Axolotians huddling at the southern end of the lake and searched the freezing waters with its capacious beak, dredging for a breakfast of eis skates.

Suddenly, as the sundial hit fourteen arc-degrees past dawn a strange rattling sound shattered the silence of the morning mists. To the gathered crowd it sounded remarkably like the noise of dried lentils clattering inside a hollowed tortoise-shell on a stick. It was.

A forlorn mantra floated into earshot above the rattling lentils, emanating from the crouching figure on the pebble-strewn shoreline as he hopped and gyrated around the wooden structure of the launching ramp.

160

It was the appointed time*, the time for invocations to be scattered towards the heavens, each begging and grovelling for a safe and successful completion to a lifetime's work.

Suon Hunntah almost wept with brimming pride as he stared at the sweeping lines of the ship's hull. It rested atop the launching ramp, chocked and ready, sizzling with majestic grace and elegant poise. Any Axolotian with an eye for anything even remotely marine would recognise this as something special. From the jauntily protruding bowsprit, past the flightily arcing outriggers, to the noble tilt of the rudder, this was a vessel built for speed. At full sail, so Hunntah hoped, the *Jocular Whelk* would skip across the wave tops, outstripping the wispy white horses which normally galloped there. Or, as it was put more colourfully locally, 'It'd go like poo off a stick.'

A crowd had gathered eagerly to witness its launch and Hunntah had waited months for the most auspicious of times for his water-borne baby to take its first dip. He had consulted a myriad local seers, pestered a dozen or so prophets and squeezed vital drips of information out of the lips of those-in-the-know, and they had all agreed that three weeks on Thursday was the best time to launch. Possibly.

But he had decided to take matters into his own hands and be the first to offer his public congratulation to Tehzho Khonna and his beautifully luscious bride-to-be Miss Khrystal Gehyz. It was a tradition, albeit an

* Actually it wasn't. The lentil rattling and atonal moaning should have started a good ten minutes ago if all the guff in 'Omen Corner' was to be believed. But unfortunately, Kwedgley, the shore-strutting warbler, didn't own a portable sundial and had lost count of time on the hike from Axolotl. But, since no one else had been keeping count and since he fluffed his feathers and rattled his tortoise with such strength of devotion, nobody actually noticed.

It was a good job for him, too. If anyone *had* noticed then he would have been blamed for the coming disaster and ritually decapitated. Properly.

incredibly ancient and almost totally forgotten one, that a blessing in the form of a water-going vessel be made in order to carry the couple's good fortune and continued happiness symbolically across the uncharted waters of trouble which undoubtedly lay ahead. It was a noble gesture, appreciated by all of Axolotl, that Suon had chosen to resurrect this tradition. Personally he was just in it for the chance of some free publicity for his ailing shipyard, but that was beside the point.

Kwedgley, the befeathered Invocator-in-Charge of Transport and Goods Handling, whirled dervish-like and made odd warbling noises with the palm of his hand on his mouth. This was his first really big public job and he was going to make the most of it.

If the truth was to be told, it was the first public job he'd had that had concerned the transport side of his employ at all. Normally he simply had to indulge in a bit of powder scattering or unguent splashing to ensure, say, a valuable crystal vase was dragged through the postal system without being mashed beyond recognition as it was shoved unceremoniously through the recipient's letter box.

So far, (Touch wood and spin round three times if it isn't true), he hadn't had any disasters. This state of affairs probably owed a significant amount to the fact that recipients of expensive vases would have known about their delivery in advance (via the *Scryin' Out* Postal Prediction Page) and left the door open. Although many Axolotians suspected this, so far none had plucked up the courage to send anything of even minor value through the post unblessed with Kwedgley's stamp of faith. It probably also helped that he worked down the post office.

But right now, he was having the morning off and was thoroughly enjoying dancing wildly about in front of a cheerfully appreciative audience, shaking his tortoise and sprinkling perfumed oils over the rocks and any of the audience that happened to get in the way.

162

Right on cue (eighteen past dawn), a gentle southerly breeze shook itself awake, yawned and went to work. Fingers pointed and awestruck gasps of approval flitted around the crowd as the sails of the *Jocular Whelk* twitched and slowly filled.

Encouraged, and not a little surprised, Kwedgley spun a double salko, threw in a spontaneous backflip for fun and redoubled his effort. A steady current of invocative grovelling spun and whooshed upwards unseen along the strands of atmospheric ether, homing in on a specific deity.

There was a grunting of irritation in the Kingdom of Heobhan as an electric shaft of entreaty whistled through a window and slammed itself unceremoniously up the nose of Khlyde, the Over-Deity for Ships and Stuff. He coughed, thrashed dozily at his tickling nose and rolled unathletically from his king-sized cloud with matching duvet and pillow set. The floor hit him solidly in the face.

A dozen creeds of tortoise-shell supplications whistled up his left nostril. It twitched, tingled as if a couple of hundred ants had suddenly decided to have formic acid battles in there and, inevitably, he sneezed. Wiping his nose grumpily on the back of his pumpkin pyjamas, he grunted and tried to avoid a swarm of solicitations.

'Alright, already. I know when I'm wanted. Give a god a bit of peace, why don't you?' he grumbled and stood stiffly. A triplet of forlorn entreaties hovered by the windowsill wondering if it was a good idea to act right now. Unanimously they decided to see how it all went.

Khlyde, it had to be said, hated early morning visitations. Especially after a hard night at Manna Ambrosia's toasting the latest recipients of a spot at the Top Table. Rubbing his chin, he tried to think back to how many bottles of Lush's finest he had put away. He remembered twelve. It was a bit of a blur after that.

163

The entreaties decided to do their stuff and dive-bombed his nostrils by way of a reminder.

'Gah! No peace, no peace,' he grumbled. He reached for his peaked cap and stepped out of the front door, vanishing in a tinselly flash of gaudy extravagance which made his unholilly tender head hurt.

Down on the shores of Lake Averjinn the crowd's excitement was growing. The southerly breeze had picked up to a steady twelve knots and the *Jocular Whelk* was straining at the tightly secured launching gear. Ropes creaked, tension mounted and Kwedgley rapidly headed towards a total blur of living colour.

Suon Hunntah's face was a study of proud father-dom mixed with extreme first-night nerves. All the signs, omens and augurs looked remarkably promising. Good wind, good crowd, great boat. And soon the hour would be upon them when finally, after months of waiting and years of painstaking construction, the good ship *Jocular Whelk* would take to the open water.

Suddenly there was a tinselly flash and a slightly larger than average-sized man appeared sporting a peaked cap and a white, close-cropped beard trimmed to the style beloved by ships' captains and other seafaring folk throughout the known world. Oddly, and much to the bemused surprise of the launch crowd, he also wore a pair of pumpkin pyjamas.

'Ho there. Shiver me timbers and all that guff.' he declared around an expansive yawn. He looked around disappointedly for the youngsters with the ear-piercing whistles who, for some reason known only to those involved in the great briny expanses, always appeared and stopped any conversation dead in its tracks by a quick barrage of a deadly three notes. He tutted under his breath as no aural assault appeared.

'No sense of etiquette,' he thought miserably, before being washed in a sudden and remarkably soothing wave of relief. After all that wine last night, he wasn't entirely sure how his throbbing head would have taken such abrupt sonic treatment.

On witnessing Khlyde's supernatural appearance Suon Hunntah had assumed the required position necessary for a successful blessing. He was flat on the pebbly beach wailing supplications and pleas, hands clamped firmly over his ears in the traditional Axolotian manner.

Centuries of empirical reasoning had gone into the adoption of this position. Hurling oneself to the ground showed the summoned deity just how seriously one was taking all this – a successful outcome was more important than a clean toga. The slamming of hands over one's ears was self-defence. Nobody wanted to hear a member of the celestial tribes of deities laughing at one's urgent request.

And so, nose to the round stones, ears shut, Suon Hunntah rattled off a cannon of eager pleas.

'...bless, if you really don't mind, this my humble vessel and all who have the modest fortune to sail her, and especially the symbolic happiness of Tehzho...'

Unexpectedly a disturbing scratching and clawing sounded from below the heather on the shore. A twitch of alarm rippled through the crowd. 'Omen Corner' had mentioned nothing about this.

Unsurprisingly, given his current demeanour, Suon hadn't noticed. '...and make my meek vessel skip lightly over the wave tops in an unostentatiously brilliant and unpretentiously head-turning fashion, now and forever...'

Kwedgley whirled to a premature halt and staggered in dizzy surprise as he too noticed what sounded like the scratching of a large creature's claws on the very rock upon which they were standing.

'...the tacking be as slick as a greased eel, the jib never droop and the bilges run with only the cleanest of fluids...'

As one the crowd screamed.

Ten feet behind the yawning figure of Khlyde the

165

ground exploded in a scattering of rubble and a jungle of thrashing claws erupted into view. A black-carapaced creature hopped nimbly sideways, landed in the heather with a clatter of exoskeleton and glared at the crowd through a host of compound eyes.

A second later two figures appeared in a cloud of stinking smoke. They stood almost ten feet high. Arms, heads, legs and tails were thick and rounded and seemingly without joints. One of them was staring intently at the strange metallic device in his claw. Two spoon-like pointers swivelled erratically around and homed in accusingly on the pumpkin pyjama'd deity.

'That's him! He's got Anti-Personnel Shrines in all his pockets!' declared Flagit. He leapt forward, snatched Khlyde in a full nelson and dragged him kicking down the belching opening. With military precision the black-carapaced creature hopped back down the hole squirting high-tensile webbing out of a dozen asbestos spinnets. In a second the belching smoke had cleared.

There was no sign of the Over-Deity in Charge of Ships and Stuff.

The silent blanket of shock descended completely over the shores of Lake Averjinn.

Well, almost completely. Suon Hunntah hauled himself to his feet and walked over to the launching ramp, eyes down in respect. Sincerely he tugged on a lever and released the launching gear.

With a rumble, and a total lack of enthusiasm from any of the crowd who were, to a one, staring slack-jawed at the gently smouldering patch of heather, the good ship *Jocular Whelk* slid forward. Sails billowed in the steady breeze, the jib stared proudly at the vast expanse of the lake and gradually it accelerated down the launch ramp, wooden wheels screeching from the gear. Plumes of dust blasted skywards as ropes snagged on piles of chains, dragging them towards the water, slowing the vessel as calculated. Suon was leaping up and down, cheering and waving a pair of little flags he had

166

brought along specially, working himself into a frenzy of delight.

Almost casually the *Whelk*'s bow broke its first wave, trundled off the end of the launch ramp and, with a terminal splash, the six-inch model boat disappeared below the surface as the chains suddenly discovered that they didn't float.

A thousand feet below, at the bottom of a freshly dug stalag-mite tunnel, a pair of devils hastily stripped themselves of a cupboardful of blankets. As they dragged a bewildered figure in a peaked cap and pumpkin pyjamas off around a corner to empty his pockets of Anti-Personnel Shrines, followed by the clattering black-carapaced stalag-mite, they were blissfully unaware of just how much luck they'd had to pull that off.

A couple of dozen centuries ago they wouldn't have stood a chance of even getting their talons on a deity, let alone dragging him into the depths of Helian in a full nelson. No chance. He'd have been wearing his Counter Iniquity Suit.

Despite being incredibly bulky, unfeasibly heavy and requiring two assisting angels to slip in and out of them, Counter Iniquity Suits had been an essential part of any deity's touring wardrobe back then. Well, even gods couldn't be too careful in those days, under the paranoid atmosphere of the Infernal Invasion. Everybody knew that the threat of the demons rising at any time to come swarming unstoppably through the gates of Heobhan was real. They were just waiting for the right time, that was all, waiting and dreaming up attack scenarios. For centuries most of the deities wouldn't even dare venture out of Heobhan to scatter blessings on their devoted followers. Until the invention of the Counter Iniquity Suit.

Encased inside its three-inch thick sacrament-strengthened padded armour the wearer was completely safe from any evil attacker who chose to try his talon. The

Suit's surface was coated in tiny strands of pure faith, each capable of delivering high current charismatic charges to any assailant. They were a huge success, for a while.

Gradually, though, when it was realised that the Infernal Invasion didn't look like it was actually going to materialise and folks were getting really cheesed off with trudging about, sweating inside bulky Counter Iniquity Suits, they fell out of fashion. Now not even the most paranoid of deities wore them. Well, except occasionally in private with consenting partners, but then, that was their business.

Meanwhile, on the banks of Lake Averjinn jaws were still hanging loose in shock.

'Well, s'pose that's that then,' said Kwedgley, shrugging his shoulders with a rattling of lentilled tortoise.

The crowd turned and glared at him menacingly.

'Now, wait ... oh no. That wasn't anything to do with me! Look, I can explain ... I ...'

It was at that very instant that Kwedgley, the Invocator-in-Charge of Transport and Goods Handling, discovered just how fast he could run.

And as the morning calm settled back across the shores of Lake Averjinn, like some vast broody specimen of poultry-kind, a single, solitary figure stared forlornly at a string of bubbles rising from the dark depths.

Baffled voices echoed inside the deserted hull of the Pact-men's hideout on the banks of the Phlegethon.

'But are you absolutely sure that's what happened?' Queazx asked with not a little concern in his voice. He stared at Fithel's hands, examining them surreptitiously for any recently received damage which would impair his fingering in any way.

'I've told you a dozen times already,' groaned the violinist. 'If something hadn't stopped him that guard devil would've handed Screed's book over to him and...' He stopped.

'And what?' pressed Queazx the composer.

'Don't know, I didn't get a chance to find out,' muttered Fithel thoughtfully. 'But it would've been good.'

'How d'you know?'

'Oh, c'mon! He wouldn't have been that disappointed otherwise, would he?'

'How disappointed?' interrupted the Really Reverend Unctuous III. 'As bad as you if you lost your violin?'

'I suppose so,' shrugged Fithel.

'That's it,' declared Unctuous dramatically and slammed his fist into his open palm. The last few hours listening to Fithel and attempting to figure what Screed was here for had finally borne fruit.

'What's it?' chorused Queazx and Fithel.

'That's why he's here. His pact! He's here to save . . .'

'No, no.' interrupted Fithel, shaking his head. 'That's what's weird about him. I tried asking him what his pact was and he kept going on about a contract.'

Unctuous's face was a study in surprised revelation. 'Contract?' he spluttered. And in the recesses of his cloistered mind a complex tapestry of understanding started to weave itself into cognition. Tableaus of the sermon on the hut flashed into view, the effect Screed had had on the mob of tortured souls as he had spoken of Sot, the captivated and cheerily swigging devils . . . a contract?

And then, in a sudden flare of comprehension Unctuous understood. But it seemed too unbelievable, too wild. Even though he had witnessed it. He shook his head. He'd heard of the Haranguist Mission, of course; their motto, 'Any time, Any Place, Any Word' was infamous amongst the more preaching oriented classes. He had even been tempted to go and join them at one point forty years into his tenure as priest for the non-existent congregation of St Absent the Regularly Forgotten, but . . . well, it hadn't seemed fair to abandon the chapel completely. And besides, he was well out

169

of preaching practice. But the money as a mercionary *was* tempting.

Tempting enough to sign up to spread the Good Word here?

Unctuous quivered as he saw the almost perverse logic to it all. He couldn't deny that there was a fair bit of potential down here. In fact, for anyone with a silvery enough tongue it could be a real soul mine. Saving the damned. Succouring them into a life after the afterlife.

And then a fizzing logic contact was made in his mind. If Screed really was here to save souls then this could be his chance. A way out.

Unctuous trembled as he thought it through. He was right. He had to be. And in that instant his mind took a vote, neurones waggled in favour and the motion was passed. He simply had to find Screed and be saved!

There were only two snags (albeit vast ones) blotting the otherwise pristine horizon.

Where was Screed right now? And why had two worryingly familiar devils kidnapped him from the Mortropolitan Malebranche Prison?

Somehow, this latter snag caused Unctuous the most distress.

If the evil, conniving monster that had conned him into a pact had been one of the pair sprinting away from the prison with Screed then nothing good would come of it.

What could a devil possibly want with a contract missionary in Helian?

It didn't bode at all well.

In the privacy of Nabob's cavern in downtown Tumor, Flagit's voice echoed off the walls. 'What d'you mean, you've never heard of Anti-Personnel Shrines?' he snarled at the pumpkin pyjama'd deity in the chair. He sneered meaningfully as he angled the lava-lamp into

Khlyde's eyes. He was two minutes into the interrogation and already over-impatient.

'No point wasting time denying it. They're no secret, we know all about them,' Flagit bluffed. 'It's no use keeping it to yourself, you'll only make it worse!'

'I tell you,' insisted the peaked-capped deity. 'I know nothing about these Anti-Personn...'

'Liar!' snapped Flagit, slamming his talons onto the obsidian table. 'The evidence is all over you. Look!' He held his DIY shrine detector up in Khlyde's face. The two spoon handles pointed in unwavering accusation. 'You've been handling them, haven't you? Where are you moving them to?'

'I don't know what you're...'

'Fine! Deny it if you will. But you'll regret it once I find that stash. I tell you, you'll be sorry!'

Flagit whirlwinded out of the door, dragging Nabob behind him with a terse, 'C'mon! They can't be that far away from there. We'll find them! Without his help!'

Screed, still bound to the stool, attempted to shrug pathetically. He failed.

As the shadow of the Axolotian sundial in Hyh'd Park crawled slowly around to thirty-one arc-degrees after dawn, the door to a tiny hut on the outskirts of the city was tugged open. A man appeared rubbing his eyes and yawning expansively. The sun, totally underwhelmed by this sight, continued trundling across the trackless blue yonder of the cloudless sky. As usual.

The man in the hut stretched himself with a series of osseous clicks, trudged down the three steps of his verandah and stared out over the hillside expanse of golden barley. Swirls and vortices of wind rippled across the sea of deaf ears, rustling in a susurrus of satisfaction. It was just like any other morning really. Hovix would always stretch, yawn and come trudging around the top of his field looking for the tell-tale signs that his barley was ready to harvest. But today he was more hopeful.

The signs were good. Well, at least according to *Scryin' Out* they were.

However, as good as the seers who worked for *Scryin' Out* were, years of on-the-job experience had taught Hovix that there were signs and there were signs. It was all well and good for townie prophets to stare into crystals or shake tea leaves in the comfort of their own temple, extracting vital omenical clues for the more agriculturally inclined of Axolotians, but Hovix knew there were other, more ancient divinatory procedures.

His back complained as he bent over and plucked a handful of cornstalks from the edge of the field. He shook them five times, blew across them and, with an emphysemic gurgle, spat a glob of phlegm onto the ground and tossed the cornstalks onto the early morning southerly. The fawn foliage writhed in airborne frenzy as the stalks tumbled over each other, drifting parallel to the field of corn. Then silently they hit the ground as a group, settling to rest in a complex pattern of glyphs, spelling out an undeniable message to all who knew the subtle skills of interpretation. Hovix stared at the three clumps of straw which showed the Murrhovian character for sickle, the swirling Ammorettan symbol for 'Party, party, party!' and the harshly angular lettering of the ancient Khambodian symbol which represented the phrase 'This field of barley is absolutely ready for harvesting, today. Any delay at all will undoubtedly result in a net shortfall of gross product and a consequent compromise of your profit margin. Break out the sickles and get chopping!'

Hovix's eyes drank in the shapes of these patterns, the analytical sliver of his mind clicked into action and in seconds he had scratched his head in confusion and walked irritably away. Murrhovian, Ammorettan and Khambodian were all languages he had never heard of.

Shrugging his shoulders, Hovix trudged on further, his eyes scouring the swaying surface of the field of corn.

And suddenly his jaw dropped as he saw it. Halfway down the hill there was a patch of flattened stems. It was as if an infinitely controllable whirlwind had been used by some celestial vandal to scrawl across the malleable surface of the field. There were circles, triangles, odd geometrical constructions and even, surprisingly, a picture of a hedgehog.

Hovix screamed, leapt for joy and sprinted off back to his hut. This was it, the sign! A complex one, admittedly, but it was the sign. Every Axolotian farmer knew that only when the crop circles appeared was the barley ready.

Now it was almost time for the harvest.

The only thing standing between him and the first swing of his sickle was the essential deitical blessing for a good harvest, but this time it wouldn't be coming from the normal deity of harvests. Oh no. This barley wouldn't be heading for the normal grinding wheels and other agricultural processes. Nope, this barley had been earmarked as soon as he had heard of the impending hitching of Tehzho Khonna and Khrystal Gehyz. This was the barley that would make the special unfermented beer that would be turned into the shampoo for the combined use of the bride and groom on their special day. This would be one of the very, very rare barley fields that would be blessed by the minor goddess Dahls'soon, the Shoulders and Head Deity Over Coiffurie.

Hovix rubbed his hands. Once blessed he could charge about ten times the normal market price for it. This was the chance he had been waiting for. It was ever so good of Tehzho to propose like that.

In a flurry of excitement Hovix screeched around the back of his hut, ripped the cloth off the top of a tiny wooden structure and lit all the candles, aromatic sticks and odd narcotics burners. In seconds plumes of aromatic smoke were rising into the morning sky and invading his nostrils.

Swaying slightly and blinking with the heady effects

173

of fifteen types of narcotic herbs on an empty stomach, Hovix knelt before his converted rabbit hutch and began uttering the correct intonations and entreaties in the general direction of where he assumed Heobhan lurked.

Stifling a yawn, a figure in a hairnet plucked a wedge of heavily seeded bread off a roaring fire, tossed it onto a plate and sneezed as a host of grovelling requests soared in through the window and blasted up her left nostril. Dahls'soon tried her best to ignore the sternutative scratching at her nasal passages and reached for the marmalade.

After a bout of fifteen acute sneezes and half a dozen hacking coughs she realised that perhaps her breakfast would be more enjoyable if she just popped down, hurled a bit of a blessing about and kept those irritating mortals happy. Then she could get back to creating *the* ultimate pigeon-loft hairstyle – a style that would knock the outmoded beehive into the proverbial cocked hat of hair-creativity.

Licking her fingers to remove all traces of thick-cut orange, she closed her eyes, held her breath and vanished in a blinding flash which would have made any budding pyromaniac green with envy.

Hovix squeaked in alarm as the column of animated mercurial droplets shook themselves into reality behind him, coalesced and turned into a silk pyjama'd being sporting a hairnet and rag curlers.

'Alright, so whose hair needs the works? C'mon, my breakfast's getting cold,' she grumbled. Idly she peered at the balding pate of Hovix, darkened by years in an open field. 'Well, it's not you, is it, dear? That's way beyond *my* help. Where am I required?'

Hovix pointed to the swaying ranks of his barley field and grinned.

'Ahem,' Dahls'soon cleared her throat delicately and peered at the golden ears. 'Is this some sort of strange parlour game, my dear? For, unless I have been doing things dreadfully wrong the past few centuries, that looks like a field of barley to me. Now I know that a great deal of styling potential *does* exist in strands of ripened barley, the traditional woven animals for instance, but I really do fail to see what it is I am doing here.'

'B ... beer and shampoo,' spluttered Hovix, spellbound. He'd never seen a goddess in curlers before.

'Dreadful combination, give you the most appalling heartburn, believe me, and the bubbles are a real...'

Hovix never did find out what the bubbles were. Before he had a chance to ask, the ground behind Dahls'soon erupted in a scrabbling shower of wild claws and a scream of 'That's her. Get her!' shattered the morning calm. In a flash of stripey blue and pink the deity was snatched by a pair of blanket-bound monsters and bundled down a belching hole, complaining about her lack of breakfast.

Hovix stared at the rapidly sealed hole and scratched his head. Was it something he had said? The wrong invocation?

His train of thought didn't succeed in developing much further, for at that very instant a screaming mob of Axolotians breasted the horizon and swept towards his field from the direction of Lake Averjinn. Hovix recognised Kwedgley in all his feathered glory and for a few moments wondered precisely why it was he was being hunted down by a wild mob, especially at this time of morning. He pondered this for just the length of time it took for Kwedgley to lead the screaming mob unstoppably into the outskirts of his barley field.

Dashing madly and dodging a variety of outflanking manoeuvres, Kwedgley led the mob on a hundred different paths of barley destruction while Hovix clutched his cheeks and watched in horror.

Precisely whose sandal heel it was that caught the two pieces of flint, ground them together and launched the disastrous spark, nobody would ever be sure, but strike it they did. Hungrily the flames dived into the tinder-dry crop, slavering tongues of yellow and crimson licking at the ripened ears.

The firework popping of magazines of kernels woke the rest of Axolotl in minutes.

A thousand feet below two devils frog-marched a silk pyjama'd deity away into the depths of downtown Tumor, cackling evilly.

The dozen Malebranche snarled angrily and cracked whips at the slower moving of the now thoroughly redundant admissions clerks as they herded them forcibly towards their new employment. Seirizzim strode imperiously at the head of the column, his heels striking occasional sparks off the rocky ground, his ears thoroughly sealed against any complaints or requests for a transfer.

He had made up his mind. The Lava and Brimstone Mines of Rubor simply had to be opened up again. It would be one in the eye for Sheytahn, if nothing else.

'A stroke of genius this, sir,' fawned Asmodeus as he trotted cheerily within the penumbric evil of Seirizzim's aura of command. 'Challenging Sheytahn's monopoly on fuel supplies with no loss of torment efficiency. Sheer genius!'

'Of course,' sneered Seirizzim, striding out arrogantly.

'It will certainly show him who is in charge.' Asmodeus attempted to sneer in the manner just demonstrated by Seirizzim. He ended up looking as if he was trying to shift something that was caught between his teeth.

'And speaking of charging, he won't be able to wriggle out of his contracted torture needs. I have him!' grinned Seirizzim. 'He should never have attempted to extort fuel payments from me! What a fool!'

'Certainly, sir,' oozed Asmodeus.

'Ha! In fact, there are two fools in this thoroughly advantageous scenario,' mused Seirizzim, scratching the back of his ear with a talon as he strode out.

'Two, sir?'

'Of course. What of the idiot who closed the mines in the first place. What buffoon ordered that?' He raised an eyebrow of curiosity, halted in mid-stride and whirled on Asmodeus. 'Now then, you've seen all the documentation from way back, which moron was it, hmmm?'

Asmodeus flushed. 'I don't think you should use words like that about . . .'

Seirizzim's eyebrows arched villainously. 'About whom?' he growled, snatching Asmodeus firmly around the neck. 'Who declared the mines economically unsound, hmmm?'

Behind him, the entire massed ranks of the admissions clerks swallowed nervously. They had never, up until a few hours ago, witnessed Seirizzim's managerial command techniques in action, in the flesh as it were. They shuffled nervously in the black dust and rubbed apprehensively at their necks as Asmodeus's hooves lifted off the ground. If he treated close colleagues like this then what would he do to them if he ever got miffed?

Asmodeus gurgled as he dangled from Seirizzim's talons.

'Who ordered the closure of the mines? Tell!'

The banker desperately whispered a name and was dropped as Seirizzim hurled back his head and laughed wildly. 'You serious?' he bellowed.

Asmodeus, on his knees, nodded.

'I *can* check,' Seirizzim threatened.

The banker shook his head wildly and almost lost his pince-nez.

Seirizzim guffawed again. 'Well, well. Foul Lord d'Abaloh closed these mines?' he crowed. 'How grossly short-sighted!'

His mind whirred excitedly as he strode suddenly on. If he could see beyond decisions made by the Foul Lord himself then why shouldn't he be promoted to that position? The whole of Helian would benefit. Oh yes, there was scope for him beyond mere Undertaker-in-Chief of Mortropolis. Too right. If he planned things

177

carefully then the stratasphere was the limit. Make Mortropolis self-sufficient and he could start making inroads into d'Abaloh's territory.

In that instant Seirizzim's stride suddenly developed a definite swagger as he saw himself inhabiting a newly built Grand Palace, not that dreadful pink thing on the banks of the Styx. Leave that to d'Abaloh.

But now, there were more mundane things to do closer to home.

He led the mob of terrified admissions clerks up and over a small rise.

"Things like that!" he thought as he stared suddenly at the long abandoned mine entrance.

'Welcome to your new job!' he declared expansively and swept the ground in a long bow of mockery.

To a demon, the clerks stared in horror at the belching mine entrance and the tiny parallel tracks vanishing down its inchoate throat. The corroding shells of ancient-looking carts lay scattered all around, bent and twisted grotesquely. Wisps of sulphurous air curled out of the hole in choking blankets of lung-rotting toxicity. Dribbles of crimson lava pulsed sickeningly from faults in rock like the weeping wounds of a battle-scarred war rhino.

With a flash of insight, the clerks knew that this was going to be a little more demanding than, say, boilpoint pen-pushing.

Seirizzim laughed.

It was, according to the Hyh'd Park sundial, sixty-three arc-degrees past dawn and, as would be expected at that time, the Grand Municipal Prophets were settling into their seats for another day's work. Grunting and creaking in various states of decrepitude, the five ancient ones assembled around the vast, ornately carved marble table and began warming up their own personal omenical bones. Some simply shook the strangely runed cubes of llama thigh, others cupped them in arthritic hands and blew across them, and one Captain Maehap lifted his

178

toga and shoved the three cubes firmly between his buttocks.

It was his belief that if you couldn't give the future a taste of what it was about to hurl your way then life was simply too unfair. It had to be said that Captain Maehap, despite, or indeed because of having spent almost ninety years as head of the Grand Municipal Prophets and seen every kind of prediction under the sun, was now something of a pessimist. Rumour had it that the day Captain Maehap made a cheery prediction then disaster would strike Axolotl. How true this rumour was nobody had a clue. Maehap had never supplied anything even remotely cheery enough to get worried about. Factual was the best it got.

'Alright, Pothet, get on with it,' croaked Captain Maehap irritably and continued sucking his teeth. 'Time to find out what the fates have in store for our dear city.'

The relatively sprightly Pothet creaked to his sixty-year-old feet, shuffled towards the top of the long thin marble table and flung his trio of omenical bones.

Then, mumbling under his breath, he shuffled down to the far end of the table and squinted at the runes, wiping his nose as he pondered their auguric significance.

'Well?' croaked Maehap after ten minutes of embarrassed silence. 'Having trouble?'

Shoulders drooping, Pothet looked up. His liver-spotted face attempted to hide a blush of professional shame. 'I ... I don't know what it means,' he confessed, barely audibly.

'What?' snapped Maehap, cupping a hand around his ear. 'What d'you say? What d'he say?'

The other three prophets at the table stared nervously around themselves, not daring to believe what they had heard. A prophet with an uninterpretable sign ... it didn't bear thinking about. It went against everything that underpinned Axolotian society. Without a glimpse of the future they were rendered totally blind. Everything

179

they held true would surely crumble before their very rheumy eyes.

Had that crack in the ceiling been there before?

'What d'he say?' croaked Maehap.

Pothet's knuckles clenched white around the edge of the table as his stare moved from the accusing trio of unfathomable runes to the irritable frown on Maehap's face.

'It's meaningless...' choked Pothet. 'Totally unfathomable. I haven't a clue!'

'Can't be!' snapped the Captain. 'Figure it out! And fast. It'll be time for morning muffins soon.'

'I can't.' Pothet trembled, sensing that perhaps he would face the end of a long and comfortable career before the muffins arrived.

'Bah! Want a job doing, pah...' snarled Captain Maehap, shoving back his bamboo chair and shuffling towards the end of the table. Each step was marked by a sucking of teeth and a wheezing breath. The other prophets watched in amazement. These were unprecedented events, no doubt.

'Call yourself a prophet,' grumbled Maehap as he hauled himself around the end of the table and coughed. Pothet hung his head and looked forlornly at his slippers.

The Captain squinted through his cataracts and forced the runes into shaky focus. The air in the hall seemed to turn to expectant syrup as his fading cognitive processes tugged at the import of the symbols, wrangling meaning from the geometric arrangements, curves and positioning. It was a hard one, to be sure, but he wouldn't ever admit that. Pulling on all his near ninety years' experience, he screwed up his already wrinkled face and wrestled with portents like some sentient prune. Gradually, the light of understanding prised its way shyly under the flysheet of ignorance and whispered in his ear.

The last thing the quartet of Grand Municipal Prophets expected to hear issue from the lips of Captain Maehap was a stifled splutter. All eyes turned to him in amazement as he wheezed, gulped a lungful of air and cackled wickedly, his hands clutching at his chest. In seconds he was on the floor laughing hysterically.

The remaining prophets stared at each other in shock, utterly unsure what to do as croaks of mirth rattled around the hall, echoing off the pillars.

'Er ... would you be so kind as to er ... enlighten us?' begged Pothet, feeling even worse now that he had failed to see something in his runes which had such an effect.

Captain Maehap rolled around on the floor clutching his ribs helplessly. 'Roll some more like that, will you,' he hooted. 'That's made my day!'

'What is it?' pleaded Pothet, squinting at the runes. 'I don't understand.'

Maehap writhed and sat up. 'Good news!' he declared. 'We shan't be pestered for predictions by that irritating idiot shipbuilder, Suon Hunntah, for a long, long time.'

The other four prophets stared in blank incomprehension.

'Seems it's going to take him at least four years to build the *Jocular Whelk II*,' hooted Maehap. 'And then another year and a half to brew up enough courage to launch the damned thing! Ha, ha, best news I've had in years.'

And then it hit them. Just as they realised that the giggling heap of ageing pessimistic prophet had issued a 'good news prophecy', their ears became horribly aware of the distant clattering of a herd of furious sandals and their nostrils picked up the unmistakable smell of inflamed barley fields.

This was it, the rumours were true. Maehap had dished out 'good news' and already there were riots in the corridors and the fields were burning. They didn't expect it to have happened that quickly, though.

The thunder of clattering sandals rumbled in mounting

181

intensity, approaching all too swiftly down the marble corridor.

Pothet panicked. They were coming. The mob. And in this room there was only one door, one way out. His heart surged a step nearer to cardiac arrest as terror mounted. It wasn't fair that he should be mashed to bits by a wild mob, not fair at all. He had always given good predictions, guiding the fortunes of Axolotl accurately and ... In that second he realised it was all wrong. Flight instincts fought with fight urges and lost in seconds. There was no way out. There was only one thing to do at times like this. Scream and ... two things. Scream and panic and ... three things.

Screaming and panicking as his heart raced, he fell to the floor in a flurry of flapping toga and went for option three in a big way. He hit the marble spouting torrents of desperate invocations and fear-ridden treaties, beseeching those on high to intercede somehow and save their proverbial bacon from the frantically sprinting mob. In a flash and a trio of dull thuds he was joined by the other three prophets. Swathes of supplication screamed Heobhan-ward from the ageing mouths of the Axolotian Grand Municipal Prophets.

Fifty yards away, beyond the solid bamboo doors of the Municipal Prediction Hall, a sweating and terrified feather-encrusted man skittered around a corner and pounded his way down the corridor in a flurry of technicolour. Five and a half seconds later the entire crowd that had so recently been standing on the shore of Lake Averjinn followed in frantic pursuit.

Desperately, Kwedgley, the Invocator-in-Charge of Transport and Goods Handling, hurtled down the corridor towards the vast arching expanse of the bamboo door, one word screaming from his panting lungs. 'Sanctuary!'

The rumbling thunder of pursuit rattled ominously in his ears.

Ten feet from the Municipal Prediction Hall he began

a screeching slide and powered into the door, bouncing off it flat onto his back. As if he was attached to the handle by some invisible elastic band he was on his feet in a blink, his fists pounding desperately on the corrugated surface, squinting over his shoulder at the seemingly unstoppable mob.

Perspiring anger plastering their faces, his pursuers thundered on, ready and desperate to show the gods just what they thought of him.

Way too late, it came to them that shiny marble floor tiles severely decrease braking efficiency.

Still back-pedalling furiously, the mob hit the bamboo doors with a vast excess of momentum. Hinges, panels and several dozen startled spiders exploded into the interior of the Municipal Prediction Hall on the bow-wave of riotous runaway Axolotians.

And at the very same instant the four prophets' invocative prayers were answered. Four columns of blinding aerosol mercury coalesced into a quartet of yawning and marginally hungover deities. Terrified silence gripped the Axolotians in a strait-jacket of stunned surprise as they stared at the celestial visitors.

'Well, what d'you want, eh?' grunted a bare-chested deity, clenched fists circling inches from his nose, which by its appearance had been reset on numerous occasions. All eyes swept from the knee-length lace-up boots up to the heavy brows of Pugil, the Celestial Being-in-Charge of Fisticuffs and Scrapping. A hundred jaws dropped. Pothet grinned. His prayers had been answered. Now let those ungrateful Axolotians try to lay a finger on him.

To all the uninvited guests it was quite obvious what had been in Pothet's mind when the panicked invocations had been sent.

The other prophets had been somewhat less pragmatically confident in their choices.

The mob looked up from the floor at Fleeh, the Over-Deity of Sprinting and Running Away Rapidly; Dehtol,

183

Mentor-in-Charge of First Aid and Bruises; and the ever popular Bauhels, Celestial Lieutenant with Particular Attention to the Non-Soiling of Undies.

Judging by a trembling prophet's expression of embarrassed discomfort, Bauhels was a tad too late.

'Well? What d'you want, eh?' growled Pugil, skipping and jabbing incessantly.

None of the Axolotians had the chance to answer.

With a cry of, 'In here. Get them!' two blanket-wrapped devils dropped a vast net from a skylight in the ceiling, tugged on draw-string ropes and snatched the quartet of deities off the floor in a writhing bundle. With a grunt of effort they set their catch swinging, smashing the netted gods through a large window, then with a remarkable feat of exquisite judgement sent them arcing neatly down a conveniently waiting belching hole.

The stalag-mite rattled and cavorted enthusiastically and readied its asbestos spinners.

The two blanket-clad ones swung through the skylight on the end of ropes and zipped almost casually through the shattered window and down the hole. They were followed by a black-carapaced creature with more claws and legs than was healthy for it.

It was only as the hole was sealed up, and the belching sulphurous smoke was stopped, that screaming hysteria broke out in the Municipal Prediction Hall.

A flash of crimson lightning arced down from the stony gloom of the stratasphere and fizzed into the oozing hydrocarbons of the Phlegethon. Unnoticed by the entirety of Helian, something bulbous and gelid struggled in the zipping discharge and died. This was a real shame. Given the right translator, it could have been very helpful as a material witness.

Not three minutes ago it had waggled a casual optical tentacle towards the shoreline of downtown Tumor in what passed as acute cephalopod interest.

Unexpectedly a devil had peered out of a gloomy side alley, scoured the vicinity for observers, satisfied itself that the coast was indeed clear and vanished into the shadows.

Moments later it had reappeared with a black scaly colleague and had proceeded to tug a writhing net out of the gloom and towards a locked trapdoor in the street. The net appeared to be stuffed with the struggling bodies of four pale and extremely miffed-looking bearded men.

In seconds the first devil had tugged the back-entrance hatch of his cavern open and the net was kicked unceremoniously down the flight of steps. One last glance over their shoulders and the scaly ones, accompanied by a large scuttling thing with legs, had followed, tugging the trapdoor shut behind them with a secure click. Unnoticed by all, a curious purple aura lingered piously around the trapdoor, squatting thickly like an overweight midnight smog.

The whole operation had taken mere moments. Any longer and they would undoubtedly have been seen by more than just the toasted creature in the Phlegethon. If not by Filch, shady denizen of downtown Tumor's less savoury back alleys, then at least by his latest victim.

Filch had been trailing the irritatingly wealthy-looking devil for the last few minutes as he had strolled further and further away from his more normal surroundings. It was blindingly obvious to even the most ineffectual of pickpockets that here was a prime target. He was lost for certain – nobody in their right mind strolls in downtown Tumor. You run, or you sneak, or you hide. *Never* do you pace measured strides down the centre of the alley with the tip of your cane counterpointing every other hoof-fall. Well, not unless you actually have an overwhelming desire to find yourself on the receiving end of a swift and merciless mugging.

It was also obvious to Filch that he was in fact carrying

185

between six thousand three hundred and ten and six hundred three hundred and fifteen obuls in a small pouch in his lower left-hand suit pocket. He could tell. Years of strenuous and devoted training had honed his aural reckoning to perfection. He could hear an obul drop at five hundred yards. During push hour. In a flame-storm.

Filch also suspected that the very same pocket contained a small clawkerchief and a Nognite parchment card offering directions to the party in Upper Mortropolis where this mug should now be enjoying free jugs of lava martinis.

Loping down the alley in covert pursuit, all he had to do was wait for the perfect opportunity to strike. Sure, he could have hit and run at any time but, well, it wasn't the same somehow, just screaming out from behind, smashing the victim across the back of the head with a handy blunt implement and the rifling through the prone victim's pockets. No, any idiot could do that. Filch preferred a more subtle approach.

And with this devil in a blue dress suit it was almost certainly going to be the classic. He'd stop and look around, baffled, stare bewildered at the card, and then hail the nearest stranger to ask for directions. Any minute now. Filch could feel it.

That oh-so-helpful stranger would be Filch and as soon as he responded the trap would be sprung. The suited one would have placed himself in Filch's debt and wouldn't ever get away with his pockets as full as they had been seconds previously. Worked every time.

And if Filch was any judge of character the moment was almost upon him. He nonchalantly hurled a large rock into the alley behind him as noisily and threateningly as possible. The devil in the blue dress suit started, looked around warily and came to a halt on a well-concealed trapdoor in the street.

An elegant claw scratched between his horns, reached into his pocket and tugged out the party invitation.

186

Filch's eyes bulged as his slitted pupils watched a stroke of unbelievable luck. The small pouch of obuls fell out of the suit pocket and landed on the trapdoor with a dull thud.

'Six thousand three hundred and thirteen obuls exactly!' confirmed Filch's ears, despite the fact that the pouch had landed in a puddle. And he knew the time was right.

Striking up a jaunty whistling, he leapt into the middle of the alley and strolled towards the dislocated stranger.

'Ahh, excuse me, my dear devil,' began the blue suited one, 'but I wonder if you could see fit to direct me towards...'

'Certainly,' oozed Filch expertly and swept close to his victim. Without glancing down he placed a hoof over the sack and bit back a grin. This was too easy. 'Where you 'eading?' A lick of the oddly purple haze caressed his hoof in a strangely pious way.

'The Stahlinn Stratascraper, Upper Mortropolis. I am to attend a function.'

'I'm sure you are,' grunted Filch and suddenly felt very peculiar inside. His hoof twitched uncomfortably on the sack of cash. 'Stahlinn Stratascraper, er, yeah. You, er ... you need to head straight obul there ... er, over there...' A bead of sweat sprang to his forehead as the purple patch of piety nuzzled its way up his leg. 'Avoid that sack alley, ahem ... back alley and keep the change ... No, keep straight on until the third on the left...'

Filch's head reeled in confusion as he spouted the directions. He had never felt like this before. Dirty inside, shaky ... dishonest.

The sack of obuls made the sole of his hoof itch and he had to fight himself not to say anything.

The devil looked quizzically at Filch and asked, 'Are you feeling right with yourself? I have a small snifter of lava martini in a small flask if you would care to...'

'No, no ... I'm fine. Feeling justice ... just as happy as I can. Just a bit tired at prison, ahem ... present.'

The obuls burnt dishonestly into his hoof as the purpleness tickled his abdomen.

'Well, in that case I shall be away. Thank you once more for the directions. I'm certain I shall be able to find my way.' The devil in the blue dress suit strode off.

And Filch nearly screamed. He was certain his hoof was smouldering. He sniffed carefully and shrugged. Then bent down, snatched the tiny sack and inhaled a vast lungful of piety. Before he had realised it he was consumed by a tidal wave of disgustingly honourable benevolence. His fingers trembled with tremors of truth, his heart pounded beneath a terrifying mass of morality, his head spun with screaming sonnets of scary scruples. The long atrophied organ of his conscience leapt into action, snatched his will and ran with it.

In seconds he was sprinting uncontrollably after the suited one, laughing, waving the sack of obuls frivolously and shouting, 'Er, excuse me, but you seem to have dropped this! Would you like it back?'

The Dominum Effect

Harsh syllables of irritation echoed around the inner walls of Nabob's cavern as Flagit barked at the row of seven figures bound securely to swivel stools.

'For the fifty-seventh time,' he squealed, 'where are you hiding the Anti-Personnel Shrines? C'mon. Speak. Answer me!'

Baffled shrugs of confusion rippled up and down the septet of prisoners.

'Answer me!' he bellowed, thumping a clenched claw onto the obsidian table in frustration. The lava-lamp pointing at them wobbled dangerously. 'You've got nothing to benefit from keeping quiet. I'll find out eventually. Ha! You're not going anywhere. Your lives in Axolotl are over. D'you understand? I'm in charge now! Where are the Anti-Personnel...'

'Excuse me,' interrupted a fidgeting figure on the end of the row, a red cross glinting at a position precisely where his lapel would have been if togas had them. 'Would you mind awfully if you could loosen these ropes a little? They are restricting the flow of blood to my wrists and I fear that permanent damage may...'

'Shut up!' snapped Flagit at Dehtol, the Mentor-in-Charge of First Aid and Bruises. 'I will not loosen anything. And I don't know what you're worrying about blood for. You don't need it down here. You're dead!'

Dehtol's eyebrows arched in confusion. 'I certainly don't feel particularly dead. I can ascertain a definite pulsing at the wrists. Yes, definitely.'

'Shut up, you're in a state of shock!' snarled Flagit.

'Oooh, no. I think you are mistaken. Shock is more sort of, well, shocking really and...'

'Shut up!' yelled Flagit.

'Messy,' finished Bauhels miserably.

And then Dehtol shook his head. What was he thinking? He was a Deity, he couldn't be dead. That was one of the perks of deitydom... Immortality.

'Where are the Anti-Personnel Shrines?' snarled Flagit again. He was getting desperate. He had never expected this to be so hard. Almost perversely it was the determination of his prisoners to keep quiet which was driving him on. If they had to keep the Shrines this secret then they must be *really* effective.

All he needed was about a dozen of the things and he and Nabob could take control of the whole of Mortropolis. Two devils against the system ... ooooh, such power! He knew exactly where to place them for maximum disruption, the secret documents had told him that. There were, he admitted with a gloat of satisfaction, some very helpful maps in that little pouch.

'Tell me where they are being stockpiled!' he ordered, angrily scowling at Dahls'soon. 'Tell me now or it's no more mister nice devil!' Unnoticed by him, a strange purple tongue of haziness licked out from the faintly visible crown above Dahls'soon's curlered head and stroked his forehead.

'Oh please, don't stare so,' muttered Dahls'soon. 'I'm embarrassed enough as it is. Just *look* at the state of my hair. And this dry heat, well, it's sure to ruin it. Split ends and frizz in minutes, just you watch. The amount of conditioning balm I'll need to apply when I've finished my breakfast ... Oh, breakfast. Oh, darling, would you mind awfully fetching a little snack, there's a dear, only I'm so frightfully peckish. Missed breakfast, you see?'

Without thinking, Flagit wheeled around and clicked his talons at Nabob, boredly snoozing on his pebble bag. 'Fetch her a rock cake!' he snapped. Flinty's antennae flicked to sudden attention and she began to dribble.

'Could I have one, too?' asked Dehtol.

'Ooooh yes, and me,' piped up another.

'And me!'

'Bring seven,' growled Flagit to Nabob, gnashing his fangs. This wasn't going as effectively as he had hoped. But they'd pay for this time-wasting. Oh, yes ... he'd see to that personally.

'I'm not sure I can carry that many,' began Nabob.

Flagit wheeled around and stomped out into a side cavern, snatching Nabob roughly by the horn and dragging him along. With a muttered series of curses relating to jobs and how it was invariably more effective to see to it oneself, they vanished.

'Well, this is a mite mysterious, shipmates,' grunted Khlyde, the Over-Deity for Ships and Stuff. 'Anybody fathomed what's going on?'

'I don't even know where we are,' muttered Fleeh, the Over-Deity of Sprinting and Running Away Rapidly, who was currently very embarrassed about having been caught by a net from the ceiling. He should really have been able to dodge it, easily outrun it. It just wasn't sporting not to have let off a pistol or anything.

Screed, perched at the far end of the row of bound deities couldn't help himself. He burst out with the answer. 'Helian! You're in Helian!'

The faces of six deities turned on him, quizzically accusing.

'Who's he?' shrieked Dahls'soon. 'A stranger! And me still with my hair not set! Oh woe.'

'Beats me who he is, me hearties,' offered Khlyde, the peak of his cap waggling. 'He was here when I arrived.'

'I'm the Reverend Screed of the Haranguist Mission,' said Screed.

'That's why I didn't recognise him. He ain't a deity,' grunted Pugil, Celestial Being-in-Charge of Fisticuffs

191

and Scrapping. 'I never forget a face,' he added. 'Specially one I've hit recently. Show me a nose I've broken an' I can tell you where an' when I done it!'

Screed's head was spinning. Deities? What were six deities doing here? This wasn't anything to do with the secret documents he'd translated. Or was it? Were they here working for Sot, too?

Fleeh was glaring at Screed suspiciously. 'If he's not one of us, then why's he here, alone with us, after all those questions? I don't like it. I don't like it at all. I think we should all just clear off out of here. Leave well alone, I say.'

'What? You think 'e's a spy, eh?' grunted Pugil mockingly.

'Yes. He's a plant, listening in to our conversations...'

'What for?' countered Pugil. 'It don't make any sense.'

'He'll steal my styling secrets!' wailed Dahls'soon.

'No, no,' whispered Fleeh with a glint of paranoia. 'I've heard of this. Remember Any Other Business a few days back? Remember those weird ideas of that Bhelbynn chap? This is all his doing, I tell you.'

'What? Him on the third table? The guy in charge of Mortal Management and Crisis Control?' spluttered Pugil. 'Can't place his face. Hmmmm, if this is all his fault I'll remedy that with a few well-placed knuckles, just see if I don't.'

Fleeh nodded. 'Yeah, it's him. He just picks deities at random and "Whoosh", before you know it you're on one of his courses. Some folks I've heard of get dropped in the middle of nowhere with a compass and twenty-three pieces of string and they've got to find their way back or build a tent. Or something. Supposed to build team spirit. But mostly they just end up scrapping all the time.'

'Sounds like fun,' grinned Pugil.

'But why are *we* here?' asked Dahls'soon desperately, a strip of curling rag unraveling before her eyes. 'This team spirit thing *can't* be more important than good grooming, surely, darlings. And what's it got to do with Anti-Personnel whatsits?'

Nobody had the chance to answer. At that instant a hoof kicked open the door and Flagit appeared with a large tray of rock cakes. He struggled over to the table and dropped the tray on it with a crash of impatience. 'There, happy now?'

All eyes stared at the seven knobbly dark grey buns. And the deities grinned. Maybe this course of Bhelbynn's wasn't going to be too bad. Okay, so the quality of the food might not be up to the same exacting standards they were used to at Manna Ambrosia's, courtesy of dear old Tohnee Fabrizzi, but, hey, it *was* waitress delivered. They could almost be on the Top Table. Almost.

'Where are the Anti-Personnel Shrines?' ranted Flagit yet again, like an interrogative parrot which knew only one question and adored the sound of its own voice.

'Er, I'm not sure if anyone's asked this before,' began Fleeh, broaching a question which really should have been addressed five hours ago when Flagit had first started ranting about Anti-Personnel Shrines.

'What is it?' snarled Flagit impatiently, glaring at him through tightly slitted pupils. Licks of steam curled out of his nostrils.

'Er . . . exactly,' answered Fleeh. 'What is it? I haven't a clue about these Anti-Personn . . .'

The tirade of shouting and swearing which was about to explode from Flagit's body was only diverted by the return of Nabob with a steaming pot of brimstone.

A wave of approval oozed from the gathered deities at the welcome arrival of more refreshments. Undetected, the purple pilot lights which squatted above the deities' heads swelled and licked urgently towards Flagit and Nabob.

Nabob put the pot down on the table and surprised

himself by smiling sweetly at the row of seven guests ...
er, prisoners. They are *prisoners!* he insisted to himself
as he curtsied away.

Flagit glared at the captives, scowled at the rock
cakes and tutted as he snarled, 'There you are, help
yourselves.'

Nobody moved.

'Well? What are you waiting for?'

Dehtol waggled his wrists ineffectually. 'We can't
come to the table right now, we're a bit, er, tied up at the
moment.'

'What d'you expect me to do? Feed you?' shouted
Flagit.

Three of the deities rolled their eyes in pleasure. The
Top Table never had such personal attention. This was
looking better all the time.

To their disappointment, Flagit vanished around the
back of them and began unravelling their Nayburn High
Tensile Hemp bindings, grumbling as he went.

'Bring us some buns,' he complained. 'Can't come to
the table. Pah! Pathetic, you are, and what have I got in
return? Nothing! Well, I really had better start getting
some answers soon otherwise I will be forced to turn
very, very nasty indeed, just see if I don't.'

Within moments half the deities were tucking into the
tough but yielding texture of Helian Rock Cakes and
grinning as they chewed. Waves of cheeriness exuded
from them, spreading and stroking at Flagit's fevered
brow, cooling his temper.

'I'm telling you, I can be very nasty, I can. You'll all
be very sorry I captured you if you don't be nice and tell
me just a little bit about where you think these Anti-
Personnel Shrines might just happen to be right now.'

All six of the deities were gnawing away almost
contentedly, paying not the slightest bit of attention to
Flagit's ranting. There'd be plenty of time to catch up on
the details later; they could always ask if there was
something about this course that they didn't understand.

There were bound to be take-home notes, or some reminder.

Unthinking, as he grumbled away Flagit unravelled Screed's bindings.

'I mean, if you don't tell me where the Anti-Personnel Shrines are,' he wittered, 'I might start to get a bit upset and...'

Screed took a deep breath, drew himself up to his full height as he slid off the stool and rubbed his wrists. He stared intently at Flagit's chest.

'Alright if I go now?' he asked. 'I mean, I've done my part of the bargain, haven't I? Fully translated text and...'

'Yes, yes. Go!' muttered Flagit, his mind elsewhere, concerned with the other six prisoners.

Nabob's jaw dropped as he heard Flagit's words. He had actually kept his word. It was unheard of! Was he feeling alright?

'That door over there,' said Flagit, pointing a curly talon. Waves of approval lapped at his anger, oozing from the cheerfully chewing deities.

'Go on, get out of here,' insisted Flagit.

Screed wasted no time at all, scurrying doorwards with excited glee. He snatched the door handle, twisted and tugged...

'Screed!' shouted Flagit.

The Reverend turned, expecting an evilly grinning face to snatch him back and lash him to the stool again.

Flagit stared at him, a wave of frivolity oozing contentedly through him like warm syrup through a freshly toasted crumpet. A strange expression trickled onto his face, almost peaceful, almost happy, very disturbing. 'Just want to say, er ... about the translation and stuff, well ... tha ... thank...'

Nabob's jaw was on his chest as he watched Flagit. What was wrong with him? Was he ill? Something he'd eaten? He stared accusingly at the rock cakes.

Screed grinned and vanished around the door. He

wasn't entirely sure what was going on but he decided to take full advantage of the situation as it stood. The door slammed behind him.

'Great buns!' declared Dehtol wiping his mouth. 'Just the ideal levels of sugars necessary to lift a body's spirits. Got any more?'

'Y ... yeah,' answered Flagit dreamily. 'How many d'you want? I'll just go and...'

He turned and swept across the floor towards the other cavern, propelled on a growing purple wave of enlightenment emanating from the deities.

He really should have looked across at his DIY shrine detector. It would have warned him of the danger. The two six-inch nails supporting the spoon-like pointers were bending backwards as the theophobic cells struggled to escape the mounting tide of shrine waves.

Nabob, quivering, ran into the kitchen and slammed the door.

Kicking and moaning in the final few moments of an afternoon slumber, 'Snuff' Douser of the Axolotian Fire Prediction Service was gripped in the all-too-real images of a shocking nightmare. Helplessly he thrashed around in his hammock, flinging his duvet across the room as he enacted the daring rescue playing out in his mind.

Another flaming wooden beam shrieked in the agony of immolation and leapt from the roof of the tower, roaring as it plunged towards him. His whole nightmare world became that flame-torn joist as it raced him down. He screamed, leapt backwards and felt the searing heat engulf him for a single heart-stopping second as the incendiary beam careered past, down the centre of the smoke-filled stairwell.

How could he have let this happen? It was unthink-able, but somehow in the nightmare, 'Snuff' Douser had completely failed to carry out his duty to Axolotian society. Why had his nostril not quivered its predictive warning of imminent inflammation? Had he lost his powers of infallible foresight? Was this the end of his career in the Axolotian Fire Prediction Service?

The nightmare inferno raged unstoppably around him, roaring like some rabid dragon with terminal heartburn. And then over the noise of combustive destruction, he heard it again. Guilt conquered panic and drove him on up the stairs as he heard the terrified whinnying of Dennis his trusty donkey.

Decades they had been together, never missing a forthcoming fire, always strolling casually up in the proverbial nick of time to empty his leather bucket of water over the smouldering acorn sparks of a wannabe mighty inferno oak, dousing their hopes forever in a lick of steam. He simply had to reach Dennis before it was too late.

Another adrenaline-soaked whinny rattled through his brain, strengthening his resolve, pushing him on up the seemingly endless flight of stairs. Two more beams soared out of nowhere on chariots of flaming tongues, pinning him to the wall as they bounced on the stairs and ricocheted down the central well, tumbling, spreading seeds of flame as they went.

With a roar, eighty feet of exit staircase ignited.

'Snuff' gritted his teeth. There was no way back down. He had to go on, heroically pushing back the fear of danger, battling the odds to save his trusty ass. As if in encouragement another whinny sounded ahead, muffled behind a wooden door.

He willed his legs into action, powering his thighs onwards up the endless flight. And then he was on the top landing, separated from Dennis by a single oak door. And a sheet of hero-toasting flame. Oh, and a dense pall of vision-obliterating smoke.

To anyone but 'Snuff' this would have been a disaster. But he laughed at it all. It would take more than such physical barriers to stand between him and his shaggy steed. Especially after he had come so far.

197

Snorting and pawing the floor like a rhino on heat, 'Snuff' wound himself up and charged.

The door caved in beneath his shoulder, hurling fragments of wood in all directions. With one bound he was across the room and leapfrogging onto Dennis's back. A whinny of delight erupted from the faithful donkey's lungs as he felt 'Snuff''s familiar legs grip tight around his midriff. He galloped forward, leapt at the window and, framed in a galaxy of spinning glass stars, they shot out into the night air.

One hundred feet up in the night air, to be precise.

The hungry rocks below grinned upwards expectantly as 'Snuff' realised just how unaerodynamic the average donkey was.

The ground began to race towards them with all the boundless enthusiasm of a mud-soaked labrador.

'Snuff' screamed, thrashed helplessly and fell off his hammock. The sudden collision of cold marble on soft nose was something of a blessed relief.

It had all just been a nightmare. Dennis hadn't been imprisoned in a flaming tower. There was no fire. He hadn't lost his precognitive abilities.

For a few moments 'Snuff' lay on the cold floor, patting it affectionately, revelling in relief as he breathed deeply. Then suddenly he coughed and sat up in alarm, his nostrils flaring uneasily.

If that had all been a simple nightmare and there had been no fire then why were his nostrils tickling with smoke? And why could he hear whinnying?

He sprinted to the window and leaned out. Dennis was in his paddock leaping and cavorting in alarm and pointing a desperate leg towards the far horizon. 'Snuff''s gaze followed. He gasped as his eyes fell on the billows of smoke rising unchecked from a burning barley field.

In a second he was out of the window and sliding down his emergency pole, straight onto the back of a champing Dennis. He tugged the stable release and was away through the gate at full trot.

Only now, as the streets of Axolotl trundled past, did he have a chance to wonder at what had happened. He should have sensed it, should have got the twitching nostrils, but ... there'd been nothing. Could the nightmare have been a warning? He doubted it. He might be as hyperstitious as the next Axolotian, but premonitory nightmares, in the afternoon? No way! Could there be a new employee in the ranks of the Fire Prediction Service? One whose duty was to keep a weather nostril on the potential conflagration of crops and agricultural supplies? If that was the case, why didn't he know about him? Grossly unlikely!

That left the third and most terrifying of conclusions. Every Axolotian worth an ounce of precognition knew that there was one class of events which was utterly impossible to predict, one group of happenings which even the normally eager premium hungry Axolotian Insurance Company wouldn't touch with the proverbial bargepole. Acts of the Gods!

But there were still two questions at the forefront of 'Snuff' Douser's mind as he trotted past the outer window of the Municipal Prediction Hall.

How the Helian was he going to put that field out? And – a sinister one, this – what would any of the gods stand to gain from torching a barley field?

'What would any of the gods stand to gain from torching a barley field?' gabbled Grand Municipal Prophet, Captain Maehap incredulously as he stood in the now crowded and draughty Municipal Prediction Hall. Outside, through the recently shattered window, there could just be heard the trotting of Dennis the donkey.

The mob of Axolotian citizens stared back at Maehap. 'What makes you think it was the gods, eh?' asked one of them with a barbed tone. He, like the rest of the gang, glared accusingly at the feather-barbed figure of the Invocator-in-Charge of Transport and Goods Handling.

'Sanctuary,' whimpered Kwedgley yet again, clutching at the ankle of Captain Maehap.

'Has to be an Act of the Gods,' insisted Maehap, patting Kwedgley's feathery head. 'Did any of you lot foresee these events, eh? The sinking of Hunntah's ship? The torching of the barley field? This gross and distasteful act of extreme vandalism?' He pointed imperiously at the shattered skylight and smashed window, barely containing a shudder as he recalled the all-too-recent invasion of the bulky net-wielding monsters. 'Did you have even the minimal quivering of whichever organ of yours it is which does the quivering, eh? Well, did you?'

There was a general shuffling of embarrassed denial.

'Well?' snapped Maehap, glaring over the arch of his wrinkled nose. 'You,' he stabbed a finger randomly at the mob. 'Did you predict any of this, eh?'

The suddenly spotlit seer mumbled and looked sheepishly at his sandals.

'Eh? What's that, speak up!' barked Maehap. 'D'you see any of it or not?'

'No, I ... er, I've been kind of busy recently. Sort of focusing my attention on ... on...' He faded away again.

'On what, man? C'mon, spit it out!'

He blushed and looked around nervously. 'On ... on Tehzho's wedding. I ... I want to make really sure it goes well. I'm his biggest fan and I really...'

'*I'm* his biggest fan,' countered a voice at the back of the mob. 'I've seen every single "Play Your Stars Right!" I have. I know all his catchphrases...'

'Pah. Call yourself the biggest fan?' argued another. 'I knew him before he ever set foot on stage...'

Yet another voice shouted in denial. 'Well *I* was the one who persuaded him to *put* his foot on the stage...'

It would have erupted into fisticuffs had not Maehap crawled onto the marble futures table, struggled to his feet and slammed his stick onto the surface with a dozen resounding cracks.

And into the ensuing silence a panting voice piped up from the back. 'Er, if it was an Act of the Gods, then it's a bit of a weird one.'

All eyes in the Hall turned and stared at this apparent blasphemy, demanding an answer.

The questioner, one very forlorn-looking Suon Hunntah, grinned sheepishly and at least had the decency to blush with embarrassment before he was shoved to the front of the mob under the instruction of Maehap's wagging finger.

'Well, what I mean is, er ... a bit of a peculiar Act to go to all the trouble of actually turning up and then, "Foooof!"'

'Foooof?' choked Maehap in confusion.

'Yeah,' answered Hunntah, who had been told all about the events on the edge of Lake Averjinn that he'd missed, owing to the fact that he'd been face down on the ground with his ears closed. 'Foooof!' He waved his arms in a way he hoped bore at least a passing resemblance to a deity disappearing, 'Vanished without a grace.'

'Yeah, didn't have a chance. They just leapt on him and dragged him kicking...' Another voice piped up.

'Who leapt on him? What did they look like?' spluttered Maehap, feeling a cold chill of terror awaken at the base of his spine and run icy fingernails up to his neck.

'Just like the things that came through that hole,' came another enthusiastic voice, pointing at the rent in the ceiling.

'Yeah,' growled a third voice, rumbling deeply from a heavily muscled hulk of citizenhood with bald head and arms the size of most folk's legs. 'Very professionally done. Minimum fuss, just snatched 'em through the window. Love to shake them guys by hand. Didn't get a chance to fight back. That's the best way. It was a bit odd, though.'

'What are you on about? Of course it was odd. It's not

201

every day you get things ripping holes in the roof, is it? What's he on about?' spluttered Maehap, pointing at the bouncer from the local night spot.

'Well,' growled the bouncer, 'the guys that vanished through the window, d'you see the look on their faces? I've seen it dozens of times, see? More or less every night actually, and I know it well. It's the one that says "No, no, I don't want to go. I want to stay here, please, please!" But it's normally the other way round. Know what I mean?'

'No, frankly,' confessed Maehap. 'What other way round?'

'How d'you know my name?' asked Frankly the bouncer, baffled, 'Oh, never mind. See. I've got this theory...' And he shut up.

'Yes? And...?' croaked Maehap, flapping his hands as if trying to stir the air. 'Let's hear it, then!'

Frankly's eyes lit up. Over the years he had learned that, because of his bulk and seismically deep voice, nobody believed he was actually capable of sentient thought much above the level of hurling folks out of doors. After having his theories laughed out of existence more times than he cared to recall, he was somewhat reluctant to air them. But this was different. If the Grand Municipal Prophet wanted to hear it then...

He took a breath. 'Them deities have been kidnapped, or deitynapped, I suppose it'd be.'

There was a gasp from everyone in the Prediction Hall and all eyes bored into Frankly the bouncer.

'What?' he rumbled. 'Oh, c'mon, don't laugh, that's not fair...'

'Would you care to explain?' begged Maehap.

'Er, oh, yes, Your Futureship, Sir. Er, well, it's my job to hurl folks *out* when they get a bit over-affectionate with some of the servin' girls, right? Pick 'em up and "whoosh" out the door. Then they always give me that "don't want to go" look.' There was a dull silence as everyone still tried to figure what Frankly was on about.

202

'Those guys that vanished out that window all had that expression, so they didn't want to go with them things that made that hole, see?'

In a flash everyone realised that the facts did indeed fit Frankly's theory. The expression of alarm on the deities' faces, the unorthodox method of departure – all circumstantial fingers of evidence pointed the same way. The deities had indeed been kidnapped.

'Well, what d'you think?' asked Frankly the bouncer. 'Have you got a better explanation?'

Maehap sincerely wished he had. His mind took Frankly's theory, shoved it under its hypothetical armpit and ran with it, spinning off a hundred different questions. A few of which went something like:

Does it matter if he is right?

It won't affect me, will it?

I won't get physically harmed, will I?

There won't be a complete undermining of Axolotian Society as everybody realises that they cannot see the future, will there?

There won't be a sudden explosion of mad panicking riots, will there?

There won't be hundreds killed in the frenzy of looting which will surely ensue once the dreadful truth gets out, will there? Will there?

Depends who's doing the deitynapping, doesn't it?

It was this last question that threw a glacier's worth of icicles up his spine in a bladder-wrenching shock of acute realisation.

There were only two answers to it. Deities or Devils!

And if it was the latter then the answers to all the above simply had to be ... yes! Writ large.

'Well, what d'you think?' asked Frankly the bouncer again, tugging Maehap's terrified mind back into the present harsh reality. 'Got a better explanation?'

Captain Maehap fiddled with his fingers and took a deep breath. 'Er, well, you see...' he began with underwhelming confidence 'Ah ... aha! It was the gods, yes, of course. I don't think there's anything we really need to be too b ... bothered about. Er, we all know how mysterious are the ways in which they work. Don't we?'

The grin he plastered across his aged features could definitely have benefitted from about a thousand gallons more confidence behind it.

'What?' asked a voice from the crowd. 'You saying this is all a symbol of something?'

'Er ... I suppose I ...' flustered Maehap, his confidence rapidly deserting him. This was territory he was far from used to. Prophetic predictions, no problem, but hypothetical extrapolations based on hearsay and eyewitness reports ... dodgy ground, steer clear. Too much chance of being caught out if the answer was wrong.

'Is that why there's a picture of the things that came in through the roof here in the carvings on the side of your table?' asked Suon Hunntah, pointing at a group of figures.

'WHAT!' screamed Maehap and, risking his knees in an uncharacteristic act of desperate recklessness, he leapt off the table and stared at the carving at the end of Suon Hunntah's fingertip, his heart pounding. If it was true he knew he wouldn't need his knees much longer anyway.

Maehap's ageing jaw dropped onto his chest as he stared at the carved Frieze of A Few Apocalyptic Things To Watch Out For. Carved over centuries, this tableau of gargoyles was the last remaining vestige from the time of the Empiricists. A time before the rise of prophecyship when the future could only be guessed at by using the painstaking collection of data on all subjects and searching for patterns. The Empiricists had invented the concept of days and nights, the theory of recurring seasons and the sure and certain knowledge that the only reason anybody doesn't simply float away if they jump high enough is that everyone is attached to the ground by a pair of invisible red strings tied around each ankle.

204

A huge number of their teachings had been incorporated easily into modern Axolotian culture. Well, they were all so blinking obvious. Everybody *knew* that everyone was attached to the ground by a pair of invisible red strings, didn't they? Why else weren't they up there in the clouds, eh?

But there were things that not everybody was allowed to know. Secret things uncovered by the Empiricists' tireless observations. Things that presaged trouble. Things To Watch Out For.

As Captain Maehap stared at the ancient carvings he desperately wished his mummy was still around.

For there they were, hewn out of solid marble in grotesquely scratchy perfection, staring accusingly at him across the centuries – a dread warning of impending disaster left him by the Empiricists. A pair of bulbous-bodied beings with huge heads, pointy noses and joint-less arms danced hideously in the midst of a whirling stone blizzard.

This was bad news with a capital ABOMINABLE.

Maehap shivered involuntarily as he recognised The Dreaded Snowthings of The Freezing Apocalypse. If they had returned, presaging The Cataclysmic Blizzards then there was only one thing he could tell the citizens of Axolotl.

Buy up all the shares you can lay your hands on in the Axolotian Hot Water Bottle Company, quick sharp.

The Mostly Reverend Vex Screed hadn't stopped to consider just how unlikely it would normally be for Flagit, or any devil come to that, actually to keep his word. He'd had more pressing matters at the forefront of his mind. Free of the countless ells of Nayburn High Tensile Hemp and out of Flagit's taloned reach, he could get back to his burning mission. The Saving of Souls.

Eager excitement had bubbled through him at the prospect of a damn good preaching, driving him down streets and alleys, skittering around corners like a man possessed. He had leapt boiling puddles of lava with single bounds and eventually erupted onto a seething street heaving with miserably trudging souls. One step further and he would have been snatched into the filthy tide of tormented ones as they shuffled off towards another session of suffering. Instead he had sprung at the nearest strata-scraper and scrabbled his way up the knobbly stalag-mite-hewn walls, hauling himself up to a tiny windowsill. There he had let his voice of salvation burst forth over the downtrodden spirits of Helian as they had shuffled past below him. With the excessive glee of evangelism powering through him he had set about haranguing them first into awareness, a secondly into attention and thirdly into the arms of angelic rapture.

After half an hour of stirring sermons extolling the delights of the consumption of ale, and the subsequent acquisition of several hundred devotees to Sot, the Deity-in-Command of Ales, he turned his mercionary expertise to other topics. Already there were a few hundred converts to the overwhelming belief that there would be salvation through the correct use of Sister Ophelia's Scrubbing Sponge and Barrel Balm (with conditioner). Several dozen worshipped the ground that could be walked upon whilst wearing Deacon Martynn's Prayer-Wear Boots and Cloistered Clogs. And he was well into double figures on converts believing the advances which could be made towards securing one's very own heavenly dwelling if mortgage repayments were made through the coffers of Reverend Loid Spank. And he wasn't ready to stop there...

'Can you not feel the urging tingle at the ends of your fingers and, oh ... talons?' he added as he caught sight of a few of Helian's larger and scalier residents casting a sly ear in his direction as they pushed armpit-deep through the pack of bodies. 'Feel the naked incompleteness of index digit and thumb! Something is missing! Can you not feel it?'

He held up his hands at chest height before him, curled his index fingers over to join his thumbs, forming a pair of rings, and splayed the remaining fingers out like plumes of feathers. Then, silently, he struck his hands together. To some of the unbelievers in the crowd it looked like a pathetic shadow puppeteer's attempt at showing two deformed parrots kissing, but to those gripped by the urges inflamed by Screed's salvationary words it was a different sight and sound. They could already hear the gentle tinkling of the imagined finger bells of faith shimmering with each collision, could see the shiny metallic discs vibrating, and suddenly ached with the longing to ring out their very own pair of Solstice Bill's Cymbalic Soul-Savers (available in crash, ride or hi-hat options).

'Or do you feel the rhythms of salvation should be more forceful?' asked Screed, curling his hands as if gripping two wooden shells, raising one hand high and stamping his heels on the windowsill as he pirouetted frantically. 'Heobhan can be yours with Pope Huansan-shez's Miraculous Mission Maracas. Yes, flamenco your way from the flames of pain to the mainly gainful plains of paradise!'

He was getting carried away. The words flowed unchecked, unthought through, but the crowd seemed not to care. The clicking of devilish hooves bore testament to that as nine-foot monsters struck macho poses, stamped the ground and clapped claws in wild paradiddles above their horns.

And as Screed stared out over the enraptured crowd he grinned. This was what he was here for. This was it!

As Flagit emptied the last of Nabob's Helian Rock Cakes out of his bun container and arranged them on the tray with highly uncharacteristic neatness, a taloned claw snatched at his shoulder and spun him angrily around.

'Have you finally gone mad?' snarled Nabob through

207

tightly clenched fangs, his nose an inch from Flagit's. 'If anyone hears of this . . .'

'Out of the way, please, I have to give these cakes to . . .' began Flagit, pushing insistently but not *too* forcefully towards the door to the rest of the cavern.

'Forget those,' snapped Nabob, slapping the tray of cakes out of Flagit's claw and wincing as they bounced off his hoof.

'But I promised them I'd . . .'

Nabob wasn't sure whether to cover his ears to the disgusting language or shake some sense into Flagit. He slapped him across the face instead.

'That wasn't nice,' sulked Flagit, showing no signs of retaliation. 'I don't think I deserved that.'

'Well, you don't deserve this either,' snarled Nabob and hit him again, harder, on the other scaly cheek.

'You're right. I don't. Please refrain . . .'

Nabob screamed, slammed his claws over his ears and screwed his eyes shut. He'd said it again. That word. That 'P' word!

There were plenty of 'P' words he could have used – punishment, pugilism, pain, pummelling, pounding – all good, healthy words that go really well with merciless, or gratuitous. But 'please'?

Nabob shuddered. Never had he heard such abhorrent language. And as if that wasn't bad enough, there was the tone of voice Flagit had used. So harmless. So reasonable!

So frightening!

Nabob opened his eyes as something brushed his hoof. In horror he stared at Flagit crawling around the floor picking up the scattered cakes and wiping them carefully.

It was suddenly more than Nabob could take.

A claw lanced out of the sky, snatched Flagit firmly around the throat and hauled him onto his hooves.

'Stop that!' screamed Nabob, an inch from Flagit's face.

'But, I...'

'What's got into you?' Nabob ranted, shaking Flagit wildly by the shoulders and punctuating the odd consonant by deft slaps. 'You been at my lava martinis again, eh? Or smoking dodgy slag? What possessed you to let him go? I can't believe you actually kept your word, it's so unlike...'

'Let who go? What word?' spluttered Flagit as his redly throbbing cheeks began to make their presence felt in the hazy confusion of his mind.

'Screed!' spat Nabob.

'But he's still out there tied to...'

'Oh yeah? Care to place a few obuls on that?' Nabob kicked open the door, swung Flagit through it and forced his baffled gaze towards the coil of Nayburn High Tensile Hemp ringing a suspiciously empty swivel stool. The very stool to which the Mostly Reverend Vex Screed should have been securely bound.

A row of six figures waved cheerily at him and in that second the flint of horrific realisation was struck. Something was most definitely teetering on the wrong side of fine and dandy.

'What the Helian...?'

'...were you thinking of?' snarled Nabob, interrupting the spluttering Flagit and dropping him in derisive disgust.

He crumpled and stared at the floor, rocking back and forth like some yashmaked devotee attempting prayers on a raft in a ten-foot swell. 'It seemed like a good idea at the time,' he whimpered.

'But keeping your word?' Nabob was reeling with incredulity. 'You even thanked him for his help!'

'I did what?' Flagit's eyes were wide with terror as he crawled across the floor, snatched Nabob's ankles and began grovelling pathetically. 'Did any one else see it? You won't tell anyone this, er, little slip, will you? I'll be really, really ruthless from now on, just you watch. Be back to my normal nasty, scheming, horrible...'

209

'Scheming? Is *that* what you call it?' sneered Nabob, kicking Flagit away. 'In case you hadn't noticed, there are a total of six illegal immigrants out there in my front cavern, sitting on my swivel stools and eating my rock cakes. Would you care to enlighten me as to how this cosy little scenario is supposed to affect Seirizzim, other than giving him a hernia by laughing so much when he arrests us for immigration violations and conjures up another marvellous community service scheme, hmmmm?'

Flagit picked himself up off the floor and shook his head, bashing the side of his ear with the heel of his claw as if trying to shake some loose bits out of the other one. Fragments of comprehension and embarrassed memory collided, tumbling over one another and landing on the smouldering flint of realisation. He had been interrogating the Axolotian six for hours, demanding where the Anti-Personnel Shrines were stockpiled. He knew that they knew where it was, they'd been handling the stuff. Traces of it were all over them, the shrine detector said so.

A modicum of doubt chewed away. The shrine detector? it questioned. Could that DIY device be totally screwed up?

'You've blown it, haven't you?' sneered Nabob with not a little delight. 'Admit it. You've been caught out by that Screed. He took you for the idiot you are! Well, what are you going to do with them?' He jerked a taloned thumb towards the door and the six prisoners beyond.

Defeat and Nabob stared Flagit accusingly in the face. He shook his head again. 'It can't be,' he murmured from behind unfocused crimson eyes. 'It was working. I saw it...'

'We could have the Malebranche kicking in the door at any minute! What are you going to do?'

'It had to be working.'

'What did?'

'The shrine detector,' pleaded Flagit.

'Oh yeah?' mocked Nabob, dripping sarcasm. 'So where *is* this stash of Anti-Personnel Shrines then, eh? All you've "detected" with that thing is half a dozen illegal immigrants!'

'It did work! It *was* detecting Shrine Waves like it's supposed to! Why else would it have pointed so squarely at Screed and those other six ... ?'

Flagit's voice trailed away suddenly as it hit him. How could he have been so blind? So eager to scamper up to the gnarly roots of the wrong infernal conifer and gaily bark himself stupid?

There was only one reason why a device designed to detect Shrine Waves would point to anything emanating those fundamental particles of pure theism. There was only one reason why his shrine detector had pointed to the six prisoners and Screed. His heart almost stopped as realisation exploded in a corona of searing crysanthemums.

They were all emanating Shrine Waves.

Suddenly it all made sense. The effect of Screed's preaching, urging him to use Wonderwear; the sudden wish to loosen Screed's bindings and now finally, incredibly, keeping his word and letting him go. He shuddered. None of it could have happened without the influence of continued exposure to high doses of theic radiation.

Unconsciously he scrubbed at his claws, scratching away the cleanliness of infectious belief as his mind shyly recalled a dreadful thought. He had wondered, ever so briefly, why the six prisoners had been picked up by the shrine detector through a thousand feet of solid rock and Screed only barely made the pointers flicker, but he had never stopped to think of precisely why this should be.

Until now.

And now, he knew.

These six prisoners were giving out thousands of times more Shrine Waves than their once captive Reverend, shining like theic beacons in the wilderness of disbelief and scorn. And what gives out Shrine Waves thousands of times more powerfully than a mere Reverend? ... Oh Gods!

Flagit went very, very pale, coughed and, still under the effects of high-dose exposure to theic radiation, he looked up at Nabob and opened his mouth.

'Er, about these illegal immigrants of ours ... There's something I really ought to tell you...'

If anyone had been listening outside the door of Filch the demon's cavern they would have heard the ringing of an almost constant barrage of hammer on metal. Perhaps they would have been baffled by the unheard of sounds of honest toil and industry issuing forth, perhaps not. If they hadn't been present at the latest of the Mostly Reverend Screed's spontaneous preachings then they really wouldn't have understood what was driving Filch to behave in such a peculiarly feverish and devoted manner.

Truth be told, Filch hadn't the foggiest what had got into him either. But he hadn't noticed his change. He was *far* too busy for any deep psychological self-analysis. That would have to wait. Right now he was desperately busy ... desperately.

Ever since he had been drawn to a certain vast crowd of jingling Helian residents' pockets and wallets like the prime larcenist he was, things hadn't been the same. He had only succeeded in relieving half a dozen devils of the burden of transporting overladen wallets when, like a bolt of crimson lightning before a flamestorm, his attention had been snatched by the words of the cassocked creature on the balcony. In moments his talontips had tingled and he was hooked, grabbed by the overwhelming urge to partake of a little metalwork.

In the privacy of his cavern in deepest downtown Tumor he chuckled to himself excitedly as he snatched a tiny disc of metal alloy from a small sack and placed it on a domed rock. In seconds he had grabbed his trusty hammer and was pounding feverishly away at the single obul coin, enlarging it carefully, spreading its soft spendability across the domed rock. His eyes held the desired plan, every second comparing what he saw with what he desperately wanted to see, assessing, shaping. His ears rang with the desired tone, their suffering easing with each hammer strike as the atonal clangour was smoothed towards a single ringing note of graceful perfection.

And after three hours it was done, a tiny cap of metal complete with a knot of looped Nayburn Hemp through its centre.

Grinning expectantly, Filch clutched the string between his thumb and index talon and spread the remaining talons in what looked like a poor shadow puppeteer's imitation of a cockatoo. He did the same with his other claw. Quivering on the brink of enlightenment he struck the two perfect copies of Solstice Bill's Cymbalic Soul-Savers and revelled in the pure, shimmering note which issued forth.

And in that moment Filch abandoned all thoughts of thievery and hung up his lust for larceny, his devilish heart brimming with the overwhelming happiness of enlightenment. He stood and headed for the door.

Only at the last moment did he stop and wrap a bright orange cushion cover round his horns. He didn't know why he'd done it, it just felt right.

And so, ringing his talon bells cheerily, he stepped out into the streets of downtown Tumor, ready to spread the tinkling truth to all who would listen.

It was lunchtime in Manna Ambrosia's and the amount of noise, the number of occupied seats and the level of nectar in most deities' blood was rising. Rapidly.

Already angelic waitresses were flitting madly about, flinging servings hither and yon, snatching them off the Holy Heated Trolley and hurling them before the salivating mouths of the lower deities.

It was the same every day. Flotillas of gods weaving Manna Ambrosia-wards. Rolling roisterously on the back of their silver clouds with randomly chaotic abandon. And every day, amazingly, they all arrived in one piece. Precisely how they managed this no-one really knew. And frankly they didn't care.

All that mattered at lunchtime was the filling of bellies and the cheerful imbibing of the finest liquid fare on offer from Lush or Sot, and the settling in for a good afternoon's supping. There was only one downer to the entire event. Everyone had to wait until the Top Table were seated before any food was actually tucked into.

It was tradition, allegedly. Although many denizens of the lower tables secretly suspected it to be a sadly pathetic way for the 'Sacred Seven' to show off as they stalked smugly towards their raised tableclothed position.

They were also served after everyone else. Again, this was traditional. Something to do with serving the best last.

And so it was, on this most undistinguished of days, after everyone had been led unnecessarily to their tables by Uscher, the Under Deity Over Seating Arrangements, that the magnificent seven hitched up their togas, grinned to the lower orders and stuck their bums on seats.

In seconds, the Holy Heated Trolley was wheeled up by a pair of panting angelic waitresses and the Sacred Bread of Heobhan was dished out in their favourite form. Deep-pan pizzas.

But something was wrong, thought Uscher, sitting at a back table counting heads surreptitiously. Something didn't add up.

Scran, the Supreme Being-in-Charge of Savoury Supplies, smiled serenely, rolled up his sleeves and prepared to utter the ancient traditional mantra of blessing, 'Ready, steady, nosh!'

214

And he would have too, but, just as he was about to grunt the last word and take the first nibble, the corner of his eye caught sight of the six remaining pizzas lurking on the Holy Heated Trolley.

'What are those doing there?' he bellowed. 'Who hasn't had their pizza?'

It was a well-known fact that only the precise number of individual portions were baked each day, thus reducing wastage and giving the cook time off. It was a system of which Jit, the Under-Deity for Making Sure That All the Things That Irritate and Annoy, Don't, was justly proud.

'Who hasn't had their Pizza?' Scran repeated crossly. To refuse for no good reason was taken as a great insult to those who decided on the menu and, since this was another of Scran's roles, he was justifiably miffed. 'Well?'

The angelic waitresses shrugged, their wings rustling in feathery discomfiture. Everyone else simply shuffled nervously in their seats and stared longingly at the table in front of them.

All, that is, except Uscher, who glanced at the naked expanse of wood next to him where a deitical bottom should be and cringed. Suddenly he knew why he felt as if something didn't add up. Something didn't add up. They were a deity short. Panic hit him as he saw the knock on effects stretching away into infinity. One spare pizza! Several glasses of wine or ale left in bottles unconsumed! A pudding unclaimed! The disposal problems were endless. But worse ... this table was unbalanced. Conversation wouldn't flow smoothly. It would have to jump a gap, and the two separated by the gap would feel exposed, insecure ... oh, it was an absolute disaster. And it was his responsibility.

'C'mon, own up!' bawled Scran.

A nervous hand raised itself slowly from the back of Manna Ambrosia's.

Scran spotted it in a second. 'Well? What have you got

to say for yourself? Grub not good enough for you now, is it?'

'It's not that ... I ...' spluttered Uscher.

'Got bored with the same old stuff day in and day out, eh?' bellowed Scran from the Top Table.

'No, no ...'

'Think you could do better, hmmmm? Well? Do you? C'mon, speak up! Say what you think. Tell me why you have chosen not to partake of the finest foods available in Heobhan. I'm ready to listen to any reasonably argued point of view regarding the choice you have made not to join the rest of us in our regular community food, but it had better be good because you are single-handedly undermining the entire basis of beneficial ...' Scran finally ran out of breath and turned crimson.

'There's an empty chair here,' interjected Uscher with the speed of decades of practice listening to Scran ranting. He always ran out of breath just when he was getting going about something he felt strongly about.

'....?' he gasped, mouth open in soundless shock.

Uscher raised the chair helpfully for all to see.

'There's one of them over here, too,' declared a diaphanously shimmering goddess. She was soon followed by four others.

Uscher's jaw dropped. It was worse than he thought!

Scran was now definitely shocked. Six deities hadn't turned up. This was terrible. Never before had any of the doyens of Heobhan missed out on any of their three square meals a day. This was unheard of!

'Well where are they?' he snarled, staring intently at Uscher. He hadn't a clue who else to stare at. 'What are we going to do?'

There was a general burble of voices, quivering with indecision.

'Have another beer!' declared Sot cheerily.

Suddenly a thin minor god shot out of his seat, quivering from behind a pair of thin glasses and a pudding-bowl haircut. He waved a stylus and several

216

vast chunks of slate. 'I would like to propose the proposal that a m ... meeting is proposed,' he announced and was greeted by complete silence.

'W ... we could utilise that meeting opportunity in order to present current issues in a manner to be discussed and readily utilised,' spouted Lofax, He-Who-Is-In-Charge of Scheduling, Meetings and Vital Appointments.

The silence dripped from the ceiling.

'I ... I can make next mannasday and ... and I believe that there is a scheduling opportunity presenting itself for maximal utilisation at the self-same temporal juncture for the overwhelmingly vast majority of you all. Er ... excepting the current shortfall in numbers of our six fellow...'

'My pizza's getting cold,' grumbled a voice from somewhere.

'My beer's getting warm,' answered another.

A heavenly belly rumbled in reply.

'I ... I take it that there is an underwhelming positive acceptance factor in most of your...' began Lofax.

'Shut it!' screamed Scran and dived on his pizza.

The angelic waitresses tugged gently at the Holy Heated Trolley.

'Er, leave that, ladies,' spluttered Scran around a mouthful of pious pepperoni. 'I might want seconds,' he grinned.

The waitresses fluttered away.

'O ... of course we could schedule or arrange a potential discussive sojourn during the latter...'

'Shut up!' screamed Scran above a cacophony of chewing and swallowing.

Lofax fell onto his chair tutting and grumbling. 'Organisation, *that's* what's needed here, definitely.'

He put that momentous thought to the back of his mind and snatched a slice of pizza from his plate.

Over the far side of Manna Ambrosia's one deity chewed automatically, his thoughts far from the pizza in

217

his mouth. Sot pondered. Could it really be a coincidence that half a dozen deities hadn't turned up on the day after he'd signed up the Reverend Screed? He had given Screed pretty much a free rein on precisely how he recruited the extra devotees. Had he given him too much? Were the two events actually connected? This wasn't somehow his fault, was it?

With a quivering of nervousness he swallowed a chunk of pepperoni.

Inchoate shadows. Pools of crimson light. Occasional flares of lightning. The constant streaming of message-carrying mhodemms buzzing in and out of an array of ports. A typical day in the shadows of the Sinful Service Stratascraper. Except for the group of Pact-men creeping around in the shadows.

'Hurry up, hurry up, I'm losing it,' begged the ex-composer Queazx, tugging at the cassock sleeve of the ex-Really Reverend Unctuous III.

'Patience,' Unctuous warned himself, his eyes scanning the alley ahead, searching forlornly for any signs of the Reverend Screed.

'Don't need patience,' growled Queazx through clenched teeth. 'Need parchment, must have parchment before I lose it!' His right hand swayed rhythmically, his toes tapped and a low humming wormed its way between his lips.

'Alright, alright.' Unctuous raised his palms in defence. Queazx had been insufferable over the last few hours, nagging constantly for more parchment. He'd already used all of his store and snaffled every spare scrap of Cassoh's. Now he was impossible.

Relieved that Fithel's recent imprisonment and release hadn't harmed the violinist's fingers, Queazx had been inspired to compose. It had gripped him like an over-affectionate fever, invading his body with alarming intensity. He had suddenly quivered violently, leapt to his feet, squealed excitedly and snatched a lump of

218

charred coal and a sheet of parchment. His right hand had then become a blur. Stripes of five parallel lines had been scrawled across Nognite expanses and populated with colonies of tiny performing tadpoles, some tied to others, some with wriggly tails.

To all but two of the Pact-men it was complete nonsense.

They could have cheerfully ignored his occasional outburst of inspirational noises as he tried to hum the ascending atonal scale of a flattened chord, or whistle a trilling glissando. They couldn't ignore him when the crisis struck. In the middle of the third movement of his Ninth Symphony for Solo Violin, Comb and Parchment, just as he was about to underscore the counterpointed main theme and sow the tonal seeds for the rising climactic movement, he ran clean out of Nognite.

It was a wonder he didn't deafen himself permanently as he screamed, bit his knuckles and flicked the pile of parchments over, desperately searching for more blank expanses, panicking as notes and harmonies backed up inside his head.

It had only taken a few hours of his moaning to convince the rest of the Pact-men that more supplies really were needed. Now.

And so here they were, crouching in the shadow of the Sinful Service Stratascraper, ready to move.

Unctuous peered out into the street which ran in front of the vast stalag-mite-hewn façade and almost leapt out of the folds of his dead skin as the shift-change Klaxon erupted noisily. Even though he had been expecting it, the sudden Mortropolis-wide blaring caught him by surprise.

Now it was his turn to fidget nervously. He had to pick the moment carefully. Just as the street was almost totally packed with the shuffling tormented souls the plan would be sprung. He peered out of the shadows and waited for the moment, focusing on the density of souls in the street. It was a shame he didn't glance up at a

219

distant balcony as a tall cassocked man readied himself for another well-deserved preach.

At that very same instant, way across Mortropolis a pair of slitted pupils peered ahead and judged the moment. The belching, infernal combustion engine-powered bulk of Captain Naglfar's ferry slewed across the final few feet of the River Phlegethon under the watchful gaze of a cheerily sneering passenger.

Immediately the jetty was within range, Seirizzim leapt across the chasm of filthy ooze and landed with a clattering of hooves. He skittered away, closely followed by a squad of Malebranche and Asmodeus the banker.

Seirizzim was in no mood to waste time down by the riverside. He had to get back to the Sinful Service Stratascraper and regale his minions with the good news that the Lava and Brimstone Mines of Rubor were open again and ready for business. With some carelessly unveiled threats regarding employment possibilities therein tossed liberally amongst those slackers, he felt sure that an increase in efficiency would miraculously appear. Twenty-five percent should do nicely. For starters. And so, with the blissful sound of hard work and suffering still ringing cheerily in his mind's ear, Seirizzim turned his back on the Phlegethon and accelerated.

The street outside the Sinful Service Stratascraper was heaving. The Reverend Screed took a deep breath, raised his hands and ... a strangely furtive motion caught his eye in the crowd below. With a deft wrist-flick Unctuous had signalled to the rest of the Pact-men, three fingers, two fingers, one. Go!

Screed blinked in surprise from the distant balcony as, with a flurry of grace notes, Fithel the violinist leapt onto a suitable hut roof and began sawing madly away. Shocked, as ever, the tormented souls stared up at the string of discord assaulting their ears, one question burning to the forefront of their hopeless minds. What new torture was this?

220

Jaws dropping, they halted and stared at the wild violinist swaying in rapture. And push-hour ground to a halt. Devils, demons and screaming souls trapped like hornets in molasses. And Fithel sawed on.

Unctuous grinned in the shadows. It was going just as it should. Now he had to keep a sharp eye on the doors of the Sinful Service Stratascraper. As soon as the security demon came out to check what was going on, he, Phaust and Spruce would be in like greased ferrets. He was ready, eager and...

Suddenly something changed. The sound of Fithel's violin altered, ringing, chiming, as if something had been added. Unctuous's attention was snatched from the door. He watched in sheer amazement as another demon tugged a pair of Solstice Bill's Cymbalic Soul-Savers out into the open and joined the first. Talons tapped gently tinkling mystic rhythms, accompanying what passed as the melody. Then a short, almost wooden rippling sound erupted to the fore on the seventh of every bar as a pair of Pope Huansanshez's Miraculous Mission Maracas joined the score.

High on his balcony Screed chuckled to himself.

And buried deep within the foyer of the Sinful Service Stratascraper, at a spot approximately three inches north of the security demon's spleen, an urge sprouted. It propagated in response to the nurturing rhythms floating in through gaps in the swivel door. It swelled proudly, expanded and blossomed into a thousand cheering flowers of delight as the security demon reached under his desk, tucked a parchment-skinned drum under his vast armpit, and leapt through the door to join the growing racket.

Unctuous's eyebrows could scarcely squirm higher up his startled brow, as he watched the vast security demon leap into the now jigging throng, pounding away at his newly painted Mantric Drum. In fact, he almost forgot precisely why he was there.

But only almost.

221

Slapping the entranced cheeks of Phaust and Spruce in a suitably attention-grabbing paradiddle, he leapt out of the shadowed alley and slithered in through the swivel door. As planned, the foyer was empty. Barely containing their excitement and only just managing not to two-step across the floor, they sprinted the distance to the desk in seconds, vaulting it easily and crouching in the penumbric gloom.

And there was their prize. Wads of virginal Nognite parchment. Cartloads of it. With glee they snatched armfuls each, scurried round the desk and were out into the street in the nick of time. Around them the cacophony clattered, percussive purgatory overlaid with tom-cat screeching strings of notes. Fithel bucked and writhed beneath the fingerboard of his instrument, thrilling to the joy of his accompanists, revelling in their inspirational synergy. This was what he had died for all those years ago. He could go on for hours, reworking themes from a vast repertoire of jigs and reels and inserting the odd bit of simply appalling discordant junk on a whim and a G-string. In fact it was just as he was gearing up to launch such a volley of violent violining that he caught sight of a rapidly advancing clump of devils who were unmistakably Malebranche.

And then, suddenly, and extremely unhappily, he recognised the malevolent sneer of the Undertaker-in-Chief of Mortropolis. With a specially rehearsed scale of alarm Fithel sawed his final few notes, and punched the air four times to keep the rhythmic cacophony going, violin jutting from beneath his chin like an extra limb. Then he bowed and leapt off the hut roof in a perfectly executed back-flip and vanished into the shadows.

Screed, alarm bells ringing deep within him, scuttled along the balcony, leapt onto a nearby roof and vanished in a flurry of billowing cassock.

But this time the motion hadn't been completely covert. Unctuous, glancing back to see why Fithel had raised the alarm, glimpsed the unmistakable cassock and was gripped with an uncontrollable urge to embrace salvation. He dropped the heap of parchment, wheeled on his sandals and sprinted after Screed, hand raised, shouting, 'Er, excuse me, I'd really like a word!'

Seirizzim saw nothing of Fithel's final bows or Screed's exit; his attention was fixed on the happily nirvanic expressions smeared across the faces of the raucous crowd. His stomach heaved in disgust.

'What *is* this? Have you all lost your minds?' he screamed, staring in horror at the grinning, cymbal-clicking devils cavorting in the street. His voice somehow obliterated the sound of suddenly violinless noise. He stood, claws on hips, scowling the deepest of dark black scowls. 'Who started it?' he bellowed, and clicked two talons behind him alerting two of the larger Malebranche. They knew what to do. Instantly they were ready, on their hooftips, looming. As soon as the culprit was exposed, they'd have him.

'Well I'm waiting!' Seirizzim snorted, pawing the ground with an angry hoof.

Shaking their heads in confusion the mob turned and pointed to a spot on a small hut roof where up until a few seconds ago there had been ... oh, he's gone. Hastily and extremely nervously they secreted their percussive items about their persons and, heads down so as, not to be recognised, they dispersed as rapidly as seemed unlikely not to arouse too much suspicion.

'Oi! Come back here!' screamed Seirizzim over the sudden stampede.

No one paid any heed. In a matter of seconds all that remained in front of the Sinful Service Stratascraper was a large cloud of swirling dust, a crushed prayer wheel, an orange cushion cover and an extremely embarrassed-looking security devil trying desperately to hide a parchment-skinned drum,

'It just came over me,' he begged as Seirizzim scowled angrily at him. 'One minute I was sitting behind my desk, the next I just had to, er ... well, join in.'

223

Seirizzim's lip curled back. '"Just sitting"?' He took a hissing breath, '*Sitting*?' he bellowed and clicked his talons. A pair of Malebranche snatched the security devil in a blur of scales, dragging him to within an inch of Seirizzim's nostrils. 'Why weren't you working?' growled the Undertaker-in-Chief.

'Well, I ... there wasn't really anything...'

'You were bored and just happened to fancy a bit of a conga. That it?' sneered Seirizzim scathingly.

'Er, you *could* put it that way, but...'

The Undertaker-in-Chief clicked his talons again and the two Malebranche monsters dropped the security devil unceremoniously, grinding his nose into the dust.

Seirizzim grabbed Asmodeus firmly around the nape of the neck and led him up the steps and through the swivel door.

'See what happens when one introduces efficiency?' snarled Seirizzim. '*This* is the thanks I get? Damn creatures find time on their claws and think they've got to use it for enjoying themselves. Now call me old-fashioned if you wish, straight-laced, even, but ... I don't want filthy things like *that* happening in my kingdom! *UNDERSTAND?*'

Asmodeus nodded as best he could from his position pinned halfway up the wall on the end of Seirizzim's trembling arms.

'Double the workload!' he ordered, dropping the banker. 'Triple it! Let nobody call Mortropolis happy while *I'm* in charge! Anybody so much as smirks and they're off to the mines! Clear?'

The crumpled banker nodded from the floor.

Seirizzim whirled on his heels and sprinted up the stairs, sparks spitting off his hooves at every stride.

Asmodeus struggled upright, frowning deeply. Right now he was probably one of the least likely to end up in the brimstone pits of Rubor. But he was far from happy. Something about the expressions on those cavorting devils wasn't right. He was sure that this wasn't just simple happiness, oh no. This was worse. Much worse. Desperately he hoped that the events he had just witnessed weren't what a set of ancient documents had warned about centuries ago. There was only one way to find out. His pace quickened as he clattered down the corridor, out of a little known side entrance and away to the privacy of his own cavern.

Alleys away and running, the Pact-men minus Unctuous were well chuffed with the whole operation, although Fithel's playing had never before been quite so effective as a distraction. Still, mission accomplished. Three vast bundles of Nognite parchment acquired. Queazx should be happy now.

Sad to say, he wasn't.

He hobbled along at the back of the group of Pact-men, his face a picture of bereft desolation. Wailing quietly, he wrenched and tore at the fifty sheets of the first two-thirds of his Ninth Symphony for Violin, Comb and Parchment. It was no good. It wasn't fair.

Secretly he had known it still needed something else but had convinced himself it was simply a case of orchestration and notes. But now he knew what was missing. He had heard it, like some revelation erupting in his mind.

Queazx knew then that he had to write his Ninth Symphony for Violin, Comb and Parchment and Full Ensemble of Bangy, Clattery Things.

It had to be a hit.

Had to be.

Asmodeus erupted into his cavern, panting, spun around the doorframe, snatched a marble chair and shoved it against the closed portal. He needed privacy for this. No disturbances.

Taut with terror he dashed across the cavern, pushed a large wardrobe three feet to the left, fell to his knees and began scrabbling around inside the suddenly revealed secret cleft. His talons tapped and dismissed a host of boxes containing several thousand hundred-obul coins, they ignored a dozen or so cases of pure eight-hundred-year-old single fault lava and then he found it. His talon snaked up to its surfaces gripped it and opened it almost immediately. He squealed and swore as he pulled his talon out, shaking it and shoving it under his armpit.

He had forgotten it was that cold.

Whimpering, he wrapped a towel around his claw and tried again. In moments he had it out and on the table in the centre of his cavern.

Streams of condensation billowed off the rolled up parchment booklet, spilling over the edge of the table like some ghostly slo-mo waterfall.

Nervously he stared at the secret index and wondered if he should open it and look. What if it was true that its predictions had started? Did he really want to know? Or should he just put it away again and take his chances with the others?

The true banker inside him reached out a pair of tongs to open the first page. He had to know if it was happening as had been foretold.

Well, it was all a case of investment!

Why else would he have bought all five volumes of the Top Secret *Malleus Nugae* – The Deadly Hammer of Frivolousness? He had to protect his business interests. What was the point of spending several centuries building up veritable obul-factories only to have them destroyed in an instant? Oh no, forewarned is fore-armed. And he had the instruction manual. The *Malleus Nugae*.

What graphically presented dangers and perils it didn't contain weren't worth bothering about. Each of the five volumes was complete, telling of a different and terrifying take-over scenario. All dreadfully possible, all disturbingly real. Each one was accompanied by deadly detailed contingency plans.

Everyone in Helian knew that Heobhan was a terrible threat, a real and brooding presence simply waiting to sweep in and undermine and destroy with frivolousness. But before the *Malleus Nugae* was written, any discussion on the subject was limited to unanswerable questions, like how? Where would an attack begin? What weaponry would be employed? How would they be deployed?

Shortly after this dread realisation filtered into the populace of Helian and started bush fires of panic, it was decided that something should really be done about it. At the height of the paranoia, when the terror of swarms of invading Religionaires abseiling down through the stratasphere and spreading the Good News to innocent babies and children was boiling at its hottest, the manual had been commissioned.

After a couple of decades, five years of which was spent simply arguing about what it should be called, The Deadly Hammer of Frivolousness was published, in the secretive language of Ancient Tallian. It was as glorious as it was terrifying. Delicately curling illuminated letters described a series of five minutely detailed attack scenarios and depicted in beautiful horror how the forces of Heobhan would attempt to bend the citizens of Helian to the Will of Frivolousness.

And if they did succeed in their take-over? If Heobhan had their way? What nightmares did that hold?

It didn't bear thinking about.

Every devil would be forced to take up crocheting, every demon knitting, and all would be forced to practise eating tiny biscuits without dropping crumbs at coffee mornings. Bingo would be obligatory, whist a must and then ... and then, there were the beetle drives and bring and buy sales. Of course, attendance would be compulsory. Everyone would be there returning the fluffy stalag-mite litter tray holder they had bought at the last one. They wouldn't dare miss – nobody wanted to suffer the dreaded tombola.

Asmodeus shuddered as he thought about it all, trembling with terror. But it was all hypothetical. Simply an extrapolation of current thoughts and snippets of information. It would never really happen.

Or would it?

Centuries ago Foul Lord d'Abaloh, after discovering that the manual was in Ancient Tallian, had dismissed it with a casual flick of a talon and had it filed. And there it had lain until an acquaintance and fellow anti-frivolist had offered it for sale to Asmodeus

Now, whenever the banker was considering a new investment, ever-wary of the ever-present danger from above, he ensured that it was not situated in a likely strategic target area. Come the revolution he wouldn't be totally obul-less.

Was the time approaching now when his scheme would be put to the test? He knew that one of the Top Secret volumes had contained something about apparent spontaneous appearances of mass frivolousness, just as he had witnessed outside the Sinful Service Stratascraper, but where was it?

He forced open the parchment document and stared at the Ancient Tallian text, squinting as his eyes attempted to adjust to the strange words.

Cohntyntf.
Vohlyume Won ... Clerycal Warr Fayre.
An Ynntroduxynne.

Nope, wasn't in that bit. He was certain.

Vohlyume Too ... Opirrafhynne Papal Droppe.

Nope, that was a complete obliteration scenario. Take no prisoners. It was grim. Total decimation by frivolity bombs. Devils laughing themselves to death. Demons tickling each other, telling jokes and setting up jumble sales willy-nilly. Volumes three and four weren't right either.

And then he saw it and his memory clicked.

228

Vohlyume Fyvve...Ye Feleftele Ovyrrlode Finnaryo.

That was it. He remembered. Construction and deployment of Anti-Personnel Shrines. Strategic emplacement.
Lines of attack. Counter Iniquity Forces. Symptoms of
the Affected.

It was a sub branch of Clerical Warfare but more
subtle, more pernicious. None of the brutality of Cloister
Bomb attacks here, oh no. This was guerilla tactics. This
relied on the Dominum Effect – Enshrine and Conquer.
By specifically targeting figures of authority and high-
powered businessdevils with Anti-Personnel Shrines, the
whole of Helian society could be completely undermined
painlessly and without bloodshed.

It was simple. Once the top ten percent had seen the
light of an Anti-Personnel Shrine they would be willing
to do anything for the good of Heobhan. And once the
crumbling started, then everything would go down with
it.

Asmodeus knew that he had to have that one. Volume
Five. Now, where had he hidden it?

Like all good bankers, Asmodeus wasn't going to take
a chance by leaving all five volumes in one place. He had
them scattered all over Mortropolis, hidden in dark,
inaccessible places, away from prying eyes.

He squinted at a small piece of parchment scrawled
with claws written characters, grunted and knew where to
go. In a flurry of tongs, towels and furniture removals,
everything in his cavern was back to normal. He tugged
the marble chair away from the door and dashed out into
the street, heading back towards the towering stratascraper of the Sinful Service.

Nabob shook his head in frantic denial and waved his
claws helplessly at Flagit. 'You can't be serious? Tell me
you're making this up!' he pleaded.

'It was an easy mistake to make...'

'Mistake?' gagged Nabob. 'You kidnap six deities

229

thinking they're arms handlers and you call it an easy mistake? Oh, sure, happens every day, doesn't it? What could be more natural?'

Flagit didn't have a chance to answer. Nabob steam-rollered hysterically onward.

'You've got to do something with them. They can't stay here. Not in my cavern. They're dangerous, too risky and ... and besides, they're in the way. It was a mistake my ever getting you involved. I should've just stayed where I was, suffering and downtrodden, spat on by Seirizzim, scorned and humiliated. I knew where I was then.' He almost went misty-eyed.

'Have you quite finished revelling in a pool of stagnant self-pity?' sneered Flagit. Nabob looked up, surprised at Flagit's abruptly dismissive tone. 'Are you just going to sit there pathetically contemplating the navel of a miserable future, or are you going to give me a helping claw to defeat Seirizzim?'

'How can you think of that when there's "them" in there?' Nabob waggled a taloned thumb towards the door and the six deities beyond it.

'Precisely because they *are* in there,' grinned Flagit. 'You can't see beyond that, can you? Can't see past one little mistake...'

'Six little mistakes,' snapped Nabob.

'Alright, alright, let's not be so picky,' flustered Flagit irritably. 'Stop thinking about mistakes and think of the untapped dams of unforeseen opportunity-potential lurking, ready and available to us!'

'Yeah ... where?'

Flagit jerked his thumb through the door.

'Them?' spluttered Nabob.

Flagit nodded with the overwhelming air of smugness always called upon by folks moments before revealing the blindingly obvious to one who is deemed utterly stupid for not having spotted it themselves.

'The Dominum Effect!' grinned Flagit, dredging the name to the forefront of his mind. A name and definition

230

translated by the Good Reverend Screed.

'The what?'

'You've felt it.' Flagit stared at Nabob, trembling in a flurry of excitement. 'That sickening feeling of wanting to do someone a favour, or the urge to skip down the street, or untie a suffering deity.'

'Or let captured Reverends go?'

Flagit coughed embarrassedly. 'That too. You see how powerful it is? It's just like the document says, "Enshrine and Conquer". We *can* still do it. We can take Seirizzim down!'

'How? We need the Anti-Personnel Shrines. You said so,' whined Nabob, getting confused.

'That's what I initially thought, but now I know better. We can make it work with those guys out there.' Flagit grinned that "Trust me I know what I'm doing" grin.

Nabob cringed apprehensively, shrugged his shoulders and, knowing he would instantly regret it, he asked, 'How?'

A flash of victory raced across Flagit's face. 'Imagine if there were sudden outbreaks of frivolousness throughout the whole of Mortropolis. Just think of the chaos it would cause if devils started enjoying themselves, or started having coffee mornings and stuff, sitting around sipping and chatting instead of dashing around beating and thwacking...'

Nabob winced. 'Disgusting,' he mumbled in cold alarm. He thought back to his slapping Flagit about as he had held a tray of rock cakes.

'Panic would spread as devils suddenly started turning blind eyes and other cheeks on each other. Terror would run rife. Everyone would look to Seirizzim to solve it, and he'd be totally helpless. There'd be a vote of no-confidence in his rule for allowing it, he'd be kicked out! And Mortropolis would be leaderless!'

Nabob gasped.

'Enter two faithful Mortropolitan citizens who, at

231

great personal risk, step in and clear up the mess. These heroes just might get elected to Joint Undertakers-in-Chief.' Flagit's eyes glowed fervid crimson with excitement. 'Sound good?'

'What heroes? Who could they possibly be?'

Flagit sobbed, pulled himself together and barked, 'Who d'you think? Us! Idiot!'

Understanding rose slowly across Nabob's face like a particularly reluctant dawn.

'We do this right and Seirizzim'll be out by Firesday!' enthused Flagit. 'Agreed?'

Nabob nodded.

'Excellent. Grab your blankets and follow me.' Flagit leapt towards the door.

'Eh? Blankets? What for?' spluttered Nabob.

'Need a bit more ammunition,' Flagit grinned and turned the door handle.

'Oh no,' thought Nabob, crestfallen. 'Not again!'

Asmodeus clattered down the deepest corridors of the Sinful Service Stratascraper, screeched around corners and plunged on towards his secret hiding place. He simply had to reach that filing cabinet and find out if his suspicions were correct. His mind whirred with dread terror as the words 'Ye Feleftele Ovyrrlode Finnaryo' flashed across his vision in those oddly curling Ancient Tallian letters. Could it be true? Was 'The Celestial Overload Scenario' being enacted? Were they, even now, under covert attack from secretly garbed Religionaires? He shuddered as he rounded the final corner, screeched to a halt outside a large slate door and shouldered his way in. He lurched three paces in towards the spot where the filing cabinet should be, trying to recall if it was behind the third or the fourth drawer down that he had hidden the document all those years ago. It was on his fourth hoof-fall that he screamed, whirled on his heel and dashed back into the corridor to check his bearings. Terror and panic mingled as he realised that it was the right store cavern, especially chosen by him for its infrequency of use – nobody *ever* went in there. His heart in his mouth, he dashed back in and stared at the three vast monolithic blocks of obsidian filling the cavern, spots of lava-coloured light blinking regularly as molten rock pulsed beneath the glassy surface.

'No, no!' he cried and fell to his knees.

'Can I help you?' came a voice as a hatch opened in the side of the nearest of Moloch's Analytical Crystals.

Asmodeus cringed as he recogised him. 'No, no!' he repeated in a firmer voice. 'That should be three inches further back. Move it before Seirizzim hears or you'll be in trouble.' He whirled on his hoof, sprinted out of the cavernful of MAC's and into the corridor, his mind racing.

The filing cabinets had gone! Eradicated in Seirizzim's efficiency drive. Of all the caverns in the Sinful Service Stratascraper, Seirizzim had to choose that one! And he hadn't told Asmodeus.

His document had gone and in its place was a dull, nagging terror. Could he remember the exact attack patterns and symptoms of 'The Celestial Overload Scenario'? Could he recall the placement of Anti-Personnel Shrines that were detailed within? It was too much of a coincidence for him that outbreaks of frivolousness were happening and the document was missing. As a banker he didn't believe in coincidences. Accountancy didn't teach such things.

He was certain the invasion had begun.

But what should he do? Without evidence would Seirizzim believe him? Or would it end in tears before bedtime?

Only time would tell.

Time and the Deadly Hammer of Frivolousness.

Decisions, Decisions

A grunt of irritation floated in through the door of Tehzho Khonna's changing room and was accompanied by a curt rustling of stubborn crinoline. He looked up from the industry of fastening his pink astronomical-pattern bandana and cocked an interested ear. Another tut of annoyance filtered through the door, buzzed irritably and dissipated in a cloud of moody anger as his darling wife-to-be struggled ineffectually with the toggle of her wedding toga.

The crumpled mess of his bandana unravelled beneath his chin as he tugged on the wrong strand. He stood, red-faced and tense, feeling suddenly naked despite his charcoal-grey matrimonial dress toga and matching fedora. A veritable bush of an ostentatious toggle-hole bromeliad sprouted from just beneath his right ear.

A stifled screech of anger blasted its unignorable way into his room and shattered any remaining veneer of calm about his visage.

'What is it?' he snapped, kicking open the door and storming into the overly flowered room. The woman at the candlelit mirror screamed, wrapped her unfastened crinoline wedding toga hastily around her generous cleavage and bellowed at her husband-to-be.

'Getoutgetoutgetout!!' In a double time of hyperstitious panic, she leapt up from her stool and kicked the door shut.

The last thing Tehzho Khonna saw before the door broke his nose was an endearing flash of cornflower-blue suspenders and matching basque.

Fortunately for Nhupshyal, the Matrimonial Chaos Co-ordinator and Impending Disaster Assessor, the door missed him by a day and a half. But despite his years of crystal gazing experience his head jerked reflexively back from his polished ball and the images of tomorrow's possibility vanished in a puff of tinsel.

His right arm snaked out, snatched a peacock feather quill, jabbed it in the jar of ink and scribbled furiously on the already vast list of dangers to avoid at all costs. 'Groom sees Bride in dress beforehand ... A big no-no! Exceedingly damaging to nasal integrity and adds to cleaning bills. Recommend blindfolding Groom.'

Quickly he sketched a suitable binocular device in the margin and decided to sneak back to about fifteen minutes before that scene in order to determine if Miss Khrystal had in fact donned her cornflower-blue undergarments in a manner of the most omenically satisfying. He sighed as her naked body shimmered into view within the crystal. "Ahhh, sure it was a terrible job, but someone has to do it." A glint of warm candlelight played across the curve of her back as she reached out and plucked the basque from the bed.

At that moment of voyeuristic safety assessment, the patch of air above Nhupshyal's head was perhaps the only few litres in the whole of the Mountain City of Axolotl not to be charged with a sense of intense nervous excitement.

The hour of Tehzho Khonna's wedding to the delightful Khrystal Gehyz rumbled ever nearer and in its bowwave, like pernicious dolphins of madness, surfed the seeds of hysteria. Ever since Axolotl's most eligible bachelor had fixed his roving eye on that particular thirty-eight inches of anatomy and shocked his faithful (and mainly female) public with that sudden announcement, the whole population had been hurled into a seething flurry of overtime divinations and predictions.

Women who had set more than just their caps at him in decades of eyelid-fluttering worship stormed into every marital diviner's offices and demanded instant consultancies. Unsurprisingly, the main subjects of snubbed interest were directed at the predicted longevity of the forthcoming union and the identity of likely future spouses. There were many tears before bedtime from hopelessly bereft would-be Mrs Khonnas. The finest marital prophets in the city foretold of a happy thirty years of suitably snuggly bliss for the new pair, the happiness only being shattered by the birth of three strapping sons.

Elsewhere, jammed in tiny blacked-out rooms or huddled over the smouldering embers of a dying fire; bow-eyed from hours spent staring through scrying crystals, or with wrists failing from the repetitive strain of hurling omenical dice at distant walls, prophets, seers and digital diviners foretold, foresaw and calculated. They predicted a million different outcomes of the interference of the hand of fate and extracted fateful flies from the vaseline of a perfect day.

The foul-luck and bloodied broken nose brought down upon the cheery celebrity couple from Tehzho's chance sighting of Khrystal had been averted due to Nhupshyal's vigilance. And his team had also re-arranged the route of the wedding procession in order to avoid being crossed by a particularly malignant black mantric gecko which would be roaming about tomorrow morning. They had foreseen the weather and rescheduled the events to take full advantage of a convenient three-hour gap in the clouds. Everything was running along tickety-boo. All they had to do now was check the wedding list.

Nhupshyal blew a blast on his official whistle, spun on his swivel seat and came nose to midriff with the predictive might of his Chaos Assessment Team. It was always satisfying quite how punctual they were. Almost as if they knew just when he was going to blow his whistle. They did.

'Okay men, down to...' In almost perfect unison they turned on their heels in a flurry of togas and marched off down three flights of stairs, past the second on the right, swung left and let themselves in to a vast cavern of a room crammed full of gaudily wrapped gifts for the happy couple.

The usual things were there: authentic towelling hair-dryers, bamboo scatter cushions, his'n'hers terracotta shaving mugs and matching stand, his'n'hers alpaca bath robes with complementary sink robes and cistern warmers ... everything the newly-wed couple could possibly want to make a hovel a home. There was even rumoured to be a little something for that extra-special society dinner party a complete set of sixteen plaice settings made from *real* plaice. But that was just a rumour.

Nhupshyal marched up to the mound and stared at it. He knew Tehzho Khonna was popular ... but *this* popular? Quickly he estimated the amount of work, then he declared, 'Right, split into two rows with a gap down the middle, each side ready to handle half of the gifts...'

His voice drifted away as he turned and saw his team sitting, ready to begin.

'Well. Get on with it then. You know what to do,' he ordered half-heartedly. There were times when he wondered precisely what he was there for.

The rest of his team knew exactly what they were there for. Post-packaging stress phenomena. Anybody who was anybody in Axolotl knew all about it.

It was common knowledge that a gift wrapped by a person of less than joyous temperament would create a concealed time-bomb of grief and misery. At some point in the future all the bottled detestation would spring forth in a sudden bolt of misuse. An irritably wrapped knitting kneedle could rear and smite one in the eye. A footstool, packaged decades previously by a tempestuous donor, could suddenly move three feet to the side and cause a nasty sprained ankle.

It was the job of the Chaos Assessment Team to seek out such packages and defuse them. And today they had their work cut out since most of the women in Axolotl held more than a passing loathing for a certain Miss Khrystal.

Enthusiastically Nhupshyal dashed up and down the gap between the two halves of his team and handed out presents to each of them, scattering half-heard words of encouragement as he went. His Dangerous Package Diviners, as one, held parcels to foreheads and began to chant, sending out their mental ferrets to track down and flush out any residue of anger held within.

It was only as the cavernous present room filled with somnolent chanting that a terrifying truth hit Nhupshyal.

He had forgotten something vital. The traditional blessing from Moh Linnekx, the Divine One-in-Command Over Appliances of Domesticity.

With a whimper he fell to his knees, clasped his hands together, and landed face down in Personal Abasement Position Number Fifty-Nine(d). He was chanting hard before he reached the prone, pleading with the great Moh Linnekx to appear and shower profuse blessings and faucets of fortune upon them and the happy couple to whom the presents were addressed.

There was a whirling whine in the air, the atmosphere filled with the taste of ozone and suddenly there was a blinding flash of light.

'Hello,' said Moh Linnekx to the prone and blinking Nhupshyal. 'I have come to ... mmmmm ... mmmhhhh!'

The pair of blanket-bound demons which sprang suddenly out of the pile of presents, snatched him around the neck and demon-handled him down a smoking hole in the floor, didn't give him a chance to expand on that.

A second later the entire Chaos Assessment Team was in the corridor, fingernails in mouths, trembling, one thought uppermost in their collective mind.

Somebody must have *really* had it in for the happy couple if *that* was anything to go by.

*

The Very ex-Reverend Unctuous III sprinted wildly through the complex nets of streets, alleys and stalagmite bored passages that was Mortropolis in hot pursuit of the man from the Haranguist Mission. His heart beat frantically as he wheeled around corners, dashed across intersections and plunged blindly onward. He knew he had to catch the Mostly Reverend Vex Screed. That cassocked man was his way out, the key to his release from this sulphurous, scalding pit of despair, his path to reincarnation.

If Unctuous had actually been a real Pact-man then perhaps it wouldn't have been so bad down here. If he had actually sold his soul for his one wish, he could possibly have coped. But he had remained utterly bereft of anything even remotely approaching his prized dream – a congregation.

It was a sad indictment of the state of religious belief in the Kingdom of Cranachan, from which he had been so unceremoniously plucked, that nobody had even so much as just popped in to the Chapel of St Absent the Regularly Forgotten. Decades he'd been waiting for a solitary worshipper, and all to no avail.

All he wanted was a second chance up there. Things would be different this time. He wouldn't just wait around for them to come knocking at the chapel doors, he'd go out and get them. Yes, that's it, he'd herd them in and ram the Good News down their throats whether they liked it or not. He wouldn't be ignored in his second coming. Now, if he could just catch up with that Screed...

He spun around a narrow alley corner, squealed and screeched to a halt as an expanse of black cassock erupted from a shadow and snatched him around the throat.

'You following me?' barked Screed angrily, pinning Unctuous to the far side of the alley.

'No ... no, er ... yes ... well, not yet, but I'd like

239

to...' spluttered Unctuous, his thoughts confused at the sudden interruption of a tightening fist around his windpipe.

'"Like to" what?' snapped Screed.

'Er ... like to, your Reverence?' hazarded Unctuous hopefully. It wasn't the right answer.

Screed tightened his grip and frowned. He'd learned over his extensive years as a mercinary that danger lurked down dark alleys. Okay, so he wasn't sure if dark crimson alleyways were any more or less dangerous than the more traditional penumbric shades of twilight he was used to, but better safe than sorry.

'What you following me for?' he growled.

'Er, I'd like to follow you, if you get my drift?' Unctuous attempted a smile of reassurance. It didn't really work.

Screed scowled at Unctuous's habit. 'Last leader let you down, eh?' he sneered.

'N ... no. Lack of congregation ... er, look, it's a long story and my throat's hurting a bit. D'you mind...?' He looked wistfully at the floor and dangled his feet in a manner he hoped was as meaningful as it was endearing.

Screed grunted and dropped him.

'Phew, you always that hard on new recruits?' croaked Unctuous, wondering if a severe rethinking of his baptismal techniques could be in order.

'Only ones who chase me down dark alleys. Now what *do* you want?'

'I told you,' sulked Unctuous, feeling hurt. 'I want to follow you. See, I caught one of your more recent, er, addresses and well, I felt quite inspired and...'

Screed, despite his suspicions, smiled inside. 'How inspired?'

'Oooh, very!'

'Enough to go out and buy a complete set of blue Wonderwear – One Size Fits All?'

'Yes, yes, yes, definitely,' grovelled Unctuous.

240

'So, where is it?'

'Er, what?'

'The complete set of blue Wonderwear – One Size Fits All, which you were *so* inspired to go out and buy?'

'Ah.' Unctuous looked at his toes and fiddled with his thumbs. 'Well, I looked but I couldn't find any, see?'

Screed's forehead wrinkled like an overweight shitsu and he leant threateningly forwards.

'B ... but I would've bought one. Honest.' Unctuous tried his endearing grin again.

'And what about a pair of Solstice Bill's Cymbalic Soul-Savers?'

Unctuous shrugged. 'Guess I must've missed that bit. But I'm really sure that they're very good.'

Screed tutted, turned and swept away down the alley. It wasn't worth wasting valuable preaching time on this buffoon. Big crowds, that was what he needed. He shouldn't be frittering his time away talking at individuals. He knew damn well that from a handy vantage point high above a captive audience, utilising only slightly more effort than he was currently, he could convert hundreds in one shimmering instant of glory.

For a brief second Unctuous stood baffled, watching the cassock sweep imperiously away, vortices of smoke circling around its bottom corners. What had he said? What had he done wrong?

Then suddenly he was dashing after Screed again. 'Tell you what, er, slow down. Why don't you tell me all about them Solsty Billy Whatsits. I'm sure I'll really believe once you've explained all about them, please. Hello? Could you slow down a bit...?'

It was Maulday morning and the miserable shuffling of parchmentwork which constantly underpinned the sighs of discontent in the Immigration Department of the

241

Sinful Service was shattered by the clattering of hooves and the kicking open of the door. As if he had been dragged in on some foul hurricane, Seirizzim followed, high-kicking joyously. The wide grin of excitement plastered across his face foretold of terrible omens.

'Stop what you're doing. Now!' he bellowed across the infernal office, revelling in the echoing authority of his voice. 'I said now!' he snarled, suddenly flicking a boilpoint pen out of a nearby clerk's claw with a deadly swipe of his talons. A sheaf of parchment cascaded floorward with autumnal untidiness. 'Leave it!' barked Seirizzim, talons planted firmly on his hips, annoyance fixed securely on his face like a surgeon's mask. 'I have an announcement. Today parchment is dead! Follow me!'

Nabob shook his head at the back of the office and swallowed nervously. This didn't sound good.

Seirizzim whirled on his hooves and stomped out towards the door. 'Well come on then.' He beckoned, a curling talon tickling the air around the doorframe. 'There's nothing to be afraid of. Put your boilpoints down and follow! Now!' He giggled secretly behind his claw as the baffled clerks stood and trailed after him, shrugging scaly shoulders.

The only sound was an occasional confused mutter, the clatter of cloven hooves and the roaring whoosh of the underfloor heating as Seirizzim led the clerks down labyrinthine passage after plunging stairwell, deeper into the bowels of the Sinful Service Stratascraper. And all the time their curiosity grew, fuelled by the overwhelming belief that an imminent meeting with yet another of Seirizzim's efficiency developments was definitely on the cards.

On this they were right, but as to the extent to which it would affect their working conditions they were utterly wrong. Only Nabob began to suspect what they were about to see as he began to recognise the familiar route they were being led along.

Ushering the Immigration Clerks on, like some wild inchoate piper before a pack of horned rats, Seirizzim halted in front of a secured slate door, grinned dangerously and turned the key. And Nabob gulped in alarm.

In a second, Seirizzim had vanished into the darkened interior, beckoning enthusiastically. The clerks filed obediently inside, blissfully unaware of the twelve bulky members of the Malebranche which appeared as instructed from a side corridor and stood waiting with ready malevolence.

Nabob wasn't precisely certain why he did it but suddenly he fell to his knees and scuttled forward, diving towards an even darker patch of shadow between two vast crystalline shapes.

'Gentledemons,' declared Seirizzim under the wraps of darkness. 'I have a little surprise.' He flicked out a talon, tugged on a lever and immediately the room warmed to the ruddy glow of lava-lamps. The Immigration Clerks gasped as three vast obsidian slabs swam into view, their surfaces imposingly smooth, unnervingly large.

Nabob squeezed himself tighter into the gap, tugging his hooves out of sight.

'Behold!' shouted the Undertaker-in-Chief of Mortropolis. 'The future! The end of work as you know it.' A cold, cruel grin slunk across his face as he turned and shouted. 'Moloch. Fire them up!'

There was a croaked grunt of affirmation from somewhere far behind and other levers were tugged, redirecting streams of hyperheated lava towards the innards of the trio of Moloch's Analytical Crystals.

In a few seconds the tell-tale pulsing of tiny crimson spots of light showed that the newly installed MACs were ready and waiting to analyse. And the temperature between the two crystals rose rapidly as lava surged through the plumbed circuitry within. Gradually Nabob began to toast.

'Welcome to the new Immigration Department!' grinned Seirizzim. 'You are witnessing a new crimson age of efficiency. From now on, all new clients' respective eternities of torment will be decided here. Their myriad differing wickednesses and heinous crimes will be assessed, correlated against a newly rehashed malfeasance index and fitted to a cocktail of personally tailored torture regimes with devastatingly efficient and faultless perfection. No more demon error! Like it?'

There was a nervous shuffling of hooves.

'Well?' sneered Seirizzim over the whooshing of lava through the pipes.

'It will be the envy of the whole of Helian,' oozed one of the shrewder clerks, attempting to worm his way into whatever passed as Seirizzim's good books. 'And anything which increases jealousy, and envious feelings should be cheered. Hip hip...'

Under other, less pressing circumstances Nabob would have spat derisively at the fawning comments. Right now he just sweated profusely with nerves and heat.

'I'm so glad you feel that way,' grinned Seirizzim, patting the glinting surface of the nearest MAC. 'I mean, it would be somewhat unfortunate if any of you harboured doubts as to the advantages these will bring Mortropolis. Already these crystals can assess and process ten times more damned souls than you lot put together, firmly establishing Mortropolis as *the* torture capitol of Helian. With this leap of efficiency Sheytahn won't ever catch up!'

'Hoorah!' cheered the shrewd one in a voice far more confident than he really felt.

Nabob dearly wished he could have had the freedom to jam a talon or two down that sycophantic throat. But right now his mind was rattling with a series of worryingly uncomfortable calculations. With such an increase in soul traffic, wouldn't there have to be a concomitant increase in fuel supplies in order to provide the correct levels of pain and anguish for which

Mortropolis was justifiably famed? A nastily smirking question slunk over the horizon. Where would this extra fuel come from? The ground beneath his hooves suddenly seemed far less secure than he would really have liked it to be.

'Of course,' continued Seirizzim with almost agonising nonchalance, 'none of these advances would have been necessary if it wasn't for your continued levels of operational, er, efficiency. And so it is with this in mind that I am delighted to announce your new positions as Permanent On-site Substance Providers.'

'As what?' panicked Nabob silently.

'Starting immediately!' announced Seirizzim with the glinting tone of relish which Nabob had long since learned meant trouble. 'Guards!' yelled Seirizzim.

And instantly Nabob knew he had been right. On cue twelve vast demons of the Malebranche swarmed in through the door and glared at the ex-Immigration Clerks.

'If you would care to follow these gentledemons, they will escort you to your new area of employment,' commanded Seirizzim in a way that somehow made it impossible to refuse.

'Er ... just one question,' spluttered the only vocal clerk. 'Just what substance is it we will be providing?'

Nabob was, for once, grateful. It was bad enough finding out that the Immigration Department was no more, but not knowing what a Permanent On-site Substance Provider was would have driven him mad with burning curiosity.

He could almost hear Seirizzim's shudder of evil delight as someone asked the very question he was hoping they would. 'Well, that just depends on which part of the mines you end up in, doesn't it?'

'Mines?' mouthed the clerk in a paroxysm of panic and Nabob in a rack of relief.

'Yes, mines. The Lava and Brimstone Mines of Rubor, to be precise. Odd, but that *is* where lava and

245

brimstone come from,' sneered Seirizzim, oozing pedantic sarcasm and revelling in every moment of this mass job transfer. 'I really don't mind too much which you choose to provide.'

'Wait a minute! You can't just ship us off to Rubor like that...' protested the clerk.

'Oh no?' Seirizzim leant forward as if interested. 'And why ever not?'

'I ... er, we've got contracts with the Immigration Department and...'

'Ah, well that's a bit of a snag right now. See, Immigrations doesn't exist any more, so your contract's not really worth that much.'

'But there was no warning!'

'All this was announced last month on infernal mail. I sent this note here outlining all the details...' He tugged a scrap of parchment out of his pocket and waggled it victoriously at the crowd of clerks. 'Everything you need to know is in here and ... Oh dear, how silly of me. I seem to have forgotten to post it. Ah well, never mind. Rubor is ever so nice at this time of year, once you get used to the smell and the heat and the cramped, agonising working conditions. Do enjoy yourselves!' He flicked his arrow-headed tail in a flurry of command and the twelve Malebranche leered forward, menacing the ex-clerks with very large clubs. Dripping efficiency, they herded them out of the MAC room double time.

Ostensibly alone suddenly, in the relative silence of the room, Seirizzim hurled back his head and laughed. Efficiency, how he loved it. The perfect excuse for the ultimate cruelty!

And now it was time to head off to the banks of the River Phlegethon for part two of his brilliantly integrated automatic soul processing system.

There was a brief clattering of hooves and he was gone, leaving nothing but a wild vapour trail of cackling victory and a terrified Nabob.

Every deity on the Top Table of Manna Ambrosia's stared at the heavily overladen serving trolley and counted the number of remaining plates. The angelic waitress fluttered to a halt and fluffed her wings nervously. It had happened again. There were left-overs. Quickly, and with the utmost surreptitiousness, she glanced back over her wing at the rest of the tables, and breathed a sigh of relief. At least the left-overs weren't her fault; every deity had a laden plate before them steaming gently.

From a lower table a terrified deity watched the scene unfold, swathed in a desperate mood of assumed guilt. Would they blame him for the empty seats? thought Uscher irrationally. It was his responsibility to show all comers to their correct seat, but was it his fault if everybody didn't turn up?

'Seven?' spluttered Scran at the Top Table. 'It's getting worse! Where are they?'

'Somewhere else,' offered Lush helpfully.

'What? They can't possibly be eating anywhere else. There isn't anywhere else!'

Uscher's ears strained to hear what they were talking about. Were they blaming him?

'Maybe they're not eating at all,' continued Lush.

'What?' snapped Scran, offended. 'Not eating? What d'you mean?'

'Er, perhaps they've gone on a diet.'

Scran clamped his hands over his ears and squealed. 'Don't *say* that. Don't even think it!' If there was one thing that really annoyed and terrified him, it was dieting. To him it was a real slap in the face. Deliberately refusing to eat? It just wasn't natural.

Still, he thought as he stared at the septet of steaming servings, one god's diet is another one's portion. Today, for the second day running he would have second helpings. Grinning, he raised his fork and readied himself to tuck in.

The anticipatory pre-prandial silence was shattered by a minor deity leaping to his feet and plunging his hand high into the air. 'It's not my fault!' shouted Uscher in fervent panic. 'If they don't turn up I can't be expected to show them to their seats, can I?'

Scran's fork trembled in mid-air.

'In fact,' continued Uscher in a high-pitched voice, 'I should be thanked for ensuring that all the correct places are filled by those who have turned up. It's not easy, you know, matching bums to seats day in day out...'

Scran stared at his cooling lunch and his stomach growled. 'This isn't the time to be discussing the absence of certain members. Bring this up again later, will you? Say during "Any Other Business".'

Another deity leapt to his feet. 'That'll have to be carried out on another occasion, since today's session has already been tabled and minuted,' blurted Lofax, He-Who-Is-in-Charge of Scheduling, Meetings and Vital Appointments. 'Although if it is raised as an Emergency Issue demanding immediate attention then it could be discussed as early as next week. Of course, the necessary channels will have to be...'

Scran was dribbling in anticipation of his lunch, his fork hovering. 'Let's sort this out later,' he whined.

'Of course we could raise this issue in an Extraordinary After-Lunch Meeting, but that would mean rescheduling Any Other Business. Such rescheduling would have to be discussed at open meeting at a prior time to be arranged at the next Agenda Scheduling Meeting,' officiated Lofax.

Gravity and Hunger got the better of Scran's fork. In a single fluid movement it arced into his nectaried pasta and swooped up towards his salivating mouth.

Right now he couldn't care if there were seven deities AWOL. They'd turn up again sooner or later. In fact, if another one was to join their absent ranks it would probably be better for everyone's digestion.

Lofax continued to spout screeds of officiousness to the suddenly deaf ears of the devouring deities.

Sot rubbed his chin thoughtfully and desperately wondered what was going on with his Believer Beacon. Was it currently burning bright with the luminous ferocity of thousands of converted souls?

He shifted uneasily in his seat. Had his scheme been detected? Had the beer-swilling members of the Parangelic Service spilled suspicious beans after the disappearance of the freshly killed Screed? Could it be that the seven deities were investigating it?

He chewed on his pasta and hoped he was wrong.

Vortices of dense smoke curled up around the flapping corners of Screed's cassock as he strode unstoppably down endless alleys of downtown Tumor. Unctuous skittered in his wake, his sandals marking double time to Screed's imperious strides.

'Look, I really can believe as well as the next soul, you know,' wheedled Unctuous. 'In fact, I can probably do better, actually.'

'Go away.'

'Go on. Tell me to believe that black is white. I'm sure I can. Just try me.'

'Go *away.*'

'Mmmm, really nice white cassock you've got on there. Such a gorgeous shade. Very rich and what's more it won't show the dirt much...'

'*Go* away!'

'Don't you just really love all these white demons that are kicking about down here...'

Unctuous whisked around a sharp corner, trotting eagerly two feet behind the billowing edge of Screed's cassock.

Moh Linnekx wrestled his way out from underneath a large blanket, coughed and looked around in total confusion, his hair wildly tousled. Lava-lamps swam into

249

view just ahead of the roughly hewn walls of the cavern and the unwelcome attention of six vaguely familiar faces staring at him. One, plastered with a mixed look of sheer horror and delight, stared at the mess of Moh's hair and calculated the huge styling potential it held. Uncontrollably Dahls'soon leapt across the cavern, whipping out an ancient bone comb with a flourish.

'What the...? Where am I? What's going on?' he shrieked and tried to sit up. 'Get off!' he snapped at Dahls'soon.

'Management Course, my hearty companion. Welcome aboard,' grunted Khlyde authoritatively in his pumpkin pyjamas.

'What? What question's that an answer to? Leave my fringe alone.'

'All three.'

Moh Linnekx shook his head, much to the consternation of Dahls'soon, who frowned and slapped him irritably. 'Get off. No, no that can't be right. I was called on to bless all the prezzies for some wedding in Axolotl and...'

'No need to tell me more, shipmate. They came at you from behind like a squally tempest and bundled you down a hole. Next thing you know you're here.'

'How d'you know that?' spluttered Moh Linnekx, staring at the peaked-capped deity around the whirling arms of his uninvited hair stylist.

'Apart from a few subtle details our courses have charted the same route.'

'What?' squeaked Moh Linnekx, a look of panic flashing across his face.

'Oh, it's not *that* bad,' reassured Dahls'soon, stepping back and admiring her latest handiwork. 'In fact in some ways, dare I say it, the service is better here. Food's not as good, but, ahhh well, can't have everything. Hmmmm, just a little more curling on the top, I think. Has anyone ever told you how thoroughly enjoyable your hair is to plait?'

'No, er, just stop that, will you,' he objected half-heartedly and turned back to Khlyde. 'But why us? What have we done to deserve this?'

'Nothing special. We was just in the wrong corner at the wrong time. I reckon we're just the first lucky ones,' grumbled Pugil miserably.

'What for? What are we supposed to be doing?' spluttered Linnekx, becoming more confused as the answers raised more questions than they quelled.

'Weren't you paying *any* attention at Bhelbynn's little chat the other day?' grumbled Khlyde who, since he had been there the longest, with the obvious exception of that Screed chappie, had assumed the mantle of authority figure. And besides, as he had pointed out already to the other captives, he was the only one with a peaked cap and all leaders should possess a peaked cap. Just wasn't nautically correct otherwise.

Linnekx shook his head again and received a sharp crack from the fussing stylist to the gods. 'What talk? I ... er, I might have been called to work. There seems to have been a spate of weddings recently. Mind you, it's always the same. None for ages, then, whoosh, dozens of them all at once. And it always seems to coincide with spring. Don't know what's so special about it ...'

'Hormones,' offered Dehtol helpfully.

'Eh? Is that what the talk was about?' spluttered Linnekx, losing the thread again and deciding that he really ought to have started all this by taking notes on one of his special Divinely Erasable Jotter and Memory Aids.

'No, no, no,' growled Khlyde. 'He'd come up with some weird ideas of how to get us working better ...'

'And you reckon this is one of them?'

'Oooh yes, dear,' agreed Dahls'soon. 'I wouldn't have had the thrill of running my comb through your curly locks otherwise, would I? Did you know that you've got a few split ends here? I don't think I've set your hair in the last thirty centuries, have I?'

'Hmmm, true enough,' admitted Linnekx grudgingly. 'So, *you're* alright. But what is it we're supposed to be doing, eh?'

'Ahhh, well, that's the snag, see? Head forward a little. That's better,' answered Dahls'soon around a mouthful of clips.

'What snag?' grunted Linnekx, his chin jammed on his sternum uncomfortably.

'We haven't a clue,' confessed Khlyde, the wind seeming to evaporate from his sails. 'Nobody seems to want to tell us.'

'Well, there you are,' grunted Linnekx. 'That's it.' He slapped Dahls'soon's hands away and a complex plait unravelled unceremoniously.

Six faces with varying degrees of hirsuitness stared bewilderedly back. 'What's it?' they chorused.

'Why we're here. It's to teach us how to make decisions. Isn't it obvious?'

The headscratching silence told him it wasn't.

'Decisions, hmmmmmm. Could be right, you know,' mused Khlyde rubbing his chin. 'We could run that idea up the mast and see how it flies, but...'

'Well, I ... possibly...' grunted Dehtol, twiddling his thumbs. 'Sounds a bit hasty, don't you think? Bit radical.'

'I'm not so sure...'

'Seems a bit unnecessary...'

'We don't need teaching that, do we?'

Ineffectual hedgings surrounded the septet of deities and filled the cavern.

'I think that answers my question,' tutted Linnekx.

'Well, I...' began Khlyde before being rudely interrupted by a swift hoof kicking open the door and two devils dragging in another blanket-swathed figure.

Almost casually Flagit and Nabob hurled their latest captive across the cavern and Flagit vanished into the kitchen for a swift half of lava.

'I'm telling you, we haven't got time,' whined Nabob

miserably as the door shut and he flaked out dramatically across his pebble bag. 'I heard what I heard! If Seirizzim carries on at this rate Mortropolis'll be deserted by the end of the week. We haven't got the time to fetch another two or three or however many it is you want. And besides, I'm feeling kind of tired with all this hard work. It's not easy deitynapping...'

'Shut it, you wimp,' growled Flagit through the door as their latest captive unravelled himself from the blankets and stared about in flustered shock, smoothing his thoroughly wrinkled robes.

'Oh, darlings,' wailed the newly arrived Rahmani, Deity Over Fashion Statements, Dress Sense and Decorum. 'Don't look at me. Simply don't look! I'm in *too* much of a state!' Fluffs of ancient blanket clung to his designer toga. Desperately he tried to pull them free.

'Don't worry yourself about that,' soothed Moh Linnekx. 'Use this!' He produced a small brush from a pouch and handed it over to Rahmani. 'Just brush away those unsightly fluffs in seconds. See! It also removes unwanted nasal hair and collects it in a handy easy-clean compartment.'

Rahmani winced as he caught sight of Khlyde dressed in his pumpkin pyjamas and peaked cap. Did he have no sense of Fashion? Pumpkin went out last century. Sleepwear should be avocado. Avocado, or nothing. Although, he was grateful that it wasn't the latter right now.

Suddenly, and before Rahmani could offer his latest fashion advice, the kitchen door was kicked open and Flagit lurched out carrying two frothing halves of lava. 'Get that down your neck,' he growled and thrust one at Nabob. In one gulp it had vanished.

'We've got to start soon, otherwise we'll be on our own,' reiterated Nabob, wiping the back of a scaly claw across his mouth. 'Eight's enough, isn't it?'

Flagit grunted irritably, tugged the secret parchment

253

document out of a drawer and riffled swiftly through it with the tongs.

Baffled, the deities looked on, wondering if this was in fact part of their decision-making course. Could this be a demonstration of how it should be done?

Flagit peered intently at each of the sheets of vapouring parchments, checking, adding up. And then finally he pulled out a single sketchily drawn map of Mortropolis.

'Well?' pestered Nabob. 'Have we got enough of them? Only my hooves are killing me. It's cold up there and...'

'Shut up, I'm thinking,' snapped Flagit. 'If we assume that each one of these deities is producing at least the same amount of shrine waves as your average field issue Anti-Personnel Shrine, then ... er, we need four more for maximum effect according to this map, here. See? It specifies twelve places where they should be placed. We need a dozen deities strategically positioned in order to start the Dominum Effect.'

'Four more?' squeaked Nabob. 'But it'll take ages to get them! We haven't got time. Look, those plans of yours assume that Mortropolis is full. If we hang around much longer than everyone who's anyone will be down the mines in Rubor!'

'Just 'cause you nearly ended up in there doesn't mean...'

'We've got to hurry up, I tell you. Time is...'

'This says we need a dozen for maximal effect. So we get a dozen. Clear?'

'And meanwhile Seirizzim's sending everyone down the mines! What's the point of trying to get a vote of no-confidence going if there's no one there to have no confidence?' spluttered Nabob and tried to work out if all the double negatives cancelled each other out.

'Ah, but there's us. *And* don't forget Foul Lord d'Abaloh!' Flagit snatched the parchment map off the table and waggled it between the teeth of the tongs. 'This says put twelve Anti-Personnel Shrines out, trigger them and, lo, they see the light, and we step in!'

Nabob's face fell as a worrying realisation hit him. 'We put twelve Shrines out?'

Flagit nodded and pointed to the deployment map enthusiastically, his claw tracing the fastest route.

Nabob shook his head very slowly. 'Er, I hate to widdle on anyone's bonfire here, especially our own grand one, but, in case it has escaped your notice, we haven't got any Anti-Personnel Shrines.'

'I've explained this to you before. Weren't you listening?' Flagit waggled a claw at the group of deities behind him. 'It's all a case of shrine waves. They are just as good at producing more than enough shrine waves to have the desired...'

'But ... but in case you hadn't noticed, they've got legs!' spluttered Nabob incredulously, wondering why he hadn't thought of it before.

'So?' shrugged Flagit.

'So! Are you really going to trust them to stand precisely on those spots? They'll walk away, I tell you!' shouted Nabob, trembling as he saw the entire plan beginning to crumble before his mind's eye.

'Well, er ... so we'll just tie them up,' hedged Flagit, suddenly feeling very uncomfortable.

'Oh sure, very good. And you really think nobody's going to notice a dozen bound deities turning up on street corners all of a sudden? Don't you think someone in the Malebranche would just be a smidgen suspicious?'

'Er ... we could disguise them,' suggested Flagit unconvincingly.

'Are you mad? I don't know how you talked me into this.'

'I talked *you* in to this? You came to me, remember?' snarled Flagit, bridling angrily.

'I did you a favour. Don't tell me you were enjoying your community service. You'd still be there if it wasn't for me.' Nabob jumped to his hooves and stood inches from Flagit, snorting heavily.

'I wish I'd never laid eyes on this damned map,' growled Flagit through clenched fangs and a tangible veil of frustration. 'Life was stacks simpler before it!' In a fit of anger he flung the parchment across the room.

It spun wildly, looped once and swooped floorwards, skittering to a gentle halt before the eight captive deities. Fourteen eyes focused simultaneously on it from beneath baffled brows. Dahls'soon squinted at Rahmani's beard and wondered what she could do with a few specially co-ordinated highlights.

'That for us?' whispered Khlyde, pointing at the map.

'Suppose so,' answered Moh Linnekx, staring suspiciously at it through a handy compact opera glass which he just happened to produce from his pouch.

'Are you sure?' asked Fleeh timidly. 'I mean, no-one's told us to look at it, have they? They might take offence if we just start squinting at it too closely. I don't want to get into a fight.'

'Me neither,' agreed Rahmani. 'Those guys' talons could really ruin my toga.'

'Let's look then,' growled Pugil. 'I could do with a scrap. Haven't had a decent bout of fisticuffs for way too long.'

'They wouldn't just fling it over here if they didn't really want us to look, would they?' asked Khlyde.

'Yeah, he's right. Nobody's told us *not* to look at it,' agreed Linnekx.

'But is that the important issue here?' asked Rahmani, suddenly getting into the spirit of the supposed management course. 'Is the looking at the document the lesson, or is it the collective decision-making process about whether we look, or not? To peek, or not to peek that is the quest...'

'Shut up,' grunted Khlyde, before stepping forward, bending over and peering at the deployment map. In seconds Linnekx and Pugil were with him, rubbing their chins in collective confusion.

'What's it mean?' asked Khlyde as curiosity fizzed amongst the other five.

Pugil shrugged, grunted baffledly and suddenly it was too much for the rest of them. As one, they bounded eagerly over to the piece of puzzling parchment and huddled closely around it.

And odd, utterly unexpected things began to happen.

The purple tongues of the shrine waves hovering above their heads struck each other, entwined and bounced off, colliding immediately with another, and another. And as more shrine waves were fed in, the air above the eight deities began to glow in a halo of purple piety.

The shrine detector started to twitch wildly, rattling noisily and sliding along the floor away from the synergistically amplifying aura of shrine waves.

Flagit shrieked in wonder as the shrine detector fell over and skidded into the wall as if it had been hurled there. His eyes flashed to the point from which it had been hurled. His slitted pupils dilated in shock.

The purple cloud hovering above the eight deities glowed deeply and crackled with an eerie ominousness. Curiously the air began to smell of incense and recently extinguished candles. And then, just as Khlyde leaned in for a closer look at the parchment, the cloud flared, throbbed and spat a bolt of purple flame at the floor.

The deities, shocked, leapt apart and instantly the cloud vanished.

It took Flagit a good fifteen minutes to close his mouth. After which he turned palely towards Nabob and whispered hoarsely, 'I think I've got an idea.'

Unseen in the smouldering pit in the floor, five thousand tiny slag beetles discovered religion and were already making plans to build a monumental nest dedicated exclusively to a recently witnessed purple flash of light which they believed to be the incarnation of

Ichor the Slag Miner. Of course, it was highly probable they were wrong but, so what, they were happy. For the moment.

The River Phlegethon slipped and slithered its bubbling black way through the intestines of Mortropolis, blissfully unaware of the significance of a strange pair of reinforced yellow booths which had mysteriously appeared on its bank. It also ignored the suspiciously watching crowd of ferrymen who had pulled up their ferries on the very same bank – ferries which hadn't carried a legitimate passenger on their final voyage for two days now.

But that was all about to change.

The first clue was the sound of pounding hooves as a crack team of stamping Malebranche herded a clump of very ex-Immigration Clerks towards the river.

Dragnazzar, the leader of the Malebranche, strode onto the river bank and swept on towards the gathered ferrymen.

'Fire up your infernal combustion engines!' he declared threateningly.

Boredly Captain Naglfar looked up. 'What for?' he grumbled around his belching pipe. 'There ain't no paying customers.'

'Fire up the engines.'

Naglfar took his pipe out of his mouth, picked at one of his hundreds of varied teeth in as irritating a manner as possible and asked, 'Why?'

Dragnazzar snorted. ''Cause I'm commandeering your ferries,' he sneered imperiously.

'What?' spluttered Naglfar, finally leaping to his hooves. 'You can't...'

'Can,' grinned Dragnazzar with a certain wicked sense of satisfaction. 'I've got orders. From Seirizzim.'

Naglfar waggled a bored claw again. 'Ha! Seirizzim is it. Well, let me just remind you that me and the lads've got a business to run here, in case you hadn't noticed.

What makes him think he can get away with not paying the going rate, eh?'

Dragnazzar leant closer to Naglfar and stared at him threateningly. 'Have you any idea where these passengers are going?' he growled.

'No, but I have this odd feeling that you're about to tell me,' grinned Naglfar through a cloud of belligerently exhaled smoke. This looked like it was going to settle down into a good argument and, as duly elected representative of the Underworld Ferrymen's Coalition of Arguing, Shouting and Generally Being Narked, he was entitled to spin such arguments out to their maximum length at full arguing fee, plus expenses.

The Malebranche leader snorted in disgust and carried on. 'They're off to Rubor,' he growled significantly.

'What they want to go there for? Immigrations day out? There's nothing but that old disused mine working and . . .'

'Wrong. It's not disused any more.' There was something in the look in Dragnazzar's eye that didn't bode well. 'And it's a one-way trip,' he added with a disturbing note of cheer in his voice.

A look of horrified comprehension flashed across Naglfar's wrinkled face. 'You mean they're going to the m . . .'

Dragnazzar sneered as he nodded very slowly. 'I think you'd find a ferry business very difficult to run if you were somehow to find yourself joining them in there. Don't you?'

Naglfar nodded reluctantly and waved a complex series of gestures to the rest of the ferrymen. Arguments were one thing, they were professional fun; but readily enforceable threats from the Head of the Malebranche, that was different. That required the tugging of proverbial forehorns and immediate action.

In minutes plumes of filthy black smoke were belching stratasphere-wards, as the ferries coughed chthonic fumocarbons out of their congested lungs.

Just as the infernal combustion engines were fired up a tall figure in a sweeping cassock strode out of a tiny side alley, came to a sudden halt and reversed sharply. Unctuous crashed into the small of his back and tripped over Screed's cassock.

'Oh, what d'you want to do that for?' he whined, picking himself up. 'You could have warned me you were going to stop so suddenly...'

'Quiet!' barked Screed in a hoarse whisper, bending low and peering out across the river bank. His nostrils quivered as he sniffed the air feverishly, like a vampire downwind from a vestal virgin on a moonlit night. In the gloom of the alley his teeth glinted through grinning lips as he sensed the huge conversion potential in the herded demons.

He knew he had to get there. Wherever they were going he was going to be there too. He stood, glanced around swiftly, plotted a perfect string of inchoate shadows between the alley and his target and, without warning, he dashed out of the alley mouth.

'Hey!' squeaked Unctuous, sprinting after him. Then he caught sight of the gathered mass of Malebranche demons, panicked and scuttled backwards into the shadow of the alley. 'Come back,' he stage-whispered in terror. 'You can't go over there. It's dangerous!'

Witnessed only by a helpless Unctuous, the Mostly Reverend Vex Screed slunk along the river bank dodging in and out of shadows, driven on by an overwhelming desire to spread some Good News among these downtrodden demons. Extensive experience had shown him that the more downtrodden an audience was then the more desperate they were to believe in something better. Looking at this lot he'd have one hundred percent conversion in a few minutes of choice haranguing. Sot would be pleased.

Of course, there was the added bonus of getting that Unctuous idiot out of his hair. What a relief!

Thrilling inside, Screed unhooked a suitable rope from

a convenient cleat with a deft flick of his wrist, glanced over his shoulder and, screwing his eyes shut, he swung across a narrow expanse of boiling black river and landed on the deck of the nearest ferry.

In seconds he had hidden himself under a large spare sail, and lay there listening as hooves were marched up the gangplanks, spurred on by Malebranche squeals and the deadly lashings of whip-like tails.

Just as the first of the commandeered ferries belched their way into the cloying current of the Phlegethon and deported the first instalment of ex-Immigration Clerks, a pair of demons strode onto the bank and strutted towards the pair of yellow booths. A clump of surly-looking demons tracked their path and made ready with prepared placards.

Realising with a flutter of angst that Seirizzim was early, Dragnazzar wheeled on his hoof and stomped away on an intercept course. Behind him, three more ferries slewed into the river and chugged their way Rubor-wards.

'All loaded as ordered,' announced Dragnazzar with a snappy salute. 'My deputies'll have the mines up and running in no time.'

'Make it faster,' growled Seirizzim. 'Every day we have to pay Sheytahn is another day wasted. And I detest wasted obuls!' He strode up to within a few feet of the yellow booths and sneered proudly. His every move was closely watched by the clump of Orientation Demons. They had watched these reinforced monstrosities being built under heavy guard and had fumed impotently – well, they'd had nothing else to do over the past two days. Ever since the flow of damned souls into Mortro-polis had ground to a halt they'd had no one to Orientate. It had been their job to snatch tormented souls as they were hurled off the ferries, beat them liberally until they admitted their allocated eternity of torture and then frogmarch them off to said area of misery. It was a job of which each was proud. They knew that their actions

261

influenced a damned soul's view of Helian immensely. First impressions had a terrific impact.

But right now the Orientation Demons had a horrible feeling that they were about to become the latest traffic casualties of Seirizzim's efficiency drive.

They weren't wrong.

With an expectant grin plastered dictatorially across his face, Seirizzim strode up to the pair of Auto Soul Booths and flicked a switch. In seconds surges of lava flowed through the circuits, a pair of yellow flashing lamps sprang into life on the booths' roofs and fifty-three Orientation Demons lost their jobs.

'Asmodeus,' snarled Seirizzim evilly. 'Demonstrate!'

The banker took a step back in surprise. 'I ... I thought the honour should be yours, sir!'

'Well, you thought wrong! Demonstrate.' Seirizzim shoved Asmodeus in through a port in the side. The Orientation Demons watched in alarm as the events unfolded.

Crimson lamps blasted down at Asmodeus inside the Soul Booth and an obsidian screen flashed up. 'Name?'

Nervously Asmodeus tapped out a series of letters on a symbol pad.

'Torture?' snapped back the booth.

Asmodeus shrugged. 'I haven't got one,' he pleaded to Seirizzim. 'I work here.'

'Just pretend you are a damned soul, you'd know by now. Make one up! This is only a demonstration.'

'I ... er ...' flustered Asmodeus.

'Gah! Let me!' Seirizzim leant forward and typed out, 'Excrement Tanks of Filth and Depravity' with a clatter of talons. Instantly, the booth began to vibrate violently, a tiny hatch opened and a buzzing vermilion creature flitted out and hovered an inch away from Asmodeus's nostrils. It beckoned officiously and waggled a very long sting.

And in a flash the Orientation Demons knew the truth. That creature was their replacement. Snarling furiously, they flung their placards in the air and swarmed down towards the booths.

The vermilion mhodemm buzzed impatiently at Asmodeus, irritated that its charge wasn't following it to the Excrement Tanks. In a flash it had looped around behind him and lanced several milligrams of four molar formic acid into the tenderest area of the devil's buttocks. Asmodeus shrieked and swatted at the mhodemm. He received another dose of formic acid in the other buttock.

'Get it off!' he squealed plaintively. 'It hurts!'

The clump of Orientation Demons swept towards the booths, waving their placards. Seirizzim turned and watched them, his tail flicking subtle commands to Dragnazzar.

'We demand that this device is shut down immediately and...' began the elected spokesdemon.

'Demand, eh?' mocked Seirizzim. 'And why's that then?'

'Because, er ... we suspect that it may well put us out of a job and...'

'Ooooh no. These Auto Soul Booths won't do that,' oozed Seirizzim in a deadly silky voice. He swept an accommodating talon towards Dragnazzar. 'In fact, if you would all be so very subordinate and follow that fellow there over to those waiting ferries I will be most happy to discuss your new terms and conditions in the delightful surroundings of an afternoon's cruise across the river.' As the request was put so politely they shrugged and obeyed.

Seirizzim snatched their placards and hurled them to the ground. 'You won't be needing those, right now.'

And as the ex-Orientation Demons began their final walk towards eternal employment in the Lava and Brimstone Mines of Rubor, Seirizzim grinned to himself and Asmodeus sprinted wildly away from the maliciously stinging security mhodhemm, his buttocks glowing red as

263

it herded him inexorably towards the Excrement Tanks of Filth and Depravity.

'Stand closer together,' barked Flagit at the eight deities.

'Oh really, must we? I must object. His pumpkin pyjamas clash so dreadfully with my toga. Pumpkin! I *ask* you,' objected Rahmani, staring at Khlyde with a sneer of arrogant distaste. 'It should be avocado!'

'I'd thump him for that if I were you,' offered Pugil helpfully. 'Swift uppercut and the old one-two and he won't call you a fashionless philistine again.'

'Please, please, I don't want to have to treat unnecessary wounds,' complained Dehtol.

'I should just run away at the first sight of trouble,' whimpered Fleeh.

Flagit snarled angrily and bellowed at the deities. 'Look, just huddle together again,' he demanded. 'This is important!'

'Is this why we're here?' asked Moh Linnekx.

'Yes, yes,' agreed Flagit, saying anything to get them to obey. 'Now come on. Closer! Huddle!' And as they shrugged and shuffled together he dashed for cover behind the now upturned obsidian table.

In seconds the purple field of extreme piety was back, glowing as it hovered above the deities' heads.

'I was right,' whispered Flagit. 'Look!' He prodded Nabob in the ribs excitedly. A flash of shorting shrine waves flared within the cloud and Flagit shrieked and clamped his claw across his mouth. 'Closer,' he yelped into his palm as the smell of incense wriggled up his nostrils. The deities leant in and the purple shimmering intensified, writhing and vibrating like a dozen ferrets in a velvet sack, elongating as if it was trying to pull away.

Flagit's eyes were wide, staring in awe at the spectacle unfolding before him, and then suddenly there was a blinding flash, a crackling of holy ozone and a single tiny dandelion clock of purple piety ripped itself away, bobbed momentarily and floated out through the wall. The deities pulled apart, their ears tingling.

'D'you see that?' vibrated Flagit, shaking Nabob firmly by the shoulders. 'See it? It's just like I said. A creed-orb! Ha. The demon that hits is in for a big shock. Like being clobbered by half a dozen Anti-Personnel Shrines. They'll believe anything after that!'

'Yeah. So what?' Nabob grunted with underwhelming enthusiasm. 'That won't make any difference, will it?'

'Have you no imagination?' pleaded Flagit.

'Not really,' confessed Nabob.

Flagit raised his eyes to the ceiling. 'Look, that only happened when the eight of them were really close together, right?'

'Right.'

'So the closer they are together the higher the concentration of shrine waves, right?'

'Right.'

'With the concentrated shrine waves of eight deities we got a four-inch creed-orb which is probably very unstable, right?'

'Right,' shrugged Nabob, wondering where all this was leading.

'So what'll happen if we get more deities together, eh?'

'Right ... oh er ...'

'We'll get a bigger creed-orb, of course. In fact, my guess is that if we get enough deities together then in one wild celebration of a Critical Mass we can have everyone in Mortropolis gripped in the belief that Seirizzim has to go! Right?'

'Er, just how many more of them do we need before we can have a Critical Mass?'

'Pah, details, details,' snapped Flagit. 'C'mon, grab a blanket!'

'I had a feeling you were going to say that,' moaned Nabob.

Flagit snatched up the shrine detector, whistled for Flinty and vanished through the door.

'Why me?' thought Nabob, and sprinted after him, his mind still spinning with pious purple dandelion clocks of pure faith.

Scran, having polished off two large portions of grub, wiped a satisfied hand across his mouth, leant back in his chair on the Top Table of Manna Ambrosia's and took a large swig of ale. Almost reluctantly, he announced, 'Alright then. Any Other Business.'

The echoes had barely died before Lofax was on his chair, waving scrolls. 'The proposal has been posted to discuss the current unscheduled absence of some of our party. This, as has already been stated by myself on an occasion previous to this present juncture, is very short notice and will require the immediate rescheduling of other less pressing business...'

'Well?' grunted Scran.

'Could you, for the benefit of those of a more exacting nature, possibly clarify, the meaning of that inquiry. Please.'

'I should have thought it was devastating in its clarity. But, for those of a more pedantic nature, I shall clarify. Are we going to discuss them now?'

'I take it that by "them" one is referring to our absent friends and that by "now" you are addressing this current session of "Any Other Business".'

Scran sighed heavily. 'Yes,' he answered, raised his flagon and suddenly headed Lofax's next question off at the linguistic path. 'To both of them.' He swallowed a deeply needed mouthful of ale.

Lofax looked around Manna Ambrosia's officiously. 'Are there any seconders to this emergency proposal?'

Dutifully, Lush raised his hand from the Top Table and smirked smugly at Sot.

'All in favour?' piped Lofax.

An indifferent show of hands waggled in reply.

'Very well,' beamed Lofax, revelling in his officiousness. 'Motion is carried. This emergency proposal rescheduling will be discussed at next week's "Any Other Business" at which time any objections and lines of discussion can be raised enabling the real discussion to proceed as efficiently and smoothly as is practical.'

Scran shook his head in amazement. That had gone through remarkably smoothly. It must be a real emergency.

Nervously Sot tapped the table in front of him and wished he knew what was going on in Helian. Secretly he began to wonder if being on the Top Table was actually worth all this hassle and worry. It had seemed such a good idea at the time.

You could almost taste the nervous tension in the air as a team of Satisfactory Seating Consultants peered forlornly into scrying crystals and shuffled tiny bits of parchment around. Each parchment fragment had a name scrawled messily across its surface.

Kharva, the head of the Table of Directors of the Satisfactory Seating Committee, plucked six names out of the ceremonial hat and arranged them in front of him. Then he waved his hands wearily over the scrying crystal, chanted a few half-hearted incantations and waited for the cataractal fog to disperse. It was replaced with a sharp image of six faces at a table in the reception of Tehzho Khonna and Khrystal's wedding.

Two bridesmaids, an ageing aunt of the groom's, two officials of the Litter Prediction Agency and 'Snuff' Douser sat around in silence, staring forlornly at the pink napkins and waiting for the first course.

'S ... so, er, did you catch the bridal bouquet?' asked 'Snuff' of the nearest bridesmaid.

'No,' spat the plain-looking girl miserably and rustled her pink dress haughtily.

'Oh, er ... was it you, then?' he asked the other.

'No!' she snapped and glared across the table.

267

'But I thought there were only two bridesmaids.'

'Yes!' they chorused.

'So who...?'

A wrinkled finger of angry accusation lanced out from the ageing aunt and pointed straight at one of the Litter Prediction Agency members. 'Him!' was all she said. The look of daggers almost tipped him off his chair.

'Look, it's more than my job's worth to allow unauthorised items of no further use to foul Axolotian pavements...' began the Litter Prediction Agent.

'But it was going to be used,' wailed the first bridesmaid. 'It would have told us who was going to get married first. It's tradition!'

'That bouquet was clearly seen to have been deliberately discarded in a manner likely to cause pavemental untidiness and increase chaotic potential of scattering...'

'If you hadn't leapt in the way with that bin of yours then I would have caught it!' snarled the second bridesmaid.

'No ... *I* would've!'

'No, me!'

'I cannot believe that you are arguing over who would grab the refuse from a simple ceremony,' grumbled the Litter Prediction Agent. 'Would you be so keen to snatch at the roasted wishbone of domestic poultry if hurled in the same casual manner?'

'Yes,' chorused the bridesmaids. 'There might be a bit of meat on it.'

'So you are approving of the hurling of useless materials into the streets in a manner likely to cause littering?'

'No.'

'But that *is* what you said.'

'Didn't. It was her!' pointed bridesmaid two accusingly.

'Wasn't!'

'Was so!'

'No, it was him. It's all his fault!' The first bridesmaid

scowled at the Litter Prediction Agent. 'Get him!' There was the sound of chairs hitting the floor as the two pink-clad warriors leapt over the table and landed clenched fists in the Litter Prediction Agent's eyes.

Kharva covered his eyes, closed down the scrying crystal and almost wept. Ninety-seven different combinations he had tried and they had all ended in punch-ups. The only difference seemed to be how long it took to get messy.

At this rate the seating arrangements would never work. It was just too hard. The best he had come up with so far was a sextet of complete strangers, three of whom had taken a vow of silence. It was a boring reception for them, but at least they survived it unhurt.

He looked around at his team and cringed as he saw the worried wincing of prophets watching other punch-ups. There was no choice. He had to call upon divine intervention. And there was only one chappie who could possibly sort this mess out and tease it into something less dangerous than a potential riot; Uscher, the Under-Deity Over Seating Arrangements.

Kharva wished he had thought of it before, but secretly he hated to admit defeat.

'Alright, lads,' he announced with a twinge of shame. 'Crystals down, it's time to bring in the big boss.'

There was a flurry of intaken breath. The big boss! Things must be bad.

Kharva lit a couple of ceremonial incense sticks, shuffled reluctantly up onto the seat of the shrine of Uscher and placed himself carefully upon it with the requisite contortions of leg joints. Ominously his knees creaked as he folded his ankles halfway up the opposing thigh.

He closed his eyes and began the ceremonial intonation, much to the delight of the two devils a thousand feet below.

Yet again the indicators of the shrine detector went wild, quivering and pointing fixedly at a spot in the roof of a now very honeycombed side tunnel. Flagit grinned excitedly, pointed to the spot in the roof and urged Flinty into a frenzy of rock-gnawing. In seconds the stalag-mite had scuttled up the walls and was attacking the granite in a flurry of shattering chips. She was smart. She knew the drill.

Flagit and Nabob wrapped themselves in many layers of blanket and followed, one brimming with sheer eagerness, the other muttering things about aching knees.

It wouldn't be very long before there were nine deities in Helian.

The Mostly Reverend Vex Screed remained completely motionless under the spare sail on the ferry until all the sounds of barked orders and stamped hooves had faded, then, feelings of evangelistic fervour coursing through his veins, he peeked out, checked the Phlegethon banks for hidden demons and skipped onto the shore. It wasn't too difficult to track the herd of miserable ex-Immigration Clerks and their captors – there was the shouting, the occasional squeal of agony and, of course, the vast swathe of hoof-prints in the dust to keep even the most inept of hunters heading in the right direction.

In minutes he found himself squatting cautiously behind a very large boulder peering covertly down over the gaping entrance of the dread Lava and Brimstone Mines of Rubor. Two parallel lines of metal slithered into the throat-like gloom, vanishing into the crimson penumbra of foul-smelling shadows. The corroding hulks of shattered carts lay strewn randomly around like the long-forgotten casualties of an exceedingly violent cart attack.

This, more than anything Screed had so far seen, was the most fitting example of just what Helian should be.

The Malebranche guards snarled aggressive commands, punctuating each one with a series of swift whinnying kicks, and Screed felt the increase in belief potential mounting minute by minute.

He was, at that moment, blissfully unaware of the skittish approach of a strange purple dandelion clock of concentrated piety whisking its way towards him, carried on the gossamer wings of a gentle breeze.

Screed watched events in the mine unfold as Malebranche guards hurled vast pickaxes at clerks. Miserably they picked them up, blisters waiting gleefully in the wings of agony, readying themselves to spring forth onto the palms of claws softened by centuries of parchment sorting and boilpoint pen-pushing. And as the Malebranche rounded the new recruits up and leered menacingly towards them, Screed saw his chance. His heart raced, his spleen wriggled and there and then he knew he just had to preach. And he had the perfect lesson in mind.

He racked his mind quickly, trying to recall the contract he had with Arma-Palms Mining Mittens and Oven Gloves – Digital Protection for the Working Masses. Had he fulfilled it? Had he succeeded in the required twenty thousand converts for which he had been paid? Somehow he felt not. But now, here was a perfect opportunity to redress that indelicate balance. Not stopping to consider where the ex-clerks would actually have the chance to purchase Arma-Palms Mining Mittens, and not caring anyway since that was the problem of the supplies department, he knew it was time to act. *Carpe demon* and all that. Strike while the trident is hot. Arms wide, head held high, he sprinted up the back of the boulder, took a breath and declared, 'Friends, demons, Helianites, lend me your ears!'

It wasn't the most original of openings but it got their attention. Everyone whirled on their hooves, eyes focusing with a snap on the cassocked figure on the boulder. Behind him a glow of purple intensity seemed to throb and grow.

'In this time of change, we all need a little comfort,' shouted Screed. 'A little sprinkling of delight upon the parched wilderness of misery's woeful desert. Wouldn't you agree?'

There was a nodding of a few heads, cautiously, nervously, under the watchful glare of the Malebranche.

'Isn't suffering something that should happen to other folk?' asked Screed. 'Isn't pain and anguish a luxury afforded to those who really deserve it? Why should you have to endure the agony of tender talons and calloused claws?'

Just as Screed shut his eyes in a paroxysm of pounding faith, the dandelion clock of pure purple piety floated over his shoulder. Silently it drifted into the natural amphitheatre of the mine mouth. He readied himself for a final few swipes of evangelistically rousing questions, highlighting the need that his audience were realising they had, cornering it and then, when there seemed to be no way out, no place to turn, he would offer them the solution, the one true way ... Arma-Palms Mining Mittens!

'Why should it be your perfect manicure that is mangled by the rigours of daily toil? Can you have unchipped talon varnish *and* labour down the mines?'

Suddenly, unexpectedly, the dandelion clock of piety crashed into an inopportunely positioned boulder. As fragile as it was and as brimming with kilo-psalms of shrine waves, it was still a surprise just how large was the flash of blinding light which erupted from it. The whole area was burnt out in a retina-searing flash of celestial proportion as if someone had mistakenly lit the blue touch parchment of a small super nova and forgotten to tell anyone about it.

Tiny doughnuts of faith formed in the searing fireball of belief and tumbled out of the sky in a spontaneous halo-storm. And in seconds the entire mob of demons had seen the light, bought the T-shirt and embraced the last words of the stranger on the rock with the fervour of a randy terrier on a favourite leg.

Why *should* their manicures be ruined? Why should

272

they toil down the mines? Why indeed! Questions had to be answered. Wrongs righted! And there was only one devil in the whole of Mortropolis who could answer any of them.

The Undertaker-in-Chief. His Imperiosity Himself, Seirizzim.

Before the Mostly Reverend Vex Screed had the chance to introduce the mob to the delights of Arma-Palms, they had surged up the bank below him, snatched him off the rock and were carrying him away towards the Phlegethon, wild in the knowledge that he had shown them the way. The one way. The way of the riot!

Crash-Test Deities

The first pathetic beams of dawn's early light slithered feebly over the horizon and trudged dozily towards Axolotl. They were about to get a very rude awakening.

'It's what?' yelled Vhyttol, the High Priest of Matrimonial Catering Supplies, his eyes rimmed red through a high octane mix of nervous tension and an extreme lack of sleep. He'd managed to snatch just three hours' shut-eye in the last week since Tehzho Khonna and Miss Khrystal Gehyz's imminent espousal had been announced. And it showed. The ends of his nerves were frayed to complete fuzzy rawness, the megaton fury of his legendarily explosive temper twitching on a fragile hair-trigger. 'The cake is what?' he repeated, teetering on eruption.

'R ... ruined,' spluttered a minion from the kitchens.

Vhyttol raised his eyes towards Heobhan and whispered menacingly, 'Explain.'

Feelo, the minion, swallowed and wiped his palms down the front of his white kitchen toga. A small avalanche of flour tumbled floorwards. Almost certain that this would be his last day in the kitchens, he took a breath and began. 'It wasn't my fault. They were next to each other. Well, they're always next to each other but ... It wasn't my fault,' he bleated in case Vhyttol was in any danger of forgetting. The ominous brooding silence and twitching cheek muscles of the High Priest didn't bode well.

'They look the same though, don't they?' whimpered Feelo. 'I mean, in an overcrowded kitchen, in the middle of a mad rush, well, one white crystalline powder looks pretty much like another. It was a mistake *anybody* could've made. They even start with the same letter...'

Vhyttol's voice, when it finally came in a hoarse whisper, rang with enforced calmness. It was either that or damage his vocal cords irreparably with a fully fledged screaming tirade of red-faced squealing. 'Are you trying to tell me that The Cake, which is needed in less than eight hours for the most important society wedding of the decade, has been ... seasoned...?'

Feelo peered out from under the peak of his cap like a terrified rodent. He nodded and wrung his hands.

'...instead of sweetened?'

Feelo risked another guiltily confirmatory nod.

A vein pulsed at Vhyttol's temple and everyone scattered. 'You put in salt instead of s ... sugar?'

'It was the finest sun-dried rock salt...' whimpered the minion, clutching at anything to lessen the punishment he would surely get.

Vhyttol closed his eyes and raised a deadly silencing finger. 'What, pray *do* tell, was the final fate of the three pounds four ounces of premier grade cane?'

'Ah, I was going to come to that,' confessed Feelo with a quiver in his voice. 'The sausage rolls will be fine if you serve them with a particularly tart mustard sauce, it'll hide the sweetness ... oh, you don't think that's a very good idea?'

The hot breath of Vhyttol's temper blasted out of his flaring nostrils, ready to strip paint at a hundred yards.

Feelo closed his eyes and abandoned his body to the whim of the High Priest of Matrimonial Catering Supplies. It was a tragic way to go, but at least he had the sure and certain knowledge that he would be diced with the utmost precision.

He heard the rustle of Vhyttol's robes as he lunged forward; sensed the pounding of blood through the vein at his temple; felt the rasping snort of fulminating breath on his neck...

And heard the door slam shut on the tail of a pair of clattering heels.

275

Feelo's eyes flicked open and locked onto Vhyttol's fluffed Cap of Office gently settling to the floor. A squeak of relief fled prematurely from his lips as his eyes darted around him, searching for any sign of the High Priest. His knees felt like custard. Milliseconds before he slithered to the floor in a meringue of blubbering relief, the door to a rarely used store-cupboard was kicked open and Vhyttol exploded through it.

Feelo's eyes were black olive vol-au-vents of alarm as the fuming High Priest stomped towards him unstoppably, closing, bearing down, hands held high.

'Carry that!' he barked, flinging a sack of rare and precious herbs into Feelo's midriff and sweeping on by.

Snatched like saffron in a sandstorm, Feelo spun and was dragged out by the scruff of the neck.

He only regained his breath twenty minutes later when Vhyttol dropped him on a strangely barren patch of scrubby heather on a high promontory to the east of the city. The High Priest fell to his knees, inches from the edge of the three-hundred-foot drop, and swept twigs and leaves off the oddly flattened rock which lay there.

'Kindling. Kindling!' barked Vhyttol desperately. 'Now!'

Feelo almost leapt out of his skin, dropped the sack and began scrabbling frantically in the undergrowth for readily flammable twiglets of heather.

In a few moments Vhyttol had piled them into a scrappy bonfire and was squatting over a small, roughly hewn indentation in the rock, spinning a flame-stick between his palms. Feelo gaped at the blur of Vhyttol's hands, blinking in awe as a spark caught in seconds and was tossed into the heather twiglets. Wisps of bluish smoke licked into the dawn air, there was a crackle and suddenly it caught.

Vhyttol whirled, snatched the sack off the ground,

wrestled its draw-string neck open and plunged his hands deep inside, closing his fingers tight around two handfuls of rare and precious herbs.

And then Feelo began to feel that perhaps Vhyttol had been overdoing it a bit lately. He did make a pretty impressive silhouette though. Flinging his arms wide, fists clenched and standing tall at the edge of the three-hundred-foot cataract, he hurled back his head and gazed imploringly towards the orange-streaked turquoise of the dawn sky. The fire blazed at his feet.

Feelo watched and secretly wondered about the state of Vhyttol's mental health. He knew something about how different folks handled acute stress. Some turned to the bottle, some to smoking herbal narcotics and others went screaming around the city on the backs of wild ibex. But Feelo had never heard of anyone doing this.

Especially with the wailing.

He listened to the desperate words of Vhyttol as they floated skywards and shook his head. 'Sad,' he thought. 'All that worry over a bit of cake and a few sausage rolls. Some folks get *so* worked up about food!'

A sudden movement grabbed Feelo's attention. Vhyttol's right arm hurled it's rare and precious herbs at the tiny heather bonfire. There was a crackling, a flare of crimson and blue, and a column of aromatic smoke snaked its way into the still morning air like a well-trained vizir's rope in a Khomun Market bazaar.

Feelo relaxed a little. It was alright, Vhyttol was unwinding in the traditional way, burning a few dried plant extracts. Okay, so he'd added a few personalised touches, but that didn't matter. He would have quite happily sneaked away and left the High Priest to it if he'd known the way back to Axolotl. It had been such a mad dash to get here, he hadn't had a chance to take bearings.

Still, it wasn't too bad up here. Cooler than the

kitchens, that was for sure, and a far better view. Wonderful the way the beams from the almost horizontal sun shimmered so well on the wings of that man hovering there...

Feelo rammed his knuckles into the pits of his eyes, blinked and stared. The grinning man fluttered nonchalantly above the three-hundred-foot drop and stroked his curling moustache thoughtfully.

Trembling, and wondering precisely which of them it was that was more stressed out, Feelo crawled into earshot.

'Salt, you say?' mused the fluttering figure.

'Three and a half pounds of the stuff!' snarled Vhyttol in a strangely pleading way. 'C'mon, Tohnee, you've got to help me?'

'Hmmm, how about double-thickness extra-sweet icing?'

'Yeurch,' heaved Vhyttol. 'D'you have *any* idea how important this wedding is?'

'Only a suggestion.'

Vhyttol gave him a withering look.

'What about soaking it in extra sweet avocado wine?'

'Nah, the icing'll stain. A pale green wedding cake, get real!'

'Well, these celebrities do funny things. Call it fashion.'

'Look, Tohnee, this is serious. What I need is a cake recipe that'll be cooked in under an hour. Can you do it?'

'Hmmmm, tricky,' mused the winged one, stroking his chin. 'We'd best see what you've got in the kitchen.' He fluttered past Vhyttol towards Axolotl, grinning. 'Makes a change to think about things other than pizza, I can tell you. You know, Vhyttol, you really ought to call me up more often.'

As Feelo glimpsed the embroidered initials "T.F." on the kitchen toga of the angel his brain clicked.

Tohnee Fabrizzi. The now legendary inventor of the Infamous Dragonzola Garlic Bread who had died in a tragic explosion the very day before opening his new

278

restaurant in Axolotl. They said that a stray spark from somewhere had ignited a bowl of the highly volatile dragonzola cheese. It was still a mystery as to why no members of the Fire Prediction or the Accident and Emergency Foreseervice had known it was going to happen. Tohnee Fabrizzi's disappearance was clouded in more mystery than the street had been in smoke that fateful night all those years ago.

Gods! thought Feelo the pastry-faced kitchen minion nervously. Vhyttol must *really* be desperate to impress Tehzho Khonna and Khrystal if he was calling up the dead for a quick-bake wedding cake recipe.

The nine-inch nail of a scaly thumb curled around a glossy black index talon and hooked itself into a flicking position with a snicking sound. A small marble sphere was dropped in place, angled carefully and shot across the cavern with a resounding whistle. Arrow-straight, it bulleted into the clump of similar rocky spheres and sent them flying in all directions.

'Will you stop that!' snapped Flagit as a projectile marble whistled between his horns.

'I'm bored,' complained Nabob, picking another sphere out of a sack by his side.

'How can you be bored at a time like this?'

'Easy. I've been sitting here on this pebble bag doing nothing but wait for hours on end for that thing to twitch.' He pointed a dismissive talon at Flagit's shrine detector. 'Boredom just comes naturally, I guess.'

'Look, it's not my fault there's no deities about at the moment, is it?' snarled Flagit, poring over the steaming parchment deployment map for the Anti-Personnel Shrines with a look of desperation.

'Well, they'd better hurry up and make themselves available. Nine just aren't enough.' Nabob launched another marble at the clump by the wall, spitting ricochets of shrapnel spheres across the cavern floor.

Flagit gnashed his fangs. He knew damn well that

nine deities weren't enough. But what could he do? Where was he going to get three more before this afternoon?

This afternoon! A surge of angry impotence knotted his infernal guts. Too little time! Foul Lord d'Abaloh was set to visit this afternoon, the perfect time to activate their grand plan, and it was impossible. With just three more minor gods he could wreak havoc on all of Seirizzim's finest schemes, undermine every newly introduced efficiency system and send his rule crashing into a million useless shards. And all right under the nose of d'Abaloh himself. Seirizzim's hooves wouldn't touch the floor.

But what chance did he stand to pull it off with only nine? Inside Flagit wailed pathetically. So close, and yet the Undertaker-in-Chiefship was slipping further away. There had to be a way to make it work. He squinted at the secret parchment, peering through the cloudy vapours of condensation as they spilled over the edge of the kitchen table. There had to be a deployment pattern of deities that would work short-handed.

Nabob shuffled noisily on the pebble bag, closed one eye and launched another projectile marble at the clump of spheres. And this time it was dead on target. The single marble cannoned into the tight packed centre and blasted them everywhere. Three rebounded noisily off the far wall and hammered into Flagit's skull.

'Right! That's *it!* If you're going to start throwing them I...' bellowed Flagit, leaping to his hooves.

'I didn't throw anything. Just flicked one into...'

Flagit froze in mid-stride, glaring at the now empty space where the marbles had been. Slowly he stared around the cavern at just how far they had scattered and an idea wriggled into his head. If solid things could be scattered so far in the aftermath of a controlled collision then just think what could happen to the ephemerally influential shrine waves.

He rubbed his chin in a final moment of ponderment, then grinned, whirled on his hooves and burst into the rest of Nabob's "Hole Sweet Hole", barking enthusiastic orders at the deities.

It could just work.

Eddies of thin mist vortexed off her wingtips as she powered almost vertically downwards, gaining speed like there was no tomorrow. Her chest swelled as muscles worked hard, thrusting her faster still, using the very pull of free-fall and the power of her flight feathers to accelerate way beyond normal safe speeds. The rush of thin air pounded at her face, squeezing tears from her eyes, snatching them in streaks across her burning cheeks.

This was what being an angel was all about. Aerobatics.

Out here on the edge of Heobhan with seemingly all the pale blue space in eternity at her wingtips, ah, this was the afterlife!

Florrie spread her wings, angled them back and pulled almost four-g in the most dangerous and thrilling of manoeuvres – the outside loop. Her chest pounded, wing joints creaking as she converted forward momentum into lift, vibrating as she soared upwards on a vortex trail of mist, shedding vapour off the tips of her wings. She roared towards the top of the loop, cheeks flapping, hair streaming behind. With every foot higher she climbed she lost momentum, gravity stripping it away, pulling her back, slowing her. The apex neared, the glory moment of free-fall swallow dive when your heart wrestles your intestines in the euphoria of zero-g, closer, higher...

And with a very unangelic curse, she stalled.

Her wings buckled, she slipped sideways and fell out of the sky in a tumble of feathers, hair and spitting. Cursing under her breath she let herself plummet for a few hundred feet, like some trapeze artist who'd missed the bar. Then, with a sigh, she flipped into a headfirst dive, flapped twice and was back in complete control. She levelled out, flipped onto her back and swooped casually through a stray cloudbank, whistling. So what if she'd spun out, there was always next time. Or the time after. That was one of the good things about being immortal, plenty of time to practise.

Throwing herself nonchalantly into a triple barrel roll on a whim, she fluttered on, ducked around a particularly dense-looking cloud and caught herself up short as she heard an odd buzzing sound. Hanging effortlessly in mid-air she cupped her ear and listened, certain that the noise had come from inside that cloud. But that couldn't possibly be right. Noises don't come from inside...

The buzzing sounded again and this time there was no doubting its origin. Florrie flitted over to the cloud, reached out a hand to push her way through and let out a squeak of surprise as she hit something solid. Baffled, she flitted around to the far side and was stunned when she came across an ornately carved door handle sticking through a haze of mist.

The buzzing sounded again.

Curiosity smouldering within her, she twisted the handle and pushed. The door swung open, the intermittent buzzing growing louder and sharper. Intrigued, she fluttered into the darkened interior and was buzzed at by a single glowing trident on a wall packed with similar unlit symbols, each of which had its own name plaque beneath.

There was a hand-written note pinned to the wall. It read:

I'm bored with this.
Told everyone they weren't coming, so I'm off.
Bye. Fibby.
P.S. If anybody reads this and any of these
things are buzzing, contact me. Urgent.

282

Florrie scratched her head. Fibby? she thought. Now where've I heard that name before? Fibby ... ah yes, he's the Supreme Being Over ... she gulped as she remembered ... Espionage, Misinformation and Spying. Uh-oh. Flashing lights, buzzers and espionage. Something didn't look too good.

She flapped through the door of the cloud and sped off in search of Fibby, more to find out what in Heobhan it was all about than from any real sense of duty.

The tiny vermillion security mhodemm hovered for a moment as it assessed the back attack route. Then it buzzed angrily, dipped its antennae, angled its formic-acid flinging proboscis into full attack readiness and performed a neat wing-over turn. It plunged wildly past blurring black scales, narrowly avoiding a vast thrashing tail and delivering yet another direct hit to Asmodeus's left buttock.

The banker squealed again, leaping several feet into the air and swatting at his backside. The security mhodemm wriggled its antennae with satisfaction and lined up for another attack. In a way it would be sad when its target finally found his way to the Excrement Tanks of Filth and Depravity where he had been sentenced. Its attacks would have to stop then. It had to be said that the mhodemm was beginning to enjoy itself in a wickedly sadistic way.

It dodged Asmodeus's thrashing talons easily as he tried to swat his irritating vermilion tormentor and dashed around a dark corner. The mhodemm buzzed dutifully after him, lining up for yet another stinging contact. Fizzing with the primal stirrings of sadism, it angled its proboscis, swooped, struck target and was splattered across Asmodeus's scaly right buttock by a scything claw.

'And don't say I never did you a favour,' snapped Seirizzim, wiping the insect-like creature off his palm.

Asmodeus looked up at the Undertaker-in-Chief of Mortropolis through newly admiring eyes. What a hero he was, saving him from that torment, risking a stinging to release him.

Of course Asmodeus hadn't a clue that the security mhodemm was programmed only to pursue a single target. Seirizzim's only risk was of spraining his wrist when he splatted the thing against Asmodeus's already throbbing rear, but since this was a bonus opportunity to inflict a little extra-curricular corporal punishment Seirizzim had bravely done his duty.

Asmodeus blinked in un-mhodemmed relief. 'But why?' he spluttered.

'I need you,' barked Seirizzim irritably. 'Have you forgotten what day it is?'

'Er...' Asmodeus had up until very recently been concerned with more pressing and insectile matters.

'The big day, idiot! D'Abaloh? Remember? Follow!'

Asmodeus galloped frantically after Seirizzim as he headed off through a tiny alley, rushing towards the Sinful Service Stratascraper and a date with a cast of thousands.

The pair of demons dipped and weaved through the crimson highlit streets of Mortropolis, Seirizzim galloping ahead, his heart racing with nerves and excitement.

This was the last chance he had to make sure everything was just right for Foul Lord d'Abaloh's inspection visit, the first which he as Undertaker-in-Chief had endured. And if everything wasn't just as d'Abaloh liked, it would be his last. The rest of eternity swung precariously in the balance of this afternoon's performance.

'Everything ready?' he barked at Dragnazzar as he burst into Sinful Square, Asmodeus close behind.

Nine-foot-six of Malebranche leader leapt to attention and conjured a snappy salute from nowhere. 'Ready,' he barked back, and scowled at his team of eleven officers as they shuffled into a semblance of readiness, shouldering their tridents across their left shoulders with a rustling of scales.

284

'Well get on with it,' growled Seirizzim through clenched fangs and dashed towards the doors of the Sinful Service Stratascraper. He got halfway, looked up and stopped in his tracks. Asmodeus ran into him in a flurry of grovelling apologies.

'Where are they?' roared Seirizzim, snatching at Asmodeus's horns and angling the whimpering banker's head up towards the naked balcony on the thirteenth floor. 'The banners? Where are they? Speak!'

'I ... er, I've been a bit tied up with ...' He rubbed his buttocks apologetically.

'*Don't* give me excuses! I want them up there. Now!' Seirizzim squealed, flinging Asmodeus away. His mind's eye watered with pride as he imagined the scene. Him, Seirizzim, duly elected Undertaker-in-Chief of Mortropolis, standing at the banner-bedecked balcony, waving talons above the crimson sheets emblazoned with the crossed cloven hooves and trident of the New Mortropolitan Regime.

'Get on with it!' he yelled to no-one in particular, and kicked his way through the door, his hooves striking sparks off the handle.

Seirizzim's Malebranche scattered down every entrance to Sinful Square, wielding their tridents gleefully and performing a few practice stabs. In moments the entire Square was utterly empty.

On the thirteenth floor Seirizzim strode imperiously across the empty expanse of what had once been Immigrations, tugged open the large windows at the far end. Swaggering onto the balcony, his heels clicking, he stared out over his territory.

Rough-hewn towers of granite writhed upwards in the crimson gloom, straining towards the rock canopy of the distant stratasphere. He sneered as he interlocked his talons and cracked his knuckles in a noisy tattoo.

'Let the show begin,' he said to himself and imagined Foul Lord d'Abaloh standing by his side. He wouldn't be disappointed.

'Well, get on with it!' Seirizzim bellowed over the balcony, his voice echoing in the cavern of the Square.

And, with only a few barely heard whispers of command and whip-cracks of enforcement, it started.

With the first massed shuffle of chains, Seirizzim's heart leapt with joy, his pupils widening as focused lava-lamp beams flashed crimson and strafed the square wildly from surrounding tower tops, stalking restlessly. 'Nice touch,' he thought around a sharply intaken breath of dictatorial revelry. 'Must be one of Dragnazzar's.'

And into the swirling strobes of blood red trudged the massed misery of the Synchronised Shufflers of the Flame-Pits, stabbed into action by demonic Malebranche majorettes wielding glinting tridents. They shuffled in perfect co-ordination, inches apart like some chthonic nightmare millipede, left, right. Even though he knew damn well that all their ankles were shackled together, Seirizzim could still convince himself that this precision was the direct result of a perfect dictatorship. Each one of those damned souls knew that if they took the tiniest step out of place they'd be tridented mercilessly from a dozen different directions. Of course Seirizzim knew that the terror of the trident was uppermost in every inmate's eternally damned mind. They would behave. The chains were just a precaution. Honest.

The lasering beams of the lava-lamps spun and focused on the mouth of a vast alley as a volley of whips cracked noisily and a deep rumbling began. Seirizzim leaned forward, eager to see what could possibly make such a noise.

A quartet of tortured souls struggled into Sinful Square, their naked torsos glistening as they laboured behind vast spheres of solid granite. Around them wild demons flicked whips like a gaggle of demented fly fishermen, yelling and cajoling. There was a brief gap and then another four vast boulders were rolled on, each propelled by a sweating body.

Simultaneously, from the opposite side of the square a

squadron of long-deceased cheerleaders strutted their manacled selves into view, pompoms of eternal flames clutched in each hand. And Seirizzim's eyes clouded with emotion. Oh, such efficiency, such suffering! It was beautiful!

A tear of pride shimmered at the corner of his eye as he imagined all this spectacle against the background of banners and thousands of cheering, flag-waving demons. He could see it all, each of them brandishing their very own crossed cloven hooves and trident emblem of the New Mortropolitan Regime, each specially coerced into a frenzy of appreciation.

D'Abaloh was sure to love it all.

In the Grand Municipal Temple of Axolotl the air was fizzing with the terrified electricity of angst. People barked orders at groups of assistants who then whirled and scurried away to bark those same orders to servants further down the ladder of minionship. Technicians up rope-ladders dangled precariously and fixed hanging baskets of pink and white blooms in the places they would normally shove curved mirrors or colouring filter gels. The band of kazoos and ocarinas would occasionally kick into action unexpectedly, cough a few random bars of a march into the frenzied air and then unravel pathetically. The conductor was losing hair by the fistful.

And the sands of time dribbled inexorably by with tectonic inevitability, sliding unstoppably towards that sparkling moment when Tehzho Khonna, darling of the popular masses, solitary professional Axolotian compere and inventor of countless tacky catchphrases, took the curvaceous beauty Miss Khrystal Gehyz, 38-24-32 and complete unknown, to be his eternally espoused. In that moment all Axolotl's eyes and thoughts would be focused on the happy couple as they dipped their tentative toes into the warm milk of matrimony and prayed it wouldn't curdle.

And it was all being brought to the city, live, in full colour, before their very eyes, courtesy of Khamran Mh'kyntosh, producer and inventor of 'Play Your Stars Right!' He wasn't about to let anyone forget it.

'Do make absolutely certain that the happy couple are flatteringly lit,' he shouted at a precariously dangling technician on the end of a ladder. 'I want to make absolutely certain that *everybody* can see them at their best, no ugly shadows or obtrusive highlights, please, luvvie!' The technician grunted incomprehensibly, kicked a concave mirror a few degrees to the left and shoved a soft-focus gauze in front of it.

The orchestra blew a couple of discordant bars in three-four time and ended in a scream from the conductor.

'Lovely, utterly lovely, darling,' soothed Khamran with only a slightly furrowed brow. 'Just one thing, though. Do you think they could all start with the same key? Small point, I know, but these little details do matter. Ciao!'

The conductor's baton creaked dangerously close to breaking point as it bent between his white-knuckled fists.

Fortunately for Khamran he was out of earshot and blustering across the stage when the conductor vented his splenetic anger. Khamran had just happened to spot the head of the tailors as she lurched out of a back room and headed for a carefully hidden bottle of avocado gin. It had been a virgin bottle only a matter of hours ago, now it was almost empty. Things hadn't been going well ever since Rahmani, the Deity Over Fashion Statements, Dress Sense and Decorum, had failed to give a decent blessing to the whole proceedings. It was a catalogue of disasters. The flax for the linen of Tehzho's special tail-cloak had gone inexplicably limp and had been abandoned in favour of hessian; somehow the widely publicised vital statistics of Miss Khrystal Gehyz had changed in between fittings and now, even though she still checked out at 38-24-32, the leopard-print ibex-wool dress which had been made out to those precise dimensions refused categorically to come anywhere near fastening; and then there was the sorry case of the extreme allergy one of the bridesmaids had to ibex. She had completely ruined the first completed dress with a wild outburst of sneezing. As soon as everybody saw the sticky mess they just knew it wouldn't wash out. But apart from that...

'Darling darling?' beckoned Khamran. 'How *are* the costume ... er, dresses coming along? All tickety-boo?'

The dread truth welled inside. She nearly spilled it, nearly blabbed, but in the nick of time she caught her tongue. None of her ladies was going to be accused of ruining dear Tehzho's day, no way.

'Tickety-boo?' she flustered momentarily, then she clenched her back teeth and simply lied herself stupid. 'Yes, yes, of course everything is tickety-boo. Everything is utterly splendid. You have absolutely nothing to worry about at all.' She felt certain he would have spotted the high-pitched squeak in her panicking voice.

'*So* glad to hear it, my dear. Keep up the good work, ciao!' and he was off to check on another unsuspecting worker.

In a second the bottle of avocado gin had been drained.

'Ah, darling, sweetie?' trilled Khamran, fluttering his eyelids in the general direction of a man who at that precise moment in time really didn't want to be caught by the producer. 'Luvvie, dear,' panted Khamran at the chief florist, 'How *is* everything? Wrapped up perfectly in ribbons and bows of Heobhanly delight, hmmm?'

The chief florist ran mentally through the fields of faux-pas and blooming catastrophes, picking randomly at them. Should he tell the producer that the pink in the aerial arrays and hanging baskets clashed dreadfully with the trimming on the bridesmaids' dresses; or that

no matter how hard he had tried to find a crysan-
themum that fitted tastefully with leopard print the
best he could come up with set his teeth on edge at
two hundred yards; or perhaps that someone had
picked two hundred and ninety-seven blue buttonhole
pansies for the male guests on the groom's side and
three hundred and eight tiger lilies for the bride's when
it should have been the other way round? No, he
wasn't going to be remembered as the monster that
ruined Tehzho's day.

He tugged his face into a wan smile and patted
Khamran on the shoulder. 'Nothing to worry about. N
... nothing at all,' he whispered.

'Marvelloso, darling. Ciao!' And he was gone again,
heading towards the main entrance to check on something or other of vital importance.

Behind him the orchestra spluttered shakily into life,
slipped through three bars of cacophany and died. 'No,
no, no!' screamed the conductor. 'Ocarinas, it's in D
minor. Minor!'

As Khamran tugged on the vast ringed handle of the
main entrance there was a mad pounding of feet from
the other side and Tehzho Khonna sprang through,
running him flat like a demented ostrich. 'Khamran,
Khamran!'

'Here,' grunted the producer, peeling himself off the
floor and staring at Tehzho's head in sheer horror.
There, instead of the cute wisps of boyish curls and his
instantly recognisable trademark quiff, was a glistening
mass of hair plastered immovably to his skull. Khamran
had never noticed before just how far his ears stuck out.
'Now, now darling, what is the matter? Touch of the
nerves, hmmm, luvvie?' he rallied professionally. He
knew just how sensitive these compere types could be,
always needed reassuring.

'This!' panicked Tehzho, pointing madly at his hair.
'It's set!'

It would seem that charred, unblessed barley wasn't

290

particularly good at making the perfect ceremonial shampoo. Although what it lacked in conditioning power it certainly made up for in hold.

'Ahhhh,' was all Khamran managed. It wouldn't be worth alarming the day's star by telling him he looked as if he'd stood upside down overnight in a bowl of treacle. Oh no, he'd be *far* too concerned about his image then. Bound to forget his lines. The day would be ruined. He'd never produce another show in Axolotl for the rest of his life!

Khamran suddenly knew what to do. He grinned his finest lying grin, clapped his hands together and skipped on the spot. '*Great* new image, darling. Utterly stupendous! Love it, love it, love it! And what timing! A new image on the day you become a new you. Out with the playboy, in with the ... er, er. Oooooh! You *are* a genius and a tease. Fancy keeping *such* an idea under your hat, so to speak!' Playfully he punched Tehzho in the shoulder.

'Y ... you like it?' spluttered Tehzho.

'Yes, Tehz! Now *do* come on, there's still *so* much to do!' And cursing his lying tongue for at least a minute, Khamran led the star away. Everyone in the Grand Municipal Temple breathed a sigh of acute relief.

All, that was, except for Captain Maehap, who was standing on the roof scanning the horizon for any signs of the Cataclysmic Blizzards which had been foretold by the sightings of The Dreaded Snowthings of The Freezing Apocalypse.

'No, no. One group of four and one of five!' bellowed Flagit irritably at the deities in the increasingly cramped conditions of Nabob's cavern.

'Er, excuse me, but you did say equal groups earlier,' said Uscher. The Under-Deity Over Seating Arrangements, and the latest "recruit" to Flagit's growing clump of kidnapped gods, grinned cheerfully at himself, happy in the knowledge that his skills could be applied to standing crowds as well as those with a more restfully seated demeanour.

Flagit scowled at Uscher, tapping his talons in impatience. 'I know that,' he whispered threateningly. 'I've changed my mind, alright?'

The other eight deities, baffled by the point of this latest management style game, shuffled about and awaited further instructions. It was odd but they were strangely excited at this, their first interactive lesson. It was like a breath of fresh air actually to be given orders by someone who really seemed to know what they were doing, instead of having to sit uncomfortably through those endless meetings during "Any Other Business" where any deity who had even a passing interest in the matter under discussion chipped in, argued, counter-argued, hummed and hahhed and eventually came to the decision which had been blindingly obvious to everyone else hours earlier.

'I want two groups, one of four and one of five. I don't care how you split yourself, just do it! Alright?' snapped Flagit imperiously. 'One group at that end of the cavern, one group at the other, clear?'

To everyone present, that was clear. However the immediate future was significantly muddier. Nabob wasn't the only one to be wondering what Flagit had in mind. Especially when he picked up the obsidian table, carried it to one side, upturned it and hid behind it.

After several more hysterically yelled orders the deities had in fact managed to arrange themselves in positions which seemed to make Flagit reasonably happy.

'Now!' he shouted, pointing a deadly curling talon at each of the groups. 'I want you to sprint towards each other as fast as you can. And no matter what happens don't even think about stopping. Clear?'

Uscher blinked and asked, 'Just sprint?'

Flagit nodded.

'Towards them?'

'Yes! Got a problem with that?'

'Well, yes, as a matter of fact: why?'

'Never you mind, you wouldn't understand. Just do it!'

Nabob watched as Flagit made final checks on the shrine detector and Uscher shrugged.

'Go on, now!' bellowed Flagit and ducked behind the table again.

The deities shook their heads in confusion, shrugged and began to lope across the cavern floor, gaining speed, picking up momentum as they closed.

'Keep your eyes fixed above their heads,' whispered Flagit urgently and ducked lower behind the table, counting furiously.

It was then that Nabob saw it. There, hovering almost innocently above each of the two groups, was a faint purple aura, barely discernible in the ruddy gloom of the lava-lamps. Amazed, Nabob stared intently, his eyes convincing him that they were growing in pious intensity as the groups converged.

The thrill of danger coursed through Flagit's body like rampant hares in spring.

The pounding of the deities' feet grew, the distance between them vanished and suddenly they collided with a dull thud. And in the instant that nine doses of shrine waves were spat towards each other the auras above their heads flared wildly, spluttering into a shimmering of violet, distorting the air into writhing vortices of faith. The unmistakable smell of incense and recently extinguished candles blasted throughout the cavern.

As Nabob and Flagit peeked over the edge of the obsidian table, open-mawed, a roar of festive choirs quivered just beyond earshot and the cavern seemed to explode with tinselly delight. A metallic squeal sliced discordantly through the comforting aural carpet as the shrine detector screeched across the floor to hit the far wall, and Nabob screamed.

His eyes bulged as a purple dandelion clock of piety swelled through the cavern, eight feet across, crackling inside like a captive thunderstorm struggling to escape from a startled jellyfish. And as it launched itself from the deities with a quivering fragility Flagit leapt for joy.

'Yes, yes, yes!' he yelped through clenched fangs, punching the choral air. 'It's perfect!'

'Have you gone totally loony?' spluttered Nabob, snatching Flagit by the neck. 'What have you done?'

'Got the answer!' he grinned back as the eight-foot shimmering plasma of piety wriggled unstoppably through the roof. 'Did you see the size of that?'

'What answer?'

Flagit peered eagerly into Nabob's baffled eyes. 'At d'Abaloh's inspection this afternoon Seirizzim gets it!' Yellow madness glinted around his pupils. 'There'll be a new Undertaker-in-Chief before supper tonight. I can feel it!'

'But how?'

'We need two of the fastest carts we can lay our talons on and all will be revealed! Go, go!'

Shaking his head in wonder, Nabob headed for the door.

Away across the Underworld Kingdom of Helian on a relatively peaceful section of the banks of the River Styx there squatted a vast pink palace complete with ornamental gardens, landing pad and stables. Borders of red-hot pokers, dethfodils and a host of horribly spiked succulents roasted under banks of cooling fans or draped their gasping selves over vast chunks of local rock. And through all this ostentatiously infernal splendour stomped a tall, grumbling devil.

His hooves crunched angrily on the marble chip surface of the winding paths as he forged his way towards the stables, the bow-wave of his reputation sweeping ahead of him.

A good ten seconds before he swept through the stable door a vast scaled creature sniffed the air, twitched its horned nostrils and waggled its pair of tails cheerily in its stall. Harpy the dactyl quivered her thirty-foot wings in anticipation of the arrival of Foul Lord d'Abaloh, her dearly demonic master. Three, two, one . . .

Handles screeched in protest as they were almost wrenched from the slate doors beneath the claws of d'Abaloh. Eddies of lichen bedding blasted into the sulphurous air as Harpy flapped her wings excitedly, cheerily noting the fact that he was wearing his flying cloak.

The sight of d'Abaloh was always a joy to the faithfully scaly beast, especially in that cloak and goggles. It always meant a quick hack about the jet black sky. Or failing that, there'd at least be a few mawfuls of finest coal-treats. She began to salivate cheerfully and frisk in the stall, although she wasn't completely sure whether this was in anticipation of the crunchy nibbles or the snug bite of the straps, buckles and myriad fastenings of her tack.

Foul Lord d'Abaloh strode across the cobbles of the stable, his face wrinkling into a cloudy smile. Today was one of those days he would cheerfully have avoided. What had possessed him to agree to these inspection tours he would probably never know. If that idiot upstart Undertaker-in-Chief from Mortropolis hadn't suggested the damn things then he could have spent all day today tending his red-hot pokers. Damn the verminous creature. Now what was the buffoon's name? Began with an "S" . . . Sheytahn? . . . nope . . . Seirizzim? . . . Yes! That was the jumped-up bureaucratic little . . .

Harpy nuzzled her nostril horns affectionately against the sandpapery palm of d'Abaloh's claw and pulled him out of his brooding mood. The Foul Lord reached into his flying cloak pocket and tugged out a clawful of treats. Harpy whinnied deafeningly, thrust her steaming crimson tongue out and was rewarded by half a dozen sulphur crunchies.

Gnashing noisily, she watched with mounting glee as d'Abaloh whirled on his heel and headed off towards the tackle room. That meant only one thing. They were going out! Oh joy! It had been far too long since their last little flap about the skies.

Truth be told, it was only the day before yesterday, but it was always too long between hacks for Harpy the devoted dactyl.

Struggling beneath a heap of tackle, d'Abaloh returned and began kitting out the noisily purring monster, barely avoiding the pair of wildly wagging tails and the lashing tongue. He had to admit, there were times when Harpy could be a little *too* happy to see him.

After ten minutes it was done. Stirrups, saddle, reins, sulphur crunchie bag, they were all there. The only thing he had missed out was the pair of Flags of Office on each of her nostril horns. Somehow he just wasn't in the mood for them today.

D'Abaloh took the reins firmly in claw, tugged on a large lever and waited as the roof doors ground open. Eagerly Harpy gazed up at the widening expanse of swirling miasmic air and longed impatiently to be up there, free amongst the eddies and vortices, the thermals and the sheer forces, frolicking.

Tugging his goggles down, d'Abaloh clicked his tongue twice and Harpy leapt upwards. Thirty-foot wings slammed down against the air, scattering tornadoes of lichen bedding everywhere.

In five flaps they were clear of the roof and climbing, Harpy straining with the thrill of infernal air under her wings.

They had been filing in for the last hour and a half and at long last the final Axolotian was asked 'Bride or Groom?', received either a blue pansy or a tiger lily depending upon the reply and was herded off to the

296

relevant side of the Grand Municipal Temple. Already the excitement was high, spontaneous bursts of cheering and applause breaking out like scrub fires in a parched tundra. If anybody could have measured the average thrill level of audience members it would almost certainly have been way up there with that experienced at the recent final of "Play Your Stars Right!". And for that a certain producer was truly grateful. This would be a day they would remember for the rest of their lives. And it was all being brought into their humdrum, hyperstitious existences, real-time and as it happened, live before capacity crowds, courtesy of Khamran Mh'kyntosh.

Already the special edition glossy souvenir hymnal and behind-the-scenes programme had sold out completely. The confetti vendors had run dry and by the end of the day every wardrobe in Axolotl would have a "Tehz'n'Khrystal's Big Day" printed toga dangling proudly within. Sales of special-bottled avocado "Happy Toaster" gin were also bubbling well as folks readied themselves for the traditional blessing swig to nudge the happy couple alcoholically adrift on the seas of matrimonial bliss.

Suddenly, the main entrance was tugged shut, plunging the whole auditorium into pitch-darkness and raising a hum of approval from those within.

Outside, a solitary tumbleweed trundled shyly down Tuatara Street feeling very self-conscious in the deserted streets. Absolutely everyone had turned out in their finest togas to be there. Even the exceedingly rare folks who secretly detested Tehzho Khonna were present, more for self-defence purposes than anything else. If anyone started ranting on about how gorgeous the whole day was and how handsome he looked or how lucky Khrystal was to have hooked a man like that, they could raise a palm and halt the gushing tirade with a simple, 'I know, I was there.' It was bound to save years of earache.

Barely audible above the speculative hum of expectation, a series of sharply whispered commands were snapped out and the massive matrimonial bandwagon was shoved into action. Right on cue the kazoos and ocarinas of the Municipal Temple Band were puffed into life and were miraculously in key. A skylight was tugged open, spilling shimmering beams of moted sunlight onto a mirror high in the rafters and passing it along to a whole array of similar optics. A circular pool of light flashed onto the thick curtains for a few seconds before they were drawn out of the way.

And, to Khamran's overwhelming delight, the crowd gasped at the stage as it burst forth onto their collected retinas. Gangs of gladioli, crysanthemums and lupins bristled in horticultural haughtiness and attempted to upstage the draping garlands of buddleia, tiger lilies and hogweed which festooned every available orifice and cranny. It wasn't simply a riot of colour, it was all-out war.

But the audience's silence didn't last long. Striding jauntily onto the stage and leaping into the spotlight, Khamran was the pin-point in the saturated solution of the over-roused audience. His sudden appearance crystallised silent thrills into tumultuous applause, cacophanous cheering and a barrage of earpiercing whistles.

It took him the best part of ten minutes before he could make himself heard.

'Ladies and Gentlemen of Axolotl, on behalf of me and my enterprises, I want to welcome you to *the* matrimonial spectacular of the year! Please, a big hand for today's Master of Ceremony, a man I'm sure you all know, the longest serving Grand Municipal Prophet ... let's hear it for the one, the only Captain Maehap!'

Thunderstorms of appreciation discharged noisily as an oddly rotund figure shuffled arthritically into the widening spotlight. Of all the gathered folk present he was probably the least happy to be there. It seemed almost nonsensical to be indulging in such excessively

298

flamboyant frivolity when, at any moment, the Cataclysmic Blizzards could come sweeping in from any direction. Well, he wasn't taking any chances. He was currently wreathed in more layers of clothing than he dared admit and rather regretting agreeing to this whole Master of Ceremony lark. But he had been asked *so* nicely by that hasty Mr Mh'kyntosh, smiling sweetly at him, telling him what an honour it would be to have *the* elder statesman of foresight to help them into the future and how his presence alone would give the whole proceedings a grand air of auspiciousness ... well, he couldn't refuse.

Khamran had been so relieved. Until that moment he hadn't found anyone to fill the role. Nobody wanted to take part, it was too much effort. You wouldn't get the full benefit of the atmosphere of the occasion if you weren't in the audience, couldn't see the whole spectacle unfold. Fortunately for Khamran, since Maehap had never even heard of 'Play Your Stars Right!' up until a few days ago he wasn't too fussed about giving up his seat in the audience and missing the whole shebang by being on stage.

Khamran sprang back into the spotlight. 'And the two folks you've all come to see. Here they are, Tehzh...' His voice was buried by a tsunami of cheering as the soon-to-be-happy-couple walked on, hand in hand.

In the depths of the audience certain clothing makers, floral arrangers and hair specialists clapped enthusiastically but kept their nervous ears open for any stray comments. They could see their flaws miles away. That hastily tacked hemline and missing leopard-print handbag, that wilting pansy and the clashing buttonhole, that trademark quiff which was conspicuous by its greased-down absence. They clapped with bated breath, dreading the damnings.

Amazingly, there were none. Almost the entire population of Axolotl had dragged themselves here to see ace compere Tehzho Khonna join Khrystal Gehyz in a whirl-wind romance of fairy-tale sickly sweetness. It didn't matter right then what they looked like, or what they wore or how many of the flowers were wilting.

All that character assassination could wait until the gossip started later on. *Then* they could get down to some decent reputation shredding between the razor teeth of scathing envy. But that was later. Now there were much more important things going on.

Captain Maehap, standing under the scorching beam of the focused spotlight, began to sweat. Although it *could* have been nerves. He wasn't used to addressing large crowds.

Without further messing about, he launched into the ceremonial speech which had kept him up all night and had occupied almost as much of his waking moments as imagined sightings of The Dreaded Snowthings of The Frozen Apocalypse.

He cleared his throat and an uneasy hush fell on the proceedings. A hush that hummed with pre-tensioned party moods and overwound shrieking.

Captain Maehap turned to Khrystal Gehyz clad in her figure-hugging leopard-print ibex-wool toga and studiously avoided gawking at her generously garlanded cleavage. A rivulet of perspiration trickled down his forehead and vanished into a suitably bushy eyebrow.

'D'you want him?' he asked in the traditional words. 'Say "Yes, Tehz."'

Her answer was drowned in the full-throated yell of the crowd as they simply couldn't help themselves and shouted back 'Yes, Tehz!' But everyone saw her lips move in that sultry way they had, so that was alright.

Maehap, his dripping forehead reflecting the spotlight almost as efficiently as the better mirrors, turned to Tehzho Khonna with his radically new hairstyle and very itchy-looking hessian tail-cloak and asked, 'D'you want her? Say "Yes, Tehz."'

'Yes, Tehz!' screamed the crowd as Tehzho simply

300

nodded frantically. His audience had answered, his public had responded in the overwhelming affirmative. And if that was what they wanted then how could he even think about refusing? It would ruin his career if he did.

It was up to the sweat-soaked Captain Maehap to wrap the proceedings up. 'She's yours,' he announced soggily in the ancient traditional way.

The sound of popping avocado 'Happy Toaster' gin corks drowned absolutely everything, except the wave of noisy gargling which surfed in after it as the thousands of Axolotians cheerfully threw their alcoholic tribute down their throats.

Khamran knew it would take an age to clear the corks up, but he didn't care right then. He just didn't care at all.

After all, the confetti snowstorms were next, and then the reception.

In a tiny alley around the back of the Flame Pits of Mortropolis, a shovel ground relentlessly, echoing hollowly within the confines of a delivery cart. For the last ten minutes Flagit had been watching from the shadows, waiting for his moment eagerly, his heart fluttering with nervous excitement.

The brimstone delivery demon emptied the final shovelful into the vast mouth of the hopper and straightened up, wiping his glistening brow and stretching his aching back with a growl and a creaking of infernal vertebrae. Running a battered forearm across the front of his nose, he then reached for the delivery parchment and leapt onto the ground with a clatter of hooves.

'All done?' grunted Flagit, appearing from the shadows and intercepting the demon.

'Aye, all fifteen tons there in th'hopper. Sign 'ere.' He held out the delivery schedule and pointed a gnarled talon at a scratchy 'x'. Flagit grinned, scribbled at it randomly and handed it back. The demon grunted, 'See y'next week,' and turned away.

He knew nothing of the shovel arcing down on a collision course with the back of his skull until he heard the clang and awoke with a splitting headache six hours later.

Flagit dropped the shovel and leapt up into the driving seat of the cart. In seconds he had smacked the reins noisily across the carapace of the stalag-mite, who was grazing on a few scraps of granite, and had spurred the beast into life.

Grinning wildly, Flagit cracked a whip recklessly in the air above the clattering stalag-mite, directing it unstoppably towards downtown Tumor. In minutes he was screeching to a halt outside Nabob's cavern, slewing to a dead stop next to another freshly stolen cart.

'C'mon, c'mon! No time to lose!' he shrieked at Nabob as he kicked his way through the door. 'Load them up. Five with me, four with you.'

Nabob leapt up off his pebble bag and herded a quartet of deities out into his cart, trying desperately to ignore any nagging doubts that wriggled irritatingly at the back of his mind.

Taking and driving away was a minor offence compared to kidnapping and importing nine Heobhanly bodies and planning to overthrow the legally elected Undertaker-in-Chief of Mortropolis in a wild and daring raid.

'Just wait for my signal, okay? Don't move without it. Timing is critical!' barked Flagit tersely. 'You know what to do. Got your whip?'

Nabob nodded. It was all he had the chance to do.

Flagit, seeming to care nothing for the risks of close-proximity exposure to shrine waves, had shoved five deities into the cart, slammed the tail-gate shut and was clattering away down the alley in a cloud of crimson dust, his mind seething with the infernal reward of a sure and certain victory. How could Seirizzim possibly stand

302

up against the critical mass of soon-to-be-released shrine waves? It was sure to be an explosive ending to a very short career.

Flagit's whip lashed violently at the speeding stalagmite, stinging it on the right side as a sharp left approached. In a second the cart was around the corner, missing a forlornly trudging figure by scant inches and only then because he had hurled himself out of the way.

The Really ex-Reverend Unctuous III lay in a crumpled heap by the side of the road and moaned pathetically as the dust settled around him. It wasn't fair. Really wasn't fair. His only hope of release from Helian had vanished across the River Phlegethon, stowing away on a ferry bound for who knew where. If only he'd had a chance to believe and be saved. Or if he'd had the courage to stow away with him. Unctuous tutted pathetically. His life had been a complete waste and the rest of eternity didn't seem to offer much hope of improvement.

Miserably Unctuous wished that he knew where the Reverend Screed was right now. He sent a silent plea to anyone who was listening to give him a clue where to find him. Rejected and dejected, he hauled himself to his feet and decided arbitrarily to wander off up the alley to his right. Right now he hadn't a clue where he was and he didn't much care. He could probably find his way back to somewhere he knew between now and the end of eternity.

Sighing, he trudged off.

He got thirty feet into the gloom before he stopped, cocked his head to one side and listened.

For a moment he felt sure he could hear the babble of enthusiastic voices and the riotous clatter of sprinting hooves growing louder by the minute. For another moment he felt certain the voices were chanting, 'Screed! Screed!' but he dismissed it as the sad delusion of a bitterly distressed soul, bereft and alone in the whirling torment of Helian.

303

He was wrong.

The chanting and clattering of hooves grew even louder, blasting deafeningly at his ears until suddenly a wild mob of very ex-Immigration Clerks wheeled around a corner and charged in relentless unstoppability towards him. And there, high up on the tidal wave of raving demons, struggled the screaming cassocked figure of Screed, carried high like a mascot atop the runaway train of demand. A demand for Arma-Palms Mining Mittens. A demand which Undertaker-in-Chief Seirizzim would have to fulfil.

Unctuous hauled himself once again out of the gutter, raised his hand desperately and, panting, shuffled off in hot pursuit. 'Oi, wait for me!' he cried plaintively. 'Come back, I really would like a word. Hey! Screed, slow down!'

Scran's silver cloud swept out of the sky above Manna Ambrosia's, decelerated rapidly and came to a halt in its labelled bay. Humming gently to himself he climbed off and headed towards the exit passage that led to the main entrance, a jaunty tune reverberating across his lips. He was in a good mood today.

He'd just finished putting the final souls figures to the bimonthly accounts and for the first time in a good few centuries it seemed that folks had actually been paying attention. Quite where they had come from he wasn't entirely sure, but suddenly, almost everyone's figures had leapt upwards. Not just the tiny upturn which normally happened a few days before major religious festivals, no, this was almost as if some overzealous missionaries had discovered a brand-new continent which had never heard of the idea of belief. The room which was filled with the Believer Beacons for all the deities positively hummed with fiery intensity as each new spark of faith added to the gleaming glow within.

Amazingly, there was even the flickering of a faint

glow in the Believer Beacon of d'Mure the Chastity Deity. Wherever these new followers were springing from it was certainly an odd place. Still, he was to find out all about it soon enough. In the meantime he was just chuffed that his deities were doing so well on the conversion front. In fact he almost felt like screaming excitedly about it to everyone.

Whistling cheerily, he sauntered on past the rows of parked silver clouds, for once not in any particular hurry to take his place at the Top Table.

Then ahead he saw a significantly overweight figure shambling towards the exit passage and he simply couldn't control himself. He increased his pace, waved and shouted, 'Hey, Sot! Great day, isn't it?'

Sot stopped dead in his tracks, shock freezing him motionless. He couldn't believe his ears. 'Great day?' Of course it was a great day. This was Heobhan.

'Is there something you want to tell me?' grinned Scran, catching up with Sot and panting.

'T ... tell you?' spluttered Sot, not a little apprehensively. It had been at least four hundred years since Scran had spoken directly to him, and that had been to ask him to pass the black pepper. Sot scratched his head. What could he possibly be thinking of? What specific event out of all those years did he want to be told about? There was only one thing on his mind at the moment, and that was *his* secret.

'C'mon, Sot, what's your secret, eh?' whispered Scran in an oddly conspiratorial way as they walked on, his eyes shining with the glint of intrigue.

'S ... secret?' spluttered Sot. Did Scran know about Screed?

'Yeah. C'mon, you can tell me. I don't need any more devotees, do I? As long as I've got Tohnee Fabrizzi up here in the kitchens I've got all the support I need from you lot. C'mon, where are you getting all these new believers from?'

Sot choked suddenly. It was true. His pet Haranguist

Missionary was coming up with the goods. 'Believers?' he hedged deliberately. It wouldn't pay to let his methods slip. Cheating did not go down well in Heobhan.

'Don't play games with me,' grumbled Scran, scowling from under his bushy eyebrows. 'What are you doing that's different to before, eh? Your Believer Beacon is positively fizzing with the flames of newly kindled faith.'

Inside, Sot leapt for joy, punching the air wildly and screaming. It had worked. His faithful band of devotees was swelling and Scran had noticed. In that instant, that scrap of news took him a firmly tangible step nearer to the Top Table. Scran had been right, it *was* a good day!

But that one answer spun a hundred different desperate questions. How was he doing compared to Lush, his arch rival? It would be grossly unprofessional of him to ask directly, but he had to know. Two weeks of waiting would be agony.

As Sot held open the exit door he asked, 'My increase in souls figures, er, is it unusual or are there others showing a similar trend?'

'What the...?' was the only answer he received as Scran crashed into the back of a snaking queue of listlessly shuffling deities. 'What's going on here?' bellowed Scran, shoving his way forward through the line and forcing his way towards the entrance of Manna Ambrosia's.

Sot attempted to reassure himself that everything was fine and dandy. Well, Scran wouldn't have been asking him about his new-found increase in devotees in the cloud park if his figures hadn't been wonderfully unique, would he?

Scran bellowed and blustered his way to the front of the queue. 'What's going on here? Why's everyone standing around out here?'

'Procedure,' answered Lofax, He-Who-Is-In-Charge of Scheduling, Meetings and Vital Appointments, officiously.

306

'What?' spluttered Scran, rapidly concluding that today was becoming less 'good' by the minute.

Lofax pulled himself up to his full height and, barely hiding a smile of self-satisfaction, readied himself to report the gross desertion of duty of a fellow organisational deity. 'Uscher hasn't turned up!' he declared. 'It would be inordinately inexcusable of us to simply assume that we know precisely where our personal seating site is to be located. Without the guiding presence of the Under-Deity Over Seating Arrangements to steer our paths we cannot enter.'

'Uscher, too! Where is he?' snapped Scran.

Lofax shrugged unhelpfully and shovelled a few more pounds of damning soil into the grave of guilt.

Scran ground his teeth as his stomach rumbled in a very ungodlike manner. 'Well, you can hang around out here for him. Me? I know where I sit!' He shouldered open the door, stomped inside and stopped dead in his tracks.

His nostrils flared, inhaled, and his mood plunged miserably into his socks. Something was definitely amiss.

Like the forlorn nakedness of a house when the Christmas decorations have been unceremoniously tugged down, the olfactory landscape of Manna Ambrosia's was utterly bereft of the comforting reek of Tohnee Fabrizzi's Infamous Dragonzola Garlic Bread.

Everybody in Heobhan heard the wailing squeals of Scran as he fell to the floor and sobbed, vowing there and then never to make rash judgements about the state of the day until his lunch was firmly steaming before him.

Suddenly, an angel soared out of the wild blue yonder, flared her wings and settled down, hovering next to a minor god wearing a long, pale grey trenchcloak and matching panama hat.

Sot watched with a growing feeling of guilty nervousness as the angel whispered in the god's ear, casting a glance in his direction. Fibby, the Supreme Deity over

Espionage, Misinformation and Spying, shoved his fists deeper into the pockets of his trenchcloak and flung an impenetrable look at Sot. Moments later he tugged his collar high up around his neck and stormed off towards the cloud park, Florrie fluttering animatedly at his side.

Sot suddenly lost his appetite as he watched them go.

The atmosphere in and around Sinful Square buzzed with resonant waves of snapping tension. Its epicentre was Seirizzim. He knew that his future as Undertaker-In-Chief of Mortropolis depended on the overwhelming approval of one devil, Foul Lord d'Abaloh himself. One ounce of marginal disgruntlement and Seirizzim knew he would be out, ostracised, expelled.

But deep in the evil gut of his guts he knew that wouldn't ever happen. Not with the perfect display of sheer efficiency and overwhelming spectacle he had personally choreographed. Every detail had been single-clawedly supervised, every demon under his command thrashed to within an inch of permanent scarring using his very own private dragon-o'-nine-tails. It was now all ready, rehearsed, honed: a perfect palate of anguish and agony with which to paint his self-image of hellish efficiency.

There was just one teensy-weensy thing missing. Foul Lord d'Abaloh himself.

'Where is he?' snarled Seirizzim, pacing up and down, his hooves clicking noisily, the tension beginning to irritate like ants in y-fronts. 'He's late, why's he late? What's keeping him? He should be here!'

Asmodeus kept his head down as he nailed the final banner to the thirteenth-floor balcony. Four vast rectangles of crimson waved imperiously now from that eyrie, each with a huge staring circle of white at its centre, a pure pearl of innocence defaced by the crossed cloven hooves and trident of the New Mortropolitan Regime. All around the edge of Sinful Square, echoes of this motif roared back in silent obeisance, waved by specially press-ganged demons who, at the given signal, were to behave in a far from silent manner.

Seirizzim drummed talons tetchily on the edge of the balcony, gnashing his fangs. D'Abaloh should have been here by now, should be standing here, on his left, brimming with the pride of the perfect dictator.

A crisis of decision loomed in Seirizzim's mind. This *was* the appointed time. Should he hold the opening of his rally until d'Abaloh arrived ... and risk looking inefficient? Or should he flick his talons triumphantly in the sulphurous air, cut the ribbon on the proceedings ... and risk d'Abaloh missing it all? But could he be utterly certain that d'Abaloh hadn't simply snuck into Sinful Square unseen, shackling this dread decision firmly onto Seirizzim's shoulders, testing, testing? He had no choice. He simply had to start, it was the safer option. If d'Abaloh turned up late then he could just start the whole damned fiasco again. It wasn't as if it was any hardship for him to sneer imperiously down over his minions just once more, reinforcing his supremacy, his power over the entirety of Mortropolis.

It was the appointed time. Let the parade begin.

With a final sneer he raised his claw in the classic two-taloned salute and sliced through the single ribbon with ease. The hastily assembled clump of demons which lurked under the name of the Mortropolitan Sinfony Torturestra smashed noisily at boiling kettle drums, raspberried darkly through their brass and screeched talons along the strings of their disorganised violins. A dozen highly paid crowd control demons (temporarily relieved of Malebranche duties) cracked menacing lashes and whipped the audience into a frenzy of appreciation. Banners waved, throats cheered. Focused lances of lava-lamps strafed the square violently. In from the left lurched the massed misery of the Synchronised Shufflers of the Fire Pits, chains clanking between their ankles.

And unseen in the sudden chaotic chthonic animation two stalag-mite drawn carts rumbled covertly up and stopped at opposite ends of the square. If anyone had taken a moment to squint sideways at the oddly clean-looking bearded figures held within, then they might have seen curious purple tongues of piety hovering above each of their heads. But nobody looked. They dared not risk the wrath of Seirizzim. Not today. Not the mood he was in.

The foundations of Sinful Square seemed to buck and writhe suddenly as the Vast Boulder Precision Display Team heaved their ton charges into view accompanied by screams of musical discord from the Sinfony Torturestra. Dragons-o'-nine-tails cracked and slashed the air around them; tridents spun in twirls of malevolent menace. And Seirizzim bounced up and down on his hooftips, thrilling in dark delight.

From the deity-packed carts Flagit and Nabob watched in gagging awe. Tiny harbours of doubt began to fill with vessels of vacillation and flotillas of faithlessness. It was such an amazing spectacle unfolding before their eyes that the rugs of over-confidence were tugged out from beneath their hooves. Suddenly both of them were utterly uncertain they could've set up something so spectacularly sinister. It was a good job they were too far apart to admit it to each other.

Swallowing silently in the whirling chaos of the New Regime Rally, they filed it all under "nerves" and readied themselves for action.

Meanwhile, carried on a gentle, sulphurous breeze high above the majority of stalag-mite gnawed rooftops, a curious purple dandelion of pure piety fizzed and crackled and drifted towards the massed throng in Sinful Square. And it probably would have drifted on by, fluttering aimlessly through the Underworld Kingdom of Helian, until it crashed spectacularly in some deserted back cavern, bringing a haven of faith and frivolity to the resident colony of chthonic gophers.

310

Would have fluttered by, that is, except for the magnetic presence of nine deities secreted within Sinful Square and the even larger pull of countless demons who had been stroked by the gently soothing caress of delighted devotion.

Despite the airstream's most valiant efforts, the purple dandelion of piety began to descend, and, as it approached, tiny pockets of spontaneous giggling erupted from amongst the press-ganged crowd. Rivulets of excitement bubbled up, coalesced and formed into tiny ponds of frivolity. Demons were gripped with the overwhelming urge to start chanting and ringing tiny bells – bells whose shape and tinselly ringing was not unlike those exhibited by Solstice Bill's Cymbalic Soul-Savers.

It only took one of the more easily influenced demons to whip out his tiny talon bells and tap them together with joy, and spontaneous outbreaks of frivolousness erupted around the square in seconds, joining in with the infernal racket of the Mortropolitan Sinfony Torturestra. Hooves began to tap uncontrollably, miraculous maracas were tugged out of pockets and Seirizzim screamed as the press-ganged audience broke ranks.

He leaned over the balcony, stabbing the air with his imperious talons, barking orders at his Malebranche, yelling himself hoarse to no avail. They simply couldn't hear him over the infernal din.

And in the instant that Flagit stood in his cart and recognised the actions of devils in the grip of moods detailed in The Deadly Hammer of Frivolousness, he knew the time was right for action. Waving frantically, he caught Nabob's eye across the square and in seconds they had both whipped their stalag-mites into action. Clouds of dust billowed from the black carapaced creatures' spinning legs as they fought for traction. Then, in a flash, they accelerated away, tugging the carts into the writhing melee of infernal chaos.

'Out of the way!' screamed Flagit frantically, cracking his whip noisily above his horns. 'No brakes! Look out!'

311

Demons squealed, leaping out of the path of the ostensibly runaway cart. And, as planned, the carts plunged in towards each other, describing a perfect collision course, each carrying a deadly cargo.

Only Flagit and Nabob knew what would happen when these two sub-Critical Masses of piety collided. Only they could foresee the sudden eruption of vast doses of shrine waves. And only they knew the effect it would all have on the unsuspecting devils of Mortropolis.

Flagit locked his mind onto two beliefs, clutching them tightly with every neuron of his will. He was certain that if he held the firmest conviction that Seirizzim would be deposed and that he would replace him, then everyone else would believe. It *would* happen.

'Out of the way!' he screamed again as a knot of cavorting demons whirled ecstatically out of the chaos and barely missed being flattened by a charging stalagmite.

And then it was too late. From behind a waving clump of crimson banners Nabob's cart erupted, bouncing and rattling noisily, bearing down unstoppably. The two carts swerved, sparks spitting from their wheels, they tipped and hit side on in a wrenching, rapid rupture of shattering wagons. The nine deities were hurled together by the wreckage, the purple flames of faith clashing, flaring and building synergistically. Flagit and Nabob scattered as they felt the rumbling of imminent detonation.

Just as they ducked into the Sinful Service Stratascraper it happened. Sheets of purple bolt lightning fizzed out from beneath the cart crash, clouds of holy smoke billowed forth reeking of the unmistakable smell of incense and recently extinguished candles. The air filled with a roar of festive choirs, and thousands of devils were slapped firmly around the jowls by the hand of tinselly delight, the flattened palm of piety.

And from the thirteenth-floor balcony Seirizzim screamed as the smoke cleared slightly and the hated figures of Flagit and Nabob were revealed standing atop the wreckage of the cart crash, grinning broadly. A wheel spun to a halt behind them.

The deities, trapped beneath the wreckage, tutted and wondered what all this had to do with management courses.

'Friends, demons, Helianites!' shouted Flagit victoriously. 'Lend me your fears.' If he had done this at any other time he would have been mown into the ground by at least half a dozen snarling Malebranche officers and charged under section three of the New Mortropolitan Freedom of Speech Act drawn up last week.*

Fortunately for him the grinning Malebranche had forgotten about it temporarily, and they simply stood there open-eared and empty-headed, each poised with a pair of Solstice Bill's Cymbalic Soul-Savers between index talons, teetering on the edge of belief.

Flagit attempted to fix everyone in the square with a meaningful gaze as he took a deep breath and readied himself to deliver what was probably the most important speech of his existence. He was minutes away from taking the Undertaker-in-Chiefship as his very own. And he knew it. His lower intestine felt distinctly uncomfortable.

'People of Mortropolis! Stand still for a moment and look around you!' he yelled through a drift of dense theic smog. Everyone could see in that glance that the infernal laws of order had been arm-wrestled into submission and had slunk away into the early bath of defeat.

'Is this efficiency? Is this what you want? We have all heard Seirizzim's plans for a New Mortropolitan Regime. I ask you, is this it? Dictatorial street parties

* Everyone knew that Mortropolis was a demonicracy and as such everyone was completely free to exercise their right to free speech under the one-demon-one-voice ruling. However, the latest ruling contained two extra words. It was now the one-demon-in-charge-one-voice ruling and any deviation, hesitation or repetition of that voice other than by Seirizzim himself would result in severe bashing.

designed to show off his supremacy over you? Bending you backwards in enforced obeisance and grovelling and all so that he can curry favour with Foul Lord d'Abaloh,' shouted Flagit, going straight for the jugular of Seirizzim's Undertakership. A distant echo of anguish rattled off the thirteenth-floor balcony. Flagit ignored it pointedly. 'And what has he done for you, brothers? Is this state of complete chaos what you have all strained and suffered to produce? Wasn't there a better time before the election of Seirizzim?' Flagit seethed excitedly inside as he sensed the first awakenings of doubt and the embryonic stirrings of civil unrest. 'If the citizens of Sheytahn could see you now, would they be impressed?'

Seirizzim bellowed incomprehensibly from the balcony, leaning far over the edge, gesturing in a manner which looked less than pleased with the whole developing situation. With a spark of heels he spun and dashed out, snarling angrily as he clattered down the stairs, thoughts of d'Abaloh shoved unceremoniously to the back of his mind.

Oddly, in a strange twist of ironic justice, Foul Lord d'Abaloh was at that moment shoving thoughts of Seirizzim and his Mortropolitan Inspection to the back of *his* mind. The thirty-foot wings of Harpy the dactyl swept powerfully through the Helian air, slicing through cross-winds and crimson cloudbanks with seeming effortlessness and d'Abaloh squinted out through his crystal goggles at his Underworld Kingdom slipping by beneath. From up here, almost touching the stratasphere, it all looked so inviting. He could see none of the swarming crowds of tormented souls which polluted Helian's glory. He could feel none of the press of filthy mobs seething between tortures for eternity. And he wished he could stay up there for ever. Just him and his pet dactyl swooping and soaring freely, thrilling on the gossamer wings of exhilaration. But he knew he couldn't. An inspection calls. He had to go.

Back in Sinful Square Flagit was stroking the fervent crowd up into a frenzy of belief. 'Why should you all be forced to obey Serizzim's every whim? Should you really trust him to support the best interests of Mortropolis? Look at the state of this shambolic mess. The most important day he's had in office so far and look at it! And do you know who will be blamed? Have you any clue?' He peered out from the upturned carts, his eyes blazing with wild fervour. 'You!' he yelled, stabbing a demonic talon out at them. 'Your shoulders will bear the disgrace of our incompetent leader!'

The crowd cheered back. This unknown demon's arguments were sharp lights in their darkened minds, flaming brands to follow across the trackless wastes. And all who heard his words, all who were submerged in the eerie purple glow of the shrine waves, heard and began to believe. Seirizzim was the worst thing ever to have happened to Mortropolis. Undertaker-in-Chief? Pah! He couldn't even undertake out the rubbish.

'Are you going to stand for it?' shouted Flagit.

'Course you are!' yelled Seirizzim, bursting through the doors of the Sinful Service Stratascraper. '*I'm* Undertaker-in-Chief! What I say goes!'

'Quite right!' countered Flagit. 'The Undertaker-in-Chief must go! Seirizzim out!'

The crowd of demons shuffled nervously and wondered what to do. It was one thing to moan and grumble and complain about leadership behind his back but, well ... action was another thing.

'Seirizzim out!' shouted Flagit again, stamping his hoof on the upturned cart.

'Seirizzim out!' came an echo from a side alley. All eyes turned and stared in amazement as the rumbling clatter of a mob of sprinting hooves rattled into pointy earshot.

And with another cry of 'Seirizzim out!' the massed mob of ex-Immigration Clerks, ex-Admissions Clerks and a host of miffed ferrymen erupted into the square carrying the Reverend Vex Screed of the Haranguist Mission aloft like a small furry mascot. Ever since they had heard his words in the mines they had known there was only one thing they had to do. Rid Mortropolis of the Dread Seirizzim. And their time had come.

'That's right!' yelled Flagit enthusiastically, if a little baffled by the mob's sudden appearance. 'Seirizzim out!'

'Dragnazzar!' screamed Seirizzim as the mob from the Lava and Brimstone Mine surged in. 'Dragnazzar! Save me! Arrest that mob!'

'Er, I ... I'm supposed to be crowd control now, remember? You said that just today. I ...' began the huge leader of the Malebranche.

'They're a crowd! Control them!' shrieked Seirizzim, gathering now that public opinion was slipping through his talons at an alarming rate.

The mob from the mine swept through the rally crowd unhindered, tossing long dead cheerleaders hither and yon, kicking shuffling souls in all directions, closing with the unstoppability of a whale on roller skates.

Seirizzim screamed again, whirled on his heel and began to sprint away, kicking at the crowd, punching his way through the black scaly mass of the press-ganged audience. Four of the faster demons broke from the mine mob, kicked hard and accelerated, whips curling and cracking above their heads like wild tongues. Seirizzim plunged on, eyes rimmed with panic, splashing at the crowd with his talons. Then suddenly a whip lashed out of the sky behind him, curled around a fleeing heel and tugged. The countless tonnage of the stone floor of Sinful Square hit him full on the nose.

Grinning malevolently, the demon with the whip hauled him in. Seirizzim bleated helplessly as he was dragged backwards, his claws scrabbling impotently at the stones, legs thrashing.

Flagit and Nabob were leaping up and down on top of

the carts chanting 'Seirizzim out!' Despite the imminent overdose of shrine waves they still couldn't really believe it.

It had worked. Any chance that Seirizzim had to remain Undertaker-in-Chief of Mortropolis had evaporated without trace. Nobody would take orders from him again.

But that was only the first part of Flagit and Nabob's plan.

Grinning like a heavyweight champion cow-toppler, Flagit raised his claws high above the riotous Mortropolesians. 'The Undertaker-in-Chief is gagged. Long live the new Undertaker!'

Unsure exactly why, the demons cheered, clapped and rang their cymbals wildly.

'But I have a question,' screamed Flagit hoarsely. 'We need a new leader! A new Undertaker. Someone who can unite Mortropolis and act as a figurehead. Someone who can rally all behind one common cause!' All the time he was pointing a pair of index talons at his chest, swelling his torso in as pride-filled and leaderish a manner as he could muster.

'Friends, demons, Helianites,' he cried, sticking out his chin in what he hoped was a strong, square way. 'Who do you want as your next Undertaker-in-Chief?'

Silence shuffled nervously across the square as everyone looked at their hooves and/or shrugged pathetically. The mob from the mine looked remarkably sheepish as they realised they hadn't actually thought this far ahead. Seirizzim bound and gagged with more enthusiasm than efficiency, writhed helplessly beneath several hundred ells of Nayburn High Tensile Hemp and was ignored.

'Who will it be?' shouted Flagit, stabbing himself in the chest painfully with his talons. 'Come on!'

The only sound was the pattering of a pair of sandals and a desperate panting as a small rotund figure sprinted into Sinful Square. Ignoring the fact that the whole place

317

was heaving with demons, he ran past the mob from the mines, scurried up to the front and stared longingly up at Screed.

'Well, who's it going to be then?' screamed Flagit, his voice quivering desperately.

'I have come!' shouted Unctuous, staring imploringly up at Screed the mascot. And still overwhelmingly under the influence of an excess of shrine waves, everyone in the confines of Sinful Square saw the miraculous sign for what it was. Their next true leader had been revealed to them. They had all felt his touch, all heard his words and all had supped of his free ale.

'Screed!' they cried as one, offering themselves unto his leadership. 'Screed!'

Flagit's jaw clattered onto his chest. 'No, no. Hang on. I meant me!' he protested noisily.

'What about me?' shouted Nabob. 'You promised me I'd...'

'Look, I'm the best choice!' squealed Flagit in the register normally associated with week-old panicking piglets. 'Hey, pay attention. Look, I'm a brilliant choice, I ... Oi, get off! No, wait ... put me down!'

Without an order being barked, the two unbelievers, the only dissenting voices in the entire mob, were snatched by four of the larger Malebranche officers and hauled screaming down a side alley in close pursuit of another quartet who were dragging the writhing Seirizzim away.

Faint echoes of wheedling reverberated out of the alley. 'This is a big mistake,' whined Flagit, trying to sound as if he was in charge. 'Look, if you put me down and let me go *right* now I will overlook this incident. I will make a perfect Undertaker-in-Chie ... oowwww!' The unmistakable sound of a hardened Malebranche fist striking delicate nasal tissue resonated painfully between the chants of 'Screed! Screed!'

The ex-Really Reverend Unctuous III couldn't believe his ears. 'No, look, you don't understand!' he shouted. 'I

only wanted him to show me the way out of here ...
aaaargghhh!'

A vast demon glared down at him, folded its face in a
very peculiar way and plunged a vast claw at him.
Unctuous screamed as the talons closed around his
throat, squeezed and pulled.

'He has shown us the way!' roared the demon, who
had obviously had far too many shrine waves for his own
good. 'He shall be rewarded!' He raised Unctuous high
above his horns and flung him onto his shoulders.

'No, no. Look. I only wanted Screed to ... hang on.
Rewarded, you say? Er, what exactly d'you mean by
that?' spluttered Unctuous.

'Under-undertaker-in-Chief!' declared the demon.

Everybody roared their approval and they all set off
on a vast lap of Mortropolis's streets, Screed and
Unctuous held high above their heads, a united congregation cheerily following behind.

High above, perched on a flapping dactyl called
Harpy, Foul Lord d'Abaloh peered down into Sinful
Square and smiled. 'Well, looks like everything's fine
down there, eh, Harpy. I, er ... don't really think we
need to actually pop in now, do we? Just flit about up
here a bit and then swoop off across to see how
Sheytahn's getting on. Sound alright to you, eh?'

Harpy bellowed cheerily and swooped into a parabolic
dive of delight. D'Abaloh took that as a definite 'yes'.

Florrie followed Fibby, the Supreme Deity over Espionage, Misinformation and Spying, into the interior of the
buzzing cloud and stared at the flashing trident.

'There, told you,' she said. 'Buzzing and flashing like
some kind of alarm. What is it?'

'Some kind of alarm,' whispered Fibby in the shocked
voice of someone who is looking at something happening
which they never, ever expected to see.

'Really? Oooh, what kind of alarm?' asked Florrie,
excited.

'The worst, the worst,' muttered Fibby, brow wrinkling, shoulders hunching closer to his ears. 'We've got to get him undercover, out to a safe cloud, away from them!' He whirled on his feet, his trenchcloak billowing around his ankles, and stormed out of the cloud.

'Them? Who's them?' pressed Florrie. 'What's going on?'

In the countless centuries since the threat of the Infernal Invasion had evaporated in a puff of boredom she had forgotten so much. Mind you, most of the complex and highly sacred surveillance systems which Fibby had been in charge of had been kept very secret. There was no point telling everyone that he'd set up an exceedingly covert way to keep tabs on trends in demonic thinking. It wouldn't be exceedingly covert then, would it?

During the height of the Infernal Invasion threat Fibby had spent weeks in his cloud, staring at the tridents, waiting for them to show they were detecting evil thoughts directed against specific targets. Every one of them was carefully tuned to the resonances of specific demonic determination. If your trident lit, it showed you were on the minds of a host of devils. And that, to Fibby's highly conspiracy-sensitive mind, meant only one thing.

They were plotting to get you!

He had to get Sot out of sight. Deep cloud cover. Now.

In the now deserted arena of Sinful Square a wrecked cart creaked, rocked a few time and was pushed over with a tattoo of grunted breaths. Khlyde and Pugil kicked at the other one, shoving shattered slateboards out of the way, and stood up.

Rahmani tutted angrily. 'Ruined! Ruined it is. I shall *never* get this right again!' he complained as he attempted to brush filthy smudges off his jacket.

Moh Linnekx rummaged about in his pouch and

handed over a small wallet. 'Handy Travel Wipes,' he grinned. 'Ideal for revitalising travel-weary garments and freshening up tired feet'.

'Got anything for this?' whimpered Dahls'soon, tugging at her fringe. 'It'll never stick up again, I'm certain of it.'

As Moh Linnekx delved once more into his capacious pouch, Khlyde shrugged, battered dust off his peaked cap and asked, 'Well, me hearties, what are we going to do now?'

'Run away,' spluttered Fleeh. 'C'mon, this way!'

'What?' grunted Pugil. 'And miss out on a decent punch-up when they come back?'

'Yes,' insisted Fleeh, and headed off towards a dark alley.

'Where are you going?' shouted Uscher.

'I'm getting out of here. This way, look.' He held up a certain familiar-looking map of Mortropolis and pointed to a tiny passageway marked 'Exit'.

'Always pays to know your getaway routes,' he added and was joined by a very enthusiastic octet of weary deities.

'Hey, it worked,' mused Uscher eventually as they trudged down gloomy back passages and little frequented alleys.

'What did?'

'This. Down here. D'you see how quickly we made a decision just then?' And the other eight knew he was right. They had sensed it.

'This way,' grunted Fleeh as he checked the map and pointed to a long-disused door in a deep pool of shadow.

'Through there?' panicked Rahmani as he looked at the cobwebs. Then he stared at his clothes and shrugged. They couldn't get much worse.

'Yup.' Fleeh shoved at it eagerly and spat when it didn't move.

Pugil grinned, stepped up and kicked it open, not

stopping to look at the faded and indistinct writing on a small sign on the wall which read:

DAN ER EEP OUT! AN I- PERSON EL S RINES.

Blissfully unaware of the boxloads of curious cross-shaped devices stored under the stairs, they began the long scamper up the spiral staircase.

The angelic waitresses of Manna Ambrosia's flitted wildly between tables despite the complete lack of anything solid to devour. Jugs of ale and wine flowed freely into flagons and thence down rapidly drunkening throats.

Scran stared miserably into his ale and longed for even the smallest scrap of Tohnee Fabrizzi's Dragonzola Garlic Bread. There was simply something too wet about ale without it, nothing to crunch on. Where could Tohnee have gone? Had he been treating him so badly that he had simply upped and vanished? But no, that couldn't be right. Only deities could do that, couldn't they? He stared into a future bereft of Fabrizzi's fare and a tear of drunken misery sparkled at the corner of his eye.

Suddenly an officious deity sprang to his feet and thrust his hand into the air. 'Is it time for "Any Other Business", yet?' asked Lofax to an audience of groans.

Scran slurped his ale and an angelic waitress emptied in another gallon.

'Sir? Is it time for...?' began Lofax again.

'I heard you,' barked Scran, his voice echoing woodenly around the inside of his flagon.

'Well?' pressed the deity with his hand in the air. 'Is it time?'

'I'm thinking,' grumbled Scran. 'I can't see how it can be, because we always have "Any Other Business" after pudding and we haven't had pudding yet so...' His train of words dribbled inconclusively into his ale.

'But it's the right time?' whined Lofax, trying to suppress a frown of irritation.

'Oh, alright then,' grumbled Scran over the hubbub of drunken deities. 'But it won't make much sense to that lot. Mind you, I'm not sure it does anyway.'

Lofax lowered his arm, grinned, took a deep breath and announced officiously, 'Any Other Business?'

'Yes, me hearties!' announced a pumpkin pyjama'd deity wearing a peaked cap and captain's beard as he lurched out of the Little Gods' Room, panting.

All eyes turned to this sudden interruption, some focusing significantly faster than others. 'We've discovered this way of making decisions!'

'Khlyde! Where have you been?' demanded Scran. He shrugged as the other deities appeared through the Little Gods' Room door. Dahls'soon followed behind, blushing. She'd never been in there before.

'It's brilliant,' enthused Khlyde. 'You need two folks in charge, one a sort of father figure to the other one and a gang of holy folk, like us. A sort of Father, Son and Holy Co.'

'Where's Fabrizzi?' whined Scran.

In a distant corner Bhelbynn sat up, rubbed his chin and began to think about Khlyde's words. It seemed a bit triangular and possibly a bit bottom-heavy, but, he mused, it might just work.

'You can't just burst in like that and announce a topic for discussion at "Any Other Business"!' shouted Lofax, waggling his motion tables. 'There's nothing entered here. You know the rules! Non-tabled motions *must* be correctly presented for debate utilising the correct procedural pathways.'

The prodigal deities shrugged and were led to their seats by a very relieved Uscher. Who needed decisions, he mused, when there was beer about and deities to be led to it?

In a darkened corner Sot breathed a vast sigh of relief. There had been no mention of nefarious schemes and his involvement in them. He was in the clear. He *would* get to the Top Table after all. With a grin of relief he flashed a gallon of his finest ale into his flagon.

323

He didn't get a chance to drink it.

A shadow moved behind him, revealed itself to be wearing a pale grey trenchcloak and matching panama, clamped a hand across his mouth and dragged him off his stool.

'Don't say a word!' barked Fibby as he wrestled Sot out of Manna Ambrosia's while all eyes were still fixed on the recently returned deities. 'You've got to keep quiet otherwise they'll find you! It's for your own good. Trust me. I know what I'm doing!'

Deep in a cavernous darkness, lit only by the gloomy crimson of lava and brimstone, three figures were handed enormous pickaxes by a massive specimen of Malebranchedom. He pointed to the brimstone-coated wall, growled and indicated an array of empty buckets gaping in the gloom like the maws of hungry baby Ammorettan Death Lizards.

'Dig,' grunted the guard eloquently and kicked the nearest of the three sharply across the backside with a deft hoof.

The chains on Nabob's ankles rattled as he shuffled towards the wall and attempted to lift the pick. 'Dig?' he whimpered. 'I can't even lift this.'

'You'll learn,' growled the guard, leering cheerily in the crimson darkness. 'Or else...' he added enigmatically and turned to leave.

'Hey!' protested Flagit, 'Where are you going? You can't leave us alone in here...'

'Shut up!' snapped Seirizzim in a harsh whisper. 'Don't you have *any* brains?' He waved cheerily to the guard. 'It's alright,' he called, 'we'll be just fine down here. You go back to your hole and have a nice evening.' Seirizzim's mind fizzed with the sure and certain knowledge that he would soon be capable of handling a pick expertly. With no guard around, and the only thing between him and freedom a pair of shackles, he could soon learn to swing a shackle-mangling implement.

'Very kind,' grunted the guard. 'Night, night. Oh, hang on, I nearly forgot these.'

Baffled, Nabob, Flagit and Seirizzim strained their ears as they heard the unclipping of a trio of tiny cages and a sudden buzzing of tiny wings.

'Oh no, he wouldn't...' spluttered Seirizzim recognising the sound instantly.

'What? Wouldn't what...?' asked Flagit, sensing a degree of alarm in Seirizzim's throat with satisfaction.

'No! Don't please!... NOOOOOO!' squealed Seirizzim as a tiny insect-like security mhodemm alighted gently on his shoulder and waggled its proboscis threateningly.

The guard grinned as he heard the screams echo satisfyingly out of the mouth of the Lava and Brimstone Mines of Rubor.

Captain Maehap stared around the inside of the Grand Municipal Temple of Axolotl and shook his head in amazement. Not at the fact that the interior had been completely refitted into a perfect venue for a wedding reception in under ten minutes; nor for the fact that Khamran Mh'kyntosh had delved into his pockets and paid for all the booze and grub for the whole of the guests; and not even for the fact that he had remembered his lines in front of such a huge audience.

No. Captain Maehap was amazed that nothing had gone wrong. After all the thousands of individual panics about flowers and clothes and seating and hair and a plethora of other hitches he hadn't heard about, everything had gone really well. Okay, so the flowers in the groom's side's toggleholes hadn't matched his toga, and five of the guests had fainted with excitement, and they were fifty-three cases of fizzy avocado gin short, but ... well, it was done. Tehzho and Khrystal were now Mr and Mrs Khonna and everyone in Axolotl was delighted.

Maehap took a sip of melon liqueur and wandered up onto a high balcony as the kazoo and ocarina band warbled discordantly away at some popular tune from thirty years ago. He sighed and peered out of the window, reminiscing already about the day and readying himself to groove the night away. Twelve more of these and he'd be anybody's...

And then, outside, something moved. The corner of his eye was hooked in alarm as a cloud of tiny white flakes cavorted gaily on a breeze. They were followed by more pure specks and his spine ran cold with terror.

Had the dreaded prediction come so soon?

Were they snowflakes ... or confetti?

Captain Maehap shivered and took a desperate swig of melon liqueur.

In an obscure corner of the outskirts of Heobhan an irate figure pounded desperately on the walls of a bare hollow deep in the insides of a vast cloudbank.

Sot had only realised Fibby's mistake ten minutes after the panama-hatted deity had locked the door and sped away. Screed had obviously been *far* busier than he should have been. Converting devils as well. Such devotion to duty!

'It's not what you think!' screamed Sot, smashing his fists against the fluffy, unyielding interior of the cloud. 'They're not after me. I'm perfectly safe. They believe in me. Come back and let me out. They're my friends. Fans! Let me out!'

Less than twenty yards away a squealing angel pulled off an outside loop, blissfully unaware of the contents of the soundproof deep-cover cloudbank around which she had just executed the manoeuvre.